The Housekeeper's Secret

Also by Iona Grey

The Glittering Hour
Letters to the Lost

The Housekeeper's Secret

Iona Grey

ST. MARTIN'S PRESS
NEW YORK

First published in the United States by St. Martin's Press, an imprint of St. Martin's Publishing Group.

THE HOUSEKEEPER'S SECRET. Copyright © 2024 by Iona Grey. All rights reserved. Printed in the United States of America. For information, address St. Martin's Publishing Group, 120 Broadway, New York, NY 10271.

www.stmartins.com

Designed by Jen Edwards

The Library of Congress Cataloging-in-Publication Data is available upon request.

ISBN 978-1-250-27262-1 (hardcover)
ISBN 978-1-250-27263-8 (ebook)

Our books may be purchased in bulk for promotional, educational, or business use. Please contact your local bookseller or the Macmillan Corporate and Premium Sales Department at 1-800-221-7945, extension 5442, or by email at MacmillanSpecialMarkets@macmillan.com.

First Edition: 2024

10 9 8 7 6 5 4 3 2 1

For Jenny,
who is always there, even when she's half a world away

The Housekeeper's Secret

You notice the noise most when it stops. When the silence comes rushing in with a force that takes your breath from you.

And then the birdsong.

Above, the sky is pale blue, endless. It's been raining for weeks, but yesterday the clouds rolled back, and they made their stumbling progress towards the front line through a dawn of limpid summer loveliness. Now, tipping his head back, it seems like he can see all the way to heaven. Like he could touch it.

High up, a plane hangs in the blue, the sun catching its wings. Like a dragonfly.

For a moment, standing on the mud-gummed duckboards of the communication trench with his face turned up to the early sun, he catches a whisper of summer—green earth and good grass—above the pervasive reek of latrines, rotting sandbags, and damp khaki (and the faint trace of vomit on Robinson's breath, behind him). His mind returns to the morning he arrived at Coldwell, walking across the park from the road, seeing the house for the first time.

In that instant, the image is more vivid than the slimed sandbag walls bracketing him, the mud-crusted pack on Joseph's back a few inches ahead.

He closes his eyes, wanting to hold on to it, willing himself back across the miles, across the years; and his hand goes to the chest of his tunic where the letters in his pocket are pressed against his body by a bandolier of ammunition and seventy pounds of equipment.

He started writing a week ago. On their last day behind the lines, when the British bombardment had just begun, supposedly smashing the enemy into submission but rattling the nerves, battering the eardrums, and shattering the sleep of their own troops in the process.

The letter has been a distraction. Writing it has filled the endless hours as they moved out of their billets and joined the river of khaki flowing into the reserve lines. It has given him something to think about amidst the noise and boredom and mounting tension, and diverted his thoughts during night fatigues carrying heavy tins of explosive through the labyrinth of mud-filled trenches to where tunnellers waited to pack it into the mine, ready to blow the enemy lines sky-high at the start of whatever is coming.

Once he started writing, he found he couldn't stop. It was like talking to her; the conversations they had never had the chance to have, the explanation he had never had the chance to give.

The forgiveness he had never had the chance to beg.

The ink was scarcely dry when he shoved the letter into an envelope an hour ago. He has no address for her, so he will put it with the other letter he has written, in the envelope marked *To be sent in the event of my death.*

In front of him the line of men begins to move again, inching forward. The Sherwood Foresters will be in the third wave to go over the top, they were told over the rum ration this morning; behind the 1st Londoners and the North Staffordshires. It'll be an easy stroll, the brass hats say.

He has written the letter for himself, really, to ease his own troubled mind. He doesn't have any hope that it will find her, because in almost five years of looking, he never has. And if, by some miracle, it does . . .

Well, it will be too late.

———— ∞∞∞ ————

7.20 a.m.
July 1st 1916
Brighton, England

She opens the door at the bottom of the area steps and stands in a slant of pale sunlight, eyes half-closed. The air is as cool and fresh as a glass of milk.

The damp gloom of the passage chills her back, so she emerges further, savouring the sun after a week of rain, and breathing in the scent of the yellow roses that climb up the basement wall. Far above the rooftops of Belgrave Place the gulls reel and glide, and today their cries sound jubilant rather than mournful. Listening, she notices the quiet that shimmers beyond the sounds of an everyday morning—the distant clang of milk churns, the spluttering throb of a motor—and she realises that the rumble of the guns has stopped.

She wonders what it means. If it is a good sign or a bad one.

She had heard them that morning, more distinctly than ever. The sound is like thunder rumbling in the distance, never getting closer. The noise is carried across all those empty miles of ocean and she can't imagine what it must be like close at hand. How anyone can endure it without going mad.

Of course, they don't. Not all of them. The hospital has had a number of men suffering the effects of the guns, not on their bodies but their minds. *Soldier's heart*, the nurses call it.

The thought of the hospital casts a cloud over the brightness of the morning. It is Saturday, which means she will spend the afternoon there, 'making herself useful,' as Mrs Van de Berg puts it: helping the men to write letters and reading out bits from the newspaper to keep them entertained. ('We must all do our bit for our dear boys, Simmons,' Mrs Van de Berg says, and has decided that her bit is sending treats to the officers' convalescent home and donating her housekeeper for two afternoons a week to the Auxiliary Hospital on Lewes Crescent.)

A cat pads languidly along the railings on the street above and settles on the top step, curling its tail neatly around its body. Two floors up, a cacophony of hysterical barking erupts, ignored by the cat, who, with a nonchalance that borders on insolence, applies itself to washing a paw. She sighs. If Mrs Van de Berg's querulous Pekingese is awake, that means Mrs Van de Berg will be too, waiting for her morning tea.

Reluctantly, she pushes away from the sun-warmed wall. As she turns to go inside, she notices that one of the rose stems is broken. She snaps off the heavy bloom, not for Mrs Van de Berg's drawing room but for the kitchen, to put in the Chinese vase that she bought on foolish impulse in

Hanningtons department store last year, while shopping for towels for the upstairs guest bathroom. She is just stepping back into the cabbage-and-carbolic-scented basement when a noise stops her in her tracks.

A muffled boom. A distant baritone blast that rattles the china on the dresser and makes her heart lurch in her chest.

The cat stops washing, paw held aloft.

Inside the house, Ko-Ko the Pekingese falls silent for a long moment before his barking resumes in a frenzy. Up in the hallway, the longcase clock strikes the half hour.

A shiver ripples down her spine. (*Someone walking over your grave*, Susan would have said.)

She doesn't allow herself to think of him these days, whatever the purchase of the vase suggests. Not thinking of him is one of the rules on which her sanity and survival depend. But as she returns to the dim subterranean kitchen, his ghost resurfaces from the past and walks beside her, so she can almost feel the brush of his hand against hers, the warmth of his skin.

She puts the kettle on the stove and closes her eyes briefly. And she hopes that, wherever he is now, it isn't there.

Spring

Chapter 1

Coldwell Hall, Derbyshire
April 1911

It had been a cool spring and the blossom was late that year.

The Chinese vase Eliza carried up to the Kashmir Bedroom contained only a few stems of lilac, just beginning to turn brown and go past their best. As she set it on the washstand a scattering of tiny star-shaped flowers fell onto the marble.

'Mr Gatley says he's sorry but that's all there is. Daffodils are over. Peonies aren't out yet. There's bluebells, but Susan said they're bad luck in the house. If you bring bluebells in—'

Mrs Furniss cut her off with an edge of impatience. 'Thank you, Eliza, the lilac will do very well.'

With the visitors about to arrive everyone was feeling the pressure, but in Eliza's book that was no reason to be rude. She watched the housekeeper reach for the watch that hung from the ornate silver clasp at her waist, snapping it open and looking at it distractedly. 'Is Davy Wells watching out for the carriages? He hasn't forgotten?'

'No, Mrs Furniss.'

Honestly, you'd think it was the king and queen they were expecting, not Mr Randolph and some middle-aged spinster he'd plucked off the shelf in desperation, and boring old Lord and Lady Etchingham. (No point in putting on any airs and graces for them; Lady Etchingham was Sir Henry's daughter and had grown up here, so knew better than most what a mouldy old pile it was.) Mrs Furniss was usually all right, as housekeepers went, but she had a bee in her bonnet about this visit and was treating them like idiots. Which was fair enough in Davy Wells's case, but hardly reasonable for the rest of them. 'Joseph went up to the gatehouse to check. Mrs Wells said Davy's had his eyes pinned to the road since Johnny Farrow left for the station. He's ready to run down and ring the bell as soon as he sees them coming.'

Davy might not be the brightest spark, but he'd lived in the gate lodge at Coldwell for all of his twenty-odd years and knew every hill and hollow of the park, and the quickest shortcuts across it. There might be precious few visitors to Coldwell these days, but that didn't stop Davy from watching out for them. It was his life's purpose, probably because it was one of the few things he could do, being mute and simple. On the rare occasions a horse or a carriage turned between the gateposts, he ran ahead of it, cutting across to the estate's little church to ring the bell and alert the servants. The carriage drive was almost a mile long and hilly; before the visitor had appeared within view Mr Goddard, the butler (who was as old as time and moved as slowly), could get his dusty old tailcoat on and make his way to the front door.

Mrs Furniss swept the fallen lilac stars into her hand. 'Good,' she said crisply. 'Off you go, then, and get the tea trays ready.'

'Yes, Mrs Furniss.'

Eliza was in no hurry to go back downstairs, where Mrs Gatley, the cook, was just as uptight as Mrs Furniss but a lot louder with it. Lingering in the stillness, Eliza caught sight of her reflection in the looking glass above the washstand. It was at least four times the size of the mean little mirror in the attic room she shared with Abigail, and the glass was clearer, so it didn't look like she had the pox. She turned her head slightly, noticing that the spring sunshine gave her hair a buttery sheen (the sun hadn't struggled up as far as the attic when she'd got dressed this morning) but also showed the spot she'd felt swelling on her chin. She touched it tentatively.

'*Eliza Simmons*—tea trays, now!'

Eliza slouched to the door with a sigh.

She and Abigail were fond of moaning that nothing ever happened at Coldwell. Thudding down the back stairs (which smelled of cabbage and chamber pots), she wasn't sure she didn't prefer it that way.

———— ∞ ————

When Eliza had gone, Kate Furniss looked around, repositioning the vase on the washstand, turning it so the two painted figures were at the front.

It wasn't the smartest vase—a cheap English factory copy, not one of Coldwell's genuine Eastern treasures—but she didn't suppose Miss Addison would notice. A couple of branches of lilac hardly made a sophisticated floral display either, but they brightened the room and distracted attention from the flaking plaster cornice and threadbare carpet. (At least she hoped they did.)

The Kashmir Bedroom was the best Coldwell had to offer to guests. It might once have been a luxurious place to stay, but the pale blue painted walls had darkened over time to a dingy grey and the embroidered Indian silk bed hangings were faded and frayed, their exotic blooms unravelling. Like the rest of the house, their glory days were long past.

Kate had checked the room already, making sure that the bed was made up to her satisfaction, that there was soap and fresh towels on the washstand and a pot in the bedside cupboard, but she went over it all one more time. It wasn't the servants' place to get involved in Sir Henry Hyde's personal business, but you'd have to be deaf or stupid not to realise that an awful lot rested on the next few days; specifically, the marriage hopes of Sir Henry's son Randolph (whose bachelor status had seemed fixed) and, by extension, the future of Coldwell Hall and all who worked there.

She went to the window, removing the handkerchief from her sleeve to rub at a smear on the pane, and stood for a moment, watching the shadows of clouds slide over the hills. Her gaze moved uneasily to the crest of the drive where the carriage would first appear.

They were unused to guests at Coldwell, and she felt overwhelmed by the task that lay ahead. Four staying guests to look after, and their servants to accommodate below stairs; five more guests for dinner tomorrow night. Three days of marshalling her small troop of girls, ensuring that there was enough hot water; that trays were prepared properly, beds aired and turned down, fires lit and kept burning, the correct linen and china taken from the store cupboards and replaced again, and that everything went according to her meticulous plan.

Kate sank down onto the window seat and rested her head against the cool glass. Everything was under control, she knew that; control was what she did best. She was too vigilant to make mistakes, too careful to leave anything to chance; but still, it felt like her head was full of jangling bells, summoning her to the hundred small tasks that needed her attention.

With only elderly Sir Henry inhabiting Coldwell's endless upstairs rooms, the staff below had dwindled to a skeleton of what it had once been—enough to look after the needs of one reclusive baronet but woefully insufficient to maintain a fifty-room mansion, never mind provide for a house party. Mr Goddard had finally accepted that they needed to replace the footman who had left last Christmas, but he had placed the advertisement in the *Sheffield Morning Post* too late to engage someone for this visit. Kate had written to Mrs Bryant, housekeeper of Sir Henry's London house in Portman Square (where Randolph Hyde had taken up residence since his return from India) to ask that a footman be sent, to ease the pressure on poor Thomas, though the London footmen tended to be overconfident and troublesome. She would have to make sure that the extra pair of hands didn't stray where they shouldn't.

She let out a breath, misting the glass by her cheek. Through its haze she caught a movement in the park beyond.

A figure was standing on the top of the hill in front of the house. A man; tall and well built. Youthful. He was wearing a pale shirt, the sleeves rolled back, a jacket and a knapsack slung over his shoulder. Without thinking, her eyes firmly on him, she stood up. The breeze lifted his hair and made his shirt billow back and flatten against his chest. She was too far away to see his face properly, but she knew she hadn't seen it before.

A stranger, then.

For a second, it seemed he looked straight at her; and in spite of the distance between them there was something dark in his stare, something searching. Instantly, she darted out of view and pressed herself against the wall panelling, the instinct to hide still overwhelming after all these years. Her heart rattled against her ribs and her palms were clammy as she waited, before edging back the stiff curtain and peering out.

He was gone.

Emerging cautiously, she looked out, and saw that he had put his jacket on and was walking towards the house with a loose-limbed, easy stride. His footsteps left a silvery trail in the damp grass.

She watched until he disappeared from view beneath the window. Taking a steadying breath, she gathered herself, brushing away the shadow of suspicion, the whisper of *what if . . . ?* She collected her pile of clean towels and went to check that all was as it should be in the remaining guest rooms.

⁕

It wasn't much of a place.

Oh, it had been once, there was no doubt about that. The house itself was a palace: a great big stone monument to wealth and power, with rows of windows stretching on forever and a huge triangular portico on the front supported by four mighty pillars. It had obviously been built to impress, and the fact that it was so hidden away just made its extravagance more arrogant. Its magnificence was not meant to be shared, its luxury intended only for a select few.

But it seemed that the plan had gone awry, and somewhere along the line seclusion had become isolation, sliding towards abandonment. Time and the elements had blackened the buff stone, and the windows were grimy, many of them shuttered. Paint flaked from frames and weeds sprouted from guttering.

Getting off the train at the tiny station in Hatherford, he'd asked directions and been told it would take two hours to walk the seven miles to Coldwell. He'd saved himself at least a mile by climbing over the high stone wall and cutting across the park, instead of following the winding road round to the gates. The ground was rough and tussocky with bracken, boggy enough to soak his boots. Labouring up the hill he'd noticed a squat stone church half-hidden by a vast cedar tree and, just beyond, the crumbling ruins of a tower.

At a distance it was impossible to tell whether its collapsed state was one of those deliberate things rich people built as novelties or an old structure that had simply been allowed to fall into disrepair. The top was crenellated, like a row of broken teeth, the high-up windows black and blind, and a tangle of brambles had been allowed to clutch and clamber around its walls. Drawing level with it, he'd seen a heavy iron padlock hanging from the door.

As he reached the top of the hill a cloud moved across the sun, extinguishing the weak spring sunlight like a candle being snuffed out. The house below shrank back into the shadows. Some recent attempt appeared to have been made to clear the weeds from the semicircle of gravel in front of the wide steps, but it had done little to dispel the air of shabby neglect or the slight sense of menace. Of something sinister, lurking out of sight.

Or perhaps he was imagining that.

A movement in one of the first-floor windows caught at the edge of his vision. He looked, and saw a face behind the glass: a pale oval, which vanished almost in the same second but left an impression of large eyes and sharp cheekbones. Blue eyes, he thought, though that seemed ridiculous. The glass was dirty, and he was too far away to tell.

But anyway, he had been seen, which meant he either had to make himself scarce before someone came after him or go through with it. Something in him recoiled at the thought of entering the great dark house, as if it might swallow him up completely, but he had come too far and waited too long to turn back now.

Shrugging on his jacket, he picked up his pack and smoothed down his hair, then set off down the slope.

Coldwell Hall had been built on the site of a remote sixteenth-century hunting lodge belonging to the Dukes of Northumberland (where, local legend had it, Henry VIII had once slain a rare white stag) on the expanse of bleak moorland that lay between Manchester and Sheffield.

The old lodge had been demolished—all except the tower of its gatehouse—and a grand baroque mansion constructed in its place by the first Baronet Bradfield, who had made a vast fortune as a colonial administrator in the East India Company. Coldwell Hall was intended to showcase his newfound wealth, do justice to his new-minted title, and house the collection of ancient Indian treasures he had amassed while imposing British rule on recalcitrant locals in Calcutta and Bengal. It had been designed to draw guests from distant London, to surprise and delight them with the contrast between the house's wild, windswept surroundings and the cultured comforts inside.

But that had been more than a century ago.

Ironically, the coming of the railways had served to cut Coldwell off from civilisation more completely: the seven miles to the nearest station made it a far less convenient destination for a country house gathering or shooting party than properties with private railway platforms placed discreetly within their parks. These days the only visitors to Coldwell were Sir Henry's physician, Dr Seymour; Reverend Moore from the parish church in Howden Bridge; and (less frequently) Mr Fortescue, the Hyde land agent. In the drifts of conversation that echoed through Coldwell's quiet corridors during these visits Kate often heard the name of Sir Henry's bachelor son, Randolph, along with the words 'irresponsible,' 'feckless,' and 'profligate.' On spidery half-written letters abandoned on the bureau in the Yellow Parlour, she read '*debauched and dissolute—like history repeating itself. Another disgrace on the name of Hyde.*'

After inspecting the guest rooms, Kate went down the main staircase, trailing a finger along the dado to check for dust, feeling the dank air enfold her as she descended into the marble-floored entrance hall. The house was set in a dip and the sun struggled to find its way into this cavernous space, where the heads of animals stared down from the walls, seeming to offer visitors more of a warning than a welcome.

The rocky ground of Derbyshire's Dark Peak district didn't lend itself to riding, so successive generations of Hydes had found their sporting pleasure in shooting grouse and stalking deer on home turf, and slaughtering more exotic prey while out on the subcontinent. Around the walls, red deer from the Derbyshire moors touched antlers with antelope and gazelle, and the fearsome horns of cattle whose faded, balding hides had once felt the warmth of the Indian sun. The centrepiece of the trophy display was a tiger, which appeared to leap out of its mahogany mount, ears flattened, teeth bared, green glass eyes fixed on the portrait of his nemesis on the wall opposite. Aubrey Hyde, the second Baronet Bradfield, secured in family legend as the black sheep, and the tiger hunter.

Kate always hurried past this portrait. There was something about the second baronet that unsettled her: something lascivious in his parted lips and the moist glisten the artist had given them; something disturbing in his watchful, hooded eyes and the way they seemed to follow her across the marble floor. His pose was relaxed, his hand resting casually on a stone balustrade beside him, and that unnerved her too.

She knew how deceptive such nonchalance could be. How quickly a hand loosely held could tighten into a fist.

The layers of silence were suddenly disturbed by the distant note of the church bell. Its thin chime was rapid and insistent, and she pictured Davy Wells hauling on the rope, red-faced and breathless from his race through the park. She felt an odd lurch of foreboding and her hand went to the Indian silver chatelaine fastened at her waist, touching the items suspended from it like a rosary—the scissors, the buttonhook, the thimble and pencil, the keys to her parlour and her desk. At the foot of the stairs she took in a breath, composing herself into the character she had taken such care to create. Mrs Furniss, the housekeeper. Calm, capable, conscientious, always in control.

All of it a fiction.

Her footsteps echoed in time to the clang of the bell as she crossed the hallway to the heavy door concealed beneath the staircase. Pushing it open, she left behind the stillness and went down the worn steps into the heat and noise of the servants' basement.

The air in the kitchen passage was damp, hazy with game-scented steam. Passing the kitchen door, she saw Mrs Gatley hefting a great roasting tin out of the range, while Susan, the sole kitchen maid, whisked frantically at something in a pan. Tension simmered in the air like fat on a hotplate. Mrs Gatley was the head gardener's wife and had taken on the job of cook as a temporary stopgap when finding someone willing to put up with Coldwell's isolation, poor pay, and lack of modern kitchen conveniences had proved impossible. Ten years on she was still there, and rarely missed an opportunity to grumble about it.

'Oi—hallboy! Let's have some help with this luggage!'

A shout sounded through the open door to the kitchen yard, its London accent jarring. The wagon bearing Mr Hyde's and Miss Addison's luggage had already rumbled under the stable arch and the Twigg boys—Stanley and George, from the stables—were beginning to unload it. The Portman Square footman clearly considered himself above manual labour and superior enough to issue orders to Joseph who, as hallboy, was at the bottom of the pecking order.

Kate was about to go and disabuse him of this notion when Mr Goddard emerged from the butler's pantry, settling his tailcoat over his shoulders and tugging at his lapels.

'Positions everyone!'

In the subterranean light of the passageway, he appeared taller and more cadaverously thin than ever, his half-moon spectacles glinting dully on the end of his long nose. 'Smarten yourselves and make your way upstairs, please.'

The London footman would have to wait. Kate turned into the stillroom passage that led to the housekeeper's room, almost colliding with Abigail hurrying the other way.

'Sorry, Mrs Furniss.' The girl's eyes were bright and her cheeks faintly flushed. Kate stepped aside to let her pass.

'Oh, Abigail—did someone come to the servants' entrance earlier? A man?'

'Yes, Mrs Furniss.'

'And what did he want?'

'He was asking about the footman's position.' Abigail began to untie the coarse work apron she wore over her black afternoon dress, in preparation for swapping it with a finer lace-trimmed one. 'He saw it in the newspaper and came direct. Eliza took him to Mr Goddard's room. Thomas is finding him a livery now.'

'He's been engaged? Just like that?'

The girl shrugged apologetically and edged away.

There was no time to verify this improbable story. There was no time to brush out her hair and repin it either, so she stood before the looking glass in the small housekeeper's parlour and tried her best to make it tidy enough to go take her place on the front steps alongside Mr Goddard, and welcome the visitors to Coldwell.

June 24th 1916
Somewhere in France

Dear Kate,

The commanding officer has told us that if there's anything we want to say to loved ones at home, not to put it off any longer. Things are happening here, the whole of the British Army seems to be assembling in these small villages and country towns, bringing guns and shells and supplies and setting up first aid posts, so I know it will be something big. Something that I might not survive.

And, Kate, there is so much I want to say.

This morning, our guns and trench mortars started a bombardment that has continued all day without stopping. The noise is indescribable. We spent the day unloading crates of shells, and in the distance the artillery bursts like fireworks, which makes me think of you.

Everything makes me think of you. For five years I have tried to look forward and build some sort of life without you, though it would never have been the life I would have chosen. Now the prospect of any sort of future seems unlikely and there's nothing to stop my mind from returning to the past.

I wish I could go back too, and do everything differently, but of course it's too late for that. The only thing I can do is try to explain. I have little hope that you'll ever get to read this letter, but I believe that setting it down on paper counts for something. If I don't come through this, at least the facts will be recorded, for what that's worth.

At least I will have let it be known that I loved you, and I'm sorry.

Chapter 2

'So where is he, then?'

Eliza spoke out of the corner of her mouth as she stood beside Abigail on the front steps, watching the carriage navigate the drive's final descent. Mr Goddard and Mrs Furniss were in place on the gravel below, and Thomas, the first footman, had come running down the steps just in time to take up his position behind them, ready to spring forward and open the door when the carriage came to a halt.

'Must be still getting himself smartened up,' Abigail replied. She didn't have to ask whom Eliza was referring to. Lads as handsome as that didn't appear at the kitchen door of Coldwell Hall every day, though Eliza would have shown an interest in any man under forty as long as he had most of his own teeth and didn't smell of horse manure, like the Twigg boys. Abigail liked to think she set the bar a bit higher, but she had to admit the new footman had exceeded even her exacting standards.

'He looked pretty good as he was to me,' Eliza muttered.

Abigail's snort of laughter escaped before she could stop it. Mrs Furniss looked round sharply, the spring breeze blowing a strand of dark hair across her cheek. Abigail pressed her lips together to hide her smirk until the housekeeper had turned away again.

The ring of hooves and harness was louder now as Johnny Farrow slowed the horses for the turn. Another figure sat beside him on the box, dwarfed by the coachman's bulk. Frederick Henderson, Abigail thought with distaste, Mr Hyde's oily valet. She remembered him from the last time Mr Hyde had visited his father. Fancied himself a cut above the rest of them, did Mr Henderson, walking around the entire time like there was a bad smell under his nose and even talking to Mr Goddard like he was there to do his bidding. She turned her attention back to the far more attractive subject of the new footman.

'He's called Jem,' she whispered. 'Jem Arden. I wonder if it's short for something?'

'He didn't look short of anything to me,' Eliza murmured.

Abigail giggled. 'I wonder what's brought him out here.'

'Who cares? Let's just hope he stays.'

Johnny Farrow brought the horses to a standstill at the foot of the steps in a jangle of bits and brass. Thomas stepped forward to open the carriage door, his red hair gleaming in the sunlight like the polished copper jelly moulds on the kitchen dresser.

'Have you seen the London footman?' Eliza flattened her apron as the wind caught it.

'Oh, aye, I've seen him all right,' Abigail muttered. He'd made it impossible *not* to see him, sauntering along the kitchen passage with his hands in his pockets, getting in the way and making out it was her fault for almost bumping into him. He'd looked her up and down, his eyes hovering over the top of her apron as he'd introduced himself as Walter Cox, his accent as foreign in these northern hills as if he'd come from somewhere far across the sea. 'Very sure of himself.'

'But handsome.' Eliza flashed her a sideways grin. 'What's that they say about London omnibuses? You wait forever, and then two turn up at once. Even in a backwater like Coldwell.'

'Aah, here we are, home sweet home!'

Below, Sir Henry's middle-aged son emerged from the carriage behind his russet spaniel and—while the dog darted about excitedly, pink tongue lolling, plumed tail waving—puffed out his chest and took an expansive lungful of air.

'The old place actually has a bit of sun on her! Not ruddy raining for once, eh, Goddard? Good show, good show.'

Mr Goddard's rickety frame trembled beneath the hearty clap Randolph Hyde landed on his upper arm, but Hyde didn't appear to notice, turning round to shout at the dog, which was lifting its leg against one of the stone pillars.

Kate stood stiffly at the foot of the steps, a smile of welcome pasted to her face. She was surprised to see how much Coldwell's heir had aged since his last visit. The spring sunlight showed up the network of broken veins on his cheeks and the puffiness beneath his eyes. He was just past forty, but years spent in the Indian sun (and in the bar of the Bengal Club) had given him the appearance of a man much older.

'Not much of a welcome party.' Hyde's dissipated blue eyes flicked without interest over the servants assembled on the steps. 'Is my sister not here yet? And no sign of the old man . . . ?'

'Lord and Lady Etchingham are coming by carriage, Mr Hyde. They have yet to arrive,' Mr Goddard said gravely. 'Sir Henry is waiting for you in the Yellow Parlour. The cold—'

'You don't need to tell me about the bally cold, having been sitting in that God-awful carriage for the last hour.' Hyde's tone was petulant and he clapped his hands together, addressing the woman who was preparing to step down from the carriage. 'Come along, my dear! Allow me to introduce you to the legendary Goddard, without whom Coldwell would quite simply crumble. And the delectable Mrs Furniss . . .'

Kate didn't allow her smile to falter, though beneath the black silk of her sleeve, her flesh shrank from the hand he placed on her arm.

Thomas extended his hand to assist Miss Addison. The woman who emerged from the carriage was neither young nor fashionable and was wearing a rather fussy ensemble of cornflower-coloured silk that managed to look both obviously new and singularly old-fashioned. Kate bowed her head respectfully, raising it to see Miss Addison step on the flounced hem of her dress and stumble. Blushing fiercely, she shook out her skirts and gave a self-conscious laugh that showed prominent teeth.

'Oh dear, how clumsy of me.'

'Come along—let's get inside,' Hyde snapped, looking around for his dog. 'I don't know about you, but I'm famished. Ready for tea at the first instance, swiftly followed by something stronger. *Boy!*'

Thomas jolted to attention, but it was the dog Randolph Hyde was calling. It came bounding back from where it had been capering on the grass, running between the horses' hooves to follow its master, who was climbing the steps to the house.

Kate went forward. 'Welcome to Coldwell, Miss Addison.'

There was a figure still seated inside the carriage. The lady's maid, she supposed—they'd been told Miss Addison would bring one. Her drab clothing made her merge with the shadows, though Kate glimpsed a flash of white on her coat. Above it, the woman's face was lost to the gloom, but Kate caught the gleam of her eyes. Like an animal, unblinking.

Deliberately, she turned her attention to Miss Addison. 'If you'd like to come with me, I'll show you to your room. I'm sure you must be tired after your journey.'

'Oh—yes! How kind, thank you.'

As Kate climbed the steps, her senses prickled with awareness that she was being watched from inside the carriage. Pausing in the hallway for Miss Addison to catch up, she noticed that the delicate gold finger of the barometer was pointing to *Change*.

The servants' basement was all noise and jostle when Kate went down after showing Miss Addison to her room. Wicker baskets were piled up in the kitchen passage, and there were trunks and valises stacked in the gloomy space beneath the stairs, waiting to be taken up and unpacked while the family were having tea.

Miss Addison's maid was hovering by her mistress's trunk, as if guarding it from brigands. When she saw Kate, she came forward with an air of brisk purpose. The flash of white Kate had noticed in the carriage was the ribbon of the temperance movement, pinned to her lapel, and for a moment Kate imagined she was about to thrust a pamphlet at her.

Instead, she said, a little testily, 'I've been waiting for someone to show me to Miss Addison's room. I have her jewellery here'—she held up a flat case, her eyes fixed on Kate with that peculiar intensity she'd sensed before—'which I'm instructed to leave in the safe. You do have a safe here?'

'Of course—Miss Dunn, is it?'

Kate matched the other woman's crisp tone. To be completely correct, a visiting maid should have been referred to by her mistress's surname below stairs, but visitors were rare enough at Coldwell to make such formality unnecessary. 'If you give it to me, I'll take care of it. Miss Addison is in the Kashmir Bedroom.' She pointed to the bell board high up on the wall. 'If you wait here, I'll find one of the girls to take you up.'

Reluctantly Miss Dunn handed over the box, which was very new and bore the name of a provincial jeweller Kate hadn't heard of. Leaving her there, she felt the woman's eyes follow her down the passage to the still-room, where Eliza and Abigail were preparing the afternoon tea trays.

Or should have been. Instead, she found them standing at the window, heads pressed together as they craned to look out into the yard, the loaf half-sliced on the table in a mess of crumbs and butter-smeared knives, the cherry Madeira cake still in its tin. They sprang apart at Kate's icy voice.

'Miss Addison's maid is waiting to be shown upstairs. Abigail, go with her to the Kashmir room. Eliza, take this to the butler's pantry and ask Mr Goddard to put it in the silver cupboard.'

Eliza took the jewellery box, and they sidled out sheepishly. Left alone, Kate moved to the window to see what they'd been looking at. The luggage cart had been unloaded and removed, and the two new footmen were out in the yard, washing in the water trough before changing into the uniforms draped over the laundry line. The London lad—beanpole tall and city skinny—had taken off his shirt to sluice his armpits, revealing skin the colour of milk with all the cream skimmed off it. Kate's eyes slid over him to the stranger she'd seen from upstairs.

He was stooping over the trough to wash his face, his braces hanging down at his thighs, the muscles of his back rippling as he moved. No wonder the girls had stared. He looked like a different breed from Walter Cox: broader, firmer, better made. Mr Goddard had reported that his character reference described him as 'honest, hardworking, and strong.' At least one of those claims was demonstrably true.

She watched as he straightened up, pushing back wet, dark hair and sweeping water from his eyes. New faces were a rarity at Coldwell.

Especially faces like his.

'Hard at work, Mrs Furniss? I hope I'm not interrupting you.'

'Oh!'

'Sorry, I startled you.'

Randolph Hyde's valet was standing in the doorway, but he came into the room now, looking past her, out of the window. 'I believe it's Mr Goddard's job to keep an eye on the footmen, but you always go above and beyond your own duties. Your thoroughness is commendable indeed.'

Frederick Henderson. She'd forgotten just how unpleasant he was. Or maybe he'd become more so since Mr Hyde's last visit. He was short but oddly stocky, with oiled hair like patent leather, and his face was shadowed by a neat black beard which was possibly intended to disguise the pockmarks on his cheeks. He observed all the correct courtesies, but there was something insinuating about the way he spoke that turned them into suggestive over-familiarities. Kate remembered that from his last stay; it wasn't what he said that set alarm bells jangling in her head but the way he said it.

To her irritation, she felt her face heat up.

'Can I help you, Mr Henderson?'

'I hope so.' He held up the garment he was carrying. 'Mr Hyde's dinner jacket needs brushing.' His eyes creased into a mirthless smile above the beard. 'Chorus girls' face powder is the very devil to remove.'

He picked a cherry from the cake on the table and popped it into his mouth, and for a second she saw the pink glisten of his tongue. There was a rumour that he'd suffered from smallpox out in India before he'd started working for Mr Hyde, but Kate didn't know if that was true. There were a lot of rumours about Mr Henderson, and she wondered if—like the beard—they weren't also designed to distract and disguise. The only things that anyone knew for sure were that he'd been Randolph Hyde's man for a long time, and his loyalty was unshakeable.

'Try rubbing alcohol,' she said coolly, moving the cake from the table onto the workbench.

'Perhaps you'd be good enough to furnish me with some?'

'It's in the storeroom.'

He had positioned himself so that he was blocking her exit. She eyed the doorway pointedly and waited for him to move aside. He did so but followed her along the corridor to the storeroom and leaned against the doorframe (again blocking her way) as she scanned the shelves of linseed and turpentine, beeswax and borax.

'So . . . what do you make of all this, then? Sir Henry's marriage ultimatum. The bachelor brought to heel. I daresay it'll be strange for you to have a mistress at Coldwell, after all this time.'

She glanced at him. 'If you're talking about Miss Addison, aren't you jumping ahead rather? Unless I'm mistaken, Mr Hyde hasn't asked her to marry him yet.'

'He's going to. Strictly between you and me, of course.' His voice was teasingly intimate and made the hairs on the back of her neck rise. 'Why else do you think he's brought her up here to present for the old man's approval?'

'Even so. You don't know that she'll say yes.'

He laughed. 'You've seen her. She's hardly in a position to say no—fast heading for forty and no hint of an offer for years. She's something of a white elephant, is Miss Addison ... father's a Shropshire ironmonger who made a lot of grubby new money and spent it on piano lessons and deportment for his plain daughter. She's quite the lady of the manor in Nowhere-on-the-Wold and too refined to be the wife of a local farmer. She must have thought all her prayers had been answered when Mr Hyde turned up at the local hunt ball.'

Kate couldn't imagine a scenario in which Randolph Hyde would be the answer to anyone's prayers but kept that to herself.

'He wasn't keen on the idea at first, I'll admit,' Henderson went on, 'but with a bit of persuasion, he saw the advantages. The ironmonger's money will come in handy. The state of this old place—' He looked around with elaborate distaste. 'It'll take a lot of cash to drag it into the modern age and make it fit for civilised habitation again. And there comes a time when the idea of settling down becomes very appealing, even to the most confirmed bachelor.' Henderson's fingers brushed hers as she handed him the bottle of rubbing alcohol. 'Things change, don't they? Priorities shift. After years of travelling around the world, a man can realise that everything he needs can be found at home.'

A sinister softness had entered his tone. For a moment, Kate had believed that the touch of his fingers had been accidental, but the way he was looking at her—with a narrowed, appraising gaze—withered that hope. She jerked her hand away and buried it in the folds of her skirt, making the silver chains of her chatelaine rattle.

'If that's all? I have a lot to be getting on with.'

She locked the storeroom. Without looking back, she walked briskly along the corridor to the stillroom where, over the usual scent of sugar, tea, and nutmeg, the smell of his hair oil lingered.

The servants' hall lay between the stone stairs and the kitchen; a long room with a fireplace halfway along one side and a row of windows along the other. (These were set high up in the wall, level with the front drive so any visitors—or their feet, at least—might be seen approaching.) Staff tea was served in there at half past five; and Jem followed Thomas, hanging back and waiting to be shown where to sit at the long table. He knew how much these things mattered in the below-stairs kingdom.

'It's not usually like this,' Thomas said apologetically, gesturing him to a chair. 'There's normally only a few of us here—me and the girls, and Joseph. A lot quieter.'

Everyone had been too busy for proper introductions, but Jem was able to work out who was who. Lord and Lady Etchingham had arrived in time for afternoon tea, and their maid and valet took seats opposite each other now, on either side of Mr Goddard. Walter Cox, the loud London footman, tried to slide into the chair between the two housemaids, but the housekeeper, passing behind, redirected him, with a tap on the shoulder, to the empty space beside Jem. Cox grinned. 'Worth a try, ladies,' he said as he got up.

Randolph Hyde's valet was the last to sit down. As everyone bowed their heads and the ancient butler recited grace, Jem could feel the valet's eyes on him. When he looked up, the man was still staring, and their eyes held. Jem looked away first.

Around him, the business of eating got underway and the room filled up with the chink of china, the scrape of cutlery. It was the same in every servants' hall; the race to swallow something down before a bell summoned you or time ran out and you had to set aside your own needs to attend to someone else's. In some houses no talking was allowed at mealtimes, which at least allowed you to get on and eat, but this clearly wasn't the case at Coldwell. Conversation was conducted in quick bursts, between mouthfuls.

'Did you hear about the break-ins?' Lady Etchingham's maid said, addressing the table at large with an air of self-importance.

'Break-ins?'

It was Miss Addison's maid who spoke. She looked as on edge in this unfamiliar place as Jem felt.

Lady Etchingham's maid glanced at her in surprise, as if she hadn't noticed she was there and was directing her story at a more important audience.

'Yes, two of them: one at Darnhall Park, one at Fellside—both in the last month.' She leaned over to fork a slice of ox-tongue onto her plate. 'They got in through a window both times and took some bits of silver and what have you. Isn't that right, Mr Burns?'

Lord Etchingham's valet didn't look up from his plate as he nodded. Miss Addison's maid put her hand to her throat as if feeling for absent diamonds, though the only adornment she wore was a white ribbon pinned to her plain dress. Looking down the table towards the housekeeper, she asked for confirmation that someone had put Miss Addison's jewels in the safe.

Opposite Jem, the blonde housemaid, Eliza, rolled her eyes. 'I did. Not in the safe—that's in the library and we're not permitted in there—but I took them to the silver cupboard in the butler's pantry. That's where we keep the valuables.'

'You don't have to worry, Miss Dunn,' Walter Cox added, with a wink at Eliza, 'I've been reliably informed that the hallboy's bed is across the door to the silver cupboard, so anyone breaking in to steal would have to get past him first.' He raised his voice to address the scrawny lad eating his tea on a chair by the door. 'Isn't that right, Joseph?'

Looking up, Jem was ambushed by a shock of emotion that sucked all the sound from the room. In that second, with his fair head bent and the plate balanced on his bony knees, the hallboy looked for all the world like Jack.

Jack, ten years ago, when Jem had seen him last.

Joseph nodded vigorously, his bulging cheeks turning pink. Everyone laughed.

Jem felt light-headed, as if he couldn't get enough air. The conversation moved on to the upcoming coronation, and whether Sir Henry would be well enough to go to the London house during the celebrations. The light outside was fading, the lamps yet to be lit, and the shadows seeping in from the passage outside seemed full of secrets and menace. The livery Thomas had found for him was on the small side across the shoulders and in the collar. Perhaps that was why he felt so constricted. So suffocated.

'So ... Arden, isn't it ... ? I must say, your arrival was well-timed. I understand you join us from a ... *railway inn*, is that right?'

Hyde's valet had been silent so far, as if the domestic small talk was beneath him. His tone now was friendly enough, but it didn't conceal the barb.

Jem cleared his throat. 'I was at the Station Hotel in Sheffield.'

'I know that place,' Thomas said. 'It's massive. Well—I say I know it— never been in, of course. Far too grand for the likes of me.'

Henderson ignored him, one eyebrow arched at Jem. 'And where were you before that—the Coach and Horses in Hatherford?'

If this was an attempt at humour, it was an awkward one. Jem decided not to rise to the valet's bait and to answer in earnest, to banish any speculation from the outset.

'Before that I was footman for an American gentleman—a Mr Randall Winthrop, in Mayfair.'

He was aware of everyone around the table listening. Sweat sprang up on the back of his neck, but he forced himself to continue. 'I've moved around a bit. I started out with Lord Halewood at Upton Priory and then I was at Deeping Hall in Hampshire for five years, with Lord Benningfield. His wife is French, so the household spent half the year abroad—'

'Did you travel with them?' Eliza asked, her eyes widening. 'To France?'

Across the table, the valet's face was in shadow, but Jem could feel the weight of his stare. He nodded, grateful for the interruption, and even more grateful when Thomas joined in, cheerfully spooning piccalilli onto his plate and relieving Jem of the burden of attention.

'Rather you than me. I couldn't go in for all that travelling abroad. In my last place, I worked with a lad who'd gone to America in his previous job. Sick as a dog all the way there and back, he was—five days each way. He said he—'

'Thank you, Thomas, that's enough.'

It was the first time Jem had heard the housekeeper speak, though he'd been aware of her all through the meal and had to make a conscious effort not to turn to look at her directly. He was certain she was the figure he had seen at the window earlier, though he wouldn't have guessed that she was the housekeeper and would struggle to believe it now if it wasn't for the heavy silver chatelaine at her waist. All the housekeepers he'd known had been twice her age and had come in roughly two varieties: the maternal sort, who ran the servants' basement like a nursery, and the sour, hard-faced ones, who clanked their keys like jailers. (He knew all too well about those.)

He'd never come across one like Mrs Furniss; an aloof beauty with a cool, blue gaze that he felt might see straight through his tissue of falsehoods and fabrications. She was the last thing he had expected in this neglected, out-of-the way place, and for some reason that jolted him.

As if reading his mind, she looked up and caught him staring at her. It seemed she was about to say something but was interrupted by the scrape of a chair from the other end of the table as the butler got to his feet, dabbing his mouth with a napkin. A murmured groan went round the table as cutlery clattered down onto unfinished plates (the standard servants' hall rule that everyone had to stop eating when the butler did was one of the reasons Jem had preferred work in a hotel). Beside him, Thomas crammed in a last mouthful of ham and piccalilli as they all stood up.

The butler drew himself upright from his habitual stoop and peered down his long nose at the rows of servants on either side of the table. 'This is an important evening for Coldwell and its visitors,' he said in his rusty voice. 'I ask everyone to do Sir Henry proud. Let us make it an occasion to remember.'

The impact of this speech was slightly diminished by the distant slam of a door and the advance of heavy footsteps. The cook's voice echoed along the passageway. 'Right, then, everyone, let's get this ruddy show on the road.'

Without turning his head, Jem knew the housekeeper's gaze was still on him. The moment she looked away, he felt it. As if some physical contact had been broken.

Chapter 3

It had been a long time since a formal dinner had been held at Coldwell.

Usually, old Sir Henry had his meals at a small table in the Yellow Parlour or on a tray in his bedroom, but that night, the dining room had been opened up; aired, dusted, and polished to within an inch of its life. When Kate brought up the floral centrepiece for the table, created from the sparse materials available in the gardens (more lilac—the poor plundered tree—filled out with plenty of trailing ivy) she was satisfied with what she saw.

With the blinds lowered against the deepening evening, the bald patches on the dark green flocked wallpaper were less obvious, and the room was alive with candlelight. It glinted off the gold rims of the Spode dinner service and Indian silverware, brought back from the subcontinent by generations of Hydes who had followed the family tradition of serving in the East India Company. The house, like some ancient dowager duchess, had been woken up and decked in the finest trappings of Empire, the best family jewels, ready to receive her guests.

It was a different story downstairs. As the family and guests assembled in the drawing room, Mrs Gatley, her face glistening like a boiled ham, shouted a mixture of instructions, invectives, and prayers through the swirling steam while Susan scuttled between stove and scullery. A trio of girls, fetched from the nearest village of Howden Bridge for pot-washing duties, huddled in the passage, whispering behind their hands and gaping at the footmen. Walter Cox strutted up and down in the formal livery he had brought with him from the London house, which was newer and smarter than the ancient ones from the Coldwell wardrobe, its brass buttons untarnished, its scarlet cuffs unfrayed. Beside him, Thomas and the new footman looked like they'd stepped out of the sepia servant photographs on the wall of the kitchen passage: the ghosts of the men who had first worn the faded, braided tailcoats and white knee-breeches to climb the same stairs and carry the same silver serving dishes more than a century before.

Kate had seen the new footman looking at those photographs. He'd turned away guiltily when he heard her approach, as if she'd caught him doing something he shouldn't. It occurred to her that he might be looking for someone in particular, someone who had worked here, in which case he would likely be disappointed: the most recent photograph was over ten years old. The tradition of the biannual servants' hall portrait was just one of the many things at Coldwell that Sir Henry had neglected to maintain.

She couldn't deny that there was something about Jem Arden that bothered her. Something that didn't quite add up. He had gone out of his way by some considerable margin to secure the footman's position (which in itself was unusual) and yet he didn't seem pleased to be here. She had watched him at teatime, noticing that he seemed ill at ease and ate hardly anything. She wondered what had compelled him to leave his employment in the bustling Station Hotel and cross the moors to this place.

Servants' halls were full of secrets. Character references were full of lies.

Maybe she was reading too much into it. Maybe Jem Arden was simply regretting his decision; he'd probably expected Coldwell Hall to be a much grander and more comfortably appointed situation. He wouldn't be the only one to find the place unsatisfactory. He wouldn't be the first to stay only a few days before heading off down the drive, back to civilisation.

Just as long as he waited until Miss Addison's visit was over, she thought grimly. It didn't matter what had brought Jem Arden to Coldwell, or whether he liked it, so long as he provided the benefit of his handsome face and fine, liveried physique for the next three days, and left the girls alone.

After that, he could join the ranks of faded, forgotten figures who had marched before him through Coldwell's basements and back stairs, before disappearing, never to be heard of again.

———∞∞∞———

Thomas didn't lose his temper easily, but Walter Cox was sorely testing his patience.

As if it wasn't hard enough, three of them serving a five-course dinner in full livery with Mr Goddard watching like a hawk from his place by the sideboard. The last thing they needed was Cox showing off and fooling about, necking wine from bottles the minute he was through the dining room door and tossing grapes in the air to catch in his mouth. Mrs Furniss had caught him in the kitchen passage, swiping an almost full glass of champagne from a tray Thomas was carrying, and given them a tongue-lashing that ended with a threat to dock both their wages.

It was ruddy unfair.

The new lad wasn't much help, either. Thomas wasn't sure how dinner was served at the Station Hotel in Sheffield, but he would have thought they'd have to be a bit more on the ball than Jem Arden had been, serving the first course. Maybe he was nervous, but that was no excuse for sloshing consommé over the side of the bowl, so it nearly splashed into Randolph Hyde's lap. You'd think he'd never set foot in a dining room before.

Maybe it was the heat, which billowed steamily through the down-stairs passages and made his shirt stick to his back. Depositing a serving dish containing the ruins of Mrs Gatley's poached salmon in the scullery, Thomas tore his white gloves off and pushed past Susan at the sink to plunge his hands under a stream of cold water.

'Just be glad those old wigs weren't fit for use,' Susan remarked sympathetically. 'They'd be the devil to wear in this heat.'

Thomas, drying his hands on the dish towel she held out, gave a grudging grunt of agreement.

It had been years since the white powdered wigs worn as part of the formal livery had last been needed, and when they were taken out from the cupboard in the footmen's wardrobe they were found to be as yellowed and patchy as the stuffed ferrets in the glass case on the garden corridor.

'Don't get too excited,' Walter Cox said knowingly, swaggering in behind him with a tray of glasses. 'When Mr Hyde takes over it's my guess you'll be getting new wigs, and new livery too. Likes his footmen to look the business, Mr Hyde does.' He winked at the village girl who was unloading the tray. 'Come to think of it, he might look to get some new footmen while he's about it.'

'You cheeky sod—'

It was the final straw. Without thinking, Thomas flicked the dish towel in Walter's direction, but Walter dodged aside and darted out into the corridor just as Mrs Furniss appeared in the doorway. She opened her mouth to issue a reprimand, but only managed a gasp as Cox nearly collided with the new footman coming the other way, a laden tray in his outstretched arms.

Time faltered and stalled.

Kate heard Jem Arden spit out a curse and saw the stack of plates teeter. The Spode sauceboat tipped. For a second, she was frozen, helpless . . . before the world jerked into motion again and she was lunging forwards, somehow managing to catch it as it fell.

Dimly, she was aware of Walter tossing an apology over his shoulder as he ran up the stairs. She would have to deal with him later, and Thomas, who was hovering miserably behind her, his face a picture of contrition. For now, her skirts were splashed with hollandaise, and the new footman was standing in front of her, his face ashen and his lips white.

'Sorry.'

'You weren't to blame.'

He gave a nod of acknowledgement and made to move past her, but she blocked his way.

'Wait—Are you unwell?'

There was a sheen of sweat on his skin. His jaw was set, and a muscle flickered above it in the hollow of his cheek.

'I'm fine.'

'You're clearly anything but fine. Do I have to spell out the consequences of drinking on duty to you as well?'

It was the only thing she could think of, though she knew it made no sense; he'd come from a taproom, not a temperance society, like Miss Addison's maid. Even if he had been stupid enough to be led astray by Walter

Cox, they'd only got as far as the entrées. He couldn't have downed enough stolen wine for it to have such an effect already.

'I haven't been drinking.'

His eyes were dark, all pupil and no iris. She could sense the tension coming from him: a taut, pent-up energy that felt a little like anger. She put the sauceboat on his tray and took it from him, nodding in the direction of the butler's pantry. 'Go and wash your face and get some water. Hurry up.'

She deposited the tray and went into the scullery to sponge the sauce from her dress. Dismayed by the oily stain it left and wondering how she might shift it (fuller's earth?) she went to find him in the butler's pantry.

He was standing by the sink, his back towards her as he drank water from his scooped hands. He turned as she came in, wiping his mouth on the scarlet cuff of his livery coat. A little of the colour had returned to his cheeks, but his eyes still had a dark glitter.

'I'll get back to work.'

He picked up his gloves and crossed the room, but she closed the door before he reached it.

'Not until I say so, Mr Arden. Do you have a fever?'

'No.' His eyes were fixed on a point above her left shoulder. His expression was one of exaggerated resignation. 'I told you, I'm not unwell.'

She gave a tut of impatience. 'I can't risk illness amongst my staff, Mr Arden. Not ever, but particularly not now.'

Reaching up, she touched the backs of her fingers to his cheek. He flinched, as if he too had felt the jolt that passed down her arm. His skin was as cool and smooth as marble. She pulled away sharply.

His eyes met hers, faintly challenging. 'Can I go now?'

She opened the door and stood back to let him pass, not remotely reassured.

It was dark when Jem slipped out of the door and into the yard. The village girls were gone and the last of the endless crystal glasses had been dried and returned to its correct place in the butler's pantry. The cook had finished, and the lamps were turned out, so the large kitchen window held only the dim glow from the passageway, not strong enough to push away the endless country blackness.

Sitting on the edge of a stone trough by the wall, he let out a long, slow breath. He felt dazed, his head full of jolting, disjointed impressions from the day. They replayed themselves behind his eyes, like a magic lantern turned by a clumsy hand.

Tipping back his head, he looked up at the sky and discovered that the darkness was spangled with stars, sprinkled like sugar across the heavens. At least they felt familiar, though it had been a while since he had seen them in such abundance. Their silent shimmer anchored him, reminding him of home.

Of Jack.

When he'd seen the advertisement, it had felt like stumbling across the key to a locked door. The cogs of the universe, turning slowly all this time, seemed to jolt forward, gears in the earth's invisible mechanism slotting into place and telling him that this was the opportunity he had been waiting for.

He just wasn't sure what to do with it.

He had set out this morning with only a broken trail of clues to follow; the stale crumbs of rumour and the gnawing need to know the truth that had tormented him for the last nine years. Hatred churned sourly in his gut and acid burned in his throat, an echo of the nausea that had almost overwhelmed him earlier. Going into the dining room, his reaction to the physical presence of Hyde had been visceral. It had taken all Jem's willpower not to grab him by his thick throat, throw him against the wall, and ask him for the truth outright. After all these years of not knowing, it was dazzlingly tempting.

But he knew better than to let emotion cloud his judgement. If he was going to find out what had happened to his brother, he had to tread carefully this time. Cleverly. If he ruined this chance, he knew he wouldn't get another.

From somewhere on the far side of the yard he heard the creak and bang of the privy door and a light appeared, swaying as it came closer. Jem stilled, waiting for whoever carried it to pass him and go inside, but at the door it stopped, then swung around in a wide arc. A voice came from behind it.

'Jem? We wondered where you'd got to. Thought you'd had enough and done a runner.'

Thomas's voice. He held the lamp aloft so that Jem was drawn into its circle of light.

He forced a dutiful smile. 'Too bloody tired.'

Thomas's laugh came from the shadows. 'Tell me about it. I thought you'd be used to it, coming from a big hotel. We've not had to work so hard for years—got used to having it easy.' The light retreated as he turned back towards the door. 'Any road, you'd better come in before Mr Goddard locks up. You'll be stopping out there, otherwise.'

Jem hesitated, lifting his eyes to the stars again. From through the archway across the yard he could just catch the faint, familiar scent of hay and horses and, in that moment, in spite of his bone-deep exhaustion, he would have willingly traded a bed inside the walls of Coldwell Hall for a coat thrown down on the straw in its stables.

He'd slept in far worse places, after all.

Reluctantly he got to his feet. 'Coming,' he said.

—⌾—

It wasn't chance that brought me to Coldwell that day.

I went to find out what happened to my brother, who had disappeared during a shooting party there in 1902, while he was in the employment of Viscount Frensham. I was working abroad when he went missing and didn't know for a year that he hadn't returned to Ward Abbey after the visit. No one could give me any answers and it took all that time to discover that Coldwell was the last place he had been seen.

From then on, I made it my business to learn all I could about Randolph Hyde. He had returned to India by then, but was well-known in London. I dug out scraps of gossip about his drinking, gambling, and discovered which gentlemen's clubs he belonged to, which brothels he favoured. Everything I found out confirmed my suspicion that he had something to do with Jack's disappearance. I just didn't know what.

I had never set eyes on him, but I hated him.

On the day I came to Coldwell, hatred had been my companion for a long time. Like the bombardment, I didn't notice that it was getting bigger and louder and filling all the spaces between. With the guns, the noise becomes every-thing. You can't think beyond it. You can't remember what quiet was like. Even when it stops you still hear it, because by then it's too late. It's inside your head and nothing will ever be peaceful again.

Does that sound like I'm making excuses for what I did?

Maybe I am.

Chapter 4

Sarah Dunn stood outside the housekeeper's room, her head tipped to one side as she listened.

It was Sunday morning; early, but the maids were already at work and she had asked the kitchen girl—the nervy one with the pale eye-lashes and the litany of superstitions—for hot water to take up to Miss Addison's room. She was sure the housekeeper would be up, but was it too early to knock?

She didn't really have any choice.

Mrs Furniss's voice came faintly from within. Entering, Miss Dunn found her at her desk, head bent over her ledger, dark hair escaping from a loose plait down her back. She was wearing a mauve silk housecoat, which Miss Dunn (who had been employed in the ladies' lingerie department of Rackhams in Birmingham before taking up the position of lady's maid) recognised as being of surprisingly superior quality. Mrs Furniss didn't look round immediately, but when she did, the early light showed shadows beneath her eyes and a deep line between her brows. She started slightly.

'Oh—Miss Dunn! I'm sorry—I was expecting one of the girls—'

'It's I who should apologise, Mrs Furniss, for disturbing you so early.'

'Is everything all right? Is there something you need?'

'I'm afraid so. Unfortunate timing, and rather unexpected . . .' Miss Dunn lowered her gaze and trailed off unhappily, hoping the other woman wouldn't press her to elaborate. It wasn't the workings of the female body that made her uncomfortable but the unshakeable sense that such matters were between her and her mistress, and she was betraying a trust in disclosing such intimate information to a stranger.

Thankfully the housekeeper needed no further explanation. 'I see.' She got to her feet, reaching for the silver chatelaine that lay beside her on the desk in a tangle of chains. 'I'll get rags. Do you need clean sheets? A fresh nightdress?'

Miss Dunn shook her head. 'Just water, for washing. I've asked the girl in the kitchen.'

While Mrs Furniss unlocked the linen cupboard (which appeared to be almost a small room in itself, accessed through a door in the panelling) Miss Dunn looked around her parlour. It had two windows, looking out onto the kitchen courtyard, but the sun had not yet reached them, and the low ceiling and oak-panelled walls made the room seem dark. It was furnished comfortably enough, with a little button-back armchair upholstered in pale blue velvet and a small table beside it, a threadbare rug beneath. On the mantelpiece there was a clock and two brass candlesticks, and a single china dog (a spaniel, not unlike Mr Hyde's, though its russet was patched with white) which looked like it had once been one of a pair and had been relegated from one of the upstairs rooms when its mate had got broken.

There were no photographs, she noticed. In fact, there was nothing that gave any clue as to the housekeeper's life beyond these walls, her history before she had come here, or where on earth Miss Dunn might have encountered her before.

Upon arrival at Coldwell, she had been struck by the sense that she had seen Mrs Furniss before. It had been a fleeting certainty that had faded into doubt when she tried to find a place or a time on which to fix it. Now, as Mrs Furniss returned with a thick wad of flannelette squares, their eyes met and recognition fluttered in Miss Dunn's mind once more.

'I hope that'll be enough,' Mrs Furniss said as she handed them over. There was a moment's pause. 'Was there anything else you needed?'

'Oh, no. No, thank you.'

Miss Dunn was aware that she was staring and forced herself to look away. 'I do apologise for disturbing you.'

'Not at all.'

As she moved towards the door, she searched her mind for a casual conversational opening; some way of discovering—without seeming to pry—if, perchance, Mrs Furniss had ever shopped in Rackhams lingerie department? But her mind remained frustratingly blank, and she found herself back out in the corridor, no closer to working out where her path might have crossed the housekeeper's.

Except, she was certain that she would have remembered the house-coat, if Rackhams had ever stocked such a garment. She had an eye for quality and knew style when she saw it (which was why Miss Addison—who had not and did not—had offered her employment).

No, it wasn't the housecoat that had rekindled the ember of a memory. It was the cool beam of that blue gaze.

———⋙⋘———

The vast old house felt different with so many strangers beneath its roof: its atmosphere altered, its age-old stillness shattered. Although Kate was exhausted by meeting the demands of the visitors (Miss Addison proved to be no trouble, but Lady Etchingham was as capricious and demanding as a spoiled toddler), she found it impossible to sleep. In the small hours of both Friday and Saturday night, her restless mind had wandered through corridors and paused outside bedrooms, seeking reassurance that nothing was amiss, and not quite being able to find it.

It was tiredness that had set her nerves on edge, she told herself, trailing back downstairs after taking a tisane up to Lady Etchingham's room on Sunday afternoon (*such terrible indigestion; your cook has a very heavy hand with sauces . . .*). Lack of sleep had brought back that old jittery, unsettled feeling, undermining her confidence, making her question herself. She was dogged by doubt, the feeling that she had forgotten some important duty or neglected some fundamental responsibility and was just waiting to be discovered.

For the punishment to come.

Crossing the hall, she felt the eyes of the second baronet idly following her. On impulse, instead of going downstairs, she turned into the library passage, to check that the girls hadn't missed any stray glasses in the billiard room. Mr Hyde and Lord Etchingham had played after dinner last night, and the room was stale with cigar smoke, redolent of whisky. She raised the sash a fraction to freshen the air and was about to leave when she noticed that the library door was slightly ajar. A ripple of unease spread through her.

The library was an impressive room, with shelves from floor to ceiling and a galleried walkway running around the upper level, reached by a concealed staircase in the corner. The air of neglect and decay that pervaded other rooms at Coldwell was absent there, but Kate still felt a chill of discomfort whenever she entered it. Perhaps it was the miasma of masculinity—cigar smoke and self-assurance—which stirred buried memories. Perhaps it was the macabre collection of objects fashioned from animal parts that made her shudder—the hoof inkwell and horn candlesticks, the elephant's foot coal scuttle and paperknife with the tiger tooth handle—or the framed illustrations on the wall behind the desk, rumoured to have been cut from a book stolen from a Mughal harem, showing naked bodies tangled together in an improbable tableaux of erotic bliss. Or the well-thumbed volumes of 'gentlemen's literature' on the shelves, interspersed among respectable and unread titles, hidden in plain sight.

Heart crashing, she pushed the door open and looked in, wary that Frederick Henderson might be in there. Seeing someone standing by the desk, she was about to make a hasty retreat, before realising that it wasn't the valet at all.

'*Mr Arden.*' Her tone was glacial—did he not know that the servants were not allowed in the library except with express permission? 'I'm quite sure you have good reason to be in here alone, looking through Mr Hyde's publications, but I can't immediately think what it might be. Perhaps you could help me?'

She had expected embarrassment; a deep blush at the very least and some expression of shame at being caught red-handed in a place where servants were not permitted alone. She wondered if Walter Cox had put him up to it. The library was usually kept locked, but gossip about pictures of concubines and naked many-handed goddesses; works of literature by 'A Gentleman of the World' or 'Madame Mauvais' inevitably circulated amongst the servantry—the men in particular. Had Walter dared the new footman to come to see for himself?

If he was uncomfortable, he showed little sign of it: only the rise and fall of his Adam's apple, the flicker of a muscle in his cheek. His face remained expressionless.

'I was looking for a book.'

'A book.' She almost laughed. At least he was honest (hadn't his character said as much?), though she had expected a more creative excuse. 'Was there a particular volume you were hoping to find, or was your interest more general?'

'A particular volume.'

To her horror, he picked it up. Heat flooded her cheeks as he held it out.

'The visitors' book,' he said tonelessly. 'Lady Etchingham mentioned it when I took up the coffee after lunch—she thought it might be in here, though it hasn't been used for years. It was wrong of me to look at it; I'm sorry.'

She swallowed and shook her head as she took the book from him, her throat too dry to respond. Instead, she opened the worn leather cover and feigned interest in the pages of illegible signatures in faded ink and scrawled messages whose meaning had been lost to time.

'The last time it was used was in 1902,' he said, his voice low in the velvet quiet. 'Were you here then?'

'No, I came the following year.'

It wasn't one of those formal visitors' books, where guests had to write in columns and on narrow lines. The paper was plain, to allow for more spontaneous and creative entries. Kate flicked past pen-and-ink sketches and snatches of doggerel verse amongst baffling private jokes (*Delighted to meet 'Lady Gloria.' What a charming young ingénue!!!*). The final entry was dated August 1902 (*Dreadful weather, decent grouse*) and the page facing it was empty, suggesting that had been the last time a house party had gathered at Coldwell. Except—looking closer—she could just make out that a leaf had been removed from the book. Cut cleanly, with a sharp knife.

Intrigued, she touched the edge with the tip of her finger and was about to remark on it when a noise from the billiard room made her jerk her hand away sharply: the rapid scutter of claws, followed by the creak of a door opening. Randolph Hyde's booming voice reached them, and she remembered that Miss Dunn had said something at lunch about Miss Addison being interested in art and hoping for a tour of the paintings.

'Fairly dismal daubs in here, I'm afraid.' Hyde sounded bored. 'Italian ruins. Some forbear or other bought the lot for a knock-down price in Italy—souvenirs of the Grand Tour. Put me off bothering with the place, frankly. You'd think Italy would be sunny but look at that for a pea-souper. Give me India any day. Still, this room's only used as a chaps' mess, so anything better would be wasted. Shall we—?'

'But isn't that another room?' Miss Addison asked. 'May I—?'

Kate's eyes flew up to meet Jem Arden's. Her heart was beating so hard that she thought he must hear it. Clasping the visitors' book against her chest, she nodded to the staircase in the corner.

He understood her meaning immediately, moving swiftly to open the narrow door in the panelling and letting her go ahead of him into the small space. It was a standard rule in most houses that servants should avoid being seen upstairs by the family at all costs, though as housekeeper Kate had a little more licence. But not when it came to the library, with its collection of explicit gentlemen's material.

The staircase was narrower than she'd recalled. Light filtered dimly down from above, and the air smelled of old paper and dust. As Jem pulled the door shut, she climbed the first two steps of the spiral staircase, wincing at the creak they made, not daring to go further. They were just in time. From outside came the frantic patter of the spaniel's feet, the excited snuffle of his nose in the gap beneath the door.

Hyde's laugh followed, abrupt and uneasy. 'Aha, you've discovered my bachelor den. Coldwell's own little gentlemen's club.'

'Oh, gosh, what a simply marvellous room! All these books . . . such treasures! I didn't know you were a reader, Mr Hyde.'

'Yes, well—matter of fact, I'm not, terribly,' Hyde drawled. 'No time for all that out in India, y'know, but one has to admit books look the part in an English country house. The second baronet created this room, dear Great-uncle Aubrey.'

'He's the one in the painting in the hallway? The tiger hunter?'

'That's the chap. Family scoundrel. Quite a character—we still have all his papers here, of course. As a matter of fact, I started going through them, years ago, writing a sort of biography thing. Fascinating chap. Must pick it up again when I have more time. Now, why don't we—'

Praying for them to leave, Kate scarcely dared breathe. Jem Arden stood below her, very still, his back against the wall and his head bent. She couldn't see his face, only the hollow at the nape of his neck where the hair grew to a soft point. Close up, she noticed that it was the tawny brown of old tortoiseshell, which looked black until you held it up to the light and saw that it was shot through with gold. He would have been blond as a boy, she found herself thinking.

'Oh—that's the tower on the hill, isn't it?' The tap of Miss Addison's feet came closer, and Kate pictured her going over to the fireplace to look at the painting that hung over it. 'The one I saw when we arrived. What did you say it was called?'

'The temple. Another of Great-uncle Aubrey's projects. It's the gatehouse of the old hunting lodge that was demolished to make the present house; dates back to the sixteenth century. They kept it as a sort of folly, but Aubrey kitted it out with carved panels from a temple in Pondicherry and used it as a gambling den.' He gave a snort of laughter. 'He used to invite chums to Coldwell to worship in the temple.'

'A scoundrel indeed,' Miss Addison said dryly. 'But how perfectly thrilling to find an Indian temple in darkest Derbyshire. I should love to see inside.'

'Oh—place has been locked up for years. Supposed to be a curse on it, because of the Indian loot. Poppycock of course. It's just a dashed inconvenience—too far from the house to be worth bothering with. Right then—if you're ready, shall we—?'

'What charming prints!' Miss Addison's footsteps advanced, until her voice was only a few feet away, on the other side of the panelling. 'They're Indian too, aren't they? They look terribly old—oh! Goodness me . . .'

'My dear Miss Addison, I did try to warn you.' Hyde's tone was blustering and defensive rather than apologetic. 'A gentlemen's club, you see. Not for ladies' eyes.'

'Nonsense.' Miss Addison recovered her composure admirably fast. 'You forget I'm a country girl, Mr Hyde, from farming stock; I'm not easily shocked. They weren't what I was expecting, that's all, but they're rather beautiful . . . It's our modern way to make a fuss about propriety and modesty and so forth, isn't it? I'm not saying it's wrong, but these are a reminder that the love between a man and a woman is very natural and as old as time, don't you think?'

'Indeed I do, Miss Addison, though of course one must be careful not to frighten the horses.' Hyde gave a bray of uneasy laughter. 'A time and a place for everything, I say.'

The silence that followed felt endless. Kate couldn't imagine what was going on a mere few feet from where they were concealed, but she was aware of the warm scent of Jem Arden's skin; its clean masculinity. His head was still bowed, and her eyes traced the curve of his cheekbone, the thickness of his eyelashes. She was close enough to see the faint stippling of stubble on his jaw, though he must have shaved that morning, and a small scar, faded and well healed, just above the edge of his eyebrow. She imagined lifting her hand to touch it . . . And then Hyde spoke again, his voice gruff and awkward.

'Talking of which . . . well, the thing is—I'm a bit long in the tooth for turtledoves and all that "language of flowers" business, but . . . Well, there comes a time when one thinks of settling down. Don't get me wrong— I'm an infernal old bachelor, too set in my ways and too damned happy in them to change much. But time is ticking on, and a man in my position has certain responsibilities . . .'

Slowly, Jem Arden raised his head and his eyes found Kate's. Breaths held, they gazed at each other, silently acknowledging that they were about to become accidental witnesses to a proposal.

'So you see, I need a wife and Coldwell needs a mistress. The last thing I want is some delicate slip of a girl who can't look out for herself, and it seems to me that you've got a bit of backbone and a sensible head on your shoulders. No silly notions. An arrangement that suits us both. What about it, Leonora? Reckon you could take on this old duffer and his crumbling old pile?'

Jem's eyes were grey. Darker at the edges, like the pools of silvered water you came across on the moors. He shook his head a fraction at the crassness of the proposal, its utter absence of romance or sensitivity, and Kate had to bite the inside of her cheeks to stifle a sudden smile. On the other side of the door. Miss Addison stammered, 'Oh, heavens . . . gosh . . . thank you! I mean, yes. Please,' and Kate remembered Henderson's words. *She's hardly in a position to say no . . .* The smile died again.

There was another beat of silence. Her gaze was still locked with Jem's when they heard the unmistakable sound of a kiss, and for a moment she forgot that it came from Randolph Hyde's damp lips. A meteor shower of stars shimmered through the darkness inside her. Suddenly light-headed, she put her free hand out to lean against the wall, but found herself gripping his shoulder instead.

'Good show, old girl, good show.'

Randolph Hyde's voice was loud, hearty with relief and self-congratulation at this tricky piece of business concluded so easily. 'Now that's settled I rather think it calls for champagne, don't you?'

Clicking his fingers, he gave a sharp whistle and the spaniel's claws skittered on the polished floor. As the dog passed the staircase, his wet nose appeared beneath the door again, sniffing frantically. Kate's hand tightened on Jem's shoulder.

'*Boy!*'

The shout was more distant now, Hyde's voice echoing back as he bore his newly acquired fiancée off like one of his hunting trophies. Kate's head swam with relief and she exhaled heavily at the same time as Jem, so she felt the tension leave his body. Hastily she withdrew her hand from his shoulder, smoothing her skirt, untwisting the chains of her chatelaine, preparing to step out of this tiny space and rejoin the everyday business of the house.

They didn't move.

She felt shaky. Unready. Slowly she held out the visitors' book and he took it from her, not meeting her eye now. She had intended to find out whether he was telling the truth about being asked to find it by Lady Etchingham, but she knew that she would say nothing. Just as he would say nothing about what had just happened. About them hiding together in the cramped space of the staircase while the future of Coldwell was forged only a few feet away.

It would be impossible to explain to anyone else; awkward and improbable, and faintly incriminating for them both. And so they were bound together in an unspoken conspiracy of silence.

Keepers of the same secret.

Chapter 5

'Thank God that's over.'

Up in the footmen's attic Thomas tugged at the knot of his white bow tie and pulled it off with the relief of a man ducking out of the hangman's noose. On the other side of the room Jem Arden was shrugging off his shirt, and Thomas tried not to stare at the well-muscled chest that it revealed.

He'd had the small space to himself since before Christmas and sharing it again was going to take some getting used to. 'You can have a decent bed now,' he remarked, nodding at the iron bedstead in the corner recently vacated by Walter Cox, who was at that moment sitting on the rumble seat at the rear of the carriage as it disappeared up the drive.

Not a moment too bloody soon, as far as Thomas was concerned.

By rights, as the visiting footman, Cox should have had the straw pallet on the floor, but the new lad hadn't been quick enough to claim the bed. He hadn't seemed particularly bothered about it neither, which Thomas couldn't understand—who wouldn't jump at the chance to put that big mouth in his place? Thomas hadn't quite worked him out yet, this Jem Arden character.

Jem shook out the shirt and slipped it onto a hanger. 'The bed'll be great, but it's the quiet I'm going to really appreciate.'

'I know. Cocky sod, isn't he? Bloody Londoners, they're all like that. Think they're summat special.' Shrugging on the fustian jacket they wore for work below stairs, Thomas stopped suddenly and looked at Jem. 'Wait—did you say you were from—?'

'London?' Jem smiled. 'No. Worked there for a bit, that's all.'

'Well, any road, I'm pleased to see the back of him. And the rest of them—including Sir Henry, though I shouldn't say it. Cocky Cox can call it boring, but I'm all for an easy life.'

It was Sir Henry Hyde's habit to stay with his daughter at Whittam Park for a fortnight at this time every year, while the house underwent its annual spring clean. Thomas, assisted by Lord Etchingham's valet, had eased him into the Etchingham carriage as carefully as a piece of priceless furniture, wadding him with blankets and swaddling him in furs.

Jem began to unbutton his trousers. 'Still got two weeks of cleaning to look forward to, though.'

'The clean isn't so bad.' Thomas averted his eyes. 'There's a lot to get done and Mrs Furniss can get quite fierce if she thinks you're slacking, but I'll take a bit of furniture shifting and carpet beating over running up and down with trays and standing in the dining room for hours.' He picked up the livery jacket he'd dropped on the bed, and the discarded bow tie. 'Right. I'll get downstairs and return this lot to the footmen's wardrobe. If you strip that bed, you can bring the sheet down. Laundrywomen are here today.'

He ducked through the low doorway and his footfalls receded on the bare wooden stairs. Jem folded the blanket on Walter's bed, then bundled up the sheet and tossed it in the direction of the door, turning over in his mind what Thomas had said about Mrs Furniss. He wondered what she might look like when she was being fierce and found he was quite intrigued to find out.

He found he was quite intrigued by her generally.

It was an unwelcome inconvenience. Even before they had been en-closed together in the small space of the library staircase, he'd been dis-tracted by her, noticing the shape of her mouth with its sharply defined Cupid's bow, the hollow at the angle of her jaw where her little pearl earring quivered. Standing close enough to inhale her scent (a mixture of roses and nutmeg and vanilla . . . not dissimilar to the potpourri in the

drawing room, but warmer somehow and deeper) had been a painful pleasure, and it had hardened an abstract awareness into something more persistent and difficult to ignore.

But ignoring it was exactly what he intended to do. He hadn't come
this far to be sidetracked by a schoolboy crush. Going over to the straw
pallet on which he'd spent the last three nights, he raised the corner and
picked up the book he'd hidden beneath it. With his shirtsleeve he swiped
the dust off the cover and traced a finger over the gold lettering.

COLDWELL HALL VISITORS' BOOK

He couldn't believe how lucky he'd been to get away with it. When Mrs
Furniss had come across him looking at it, he'd assumed the game was up
and he'd be asked to leave immediately—especially if she also discovered
the cigarette in his pocket, pilfered from the box on Hyde's desk. That's
probably what would have happened if Hyde and Miss Addison hadn't
appeared, putting them both at risk of being caught in the wrong place.

Taking it over to the window he turned to the last written page,
where the leaf had been removed. He lifted the book, tilting it so the
light fell on the paper. It was thick and expensive and bore the faint
imprint of writing.

The windowsill was dusted with grime. He tapped his fingertip in the
dirtiest corner, then rubbed it lightly over the paper, so the impression
made by the pen stood out against the smear, like words whispered from
the past.

GENTLEMEN'S INDIAN HOUSE PARTY.
NOVEMBER 14TH–17TH 1902

His heart had begun to thud more heavily as he repeated the method,
brushing his finger over what looked like a guest list, printed beneath.
Goose bumps rose on his arms as the page gave up its secrets and the
second name in the column was revealed.

Frensham.

No title because that would be vulgar, no first name because that would
be common, but Jem knew who it was. Tobias Forbes, Viscount Frensham,

was Lord Halewood's eldest son. The man whom Jack had worked for at Ward Abbey in the autumn of 1902.

'Bull's-eye,' he murmured.

———❧———

For Kate, there was no time to relax after the carriages had made their swaying way up the drive. As soon as the visitors had departed, and their breakfast dishes were washed, their beds stripped, and the sheets carried across to the steaming laundry, she had to turn her attention to the next task, which was the biggest and most labour-intensive of the housekeeper's year.

The annual spring clean was the time when the windows were thrown open to air stale rooms, carpets were hauled out into the sun to have the dust beaten from them, mirrors and ornaments were cleaned, chimneys swept, floors polished, walls washed down. All the main rooms on the ground floor needed to be worked through, except the library. It alone remained locked, its scandals hidden from the eyes of the servants.

This year, with a wedding suddenly in the offing, it felt like they were doing more than simply shaking off the layers of winter grime. It wasn't only a change of season that they were preparing for but a change of pace at Coldwell. There had been sherry in the servants' hall when Mr Goddard announced the news of Mr Hyde's engagement and proposed a toast to the good health of the happy couple. Mr Hyde would likely be spending a lot more time in Derbyshire when he was married, Frederick Henderson had said, looking pointedly at Kate.

Watching Jem Arden out of the corner of her eye, Kate noticed that he didn't join the dutiful chorus of good wishes, but downed his sherry in a single mouthful with a grimace that suggested he was sealing some private vow, not drinking a toast.

She didn't want to notice. She tried not to, but she found that she was oddly conscious of him. In spite of the demands of the spring clean, the extra staff to supervise, and the list in her ledger (covering two pages and stretching on to a third) of tasks to tick off, she was powerless to stop the prickling awareness of his presence, his movements, almost as if those strange, suspended moments they had shared in the library had left her with an unwelcome sixth sense where he was concerned.

Or, she told herself briskly, maybe it was that she wasn't as easily taken in as Mr Goddard and the others. She had made the mistake of being too trusting before, and taking someone at face value. She wouldn't do it again. She'd let the visitors' book incident go unchallenged for her own sake, not because she believed him. And because she'd half expected him to give notice anyway.

But he didn't.

He showed no sign of it. In the days that followed, as the work got properly underway and the kitchen yard rang with the voices of the laundrywomen and village girls who'd been drafted in to help, the epithets of 'hardworking' and 'strong' in his character proved well chosen. Furniture was hefted away from walls and rugs were rolled up and carried outside more quickly and efficiently than in any previous year Kate could remember.

In addition, he was easy company in the servants' hall, diffusing the petty squabbles that erupted when days were long and tempers short. He made sure to compliment Susan, left in charge of cooking for the staff while Sir Henry was absent, on the meals she rather erratically produced; and in the evenings, while the others dealt hands of cards and gambled for matchsticks, he taught Joseph to play chess. Joseph the skinny hallboy, who had come to Coldwell from the Sheffield Union Workhouse, who slept on a shelf in front of the silver cupboard, and whose job was to do all the things that no one else wanted to. Who was usually left out of servants' hall games or permitted only to take the role of scorer, ball retriever, or referee.

Arden was troublingly handsome too, which was the most highly prized asset for his role (she had overheard an exchange between the laundrywomen one day, with one remarking that he'd fill a livery suit very nicely indeed, and the other one commenting that he'd look even better without it.) All in all, he appeared to be the living embodiment of Mrs Beeton's ideal footman.

So what was he doing at a lonely, left-behind place like Coldwell Hall?

The rhythm of the year was such that the end of the spring clean fortnight always coincided with Howden Bridge Fair, held on the first Monday in May on the expanse of open ground at the edge of the village.

Howden Bridge itself was small and unremarkable; a huddle of grey stone houses tumbled at the foot of the hillside, with a pub called the White Hart (a reference to Henry VIII's legendary hunting coup); a school; a blacksmith's forge and police house; and a tiny, cave-like village shop, poorly stocked with basic provisions. However, its position where the toll road to the north met the old packhorse route running from east to west had long made an obvious place for the trading of livestock. Over the years, the May sheep fair had grown in size and sophistication, drawing farmers, their wives, children, labourers, and maids from every village and lonely moorland farmstead in the Dark Peak, to enjoy novelty stalls, entertainments, food and ale, as well as the business of buying and selling animals. In this remote spot, it was the high point of the year.

It was also an incentive for the Coldwell staff to work hard on the spring clean; and after two weeks, all the major rooms had been turned out. Paintwork had been washed, floors waxed; every delicate china figurine had been wiped over; every gilded picture frame cleaned; and every item of intricate Indian silverware polished to a gleaming shine. Even the animals in the hallway had enjoyed their annual grooming, with Thomas and Jem taking turns to climb the ladders to rub oil into dull horns, brush clouds of dust from dead fur, and buff the tiger's bared teeth so that Mrs Furniss could find no fault and Mr Goddard had to grudgingly agree to a rare day off for the whole household to attend the fair.

The spell of good weather held. Warmth was already thickening the air beneath the sloping attic ceiling as the girls got ready. Eliza had decided she was going to wear the muslin blouse with the embroidered daisies on the collar that she'd bought for two shillings from a former housemaid (whom, except for the blouse, she would have entirely forgotten), but Susan eyed her doubtfully as they hurried down the stairs.

'Aren't you going to put a coat on?'

'No need,' Eliza replied airily, by which she meant *no way*. The blouse was far too pretty to be covered up with her ugly old blue coat, which would also look daft with her summer hat, newly trimmed with the spray of paper violets she'd bought last time she'd made the long trek to Hatherford on her day off.

'It looks fine now, but you know what they say,' Susan warned, hitching her own coat more securely over her arm. '"*Cast ne'er a clout till May be out.*" It could turn nasty yet.'

Eliza had no intention of letting Susan's pessimism spoil either her outfit or her mood. Johnny Farrow was already waiting with the wagon in the stable yard, and Joseph had been sent to hurry them up. 'We'll be going without you if you don't get a move on!' Thomas called as they emerged into the bright dazzle of the yard.

Eliza was surprised to see Mrs Furniss sitting on the front bench beside Johnny Farrow; she didn't usually bother with the fair. But then she remembered that Johnny had agreed to take the housekeeper on to Hatherford to settle the accounts and place orders, tasks which had been postponed over the past fortnight. Mrs Furniss gave a pointed look when she saw the tussle between her and Abigail as they both tried to get the seat next to Jem Arden.

'Hurry up, girls,' she snapped. 'We've waited long enough already.'

She'd been in a sour mood for the last two weeks. Behind her back Eliza pulled a face, feeling a little buzz of satisfaction as Abigail made way and she was able to take the place beside Jem. She folded her skirt neatly about her knees, hoping he'd notice how different she looked when she wasn't in her dowdy uniform. For once—feeling pretty in her pin-tucked, daisy-sprigged muslin—she didn't envy the housekeeper, or wish she could change places. Instead of her usual head-to-toe black Mrs Furniss was wearing a cream cotton blouse with a high lace-edged collar and a dark blue skirt, but she still looked uptight. Like her laces needed loosening.

The wagon creaked and rocked as the others climbed up, Joseph the last to scramble into place. Johnny Farrow flicked the reins and they jolted into motion; and Abigail, still settling herself, pitched sideways and was caught by Thomas. 'You can sit on my knee if you like,' he joked. 'All you had to do was ask.'

'In your dreams, Thomas Booth,' Abigail retorted, throwing Eliza an accusing glare.

But nothing could tarnish the shine of that bright morning. Not even Thomas launching into the tired old story about the year Stanley Twigg got so drunk at the fair that he was sick on a swingboat and fell asleep under Black Tor on the way home.

'What's Black Tor?' Jem asked.

'Dirty great pile of rocks on the track across the moor to the village,' Eliza said, aware of Jem's long thigh inches away from hers on the bench. One hand rested loosely in his lap, the other—thrillingly—stretched along the back of the seat behind her. 'There's an overhanging stone where travellers used to shelter from the weather.'

'Davy Wells saw him wandering home at first light and thought it was Samuel's ghost.' Thomas laughed, finishing the story. 'Gave him such a fright they had to send for the doctor to give him something to calm down.'

Jem turned to Eliza, one eyebrow raised in faint resignation. 'Davy Wells?'

'Mrs Wells's lad, from the gate lodge. Grown-up, but not right in the head. You'll see him wandering around the estate. If you speak to him, don't be offended if he doesn't answer. He's mute.'

Jem nodded. 'Right. So that just leaves Samuel. Or his ghost.'

Abigail gave a gasp of mock horror. 'You mean no one's told you about Samuel?'

'Shows how busy we've been,' Susan remarked. 'Go on, Thomas, you tell it best.'

'Well, it should be told at night, really,' Thomas said, 'but anyway . . . It all starts with Sir Aubrey, the second baronet—the one whose portrait hangs in the entrance hall. He worked out in India, same as the present Mr Hyde, and when he came back to Coldwell, he brought a lot of the things you see around the house today: hunting trophies and fancy silverware and all manner of artefacts, including a young Indian boy called Samuel.'

'That wasn't his real name,' Abigail interjected, 'but what Sir Aubrey called him. His English name.'

Susan nudged her to be quiet. 'Whatever you want to call him, Sir Aubrey used him as a tiger—carriage groom, you know? Unsurprisingly, the lad didn't take to Coldwell—homesick, I should imagine; missed the warmth—and the story goes that during one of Sir Aubrey's long house parties, he tried to escape. But, here's the thing—' Thomas leaned forward in the swaying carriage, lowering his voice. 'It was winter, and the boy wasn't familiar with the landscape. He lost his way in the snow, and his body was found by poachers in the woods behind the temple, stripped naked and frozen to death. It's said that on winter nights when the moon is bright, you'll see his ghost running between the trees as if pursued by the hounds of hell . . .'

For a moment, they clipped along in silence. They had crested the rise now and the house was lost from sight, though the tower was still visible.

Jem turned his head to look at it, and Eliza saw that his expression was oddly tense. Usually, the ghost story generated a thrill of excitement, but somehow it had fallen a bit flat. Thomas was right: it was best told at night, when the circle of lamplight made all the listeners huddle together in awareness of the shadows at their backs.

'His grave is in the churchyard,' Abigail offered. '"Samuel, Tyger to Sir Aubrey Hyde, Second Baronet Bradfield" it says on the stone. Tourists come and look for it sometimes.'

Just then, a movement ahead caught the corner of Eliza's eye, a white flash breaking cover from the gloom of the coppice to the right. The horses saw it too; one faltered and tossed its head, making the wagon lurch. There was a beat of air. On the seat opposite, Susan gave a screech and buried her face in her hands as the bird swooped silently across the path.

'Saints alive,' Thomas stuttered. 'What was that?'

'It's all right,' Jem said. 'It was just a barn owl.'

Susan's face was white as she lowered her hands and crossed herself with trembling fingers. 'It's bad luck to see them in daylight, didn't you know? A barn owl flying in daylight foretells a *death*.'

'Oh, for God's sake,' Eliza muttered.

That girl could spot the Grim Reaper behind every corner and suck the fun out of anything. As they approached the gate lodge Eliza saw a figure move in the shadow of the wall and felt her own heart kick with fear, until she realised it was just Davy Wells, keeping watch, as he always did. He sprang forward and opened the gate, turning his wary, unsmiling face towards them as they passed.

It was surprisingly cool out of the sun. Goose bumps stippled the skin beneath Eliza's daisy-embroidered blouse, and she found herself wishing that she'd brought her coat.

June 26th

The guns are still going on. It's very wet and we're back in the reserve lines. The countryside here reminds me of where I grew up in Oxfordshire—meadows and copses and farmhouses, gentle and green, not at all like the hills and moors around Coldwell. The farmhouses are mostly ruined now, by shelling and army occupation.

As I came back from night fatigues this morning a barn owl flew low over our heads, following the line of the trench. They nest in the ruined buildings and probably can't believe their luck with all the fat rats here. I thought of the day we went to the fair at Howden Bridge, and what Susan said when that owl broke cover from the wood.

In this place, I think there's a good chance she'd be right.

Chapter 6

The smell of a fair assaulted her nose: roast meat, trampled grass, spilled ale, horses, and hot humanity. Kate picked her way through the crowd, around fractious children and snappy mothers; stocky farm workers whose cheeks were crimson with warmth and beer. Her throat was dry and beneath her hat the hair at the nape of her neck was damp. The clouds had swelled, swallowing up the blue sky and blocking out the sun. It was warmer than ever; a dull, sticky heat.

She had finished her business in Hatherford quickly, aware that Johnny Farrow had not hitched the horses and gone into the Bull's Head for his usual pint, but was waiting on the wagon outside the bank. She had seen him through the pyramids of cocoa tins and tea packets piled in the window of Pearson's the grocers as she'd placed her orders, flicking his whip moodily, impatient to return to Howden Bridge where the aroma of roasting hog was already filling the air when they'd dropped the others off.

She had also seen herself reflected in the window's glass—a stiff-shouldered, pinch-faced spinster in an unbecoming hat, whose image stayed with her as she made her way through the crowds at the fair. She would have liked to go into the tent where tea was being served, or join the queue for homemade cordials at a penny a glass, but she felt self-conscious and exposed. Each casual, curious glance of a passing stranger was like a blow on an old bruise.

And there were so many strangers. So many men whose eyes sought out a woman alone, who looked, and kept on looking, just because they could. It was idle interest, that was all, not purposeful scrutiny. Even so, she saw *him* everywhere; in a set of narrow shoulders or the curl of black hair on a collar. A purposeful walk, the flick of a hand. A shouted greeting in a Scottish accent set her heart rattling.

It made no sense, of course. Alec Ross had his fingers in many business pies, all bigger and more richly filled than trading animals at a rural fair. There was no logical reason to suspect that he might appear in Howden Bridge; but fear, once it had taken root, didn't need logic to spread and flourish.

Slipping through the knots of people, she lowered her head and quickened her pace, not slowing until she'd crossed the packhorse bridge and left the fair behind. Her blouse stuck to the skin between her shoulder blades and her scalp prickled. The day's mood had changed; the light had congealed and the summer warmth had thickened into something oppressive. Clouds billowed and boiled above the hilltops.

If the weather was fair, she rather enjoyed the two-mile walk between Howden Bridge and Coldwell. The path followed the river for a little way as it rushed and crashed over rocks (the water brown with peat, like coffee) before they parted company and the path twisted upwards between rocky outcrops, thickets of bracken, and purple heather to cross an exposed stretch of moorland, with the hills of the Dark Peak circling it like an amphitheatre. Today the climb felt arduous, and she longed to be in her room, where she could peel off her heavy clothing and drop her mask of respectability. She wanted to shut the door, unhook her corset, and lie in luxurious cool and quiet, safe from prying eyes.

She felt the first drops of rain as she reached the top of the ridge. A shiver of wind went over the clumps of coarse cotton grass and rippled through the heather. Black Tor was a little way ahead, a dark shape against the pewter sky. She broke into a half run as, with a rushing sound, the heavens opened. The world's edges dissolved into a hazy blur, its details lost behind sheets of teeming water.

She stopped and tipped her face up, surrendering to the downpour. Within seconds her shoulders were soaked, the cold water seeping onto her skin, dripping down her face. After the fears and frustrations of the day the force of the rain seemed unsurprising, and almost personal—one more challenge to overcome—and there was something liberating in refusing to run and simply giving in. But she couldn't stand there forever. Unpinning her hat (made of black raffia and not intended to withstand such a soaking) she walked on, shaking back her head and hitching up her wet skirts, wading over the splashy ground.

The gritstone rocks that made up Black Tor had not been positioned by human endeavour but carved from the landscape by a million years of weather. It was rain and biting wind that had created a shelter between the massive stones; a sort of cave, like a cupped hand, which had offered centuries of protection to drovers and their animals. Rain bounced off the flat stone that formed its roof. Inside it smelled of earth and wet and sheep.

And . . . tobacco smoke?

She peeled off her gloves, freeing her reddened, work-roughened skin from the chafe of damp cotton. The roar of the rain was hushed here, so she heard the soft inhalation of breath before she noticed someone leaning against the back of the cave, smoking a cigarette.

She stiffened, her heart cartwheeling as he straightened up and came forward, so she could see him properly.

'Nice day for a fair.'

Jem Arden. He had taken his coat off and his shirtsleeves were rolled back. He was almost as wet as she was, and she wondered where he'd come from; she hadn't seen him on the path ahead of her. He held up his cigarette and muttered an apology before stubbing it out against the rock, then he pinched the end and carefully tucked it into the pocket of the coat slung over his arm.

She turned away, aware that her blouse was soaked almost to transparency and her hair was coming loose at the back. Clamping her ruined hat beneath her arm, she attempted to push the pins back in. 'It'll pass quickly. Sudden showers always do.'

As she said it there was a fresh onslaught, a crescendoing hiss from the silvery world beyond their shelter. Water cascaded from the overhanging stone above their heads.

He laughed. 'You were saying?'

She pressed her lips together, irked by his ease and the way he talked to her, as if she was . . . an equal. A fellow human being, rather than the housekeeper. The others wouldn't dare address her so informally. For a long moment, neither of them spoke. Inside her head, she grappled for the words to reprimand him. And then the image of the woman in Pearson's window came back to her—that joyless stranger with the pursed-up mouth and lines between her brows.

'It must have caused quite a disruption at the fair,' she said instead, in a grudging concession to conversation. 'It seems we left just in time.' Realising that her wet blouse told a different story, she hurried on. 'Are the others still there?'

'I imagine so. They seemed to be enjoying themselves when I left.'

'And you weren't? Enjoying yourself?'

'Ah—I'm a good bit older than them. I think I've reached the age when swingboat rides and the helter-skelter have lost their appeal.'

She arched an eyebrow. 'You make it sound like you're ancient.'

The noise he made was somewhere between a laugh and a sigh. 'It feels that way sometimes. I'm twenty-seven—I discovered the other day that's five years older than Thomas; eight years older than Eliza. Closer to your age than theirs.'

On any other day she would barely have registered the comment, but the ghost woman in Pearson's window floated before her, a taunting contrast with the laughing girls spilling out into the yard that morning in their sprigged dresses and pretty hats. On this day—this date, that she had been trying so hard to ignore—his casual comment found the chink in her carefully assembled armour.

He must have noticed her stiffen, or perhaps he felt the weight of the silence that followed, because he said, 'I'm sorry. I've offended you. I didn't mean that *you're* ancient; the opposite, in fact. You're surprisingly young for a housekeeper.'

'And *you're* surprisingly forward for a footman.'

It came out far more sharply than she'd intended, but she didn't want his apology. She didn't want his pity or his curiosity. She didn't want him to speculate about her age or where she'd come from and what had brought her to be keeper of the keys in a house full of silence and shadows. She didn't want him to know that today—unmarked and uncelebrated—was her thirtieth birthday, and to look at her with those eyes—granite-grey and shimmering with reflected rain—and remind her of who she used to be and what she'd given up.

She didn't want him to see her at all.

'You're right. Forgive me.' He turned away, his voice subdued but edged with bitterness. 'A footman . . . of course. I'm only there to carry their trays and clean their boots and pour their wine and stand in the dining room. I forget sometimes.'

'I'm sorry. I didn't—'

'No, it's my fault. I know how it works. We don't have eyes, or ears, or opinions, or feelings. Especially not *feelings*. What did Thomas say this morning, about Hyde's ancestor? He brought all sorts of *artefacts* back from India—including a boy. We're possessions, aren't we, in our uniforms and crested liveries? We mustn't be allowed to see each other as human beings. Even downstairs we play the game. We *know our place*.'

As he spoke, she felt the heat rising in her cheeks and something like panic tightening her chest. She had to fight the urge to clap her hands over her ears and shout at him to stop. Because not only had he *seen* her . . . It was as if he had looked into her heart and read aloud what was written there, putting all her loneliness into words.

'It's—it's not—'

Her throat was tight with emotion, making it hard to speak, but he cut her off anyway.

'Look—the rain's stopping. We can go.'

They walked back together in the hazy aftermath of the downpour, as the ground steamed and the bracken shimmered with diamond droplets.

Jem sensed that she would have preferred to go on alone, but with them so obviously heading to the same place it was difficult to think of an excuse to walk separately. It made no difference to him; his plans had been disrupted the moment she'd appeared through the deluge. He'd been banking on taking advantage of an almost-empty house (Mr Goddard hardly emerged from his room) to have a good look around, but it was better to have come across her unexpectedly out here, rather than at Coldwell, in an upstairs room where he had no business.

The sky above the hills was still bruised, painted with a watercolour rainbow. The washed-clean world was loud with birdsong, and clouds of insects hovered above the grass as they descended the ridge to the road, and the Coldwell boundary beyond. The ground was spongy, but she walked briskly, her posture upright, the space between them observed as rigidly as if Mr Goddard had appeared with the ruler he used to measure out place settings in the dining room. Nothing about her invited conversation, so he didn't attempt it.

God forbid he was too *forward*.

In the servants' basement she seemed so severe and aloof—a pillar of black—but out here, with her hair slipping out of its pins and her damp blouse showing the lace of her chemise beneath, she seemed softer and slighter. He suspected that was the last thing she would want. He smothered a sigh, turning his head to look out across the heather. It was the last thing he needed too. It took enough effort not to notice her when she was dressed in her housekeeper's armour, with the silver chatelaine at her waist like a crucifix to a vampire.

He spent a lot of energy not noticing, and wasn't always successful.

A dragonfly appeared, blundering through the blue like a drunk at the fair, and she recoiled sharply, batting it away. Caught by the air current, its glass wings stuttered and it plummeted, tangling in her hair. With a little cry, she came to an abrupt halt.

'Hold still.'

He went to stand in front of her, reaching out his hand to cup the insect. Her eyes were closed, but he could sense her agitation and feel the tremor of her body as his wrist rested lightly against the top of her head.

'Ugh. Please, get rid of it.'

He was close enough to catch the scent of her skin. Vanilla, nutmeg, roses—the scent that had haunted him since the afternoon in the library, overlaid now with rain. Gently, unhurriedly, he closed his fingers around the dragonfly and cupped it between his palms.

'I've got it.'

A little of the rigid tension ebbed out of her.

'What is it?'

'A dragonfly. Look.'

Slowly he opened his hands. The insect trembled on his palm for a moment before launching itself skywards in a flash of iridescence.

'Thank you.' Her smile was small and reluctant, her eyes as blue as the dragonfly. 'On its behalf as much as my own. If you hadn't been here, I would probably have swatted it.'

They resumed walking. 'That would have been a shame,' he remarked. 'They only live for a week or two. Imagine that—having a matter of days to live your whole life, and being cut down before you've had half of it.'

Imagine that.

'I would never have forgiven myself,' she said, in a tone that was laced with enough irony for him to know that she was teasing.

It felt like a small breakthrough. A minor victory.

The hillside got steeper and stonier as it dipped down to meet the road. Gathering up her skirts, she cast him a quick sideways glance. 'For someone who spends their life carrying trays and standing in rich people's dining rooms you seem to know quite a lot about nature.'

'That's because I grew up in the countryside.'

When they reached the drystone wall their steps slowed and he held out his hand to help her over the stile. She ignored it, as he had half expected she would, and used the wooden post to steady herself instead.

'Whereabouts?'

'Oxfordshire.' He jumped down from the stile. 'The Upton Priory estate. My father was coachman to Lord Halewood. I started in the stables there.'

'As a groom?'

'Carriage groom.'

'Ah. A tiger.'

It was the second time he'd heard that word today; an old-fashioned name for the young lads who helped with the horses and sat on the back step of carriages in their gold-striped waistcoats. It made him think of the disembodied head snarling from its mount in Coldwell's godforsaken hallway. You hardly heard the term now; it was dying out, along with the role. These days, the wealthy and titled had mostly exchanged their horse-drawn vehicles for motorised ones and had no need of boys to run alongside and fold down steps.

'What made you swap the stables for the servants' hall?'

The rutted road was all puddles. He glimpsed the white hem of her petticoat as she lifted her skirt clear to pick her way between them.

'I was poached by one of Lord Halewood's guests. Offered a job as a footman at a place in Hampshire.'

'The French countess?'

'That's right.' He felt a pulse of surprise (and foolish pleasure) that she remembered, and tried to recall exactly what he'd said in the servants' hall that first night: his employment history was more pitted with dangerous potholes than the badly made road. 'I didn't particularly want to leave, and I certainly never wanted to work indoors, but the wage was too good to turn down. And my mother wanted me to take it.'

Lucy Arden had always been proud of how well her oldest boy had done at school. She was fond of saying that he might look like his handsome, feckless father but he took after her with his reading and writing, and he was wasted in the stables. When Lord Benningfield made his offer, she must have known she was unwell, but she kept that from him, urging him to take the job for Jack's sake as well as his own. 'I had a younger brother who was old enough to start work by then. Moving on meant he could have my place.'

On the other side of the road, the high wall that formed the boundary to the park stretched away into the distance in both directions. There was a little gate set into it, weathered and furred with moss. He went ahead of her to push it open and stepped aside to let her go first.

'Is your brother still there? In your old place?'

The question caught him off guard. 'No,' he said, more abruptly than he'd intended. 'No, he—He's not there, he—'

She had been walking in front of him, along a path through rank-smelling, overgrown shrubbery. Emerging, she gave a sudden, strangled cry and startled back, so that he almost collided with her. Instinctively he stepped forward to put himself between her and whatever had frightened her, and saw it was only the lad from the gate lodge.

'Davy . . . !' Mrs Furniss's voice was breathy with relief. 'You gave me such a fright, lurking in the undergrowth like that. Were you waiting for me? Was there something you wanted?'

Davy Wells shrank away, staring intently into a rhododendron bush. His face was crumpled into a scowl, but he nodded.

'What is it?'

Her voice was gentle. Jem hadn't heard her speak like that before, and he almost envied Davy. The lad shifted on his feet, folding a rhododendron leaf over and over, snapping it into pulpy fragments, which he brushed from his green-stained fingers. He pulled a crumpled piece of paper from the pocket of his too-small jacket and thrust it out.

'A telegram? Thank you, Davy. You took this from the telegram boy, today? I expect he was very glad that you saved him from cycling down to the house, but next time that's what he must do. It says 'Coldwell Hall' on the front, you see, so that's where he should have delivered it.' She smiled at him kindly. 'He's lazy, that telegram boy. He's lucky you're so trustworthy and reliable. Thank you.'

Davy nodded fiercely, backing away, then turning and breaking into a shambling run. Mrs Furniss turned the telegram over. The envelope flap was loose. She lifted it and slid out the paper.

'It's from Whittam Park—Lady Etchingham's house.'

Jem watched her. He saw the flicker of shock cross her face and her hand fly to her throat. Her eyes rose to meet his and she handed him the telegram.

LORD ETCHINGHAM DEEPLY REGRETS TO REPORT SUDDEN DEATH OF SIR HENRY HYDE STOP MR RANDOLPH HYDE INFORMED STOP PLEASE MAKE PREPARATIONS FOR MOURNING

Yesterday we were given orders to dig the graves of three Welshmen who were killed in their own trench when an enemy shell hit a box of hand grenades. It was raining and the ground was heavy and wet. As I dug, I thought of the words on that telegram. MAKE PREPARATIONS FOR MOURNING.

It's astonishing to remember the lengths we went to that summer for one friendless old man who died peacefully in bed. Black drapes and armbands and stopped clocks. Out here the dead don't even get coffins. The Welshmen were sewn into blankets before being lowered into the mud, and that's far more ceremony than most of us will get.

No one likes being picked for jobs like that, especially the ones who haven't been out here long. I don't mind so much. It turns out life in service was good preparation for life as a soldier. I'm lucky that I'm physically suited to the work, which men from offices or factories often are not. I'm used to following orders, even when I have little respect for those issuing them. I don't question what we're told or argue with senior officers.

I don't have eyes or ears or opinions or feelings.

I know my place.

Chapter 7

The house was a solid slab of darkness in the indigo dusk as they barrelled down the hill, stumbling over tussocks of grass. After the noise and life of the fair the park seemed eerily still, and it was all too easy to believe that Samuel's ghost might be flitting through the trees as they skirted the woods by the temple. To Susan's ears, every rustle of leaves, every fox bark and sheep call turned into the sound of his lost soul wandering, and she stayed close to Thomas (though what he could do to protect her from restless spirits she couldn't rightly say).

Eliza stamped along in front of her, white blouse bobbing palely in the gloom, bad temper stirring the air in her wake. She'd been in a mood since the weather turned, and Susan had pointed out that she should have worn a coat (which was true; there was no need for Eliza to bite her head off). In fact, she'd had a right face on her even before that, ever since Jem Arden had announced he was heading back. Getting soaked had only put the tin lid on it.

When she reached the bottom of the slope, Susan saw her turn and look over her shoulder, to where Joseph trailed miserably behind. He'd eaten an entire quarter of liquorice and a helping of pigs' trotters and been sick when he got off the gallopers. On the walk home he'd slowed everyone down.

'Hurry up, for pity's sake. We're almost an hour late. She's going to kill us.'

Thomas flashed a swift grin at Susan. 'That'd be why we saw that owl this morning.'

'She'll understand,' Abigail said breathlessly. 'It's not our fault Joseph was taken bad.'

'We should have left earlier,' Eliza snapped.

They all fell silent as they walked round to the stable yard, preparing for apologies and admonishment and a lengthy lecture on trust and timekeeping. The yard was in darkness too (the outdoor staff, not being tied to Mr Goddard's strict door-locking curfew, wouldn't be back for another couple of hours at least); but as they passed through the yawning mouth of the archway, the kitchen window spilled light onto the cobbles.

'Here goes . . .' Thomas muttered by the back door.

They filed into the passage, heads bowed. The light of the oil lamp seemed very bright after the dark outside. It made Thomas's copper hair gleam more brightly and showed up the greenish pallor of Joseph's face, the shadows circling his eyes. Susan had expected either Mr Goddard or Mrs Furniss to be waiting; to appear with that look—disappointment mixed with chilly disdain—that left you no doubt that you were for it (at least Mrs Gatley came straight out with it), but the corridor was empty. Following Thomas, she and Abigail exchanged a puzzled look.

Jem Arden was sitting at the table in the servants' hall, his shirtsleeves rolled up and a book open on the table in front of him, an empty teacup at his elbow. He got up when they came in. It was funny, Susan thought; they'd all been at Coldwell longer than he had, but there was something about him that made it seem like he was in charge. Like he had more authority than Thomas even, though he was first footman.

'Mrs Furniss asked me to let you know that a telegram came this afternoon from Whittam Park,' he said gravely. 'I'm afraid it brought bad news about Sir Henry. It seems he died, very suddenly and unexpectedly, while staying with Lady Etchingham. We don't know any more than that for the moment.'

Susan's stomach swooped like it had on the swingboats earlier. She felt the beat of the owl's wings inside her head and its shadow seemed to fall across the lamplit room.

———∞∞∞———

In the housekeeper's parlour Kate sat up late over her books and her ledger, making lists and writing letters: to Lady Etchingham's housekeeper, extending her sympathy (she could imagine the disruption to the Whittam Park household), to Jay's on Regent Street ('The Mourning Warehouse') to order armbands and black cotton gloves for the male servants and a bolt of black crepe to cover Coldwell's numerous mirrors, and to Mrs Bryant in Portman Square to solicit the older woman's advice on how to run a house in mourning.

She herself had little close personal experience of death. She'd had a brother once, but was too young to remember the loss of the child who had embodied the best of her parents' hopes and ambitions, much less the etiquette surrounding his burial and mourning. Her parents, as far as she knew, were still alive, although they had been as good as dead to her for the last ten years, on account of their rigid belief that she must remain lying in the bed she had so rashly made for herself.

There was no ceremony and no ritual to mark a bereavement of that kind. Just silence, and absence, and bitterness.

It was after midnight when she went through to the little panelled chamber that opened off her parlour and got stiffly into bed. Mrs Walton, her elderly predecessor, had moved her bedroom down here from the maids' attic when the stairs became too arduous for her to manage. Mostly Kate was happy with the arrangement—in winter, it was warmer in the passages near to the kitchen, and in the summer, the stone flags and lack of sunlight kept her room cool. But tonight, the confined space made her feel trapped. Its wood-panelled walls were like the inside of a coffin.

The day behind her seemed to have been stretched out of all recognisable shape; it felt like a week since she had departed for Hatherford, and the fair. As she lay in the dark, a procession of images flickered through her head, like the jerky moving-picture reel she had seen at a travelling fair on Clifton Down one summer. When she finally slipped into uneasy sleep it was to find herself walking through a crowd of stiff-limbed figures in mourning black who turned to stare at her with accusing eyes that said, *That's her.*

She woke suddenly, disorientated and damp with sweat.

Her shadow lurched across the panelled wall as she struck a match and held it to the candle, driving back the darkness. Gradually her heart slowed and the blood beat more gently in her ears, but the feeling of disquiet persisted: a primitive instinct for danger which wouldn't be dismissed.

She got up, wincing at the cold of the floor, and took her candle out into the parlour. Before she had reached the door a faint noise stopped her in her tracks: a high-pitched creak, familiar and unmistakable. The noise made by the hinges of the green baize door at the top of the basement stairs.

Her pulse rocketed again, but after a moment's hesitation, she covered the remaining distance to the door and opened it softly. Out in the passageway the candle flame dipped and guttered in an invisible breath of air. She moved silently, holding the candle high in front of her, though it was difficult to see anything beyond its circle of light. Her blood felt hot and stinging in her veins. The light crept ahead of her into the kitchen passage and licked at the feet of a figure on the stairs.

She glimpsed it for a second only before the panicked jolt of her hand made the candle splutter and go out.

'It's all right. There's nothing to worry about.'

Jem Arden's voice came from the shadows, steady and low. She heard him come down the last few stairs and could see the white of his shirt, though the rest of him was lost to the darkness.

'What are you doing down here?'

'I swapped places with Joseph. He was done in when they came back, and not feeling well, so I said he could have my bed. Just as well. I heard something upstairs and thought I should check.'

They were whispering. Mr Goddard's bedroom was beyond the butler's pantry at the far end of the kitchen passage; but even so, the lateness of the hour, the stillness of the house, the darkness—as velvet soft and quiet as a cat's paw—made their voices so low they were little more than a breath.

'Was someone there?'

She remembered what Lady Etchingham's maid had said about the break-ins, and suddenly had that old, unwelcome sensation of being watched. Her eyes darted around, probing the shadows.

'I don't know. I've checked all the main rooms and can't see anything amiss. I can't get into the library though.'

Sleep-slowed thoughts tumbled over each other in her mind. The disquiet from the dream still lingered, along with the irrational fear that it might have been more than a dream. A premonition. Her husband and tormentor had slipped out of the past and finally found her, as he'd said he would. He was here, at Coldwell.

You made a promise, don't forget. To honour and obey, till death do us part. I never go back on my word, and I expect the same from other people, Katherine. No one breaks a promise to me and gets away with it.

She shook her head, trying to dispel the demons. Alec Ross was miles away, in Bristol. There was no way he could have discovered her, much less broken into the house in the middle of the night to reclaim her. She was being ridiculous. Hysterical and unhinged, like he'd always said she was.

Jem Arden touched her arm, just lightly, and his hand was warm through the thin cotton of her nightgown. 'I didn't mean to wake you,' he said softly. 'I'm sorry to have caused you alarm. Go back to bed. I'll have a proper look around outside, just to make sure, but it was probably only the wind. It's quite safe, I promise.'

After a moment's hesitation, she nodded and did as he said. It was a relief to return to her room, knowing that he was there and had taken charge. His presence—his certainty—reassured her, and as she got back into bed her mind was easier.

This time her sleep was undisturbed by dreams.

Sir Henry Hyde returned to Coldwell on a bright May morning in a black carriage with the blinds pulled down, drawn by four black horses. Word of his death had spread; and although he couldn't be said to be a popular figure in the locality, the roadside by the gate lodge was lined with people—tenant farmers and villagers—drawn by old custom, superstition, and curiosity. They fell silent, pulling off their caps and bowing their heads as the carriage rattled past.

Inside the house it was as dark as an endless winter's evening, with the blinds drawn and the mirrors draped in black. Mr Goddard, stooped and stricken, made his usual ponderous circuit of the Coldwell clocks, but instead of winding them, he silenced their ticking and circled the hands back to the time of Sir Henry's passing (or the time that it had been discovered, the old man having slipped away quietly at some point between his bedtime brandy and morning tea).

Mrs Bryant had sent a lengthy reply to Kate's letter, though its erratic spelling and complete lack of punctuation made her instructions difficult to understand. Fortunately, it transpired that Susan was a mine of information when it came to the rituals of mourning. On her authority, the few photographs of the deceased had been laid face downwards and his portrait in the dining room covered, though it turned out her expertise didn't make her any less jittery about having a corpse in the house.

Sir Henry's open coffin was carried up to the bedroom he had so recently occupied and laid in the centre of his vast four-poster. As the family arrived for the funeral—along with Miss Addison and Sir Henry's land agent, physician, and solicitor—Kate found herself once more in the position of managing a house party, but one for which she'd had no chance to prepare. In the kitchen, Mrs Gatley stomped around, muttering darkly about the impossibility of producing a succession of lunches and five-course dinners at a moment's notice, and with only the chime of the clock in the stable yard to help her with timings. She didn't quite come out and say that Sir Henry might have had the decency to die with a bit more warning, but it was clear the thought was in her mind.

The day before the funeral chairs were placed around the bed in Sir Henry's room, for the family to gather and pay their final respects. For the most part, they remained empty; Sir Henry's nearest and dearest passed dutifully through the room but didn't linger. However, custom dictated that someone must sit with the body throughout the night before the burial. Mr Goddard (who, it seemed, was the only one who felt any genuine grief at the old man's passing) went up to take his turn as soon as his presence in the dining room was no longer required. He maintained his private vigil with the man he had served for thirty-two years, until midnight, when Thomas and Jem took over.

'Rather you than me,' said Abigail with a shudder, as they emerged from the footmen's wardrobe dressed in their formal livery. Thomas's face was as white as his shirtfront, making his freckles stand out like a sprinkling of nutmeg on a milk pudding.

'The dead can't hurt you,' Jem said grimly, slipping a small pewter flask into his inside pocket. 'But they're really boring company. It's going to be a very long night.'

—◦◦◦—

He knew it would happen.

Jem had shared the attic bedroom with Thomas for long enough to have been able to predict, with absolute certainty, that he would effectively be conducting most of this nocturnal vigil alone.

Thomas was blessed with a childlike ability to be able to drop off within seconds and slumber peacefully through just about anything, including Walter Cox's warthog snoring. In his case, the word *wake* was tinged with heavy irony. Within a couple of hours Thomas's head had fallen back against the wall, and he was breathing softly, mouth open.

The brandy had played its part, of course. Jem gave the flask an experimental shake: Thomas had been so keen to take the edge off his unease that he must have downed three-quarters of it. As Jem had predicted.

He unscrewed the cap and took a swig of what remained.

Thomas was positioned on the other side of the bed, on a chair by the door. Jem got up and went tentatively over, circling the flask in front of Thomas's blank face. When his eyelids didn't flicker, Jem let out a long breath, and, treading softly, went to the heavy mahogany cabinet by the window.

Candles burned low on each side of the bed, but their meagre light didn't reach the shelves behind the glass. He reached to pick one up, and the movement caused the flame to waver, so that it seemed almost like, inside the coffin, the old man's waxy face had twitched. Jem's heart faltered.

He was more nervous than he thought.

Only because this was the kind of chance he'd been waiting for, he told himself. A golden opportunity to look for personal papers, photographs, letters—anything that might reveal information about Viscount Frensham's visit to Coldwell in November 1902. And this time he wasn't going to let anything distract him, as it had on the night of the fair when he'd swapped beds with Joseph.

He hadn't realised Mrs Furniss would wake so easily, or that she would be so shaken by the excuse he'd invented for creeping through the upstairs rooms of the sleeping house. He hadn't been prepared for how guilty he would feel about lying to her; guilty and ashamed and faintly grubby. Nor had he known that glimpse of her before the candle blew out—in her nightgown, with her hair coming loose around her face—would stay with him as vividly and disturb him as much.

He could have asked her for the key to the library—she would almost certainly have given it to him, along with a cast-iron excuse for going in there, but in that moment his conscience had got the better of him. He'd regretted it afterwards.

Now was his chance to make up for it.

He moved the candle along the cabinet's shelves, so the flame illuminated the yellow spines of Wisden's cricketing almanacks, books about native Indian birds, fly-fishing, and dog breeds, as well as several small blue cloth-bound volumes that looked like prayer books. They jostled for space alongside a delicate bird's skull, a piece of rock, and an ivory statuette of an Indian god.

Jem's eyes swept over them without interest. Putting the candle down on the small ledge in front of the glass doors, he opened one of the drawers and was confronted with folded silk handkerchiefs, a leather collar box, and a tray of shirt studs. In the drawer below he found striped nightshirts, and was about to shut it again when he noticed more of the little blue volumes he had thought were prayer books tucked against the side of the drawer.

No one needed that many prayer books.

He pushed the nightshirts aside. Bringing the candle closer, he took one of the books out and flipped it open. The pages were densely covered in a spidery scrawl, smudged and splotched in places, almost impossible to read. However, at the top of each page was a printed date.

Diaries.

Jem's fingers were trembling as he turned the brittle pages to the beginning. He'd hardly dared hope to hit the jackpot so easily. On the reverse side of the marbled flyleaf Sir Henry had written the year: 1897. Holding the book next to the candle Jem attempted to read the first page.

January 1st. Rain all day. Blasted gout giving me bother. Staff on poor form after last night's servants' ball—vexing. Telegraphed back to R., refusing request for funds. V unsatisfactory. Wish he would come home

*and face responsibilities here instead of gadding about India. C. very low
about the whole affair. Poor show.*

It took a long time to decipher the crabbed writing, and hardly repaid
the effort; Henry Hyde wasn't much of a diarist. Jem assumed R. must be
Randolph and C. his mother (Constance? Clarissa?). He flicked through
the book, trying to pick out more mentions of R., but Hyde seemed to
be more preoccupied with his gout (*Confounded pain in my foot . . . Had
Seymour out <u>again</u>—wish to God he could do something for me . . . Quack suggests the spa baths at Harrogate for my gout . . .*) and the weather, which he
recorded in monotonous detail.

Jem slid the book back into its slot and removed one four volumes
along. The date was underlined with a sweeping stroke on the endpaper.

<u>1902</u>

The year of the last entry in the Coldwell visitors' book. The year after
Jem had moved to Hampshire and Jack had taken his place. The year that
Viscount Frensham had taken up residence for the winter at Ward Abbey,
one of his father's smaller estates in Norfolk, and Jack had been amongst
the servants to go with him.

The year he had disappeared.

The window was open and (at the advice of the undertaker) the room
was cool, but Jem could feel sweat on his upper lip, his forehead. He opened
the book randomly, skimming the entry for 18 May: *Easterly wind. Cold.
Indigestion very bad, leg swollen. Saw no one but Goddard. Miss the old girl.*

His wife's death at some point in the intervening volumes must have provided some variation in Hyde's daily observations, but Jem didn't have time to
look. He turned a wedge of pages, and his eye caught on an entry in August:
Sir Henry had received a letter from Randolph, saying that he was returning
to England, setting sail from Bombay the following week. *No explanation, but
one imagines a tight spot of some sort—finances or females. Etchingham may have
heard word. Perhaps just as well his mother is not here to see it.*

Spots danced before Jem's eyes. He looked up from the book and took
a breath—in and out. The stopped clock gave him no clue as to the time,
but light was beginning to seep beneath the edges of the blind; the house

would soon be waking up. His hand was shaking properly as he flicked through the pages.

A noise.

Alarm ricocheted through his body as he listened and heard the creak of floorboards beneath the thick carpet of the corridor. He shoved the book back into the drawer, ramming it shut, and by the time the door handle moved, he was beside the window, leaning back against the folded shutter, as if he was just stretching his legs and getting some air.

Hyde's valet slipped into the room like fog. Beneath his slicked-back hair his high forehead creased as he saw Jem at the window. He looked down at Thomas, slumped in the chair at his side. His eyes moved to the cabinet. Following his gaze, Jem saw that the drawer was open a fraction, the cuff of a nightshirt trapped in it.

'Everything all right?'

Henderson's tone was bland, but he looked at Jem with unconcealed dislike.

Jem nodded. It felt like there was a boulder in his throat. 'Just needed some air.'

It was plausible enough. The window was open but the sickly-sweet smell of death pervaded the room. Henderson stared at him, his expression obscured by his beard. Then, without advancing into the room, he gave Thomas's shoulder a shove, jolting him back to consciousness.

'Eh?' Thomas blinked, sitting bolt upright and looking wildly around. Seeing Henderson, he rubbed a hand over his face as his ears turned pink. 'Sorry. What time is it?'

'Time for you to do your job and show some respect,' Henderson said coldly. 'Your friend here has been keeping watch on his own.' He opened the door, adding, almost under his breath, 'Though some might say he's the one who needs watching.'

Thomas, sitting upright, rubbed his palms down his thighs, as if readying himself for action of some sort. 'Right, then.'

With a last look at the drawer, and the fold of white cotton caught in it, Henderson left. As he closed the door behind him, a current of air tugged at the candle flame so it cast a brief glow of warmth over Sir Henry Hyde's cold flesh in its nest of blue satin.

When the undertaker had brought the corpse up, the jaw had been tied beneath the chin. The bandage had since been removed, but the old man's lips remained clamped, sealing in the family's secrets.

———— ❧ ————

I don't blame Henderson for not trusting me. He was quite right.

I lied to you that night, after the fair—there was no intruder. I was used to making up excuses for being where I shouldn't—I didn't think twice about it. I didn't always get away with it, of course. I was framed for theft when I was found in Frensham's house. I served six months with hard labour and was only sorry that I'd got caught.

It was the first time the dishonesty bothered me—that night at Coldwell. I vowed that I wouldn't put you in that position again. But one lie all too easily leads to another, and my life is littered with promises I failed to keep.

I never got the chance to tell you the truth.

———— ❧ ————

July 1st 1916
France

It's not supposed to be like this.

As they come out of the trench, they have to step over the bodies of their own men. The blue day has blackened. Smoke enfolds them. The grass is long and still wet with dew and the undulating field erupts in front of him in plumes of earth. Blinded by smoke, he trips over men and stumbles into craters.

Walk, don't run.

Joseph looks back, the whites of his eyes wild, his whole face a terrified question. *What do we—?*

The man to his right is thrown backwards in a convulsion of bullets, a shower of scarlet. Joseph flinches wildly, his mouth stretching and gaping. Jem catches hold of his arm and yanks him back.

Stay behind me and keep going.

That's what they have been ordered to do. That's what they are here for. The Big Push. They have left their streets, their homes, their sweethearts to cross this field—now, today. They have spent six months stabbing sacks with bayonets and drilling squares for this. It's all part of a plan.

But it's not supposed to be like this.

His mind shrinks, so there is only room for the same refrain. He feels the guns now, rather than hearing them. All he hears is the sound of his own heaving breath and those words.

ITSNOTSUPPOSEDTOBELIKETHIS.

They were told it would be easy. The German artillery would have been destroyed by the bombardment, they said. Eight days of heavy shelling. There would be no one left in the enemy trenches—not even the rats. That's what they were told.

He goes on. Walking not running. Stepping over bodies in the grass.

He feels as if he's looking through a tunnel. Or that he's wearing blinkers, like a dray horse. He hears the thud of men being hit, the whistle of bullets; he feels the rush of air as they pass him. He is braced—balanced between calm acceptance and utter disbelief—certain that at any moment he will be hit.

His hand goes to his heart, the pocket where the letter is, and he keeps walking, into the rain of fire.

Brighton

The hospital is in two houses on Lewes Crescent, one of the town's grander addresses. She walks there, along the seafront, where it is business as usual despite the rumble of guns from across the Channel. There are still deckchairs around the bandstand and people strolling on the pier, though many of the men are in khaki uniforms or hospital blues and the women are in groups together with mothers, friends, and sisters instead of husbands, sweethearts, and sons.

From the street, the hospital still looks much like an imposing residence (white stucco behind black-painted railings, steps scrubbed clean), though its door stands open and there are two army ambulances parked outside. As she approaches, Sister Pinkney appears ahead of two orderlies carrying a stretcher, which they load carefully into the back of the ambulance. Jumping down from the vehicle's back step, one of the orderlies—a man called Corporal Maloney, who seems to believe that flirting with the VADs is part of his job description—notices her and gives her a wink.

'Morning, Miss Simmons,' he says, once Sister Pinkney is safely back inside. 'Lovely day for it.'

She suspects she's supposed to ask for what, but she doesn't want to encourage him. She's more lowly than the VADs, and older, so he probably thinks she should be flattered by his attention. He couldn't be more mistaken.

The elegant circular hallway looks much as it must have done before the war, except a large desk piled with manila folders and papers has been placed in front of the empty fireplace, and there are several stretchers stacked beneath the staircase that sweeps upwards round the walls. Instead of potpourri and polish, the air smells strongly of carbolic and Lysol, and beneath that, of something rotting. Usually, she arrives in the quiet spell after lunch, when the doctors have completed their rounds; when dressings have been changed, treatments administered, and patients washed and shaved; but today she immediately senses a shift of atmosphere. Up on the galleried landing two nurses manoeuvre a mattress, and she hears the clang of trollies and the muted bark of orders from distant rooms. She hesitates at the foot of the stairs, waiting to let a VAD come hurrying down before making her way up.

Matron's desk is on the landing, beneath a vast portrait of a woman with a tiny waist, swathed in white muslin and whimsically clasping a posy of violets. (Her rosebud-lipped simper is starkly at odds with Matron's basilisk glare: Matron is a woman who does not suffer fools.) Today Matron is not at her desk.

Going hesitantly through to Hawke Ward, the former drawing room at the front of the house, she finds most of the beds are empty, stripped of their linen. Two VADs are vigorously scrubbing the exposed rubber sheets, talking in low, disgruntled voices, which stop abruptly as she walks in.

'Oh, it's only you,' says one of them—a girl called Nurse Williams, who comes from the Welsh valleys and whose lilting, singsong voice is breathy with relief. 'I thought you were Sister Pinkney. Or Matron.'

'What's happening?'

'We've been told to prepare for a big rush of wounded,' says the other

VAD, dragging the back of her wrist across her forehead. 'The last of the convalescent cases have just gone and we've got to get ready for men straight from the front. There's something big going on—you can hear it, can't you?'

It is not just her cut-glass accent that advertises her well-to-do background, but everything about her, from her delicate hands and peaches-and-cream complexion (reddened now, with heat and exertion) to her air of schoolgirl earnestness. 'Sister Pinkney's in a frightful bait. She gave me such a dressing-down for putting kisses when I signed sweet Private Findlay's autograph book. It's supposed to be my afternoon off and I *was* going to a show at the Hippodrome, but now we've got all these beds to make up . . .'

'Let me help.'

'Oh—that's kind,' Nurse Williams says hastily, shooting the other girl a look. 'But Sister Pinkney's ever so exacting about how it's done. It's part of the training, see—how to fold the sheet and do the corners, just so . . .'

'I was in service, before the war, in a big house.' She smiles gravely. 'If there's one thing I know, it's how to make beds.'

'Oh, how marvellous! You're an angel sent from heaven.' The peaches-and-cream girl beams. 'I'm Millicent, by the way—Nurse Frankland, here.' She rolls her eyes slightly. 'What's your name?'

'Simmons,' she says. 'Eliza Simmons.'

France

He knows the exact moment it happens, almost as if he sees it unfold in the second before impact. He hears Joseph's high, anguished cry and turns in time to see the bright blossom of red on his thigh as he jerks and crumples.

It's instinct that throws him back, arms outstretched to catch him. Joseph is clutching his leg and blood is oozing through his fingers. He is making rapid, keening sobs.

Jem—Jem—

It's all right, it's all right.

He is kneeling in the grass. Everything is muffled and slow, like being underwater. He wrestles his pack from his back to find the field dressing kit. Joseph's helmet has rolled off and his hair is blond against the churned-up earth. Jem looks around, but there is nothing to see except smoke and mud, until a figure looms, mad-eyed, revolver raised.

On your feet, man! Forward! FORWARD!

It is what they have been ordered to do. It is part of a plan. Walk don't run. Don't stop for the injured. Keep going.

The barrel of the gun glints dully as the smoke shifts around them. He can choose whether to be shot by a British bullet, or live a few minutes more to be got by a German one. The outcome will be the same, but he'd rather Joseph doesn't see it.

I'll come back, he roars, prying Joseph's fingers from his sleeve. *I'll come back for you, I promise.*

Jesus Christ, it's not supposed to be like this.

Summer

Chapter 8

As far as Randolph Hyde, fifth Baronet Bradfield, was concerned, his father couldn't have chosen a more opportune moment than the early summer of 1911 to shuffle off this mortal coil.

It was very unlike the old man to be so obliging. Not only had the contentious matter of inheritance just been settled, but the weather was glorious and Coldwell at its best, a welcome contrast with the oppressive heat of London. The cherry on the cake was that the death of 'Good Old King Teddy' the previous year meant that a coronation was in the offing. As a baronet, Sir Randolph Hyde was not a peer of the realm and had no ceremonial part to play, but with the great and the good descending on London from every corner of the empire, the occasion would provide the perfect opportunity for him to impress his acquaintances from India with his newly acquired title, fiancée, and respectability, and to relaunch himself in society.

After the funeral, when the small party of visitors had departed and the house had shaken off the trappings of mourning, Sir Randolph Hyde stayed on at Coldwell (also shaking off the trappings of mourning; though custom dictated he should wear a black tie for six months at least, he declared the weather far too splendid). Mr Fortescue, the land agent, postponed his return to London, and Amos Kendall Esq, 'sanitary engineer,' was summoned from Sheffield.

The three men strode through the upstairs corridors, discussing which dressing rooms might be turned into bathrooms (with proper cast-iron bathtubs supplied with hot water, and flushing W.C.s) and where pipes and water tanks and geysers might be placed. Sir Randolph's booming voice disturbed layers of stillness in passages that had long been silent as he called from one room to another or shouted for his dog. (Joseph was constantly on edge, jumping every time *Boy!* rang out through the house.)

As one warm, blue-skied day followed another, Coldwell Hall crackled with the energy of change. The girls were giddy with excitement at the prospect of an end to emptying chamber pots and carrying cans of water up the back stairs. They made it their mission to find things to do on the bedroom corridors so they could eavesdrop on the plans being made, until Kate's patience snapped and she ordered them to stay downstairs.

Unlike them, she felt profoundly unsettled by the changes, and unnerved by the pervasive presence of Frederick Henderson. He seemed to shadow her through the servants' basement, looking at her as if she was an item he was considering for purchase. She had come to Coldwell to escape scrutiny, but as the hot summer days wore on, she felt more watched than ever.

She wasn't alone in her agitation, or her resistance to the new routine. Mrs Gatley, struggling with the unusually warm weather, was further put out by Sir Randolph's culinary requirements, which were considerably more elaborate than his father's. His appetite at breakfast was fickle (and dependent on how heavily he had indulged the previous evening), so he expected a variety of dishes to choose from, meaning Mrs Gatley was required to huff down from the cottage in the kitchen garden early, to oversee Susan whisking eggs, frying kidneys, boiling rice for kedgeree, and poaching kippers. (Most of this feast came down again cold and untouched, and was greedily snapped up in the scullery by Joseph, Thomas, and Boy the spaniel.) Sir Randolph usually liked a hearty lunch, but the warm weather put him in the mood for picnic food, so Mrs Gatley's afternoons—formerly passed with her feet up in her own parlour—were now spent making pork pies, Scotch eggs, galantines of veal or chicken, and fruit tarts, before attempting to re-create one of the dishes from the London restaurants he favoured for dinner.

Mr Goddard, whose entire life's purpose was loyal service, uttered no word of dissent, but his values were those of his old master. Disapproval of Sir Randolph's wasteful extravagance was stamped on his face every time he trudged up from the cellar with bottles of port, claret, champagne, and brandy, and trailed down from the dining room in the aftermath of yet another lavish meal.

Thomas, eternally oblivious to any negative undercurrents, brought gossip from the stables. 'George Twigg says Sir Randolph was in the coach house this afternoon. He's getting rid of the big carriage and the old brougham. Making room for a motorcar, George says.'

It was teatime. Around the table, eyes widened.

'Does Johnny Farrow know how to drive a motorcar?' Susan asked.

Frederick Henderson gave a short, scornful laugh. 'The man's barely mastered eating with a knife and fork. Don't worry—I don't suppose he'll be sent packing. He'll be needed to drive the shooting brake and the wagon.' He looked down the table at Kate. 'Mrs Furniss will hardly be taking her fortnightly trips to Hatherford in the back of a motorcar, like Lady Muck.'

Kate felt the heat seep into her cheeks as, along the table, heads turned in her direction. He made it sound as if she had suggested otherwise. As if she was getting above herself.

Jem Arden was sitting next to him. At that moment, reaching for the water jug, he knocked over his glass and water cascaded into Henderson's lap, soaking his neatly pressed trousers and making him splutter to his feet in indignation.

'Sorry,' Jem said blandly.

After tea, when the girls were still crowded in the scullery washing the pots, Joseph took the knives to the butler's pantry, where the rotary knife-cleaning machine was kept.

The butler's pantry smelled of silver paste and chamois leather, but this evening he followed a faint drift of the roses and vanilla that scented Mrs Furniss's rooms. Sure enough, the door to Mr Goddard's room was open a crack. Through it he could hear the butler's creaky voice and see the hem of Mrs Furniss's black silk skirt.

Joseph put the knives down carefully, laying them on a piece of linen cloth to hush their clatter, and listened.

He knew it was wrong, but since he wasn't important enough to be told anything, it was the only way to keep up with goings-on in the house, and he liked to keep up, just in case. Coldwell was a good place—a paradise compared to the Sheffield Union Workhouse and what had gone before it—but you never knew. Things could turn bad in an instant. People you thought were all right could show a different side. It didn't do to get too comfortable.

It was hard to make out what Mr Goddard was saying. His voice was dry and raspy, like the rustle of autumn leaves, but Joseph—staring down at the worn quarry tiles and concentrating hard—picked out the name of Mr Dewhurst, who was the butler in the London house, and the word everyone was saying lately—*coronation*. Holding his breath, he slunk closer to the door.

'. . . Ten days, all told. No point in taking on more staff in Portman Square when Sir Randolph plans to spend most of his time here. You and I will stay to oversee the renovations, but the rest of the staff—'

A shadow fell across the tiles and a pair of gleaming shoes appeared at the edge of Joseph's vision.

His heart kicked like a rabbit in a trap. Old instinct—beaten into him from beyond his earliest recollection—made him cringe and cower from the anticipated blow. But Mr Henderson had only raised his hand to pull Mr Goddard's door shut, sealing the voices inside.

'I think you'd better get on with cleaning those knives, don't you?'

Joseph scuttled back to the rotary machine and reached for the box of powder to tip into the little trap at the top of the drum. His breath stuck in his chest as he waited for Henderson to leave. But he didn't. His shiny shoes tapped on the tiles as he crossed the room and stood by the lead-lined sink where Mr Goddard washed the crystal glasses. His hand, resting on the wooden draining board, was soft and pale, like a fish.

The girls' voices floated along the passageway, raised above the splash of water and the clang of dishes. In the butler's pantry the silence seemed to thicken the air, like the dust motes that swirled in the evening sunlight.

'Not as daft as everyone thinks, are you, eh, boy?'

The valet's voice was as soft as his flesh. Joseph kept his eyes fixed to the knife-cleaning machine, slotting the blades carefully into the mechanism, making his movements as small and spare as possible. He didn't know how to reply to the question, or whether a reply was expected. Or if that white hand was about to snatch him by the collar and shake an answer out of him.

'I reckon you know a lot more than you let on, don't you? More than everyone gives you credit for.'

'No, sir.'

The hairs were prickling on the back of Joseph's neck, warning him that, in this situation, being seen to know things was bad. He risked a swift glance at the valet, and found that he was regarding him thoughtfully, stroking his beard with those soft, white fingers.

'Well, it seems you're the first to know that all the indoor servants are being sent to Sir Randolph's London house to help with the coronation entertainments, doesn't it? You've learned that at the same time as Mrs Furniss and before any of the others. What other secrets do you hear, I wonder?'

'None, sir,' Joseph mumbled.

Mr Henderson's laugh took him by surprise. 'Very good. Just as I suspected—the soul of discretion.' The valet's hand slid into the pocket of his waistcoat. 'Do you know, Joseph, discretion is a fine quality in a servant, and one Sir Randolph prizes very highly. A boy like you could do very well at Coldwell. Very well indeed. Loyalty is always rewarded . . .' He took a step forward and leaned in, so Joseph felt his cigar-sour breath on his cheek. 'Remember that.'

Joseph recoiled. It was only when the valet's footsteps were echoing along the passageway that he noticed the glint of a silver sixpence on the edge of the table.

Chapter 9

As the day of the servants' departure for London approached, it felt to Kate that the outside world itself was slowly edging closer to Coldwell.

Sir Randolph's programme of modernisation got underway, and an invading army of tradesmen's motors and carriers' carts rumbled up the drive. The sound of sawing, hammering, and shouting echoed along corridors and down stairwells, shattering a century of stillness, and making it feel like the clamour of progress had finally found the house, sleeping amongst the sheltering hills.

With the unprecedented thrill of a trip to London in the offing, the girls embarked upon their own programme of improvements, poring over a dog-eared copy of *Home Chat* magazine for hair-styling advice and rummaging in the attic sewing room for ribbons, feathers, and silk flowers to trim hats and pin to their coats.

But by the eve of their departure, excitement had tripped over into irritability, and tensions were running high. Kate's nerves were stretched tight by the mess and disruption of Coldwell's usual steady routine. Part of her longed for the quiet that would settle when the servants' hall was empty, but another part dreaded it. She couldn't stop her mind returning to what Lady Etchingham's maid had said about break-ins and the noise

Jem had heard on the night of Sir Henry's death. Was someone watching the house, waiting for the right moment to come back?

The weather made everything more arduous. As each oppressive night was followed by another sweltering day, June no longer felt like the blue-skied overture to a gentle English summer. The temperature rose, but by mid-morning the sun was a pale smudge in an opaque sky; and the air was heavy, not like air at all. If it was like that at Coldwell, in the hills of the Peak District, what would it be like in London?

'Awful,' Susan moaned, as they sat in the servants' hall after dinner the night before they were due to leave. 'The kitchen in the London house is half underground, isn't it? And poky compared to ours. We'll steam inside our clothes, like puddings.'

Eliza was replacing a loose button on her best blouse. 'Oh, yes—I re-member Walter Cox saying that the kitchen looks out on a brick wall and all you can see is shoes going by on the street above. He said it gets as hot as hell itself.'

'Ugh—Walter Cox.' Thomas groaned. 'I'd forgotten he'll be there. You know what—you can keep your city goings-on and your fancy coronation parade. Reckon I'd rather stay here, if I'm honest.'

'You'd rather stay here than have a chance to experience one of the biggest events of the century?' Henderson scoffed, coming in with a hat-box and a newspaper. He brought with him the smell of smoke, which had hung around him for days, like the devil trailing sulphur. (It made a change from hair oil.)

Immediately after the funeral, he and Sir Randolph had begun clearing out Sir Henry's suite of rooms, which Sir Randolph intended to take as his own, and a huge bonfire had been kept burning in the overgrown yard by the abandoned joiner's workshop. The Twigg boys supervised the blaze as Henderson and Sir Randolph fed it with a lifetime's papers, magazines, letters, and diaries.

There was something quite brutal in their thoroughness, Kate thought. As if Sir Randolph, who took such an interest in his more distant ances-tor's personal papers, wished to obliterate all trace of his father's.

Henderson opened the newspaper and spread it on the table, then took Sir Randolph's top hat from the box. 'The eyes of the world will be on London in the coming days,' he said, with an air of self-importance.

'Preparations have been going on for weeks—streets hung with flags and shop windows done out with pictures of the new king and queen. It's quite the spectacle. Count yourself fortunate to be part of it.'

'*Part of it?*' Jem echoed with amusement. 'I'm pretty sure *Sir Randolph*'—studying a catalogue of household linen sent to her by Mrs Bryant, Kate heard the slight sneer in the way he said the name—'isn't inviting us as guests. The only thing we're going to be part of is a lot of fetching and carrying in a different house.'

Henderson had been rubbing the top hat with a velvet pad, stroking the silk to a soft sheen, but his hand stilled as Jem spoke. Two spots of colour appeared on his pitted cheeks above the line of his beard.

'I should say you're very lucky to be able to do that, in the house of a gentleman like Sir Randolph. Wouldn't you, Arden?'

The softness of his voice, and its reasoned tone, were at odds with the undercurrent of threat the question held. The distant thunder that had been rumbling over the hills all day seemed to come a little closer, and hostility sparked like lightning in the heavy air.

Jem, who had given in to Joseph's hopeful request for a game of chess, retaliated by completely ignoring Henderson, telling Joseph that if he made that move with his castle, he was leaving his king exposed. The long, low room was suddenly very still. Kate watched Henderson's brows pull together.

'A word to the wise, Arden . . .' Holding up the top hat, he examined it through narrowed eyes. 'That disrespectful attitude of yours might have been acceptable in a railway inn, but it won't get you far in a good household like this. The old man might not have noticed, but Sir Randolph expects a bit more. To be perfectly honest, I'm not sure you're the right fit for the job.'

Kate had been looking at the same page of eiderdowns for ages but couldn't have described a one of them. Out of the corner of her eye she saw that Eliza's needle had stopped in mid-air, as she and Abigail exchanged looks. The windows were all open, though there was no breeze on the heavy, smoke-scented air. The evening had darkened, but no one moved to light the lamp.

Jem didn't raise his eyes from the chessboard.

'Your turn, Joe.'

It was as if he had forgotten about the valet, or hadn't heard him. Joseph's eyes were wide and wary as he looked between the two men. He reminded Kate of Sir Randolph's spaniel, eager to please but sniffing the air for danger.

Henderson's face hardened. The forward jut of his jaw was more pronounced than ever. Joseph bit his lip as he surveyed the chessboard, his hand hovering over the pieces. Touching the queen, he looked questioningly at Jem, who sucked in a breath. 'Remember—she's the most useful piece in the game,' he said quietly. 'And the most powerful. Use her carefully. Don't expose her to danger. You don't want to lose her too soon.'

No one else spoke. The silence bristled with tension as Eliza bent her head to resume her stitching. Kate turned the page and stared unseeingly at some 'bedspreads, finest quality.' And then, from out in the passageway came a strident jangle that made them all jump.

Jem glanced up at the row of bells.

'Library,' he said calmly, glancing at Henderson.

Henderson's chair scraped loudly on the flagstones. As he passed Jem, he bent down, placing his mouth close to his ear. Even so, everyone heard quite clearly what he said, hissing the words through his teeth.

'I've got my eye on you, Arden. Watch your step.'

Outside, leaning against the back wall of the stable block, Jem took a deep drag on a cigarette made from the last little bit of his precious tobacco. The taste was tainted by the drifts of more acrid smoke that came from the bonfire, still smouldering in the corner of the weed-choked yard.

The light had almost gone, swallowed up by the swollen clouds that massed above the trees, as if all the smoke from the fire had risen and was trapped beneath the great oppressive blanket of the sky. He tipped his head back and breathed out a long column of his own smoke, watching it dissolve slowly in the still air, undisturbed by any breeze. In his mind he replayed the scene in the servants' hall.

I've got my eye on you, Arden.

It was a threat, but it filled him with a strange exhilaration. After all this time spent moving from place to place, asking questions, telling lies, following a trail of clues and connections so tenuous it had at times vanished altogether, it suddenly felt like he was getting close to the truth.

Dangerously close. Which was why all that remained of it was a pile of smouldering ashes.

He drew on the last bit of cigarette and walked over to the bonfire to drop the butt into its glowing heart. He knew what they had burned there. He had seen the Twigg lads chucking those small blue cloth-covered books into the flames, one after another, and he knew why Sir Randolph and his flunky wanted them gone.

They could try to burn the evidence, but he was onto them now. He knew that the answers he'd been looking for were here at Coldwell. The truth wouldn't stay buried forever.

Frustration simmered inside him at the thought of leaving for London in the morning. After almost ten years, another ten days hardly made a difference, but it killed him to think of being down there, in close quarters with that bastard Henderson, while here the house would be all but empty.

A pale shape glimmered beyond the bonfire's smoulder, lurking at the corner of the old joiner's workshop. Jem squinted through the sting of lingering smoke. He recognised the hunched shoulders and uneven movements of Davy Wells and called his name, only for the lad to dart out of sight behind the tumbledown building.

Jem kicked at the ashes, sending a shower of sparks and dark flakes into the dusk. Watching the rose-gold embers fade, he turned his attention to the idea that had materialised at the edge of his mind, and was slowly beginning to shape itself into a plan.

———⟨∞⟩———

In her parlour Kate was having a last look at the list of supplies Mrs Bryant had requested and checking them off against the baskets she had packed.

She felt cross and jumpy, out of sorts. The scene in the servants' hall had unsettled everyone, and the thought of what it would be like after Sir Randolph's wedding, when Frederick Henderson would be at Coldwell so much, was increasingly difficult to ignore. People would look for positions elsewhere. No one would put up with his aggression, his disagreeableness for long.

Except her, because what choice did she have? If the idea of living with

Mr Henderson was unpleasant, the thought of leaving Coldwell and seeking another place—having her face scrutinised, her background examined, her character reference picked over and its fictions exposed—was, well . . . unthinkable.

Of course, staff resignations meant finding replacements, a perennial problem at Coldwell. They exasperated her, her girls, with their mercurial moods and butterfly minds, but she was fond of them. They had formed, during these past few quiet years, a family of sorts, as servants often did: flawed and at times fractious, but steadfast. Loyal. If one of the girls left, the bond would be broken and the others would surely follow, as would Thomas, who was cheerful and dependable but who hated a bad atmosphere. Even he had his limits. And as for Jem . . .

There was nothing to keep him here. In fact, he was leaving for London tomorrow—what were the chances that he wasn't intending to come back? That would explain why he wasn't making the slightest effort to stay on the right side of Henderson and why he wasn't afraid to goad him. Jem Arden, the dark horse, who kept himself a little separate from the others and hid his thoughts and feelings behind that handsome mask of courtesy, would no doubt be planning to take advantage of paid passage to London, where any number of employment opportunities awaited a footman with his looks and skill.

It seemed so obvious; she wasn't sure why it hadn't occurred to her sooner.

Or why she should mind so much.

The answer came to her in the next heartbeat. It was because she felt safer, having him there. On the nights when her sleepless mind roamed out into the parkland, conjuring watchers in the woods, or hearing Henderson's footsteps outside her door, it was a comfort to know that Jem had taken Joseph's place on the pull-out bed by the silver cupboard. On nights when the past came back to her in heart-jolting dreams she was reassured by his nearness. She drew comfort from recalling his voice.

It's quite safe, I promise.

Well, she should know better than anyone that it didn't do to rely on anyone, for comfort or for anything else.

She gathered herself, smoothing her skirts in a jangle of keys. Looking briskly around the room, she took her list to check it one last time against the hamper that had been left in the kitchen passage, ready for loading onto the wagon tomorrow.

It was dark—the velvet blue dark of summer—and the lamps had been lit at the bottom of the basement stairs and in the corridor outside the kitchen. Going past the servants' hall, Kate saw that it was empty, the chairs pushed back as if everyone had left in a hurry. It was stuffy and still, and the smell of the haddock Mrs Gatley had poached in preparation for tomorrow's breakfast kedgeree lingered in the air. In spite of the heat, it appeared the windows had all been shut.

Hearing voices, she went into the kitchen. The girls were coming back through the door that led to the game larder and the bakehouse, huddled together, talking in low voices. Susan, seeing Kate in the doorway, grasped Abigail's hand and gave a little shriek.

'It's Mrs Furniss, you daft goose,' Eliza snapped, pressing her hand to her chest. 'You're making me jumpy with your squealing.'

'What's going on?'

'Jem saw someone,' Abigail said quickly, keen to be the one to relate such dramatic news. 'Lurking along the side of the house by the garden corridor.'

'Poking around in the dark,' Eliza cut in. 'Shifty as you like. He thought it was Davy Wells at first, but he realised it couldn't have been when he saw Davy over by the old joiner's shop a bit later. He told the stable boys, and Stanley Twigg came to tell us.'

Kate's heart lurched and seemed to lodge in her throat.

'The stable boys are looking outside,' Susan said, sounding almost tearful. 'Mr Henderson went up to the garden corridor. We've shut the windows and made sure they're all fastened. I can't bear the thought of someone climbing in when we're sleeping, creeping along the corridors—'

'That's enough, Susan.' Kate's voice was sharp. Despite the heat she felt clammy, as though her body had been doused in ice water. Suddenly, the face she had spent years trying to forget loomed in her head; and as she looked up at the high window it seemed to appear there, looking in at her from the darkness. 'I'm sure there's nothing to worry about.'

But even as she spoke, a distant shout echoed faintly through the house. The girls clutched at each other in alarm.

'Where did it come from?'

'Upstairs . . .'

Kate forced herself forward. Her head buzzed, like a hive full of bees. As she went up the stone steps to the green baize door she felt for the chains on her chatelaine, grasping the scissors and opening their blades.

'Bring a lamp,' she said, over her shoulder, and was impressed at the steadiness of her own voice.

The hallway was washed with shadows, painted in shades of inky blue. The animals on the walls seemed to be listening too, quivering and alert, their glassy eyes wide. All the doors leading off the hall were shut, and the stairs stretched up into darkness (for the first time Kate could see the advantages of Sir Randolph's plan to have electricity installed), so she turned in the direction of the garden passage.

There was someone there.

A figure. No more than a silhouette, though her imagination imposed on it the face she dreaded seeing. The bees in her head swarmed, and her grip tightened on the scissors as she tried to stifle a whimper.

'Mrs Furniss—'

Frederick Henderson's voice. Dizzying relief swamped her.

'No need to panic. There's been a slight accident.'

'What's happened?'

Abigail was holding open the baize door for Eliza, who was running up the stairs with a lamp. Her hurried steps made the shadows jump. Panic had given way to a different kind of dread as Kate went forward, pushing past the arm Henderson held out to restrain her.

'*Jem?*'

He was on the floor, by the doors that opened out from the garden passage onto the veranda. She could see his shirt, ice white in the blue summer dark. And then Eliza was there with the lamp and Jem was unfolding himself and looking up, and she saw that the front of his shirt wasn't white at all but splashed with scarlet, and there was blood oozing between the fingers of the hand he had pressed to his mouth. His face was oddly lopsided, his right cheek puffy and glistening.

Henderson had followed and stood a little distance away, beyond the circle of lamplight.

'Like I said, an accident.' His tone was offhand. 'It was dark. I mistook him for the intruder. I'm sure it looks worse than it is.'

They took him down to the servants' hall, Thomas and Kate supporting his weight between them, while Abigail and Susan went ahead to heat up water and find flannels.

Jem slumped in Mr Goddard's chair at the head of the table. The brighter light hanging overhead showed up the damage: a split lip and a bleeding nose; a bruise purpling on his cheekbone, forcing his right eye half-shut. His face was the same colour as his shirt, making the blood stand out more starkly.

There was a lot of blood.

The smell of it, the stickiness, churned up buried memories. Kate moved automatically, dipping a cloth into the basin of cold water, watching it turn pink. 'It's going to need ice,' she said. 'For the swelling. Eliza, would you get some, please?'

'From the ice trunk?' It had been filled that afternoon by the garden lads with blocks brought down from the icehouse, and a whole salmon—gutted, cleaned, and packed with fennel—was now suspended within it, ready for the journey to London. 'Mrs Gatley said it mustn't—'

'I know what Mrs Gatley said.' Kate cut her off tersely. 'It'll only be open for a second. Thomas—get the brandy from the top shelf in the pantry.'

After they'd gone Kate took hold of Jem's hand and gently pulled it away from his face. Above the blood and the swelling his eyes glittered darkly into hers. Her heart lurched.

It was natural that she should want to put her arms around him, to stroke his hair and soothe the shock; that's what she told herself. She had felt that pain and remembered too well the disorientation; how a blow could scatter your senses so it felt you might never recover them. Leaning closer to examine his lip, she exhaled softly and hoped he couldn't hear the thud of her heart.

Chattering voices in the corridor heralded the return of Susan and Abigail, bringing hot water and more cloths. It was only when Kate went to take a clean flannel that she realised that her fingers were still twined with Jem's. She withdrew her hand, but before he let it go she felt his grip tighten for a second.

Warmth pulsed through her. She didn't notice Eliza come in.
'The ice, Mrs Furniss.'

It looked like a picture she remembered from the Sunday school Bible: Mary Magdalene kneeling before Jesus. Mrs Furniss wasn't kneeling, but she had the same dark hair as the woman in the illustration, the same expression of fierce tenderness. Eliza felt like she was intruding. Like none of the rest of them should be there.

'Here we are, pal.' Thomas came in, oblivious, and handed Jem a glass with an inch of amber liquid in the bottom. 'Not quite Sir Randolph's finest, but Mrs Gatley's best cooking brandy.' He puffed out a breath. 'Doesn't look like you'll be fit to come to London now. Not with a shiner like you're going to have.'

Eliza looked away, following the trail of crimson splashes on the flagstones, and realised with a sick thud of disappointment that he was right.

Ever since they'd found out about going to London, she'd been looking forward to it, for all that what Jem said was true and it was just scrubbing in a different kitchen, toiling up a different set of stairs. But she'd thought that, away from Coldwell, she might be different too. Someone he might notice.

She was so sick of this old place. Of the drudgery and the sense that life, in all its colour and excitement, was happening somewhere else. Going to the London house at coronation time had seemed like an opportunity to glimpse it for herself and she'd felt sorry for Mrs Furniss, being left behind. Stuck at Coldwell with miserable old Mr Goddard.

Now, watching the housekeeper gently sponging Jem's bloodied cheek, she felt cheated. Tricked. As if she had been winning at a game when the rules had suddenly changed. And once again, she found herself the loser.

That night there was thunder.

Sleepless beneath the sheets in the airless footmen's attic, Jem listened to the rain on the window and the throb of his blood in his pounding head.

Thomas had offered to take the bed in the silver cupboard, and every now and then the lightning lit up Joseph's sleeping face a few feet away.

It reminded him of Jack.

His plan had paid off. In a dark corridor with no one watching and the perfect excuse, Henderson hadn't been able to stop himself from letting fly with his fists, punishing Jem for his disrespect. Jem had sensed that in him—the need to control and subjugate, that instinct for violence. He'd met men like Henderson before. Too many of them. He'd known how Henderson would respond and predicted that he wouldn't realise until it was too late that he'd played right into Jem's hands.

He'd been right.

Everything hurt. But an ember of triumph burned in his heart.

<hr />

There are plenty men here who do what I did that summer. There are lots of ways to injure yourself just enough to be taken out of the line, or—if you do it properly—get sent home.

You have to be clever though. The officers are wise to an 'accidental' gunshot wound to the foot or the hand. They'll court-martial you, if they suspect. They'll put you in front of a firing squad and shoot you at dawn.

Chapter 10

The servants' basement was eerily still in the aftermath of their departure. The silence was as thick as cream. Going to the larder in the middle of the afternoon, Kate poured a glass of lemonade from the jug and listened.

Amos Kendall and his men were working in the late Lady Hyde's rooms—known as the Jaipur Suite—installing a bathroom in the old dressing room. Mr Goddard had opened up a long-disused door below the nursery corridor, once used by nannies to take the children out to the gardens, and Mr Kendall's invading army had decamped to the back of the house, removing the worst of the disruption from the servants' basement. Sipping her lemonade in the cool of the larder, Kate could just make out the rhythm of their saws and hammers, like an echo from another time, made by the ghosts of the workmen who had built the great mansion more than a hundred years before.

But there were other noises too, closer and more worldly. The stable lads were clearing out the coach house and a block of empty stalls to make way for the new motorcar and its driver (not assisted, Kate gathered, by Johnny Farrow, who was refusing to facilitate his own replacement), and she could hear their activity. Nearer still, there was a steady thud: a little slower, a little less regular than a heartbeat. Taking her glass of lemonade she went to the stillroom, from where she could see out into the yard.

Jem was there, outside the woodstore, and for an unguarded second, she felt a spark of relief that he wasn't on the train speeding away from Coldwell.

She quickly extinguished it.

The pitch pine dividers that had formed the horses' stalls had been hauled out and leaned against the wall in broken pieces, which he was chopping into kindling splints. Sipping her lemonade, she watched. He worked slowly and without enthusiasm, which she initially assumed was because of the heat of the day and the tedium of the task. But then she noticed how he bent stiffly to pick up each post and hesitated before raising the axe. She couldn't see his face, but his shoulders were tense and hunched and he paused often, pressing a palm into his side.

Returning to the larder, she poured another glass of lemonade, before going out into the dusty heat of the yard. The smell of burning lingered but was overlaid with a resinous tang. As she crossed the cobblestones, she had a clear view of Jem's battered face in the second before he looked up. She saw the way it contorted in pain as he swung the axe.

'I thought you might be thirsty.'

He set the axe down, carefully, and took the glass.

'Thank you.'

She could go back inside now; there was no reason not to. If it had been Thomas chopping wood, would she have done that? Not if he appeared to be in pain, she told herself briskly. She wouldn't be doing her job if she did. She was the housekeeper. She had a duty of care.

'It looks like it's healing all right,' she said, watching him drink. His swollen top lip meant that he could only sip slowly, and he pressed the back of his hand to his mouth as he lowered the glass. 'Is it still very sore?'

'It's fine.'

She shook her head, looking down at the ground. The hem of her skirt was fringed with dust and she shook it out absently, making her chatelaine chime. 'Henderson did a lot of damage, for an accident. Two blows to the face before he realised his mistake . . . ? And I don't think that was all, was it?'

'It doesn't matter.'

'It does if it means you're struggling with your work.'

'I'm not struggling—'

She sighed. She wasn't going to tell him that she recognised the signs. That she knew, with a weary certainty born of experience, that for every visible bruise a man left with his fist there would be twice as many where they couldn't be seen.

'Where else did he hit you?'

'He didn't—'

She gave a tut of impatience. 'Lift your shirt please. Show me your chest.'

She wondered if he too was reminded of his first night at Coldwell, after the incident with the sauceboat, when she'd sent him to wash his ashen face. He hesitated, as he had done then, before reluctantly doing as she asked, looking past her as she let out a long breath and came closer.

'Oh, *Jem* . . .'

A livid bruise blossomed on his side, spreading up over the bars of his ribs and round to his back, dark purple and mauve and blue with a mottled halo of red. Without thinking, she reached out and brushed her fingertips across it.

Instantly he flinched away from her touch.

She snatched her hand back. 'Sorry. Did I hurt you?'

'No.'

He moved away, gingerly touching his swollen cheek. Kate's chest burned inside. She sensed that he wanted her to leave, but she couldn't. Not without finding out more.

'He didn't just punch you, did he?' In her mind's eye she saw him, slumped on the floor in the moonlight, and pictured Henderson's polished shoe thudding into his ribs. She raised a hand to her throat, pulling the high collar of her blouse away from her neck. Jem stooped to collect up the kindling he'd made. This time his face didn't alter, but his jaw was set and a muscle pulsed above it.

She bent to help, her greater efficiency forcing him to step back and make way. He didn't protest, though she sensed how much he wanted to. The chains at her waist swung forwards as she stooped.

'What is it between you two?' she asked in a low voice.

'What do you mean?'

She carried the haphazard armful of split wood into the woodshed and dropped it into the old zinc trough where it was kept. 'You and Mr Henderson,' she said, brushing splinters and sawdust from her skirt as she emerged again. 'You clearly don't like each other.'

'I'd say you'd have more to worry about if I did like him.' The corner of his mouth on the undamaged side lifted into a wry smile. 'I mean, do you?'

'Like him? That's not the point. I don't get into fights with him that disrupt the running of the house. So far he hasn't smashed up my face and broken any of my ribs.'

It was intended to sound far-fetched and ridiculous, but as she said it, her throat tightened. Swallowing, she went on. 'I don't think anyone likes him, but we manage to keep things civil. Is there . . . some history between you?'

He didn't answer straightaway but shook his head slowly. 'Not as far as I know.'

'As far as you know? What does that mean?'

'Nothing.' She sensed something closing off inside him. 'I'd never come across him before I came here. Why would I? He was out in India for years with Sir Randolph, wasn't he?'

It was true. Sir Randolph had retired from his post and returned last year, taking up residence in Portman Square. She remembered Jem saying that he'd worked in Mayfair and wondered if their paths could have crossed in London. But why would neither have mentioned it? Why would Jem be lying now?

He bent to pick up the axe. 'It's just as you said. He doesn't like me, that's all.'

High overhead swallows circled and swooped through infinite layers of blue. The afternoon sun gilded his forearms, bared by his rolled-up sleeves, and found the golden lights in his hair. She looked away.

It was plausible enough. Looks might not have been so important out in India, but—rightly or wrongly—in the grand houses of England they meant better pay, increased opportunity, and greater respect. It was easy to see why Henderson, with his pitted face and short, stocky stature, would hold a grudge against someone like Jem, who had been blessed with more than his fair share of physical advantages. It wasn't hard to understand how Henderson might seek to assert his superiority in other ways.

'Yes, well . . . Try to stay out of his way in future,' she said crisply, though the minute the words left her lips she regretted them. It wasn't Jem's responsibility to appease Frederick Henderson, to avoid triggering his temper, or undermining his sense of self-worth.

It had taken her a while to realise that no one should ever have to do that.

She picked up his empty glass and took it inside. Rinsing it under the scullery tap, she ran her fingers over the place where his lips had touched and wondered for the hundredth time who Jem Arden really was and what he was doing at Coldwell.

Damn.

Jem swung the axe and winced at the retort of pain that shot through his chest. He turned to look at the open mouth of the kitchen door and thought about going after her.

I don't know him, he could say, *but I think he knows me. I think he's worked out that I'm the brother of a boy who went missing here nine years ago. I think he suspects that I've come here to find out what happened. And if he does, I'm sure he intends to stop me, by whatever means it takes.*

He kicked the shards of split wood into a rough heap, trying to imagine how he would explain. He pictured that slight frown—the two faint lines that appeared between her fine brows when she was thinking—as she listened. It sounded so far-fetched; that a lad could have come here as part of an ordinary Friday-to-Monday party and just . . . disappear. How could he expect her to believe it when he couldn't really make sense of it himself?

She would ask for evidence, and he would offer her . . . nothing solid. Only the sparse collection of facts he had gathered about Jack's movements that autumn, supplemented with the things he had heard in London when he'd worked for Mr Winthrop: the servants' gossip and rumour that had led him to Sir Randolph, and Coldwell . . .

She would think he was unhinged.

He swiped the back of his hand across his sweat-slick forehead. He'd seen how alarmed she was at the idea of an intruder. She was hardly going to give a sympathetic hearing to someone who had conned his way into the household with the intention of seeking justice for an old, unproven crime. She would think him a fantasist or a fool, possibly both. At a single stroke he would sever the cautious connection that was growing between them and she would order him to leave.

He couldn't risk it.

After what had happened before, he'd vowed not to involve anyone else in his search, but as the keeper of the keys, she had access to all of Coldwell's shuttered rooms and the power to unlock its secrets.

Like the queen on the chessboard. The most useful piece in the game.

Kate passed the remainder of the slow, hot afternoon making potpourri.

In the days of the late Lady Hyde there had been a rose garden, and though it was now tangled and neglected (Gatley couldn't spare hands to tend a space that the family never set foot in), the old-fashioned bushes still bloomed, untamed and unseen. After last night's rain, the damask roses were heavy-headed and ready to drop, ripe for gathering in fragrant fistfuls and spreading out in the stillroom to dry.

At six o'clock, when the heat was subsiding and the basement passages were filled with perfume, she went to the pantry to cut bread and cheese for tea. Mr Kendall and his troops had finished for the day and the silence was as thick and golden as honey. She could hear a fly buzzing drowsily against a windowpane somewhere, the clock ticking in the empty kitchen, but nothing else. It should have been peaceful, but somehow it felt like the house holding its breath.

Waiting.

For what? she asked herself crossly. Precious little happened at Coldwell, even when the full staff was in residence. What on earth was she expecting when the place was empty?

Without the structure of routine, there was too much time to think, too much space inside her own head to fill with things that weren't helpful. When she'd eaten, with the light summer evening stretching ahead, she opened her ledger to apply herself to the household accounts, working steadily down the columns of figures and sorting through the invoices for items for the Jaipur Suite and its new bathroom, until her neck was stiff and her fingers cramped from writing.

The pinkish light washing the room told her she had missed a beautiful sunset. She stood up, arching her back and flexing her aching shoulders, suddenly restless. Impatient to get out of the small, stuffy room and go up and look for herself at the suite of rooms where all the items she had chosen would be displayed.

The passageway was haunted by the scent of roses. She closed her door firmly, so the sound rang out, and made no attempt to still her jangling keys or soften the retort of her footsteps on the back stairs as she climbed up to the second floor. As she walked along the ladies' corridor, her shadow slid along the wall at her side, hunched and black, like a premonition. She suddenly saw herself, an old woman, dressed in the same sober black, walking the same corridors, her frame as shrunken as the narrow horizons of her life.

She flapped the unwelcome image away, like a crow from a freshly turned field.

Inside the Jaipur Suite the smell of plaster dust and sawn wood had banished the lingering whisper of old Lady Hyde's favourite lily of the valley scent. The rose-coloured silk (Jaipur was known as the Pink City, apparently) that had been hung when Coldwell had its last revamp in 1819 had been pulled down from the walls in the adjoining dressing room and piled in a heap on the floor, ready to make way for the peacock-print wallpaper Kate had ordered. The room had been cleared of its furniture—all but the bed, which was too large to move, but had been covered in holland cloth and stood in the centre of the space like a tented pavilion. Lengths of lead piping lay on the floor, and ladders leaned against the walls. Standing at the door to the dressing room Kate saw that a section of the ceiling had been pulled down and the floorboards beneath lifted, where the pipes for hot water would be laid.

She tried to imagine what it would be like when it was finished, and her mind was unwillingly drawn back to another house, another bathroom. Piped hot water. A deep bath, panelled in mahogany. Dark green tiles with a patterned border of lilies, and a white porcelain sink as wide as the tin tub most people still bathed in . . .

Nothing but the newest and best for you, my angel. Didn't I promise you would have the finest home in the city?

The echo of his voice in her ear was as close as if he was standing behind her. She could almost feel his breath on her neck. She squeezed her eyes shut, but above the whooshing in her ears she still heard footsteps. It was ridiculous that her mind could still play such tricks, after all this time—

'Oh. Sorry.'

Her eyes flew open, and she turned to see Jem standing just inside the bedroom door. Embarrassed heat exploded in her cheeks as he held up a ring of keys. 'Mr Goddard asked me to lock up. I didn't know you were here.'

'I came to see how the work was progressing, and check that everything was secure.' She took refuge behind her mask of brisk efficiency, shutting the dressing room door and folding the shutters across one window, then the other, so that darkness enfolded them, hiding her embarrassment. 'I haven't heard about any more break-ins, but we can't be too careful.'

They went out into the corridor. She would have gone back the way she had come, but he had turned in the other direction, towards the nursery wing and the staircase the workmen used, and she found herself following. He walked stiffly, one arm folded across his chest, his shoulders tense. A heavy door separated one part of the house from the other, and he propped it open for her with his foot rather than use the hand that was tucked under his arm. In the mauve dusk his face was drawn, the bruising beneath his right eye matched by a blue shadow of exhaustion under the left.

She looked away, thanking him as she passed.

The two worlds on either side of the door couldn't have been more different. Where the ladies' corridor was hung with red striped wallpaper (faded now to soft rose and claret), the walls in the nursery wing were painted: hard, shiny brown on the lower half where grubby fingers could reach, cream above. There were no gilt-framed portraits here. Cleaner squares on the scuffed paintwork showed where pictures had once hung, though for the most part they had been taken down. Only one remained, hanging crookedly in a broken wooden frame.

Jem paused as he passed it. It was a print of a golden-haired little girl in white-frilled petticoats holding a basket of kittens, but its Victorian sentimentality was somewhat marred by the rash of pale scabs that appeared to have broken out on the child's face. He lifted a hand to run his fingers over the dusty glass.

'Wet paper pellets, apparently,' Kate said, answering the question before he asked it. 'Fired through a straw. You find them all over the place in the nursery wing.'

'Randolph Hyde?'

'Who else?'

She continued along the corridor and heard his exhalation of impatience and disgust as he followed.

'I've never been in this part of the house before.'

'Not many people have. It's been closed up for years.'

'Since he and his sister were children?'

'Not quite that long. When Sir Randolph and Lady Etchingham left the nursery and the last nanny moved out, it was used for visiting servants when the family had house parties.' She stopped beside the last door and opened it. 'See?'

It was a large, square room, and with no furnishings or carpet to be damaged by the sun, its shutters had been left open. The last of the day's light fell on the collection of thin, straw-stuffed mattresses that were haphazardly piled on the dusty floor and leaned against its flaking walls.

She'd expected him to glance in without much interest, but he stepped past her. Going across to a few lumpy pallet mattresses that were stacked against the walls, he began moving them with his free hand, examining them as if he was looking for something on their stained canvas covers.

'Did they have a lot of parties?'

'Not by the standards of many houses; this place is too inconvenient for guests to get to. But Sir Randolph has always been a great one for parties, so I believe when he was at Cambridge the house would be filled with his friends for long stretches in the holidays—much to Sir Henry's disapproval. Apparently when Randolph entertained, it was always on rather an epic scale. I understand that was why Sir Henry sent him to India, in the hope that a job would make him mend his wild ways.'

She was talking too much, trying to smooth over the earlier awkwardness and compensate for her nervousness at being with him like this, the two of them alone in the vast house, with the day dying away to an echo outside.

Jem let the mattress he was holding fall back onto the others, raising a cloud of dust and a waft of musty straw.

'And did it?'

'No. Quite the opposite, I believe. But it removed the problem from Coldwell. Mostly, anyway. On the rare occasions he came home I think it was worse than ever. He used to get together with his old Cambridge friends here. Apparently the parties used to get rather out of hand.'

'In what way?'

'I don't know exactly . . . Mrs Walton was too loyal to gossip, but she was getting a little confused by the time I knew her. Sometimes she used to say things without realising, as if she'd forgotten she was speaking out loud.'

'What sort of things?'

'Oh—I don't know . . . She'd mutter under her breath about young Mr Hyde's sins finding him out, and God knowing the secrets of our hearts, that sort of thing. She was very devout, and very loyal to Sir Henry— like Mr Goddard—but that loyalty didn't extend to Randolph. She barely bothered to hide her disapproval of him. When I first arrived, they were very short-staffed, and I always got the impression that she blamed him for servants leaving. If it was because he'd been inappropriate with the maids, I think she would have said . . .' She gave an awkward laugh. 'Perhaps he brought ladies of ill repute here or something. I suppose that would explain why those pages were removed from the visitors' book, wouldn't it?'

The light was almost completely gone now, and the room was full of shadows, making everything melt into the dusk. She could see the outline of Jem's shoulders against the window, but it was impossible to see his face or read its expression.

'Did Mrs Walton keep records? Of visitors and their servants—that kind of thing? If so, you could find out who was here when those pages were removed.'

'Her bookkeeping was very erratic, especially by then—much to Mr Fortescue's exasperation. She always said she held all the information she needed in her head, but that got rather erratic too. Poor Mrs Walton . . . Her mental decline must have been underway already, but it became quite rapid after I started.'

It was through helping her with the figures, keeping track of invoices, and taking charge of paying bills that Kate—for all her youth, inexperience, and 'borrowed' character—had learned the responsibilities of a housekeeper and been in a position to take over. But she didn't want to admit that to Jem Arden, who had a habit of drawing too much out of her as it was. Her keys chimed softly as she straightened up. 'We'd better go, before it gets too dark to see.'

She went ahead of him down the stairs, holding up her skirts and treading carefully so she didn't miss her footing in the gloom. Outside the air was soft, scented with summer. She waited as he locked the door with one of the giant keys on the ring Mr Goddard had given him, and they walked back, along the side of the house, beneath the shuttered windows of the library and the billiard room. The tower on the hill looked like an illustration from a child's storybook against the pink-streaked sky. A single star glinted above its turreted roofline.

Back inside the familiar below-stairs world, the silence lay heavily over everything, like the dust sheets upstairs. Mr Goddard hadn't lit any lamps, and the blue dark was scented with roses. In the corridor outside the butler's pantry and the footmen's wardrobe Jem stopped.

'I'll say good night, then.'

'You're sleeping down here?'

'Of course.' His swollen mouth made his smile more lopsided than usual, but as he straightened the arm that was crossed over his chest, he winced. 'Trying to sleep, anyway. Can't leave the Coldwell treasure hoard unattended.'

She knew how hard the pull-out bed by the silver cupboard was. How narrow. It was intended for a boy of Joseph's size rather than a man of Jem's, but it wasn't her place to go above Mr Goddard and give him leave to sleep upstairs. And a selfish part of her was glad he was there, close by.

She nodded. 'Good night, then.'

Glancing back as she turned into the stillroom passage, she saw that he was still standing there, dissolving into the summer dark like a ghost.

———⚬⚬⚬———

In his defence, Jem did try to return the keys to Mr Goddard.

After she'd gone, he knocked softly on the door to the butler's pantry, but no light showed beneath it and no sound came from inside. Mr Goddard had been instructed to carry out an audit of the wine and spirit cellars during Hyde's absence, jettisoning anything that had gone off, working out what required replenishing before the wedding. When Jem had gone in earlier, there had been several dusty bottles on his desk and a crust of purple on the old boy's lips. He wasn't surprised when there was no answer to his knock.

And so, when he was sure all was quiet, he went quietly up the back stairs and along the ladies' corridor, through the door to the nursery wing. In the room Mrs Furniss had shown him, he lowered himself gingerly onto one of the straw-stuffed mattresses on the floor, gritting his teeth against the jagged shards of pain that speared his ribs.

The pain was so much stronger than it had been at first, and worse when he tried to lie down. And so, he sat, propped up against the wall with his arms wrapped around his chest, looking at the star-scattered sky, and wondering if Jack had been here, in this room, in November 1902. If he had slept on one of these stained pallets, squeezed in amongst the snoring bodies of other footmen and carriage grooms.

And if he had, what the hell had happened after that?

Chapter 11

Kate's dreams were vivid and uneasy.

Through the hot, airless night she flitted through half-familiar landscapes, full of contradictions and urgent imperatives she didn't understand. In one dream, she was writing in her household ledger, her pen scratching rapidly along the lines, but when she looked back the ink had faded until all the pages were blank. In another, she was hurriedly trying to fasten her corset but each time she managed to secure one hook another would come loose. And then, her frustration turned to dismay as she realised that the reason it wouldn't close was because, beneath the corset, her ribs were sticking out from her open flesh. And *he* was there, watching her.

Alec.

It's because I love you—can't you see that? All of this—everything I do—is for you. Why can't you just be grateful?

His voice jolted her awake. She lay, not moving, her rapid breath steadying as she realised it was a dream. The room was empty.

Soft light was filtering through the curtains. She knew she wouldn't sleep again so she got up, sliding her feet into silk slippers at the side of the bed. Opening the curtains, she saw that sunrise was still some time away, and the air was pearly and damp.

With no Susan to set water to boil and no Abigail to bring her tea, Kate shrugged on her housecoat and went to see to it herself. The passage was cool, the row of bells high up on the wall silent and swathed in shadow. The clock ticked sleepily in the kitchen. Passing the servants' hall she glanced in, and felt her heart stutter in alarm as she saw a figure, slumped in Mr Goddard's chair.

'Jem?'

Her first, panicked thought was that the intruder had returned and Jem was hurt. His head was turned away, his hands resting on the arms of the chair and his back oddly straight, but as she approached, she could see that he was asleep. Or he had been. Her voice jolted him back to consciousness, as if she'd thrown a bucket of cold water over him.

'Sorry. I didn't mean to wake you.'

His rigid shoulders relaxed a fraction. He dropped his head into his hands. 'Better you than Mr Goddard. What time is it?'

'Early. Not yet five.' They were speaking softly, almost in whispers. 'Is something wrong? What are you doing here?'

'I didn't mean to fall asleep.' He levered himself upright in the chair and his bruised face contorted with pain. 'Didn't think I'd be able to.'

'Your chest? Is it very sore?'

A nod, almost imperceptible. 'I can't lie down.'

Guilt needled her. She wasn't surprised he couldn't lie comfortably on that shelf by the silver cupboard; she should have taken charge of the situation last night and given him permission to sleep elsewhere.

'Would you allow me to bind it?'

With a sigh, he went to rub a hand over his eyes, pulling it abruptly away as his fingers encountered the swelling. The bruising was darker today, though its florid kaleidoscope of colours was changing. 'I'd allow you to do anything that stopped it hurting.'

She remembered that pain. Like an oyster knife slipped into the gap in the shell and twisted. Her corset had eased it, she recalled. It had held the broken pieces of her together.

She returned to her room to get bandages from the medicine chest and calico and safety pins. When she came back, he was standing beneath the window with his back to her. He didn't look round when she came in, or when she said, as matter-of-factly as she could, 'You can take your shirt off now.'

Out of the corner of her eye she was aware of him unbuttoning it, easing it carefully off his shoulders and down his arms. She busied herself with laying out the calico on the table, folding and refolding to create a square the right size and thickness to place against his ribs.

'Ready?' she said, and he nodded.

In the milky light his skin was colourless, except for the livid bruising. It was best to avoid meeting his eye, to focus on doing the job quickly and efficiently, but that meant concentrating on his body. It reminded her of the paintings she had seen in the National Gallery on trips to London as a girl, when she had stood in front of huge canvases of gods and saints and soldiers. Of Christ on the cross, all lean, sinewy grace.

But the body in front of her was not conjured by the paintbrush of a master. It was flesh and blood. Solid. Silk skinned and warm to the touch.

A pulse throbbed in her wrist, her throat.

'Can you lift your arms?'

He did as she asked. Skin moved over muscle, the hard ridges of bone. She swallowed. Tentatively she laid the calico wadding over the worst of the bruising and held it there with one hand while she unfurled the bandage, pinching the end so she could begin wrapping it around him.

There was no way of doing it at a distance, or without circling her arms around him. He stood completely still as she reached to pass the roll from one hand to the other, his chin raised as her cheek almost came to rest against his chest. She breathed in the warm scent of his skin and tried not to register its dry masculinity. Tried not to register anything about him at all.

'Too tight?'

His face was impassive, but his jaw was set.

'No.'

If only he'd revealed this injury on the night that it had happened. She could have been doing this with everyone else around, the girls looking on with compassionate curiosity, jostling to be the one to hold the wadding in place and pass the bandages while Thomas cracked weak jokes to lighten the atmosphere. How much easier it would have been. How much more . . . appropriate . . . than this quiet room with the rose-tinged dawn spreading outside and the two of them—she in her nightdress still, uncorseted, her hair unpinned—not speaking, not meeting each other's eyes.

His chest rose and fell inches from her face as she reached and wrapped, and sometimes she felt the warmth of his breath on her hair. He had laced his fingers together, and his hands rested on the crown of his head, as if he was standing before her in surrender. As she pinned the bandage in place and looked up at him, she saw that his face wore an expression of weary suffering.

'There. Has it made the pain worse?'

'I don't think so.'

She moved away, picking his shirt up from the back of the chair and holding it out to him. 'Good. Go and get some sleep.'

'But Mr Goddard—'

'Leave him to me. I'll explain. You've been on duty all night, after all.'

She watched him go, easing his shirt over his shoulders. At the door, he turned.

'Thank you.'

After that, she went out of her way to avoid him.

It was easy enough. The servants' basement was large, and they each had their own duties, carried out in different parts of it. Houses like Coldwell were designed to segregate the sexes. The male domains—footmen's wardrobe, butler's pantry, lamp room, coal store—were positioned at the other end of the warren of rooms from the stillroom and housekeeper's stores. Nevertheless, it was impossible not to be aware of him. To listen for his footsteps and to hear his voice.

And so, the days became a sort of dance, where she sensed his movements and co-ordinated her own around them, maintaining a careful distance. She applied herself to the list of tasks she had drawn up and progressed steadily through them: conducting a long-overdue inventory of the linen cupboard, reallocating worn sheets and tablecloths from 'best guest' to 'family,' and from 'family' to 'servants,' and setting aside pillow-slips and tray cloths that needed the attention of a needle. Trying to keep her mind from drifting back to the servants' hall in the pearly dawn, and remembering.

Imagining.

In the slow, sultry afternoons she found it annoyingly difficult to stop herself from imagining. She didn't always manage it.

In the Jaipur Suite and Sir Henry's old rooms the work progressed steadily. Every day Kate made it her business to see how things were coming along, so she could report back to Mr Fortescue. A cast-iron bath appeared in Lady Hyde's former dressing room one day—even Mr Kendall's army couldn't manhandle it up the stairs and they had to attach ropes to it and call Johnny Farrow and the Twigg boys to help. When she went up the next afternoon, it had been fitted beneath the window, with taps connected to the water pipes and a new copper geyser, which Mr Kendall proudly demonstrated.

She always made sure to go up before Mr Kendall left at the end of the day, so there was no chance of encountering Jem as he carried out Mr Goddard's duty of securing the house. No chance of being alone with him in that room with the huge bed, swathed in dust sheets, which had provided—to her scorching daytime shame—the setting of a particularly vivid dream one sticky, restless night.

Sometimes, in the late afternoons, she would see him crossing the kitchen yard in his shirtsleeves, or, if she went up the back stairs to check the work in progress, she might catch a glimpse of him through the door of the footmen's wardrobe. Once, passing the lamp room, she paused to ask him how his ribs were.

'Improving, thank you.' The bruising had faded on his face, and his split lip was healing, though still a little swollen. She found herself looking at it as he told her he was managing to sleep more easily. He didn't say whether he had returned to the silver cupboard, and she didn't ask.

The male servants were Mr Goddard's responsibility.

Really, it was none of her business. No concern of hers at all.

There were worse places to spend a hot week in high summer, Jem knew that all too well.

The hills were purple with heather and above them the sky was an endless arc of blue. Buried deep in its overgrown park, Coldwell dozed in the sunshine. Despite the disruption of the tradesmen, it was hard to imagine a more peaceful situation.

And yet he was far from at peace.

It reminded him of another summer, seven years ago, of another empty, dust-sheeted house, when his search for Jack was just beginning. He had gone to Ward Abbey in Norfolk, the last place he knew his brother to have been, but had found the house closed up, the skeleton staff on board wages.

Undeterred, he had got work at the home farm, as a casual labourer helping with the harvest. He'd loved being outside and working on the land. The job was more physical than he was used to; more exhausting, but infinitely more rewarding than carrying trays and polishing silver, and he'd put in the effort to involve himself with the other workers, no matter how tired he was. He eavesdropped on their gossip, asked guileless questions about the abbey and the Halewoods, and went with them to the tumble-down pub in the little hamlet when work was done for the day. He played on their cricket team against a neighbouring village, as the maids from the big house draped themselves along the railing of Lord Halewood's pavilion to watch.

He wasn't proud of what he did that summer, and he knew his mother wouldn't have been proud either. He'd never thought of himself as the kind of person who would pretend interest in a girl and use her to serve his own ends. Especially not a girl like Annie Harris: sweet, naïve, willing.

She had been so eager to impress Jem that it hadn't been hard to per-suade her to sneak him into the empty house. In the glowing evenings she led him through its staterooms and up its staircases, uncovering its trea-sures. Unlike Coldwell, there were no locked doors at Ward Abbey. Tobias Forbes (*Frensham*) was either too arrogant or too stupid to guard his secrets carefully.

Jem had got complacent. Overconfident. It had been too easy.

Until it had all gone spectacularly wrong.

It had been a charge of larceny that had got him arrested. He'd been dimly aware of the stable lad who was sweet on Annie Harris but had dismissed him as insignificant, an easy rival to overcome. That was his first mistake. The silver spoons with the Halewood crest they claimed to have found beneath his mattress in the hayloft had been planted during the search . . . he was no thief. But he couldn't claim to be guilt-free either. He had hung around after Annie had seen him out one night and climbed back into the house through a window that he'd unlatched. And he had quite deliberately used the girl and led her on too, though that crime didn't appear on his charge sheet. The law was much less concerned about a servant girl's heart than an aristocrat's silverware.

The judge at Norwich Assizes had instructed him to 'reflect on his poor choices and learn from them.' It was wise advice. In the six months that followed, in the narrow, stinking cell and the dripping exercise yard of Norwich Gaol, Jem had plenty of time to go over what had happened at Ward Abbey and identify where he'd slipped up. He'd reflected and he'd learned.

He knew better now.

And so the long days passed slowly, marked by the ticking clock in the kitchen, the distant deathwatch tap of Mr Kendall's hammers, and the fizzing drone of bluebottles in the pantry. He carried out the mundane tasks Mr Goddard set him and helped the stable lads prepare for the motorcar. He slipped through the house at dusk, checking that it was secure. Resenting every locked door he tried and looking for a chink in Coldwell's armour of secrecy.

There was too little to stop his thoughts straying to Mrs Furniss. Remembering the feel of her fingers on his bruised skin. Remembering the way her hair, when it wasn't pinned up in its daytime knot, curled softly around her face. Remembering the glimpse of her collarbone at the neck of her nightdress and the way she'd looked at him, all her brisk certainty gone.

He could relate to that.

It was a feeling he was beginning to know very well indeed.

⟨∞⟩

June 27th

The rain isn't stopping. Whatever action is planned has been delayed because of the weather, and so we are waiting. Everyone feels the strain, but some find it harder than others. The bombardment continues, and the noise makes it worse. Joseph is not coping well. I'm worried about him.

He joined up right at the start. August 1914. He saw it as a chance to be a hero, I suppose, and make up for what he did, or perhaps run away from it. He didn't even have to lie about his age. The recruiting sergeant asked for his date of birth and Joe said he didn't know exactly. The sergeant signed him up without any further questions.

The trouble is, there's nothing heroic about army life. Boys like Joseph wouldn't be so keen to join up if they knew how much time you spend sitting around listening to other men playing the mouth organ badly and arguing over cigarette cards. There's too much time to think.

That's why I'm writing this, even though you'll never read it. In these long days of waiting, it feels better to do something. It's a relief to put it on the page after keeping it in my head for so long.

And it gives me an excuse to relive every moment of that summer.

Chapter 12

After the weeks of unbroken sunshine leading up to it, coronation day began with lowering clouds and a strange heaviness in the air, which was as warm and thick as porridge. For Kate, it also began with a dragging ache, low in her stomach, and a scarlet stain on the bedsheet.

Later, coming back from lighting the fire under the copper in the laundry (she knew all too well it didn't do to let bloodstains set), she encountered Mrs Gatley, decked in her best coat and hat and bearing a cloth-covered tray. She frowned when she saw Kate, stopping suddenly, so that Mr Gatley, following in her wake, almost cannoned into her and upset the trug of strawberries he was carrying.

'You're not ready! Ten o'clock sharp, that's what I was told, so's we'd be in plenty of time to find a good spot to watch the procession. You'd better be quick.' She seized the trug from her husband and set off purposefully again towards the kitchen door. 'I'll just put these in the larder and tell Johnny Farrow to wait. I'm up to my ears in strawberries up there. You'll have to make jam tomorrow. They won't keep beyond that.'

Kate followed her inside. 'I'll do it this afternoon. I'm not coming to the coronation parade.'

'Not coming? Whyever not? I'd have thought you'd be glad of the chance to get away from this place. Change of scene.' In the gloom of the larder Mrs Gatley peered more closely at her. 'Not sickening for something, are you?'

'No.' Kate gave her a resigned smile. 'Only the regular thing.'

Catching her meaning, Mrs Gatley's chins wobbled in sympathy. 'Oh, well, in that case maybe you're best off staying put. Get your feet up. Make the most of the peace and quiet—it's rare enough.' She clattered dishes down on the slate shelf. 'I made a cheese and onion flan for Mr Goddard's tea when he gets back—I shouldn't think he'll want to stay once he's done his tree planting—but there's enough for you to have for your dinner too. I'd have brought you down a slice of my lemon cake, if I'd known. I always needed a bit of something sweet at the time of the month. That's all well and truly in the past now, the Lord be thanked . . .'

Kate went out to the stable yard to see them off; Gatley, Mrs Gatley, and Mr Goddard in one wagon with Johnny Farrow at the reins, and Stanley Twigg driving the smaller cart, in which Jem had joined the grooms and the garden lads. She didn't look at him, though somehow she still managed to be aware that the bruising on his face was much less noticeable, and he was wearing the soft-striped collarless shirt he had worn on the day he arrived. His hair was lighter than it had been then, where the sun had painted gold into it.

Johnny Farrow raised one heavy eyebrow at her. 'Shall I wait?'

Kate shook her head. 'Someone should stay here. In case of intruders . . . We shouldn't leave the place empty.'

It was an excuse, but as the horses' hooves echoed under the archway, she looked around uneasily.

Wrapping her arms around herself, she went back into the silent house.

The Union Jack flags along the dusty main street in Howden Bridge were motionless in the heavy air. The garland of flowers around the door to the village school, where teas were being served, wilted and dropped their petals in the heat.

Jem watched Mr Goddard perform his ceremonial tree-planting duty on the playing field behind the school. The school itself had been built with the money and patronage of the third Baronet Bradfield (who, Jem guessed, was keen to repair some of the damage his predecessor had done to the family name); and tradition apparently dictated that significant occasions were marked with the planting of a tree by someone from the Big House. Sir Randolph had been only too glad to defer the duty to Mr Goddard, who shakily shovelled soil over the roots of a spindly beech tree a stone's throw from the fledgling ash planted by his late master nine years previously.

It was strange, seeing him outside of his kingdom at Coldwell. Alongside the sturdy villagers and farm folk he seemed older and frailer, his stature diminished amongst people over whom he had no authority, his skin like yellowed parchment alongside their outdoor ruddiness. He made a short speech, but his rusty voice didn't carry as far as Jem, standing at the back of the small, inattentive crowd.

Jem's gaze moved over the assembled villagers, picking out the few he recognised: one of the laundrywomen who came up to Coldwell on Mondays (impossible to miss, with her sleeves rolled back over her mighty forearms and a solid infant wedged on her hip), the wizened old man who kept the village store, and several children who'd had prominent roles in the parade that had opened the celebrations that morning and who were now impatient for the jam tarts and ices and sports that were scheduled to follow tea.

A ripple of very half-hearted applause signalled the end of Mr Goddard's speech. Turning away, Jem saw Davy Wells from the gate lodge, looking smart but uncomfortable in a suit that appeared to have been made for someone considerably smaller. He was with a stout, harried-looking woman in a hat that looked like some ungainly bird had roosted on her head. His mother, Jem presumed, picking his way through a skirmish of children towards them.

'Hello, Davy.'

Davy flinched away from the greeting, turning his head as forcefully as if Jem had slapped him.

Mrs Wells tutted. 'That's not very nice, Davy.' She gave Jem an apologetic smile. 'I don't know what's got into him today. The heat I expect.' Sweat beaded her hairline beneath the hat, and she fanned herself with her gloves. 'Wasn't the parade lovely? I do like to see the little ones in their costumes. You were in it last time, weren't you, Davy? Pride of place, at the front.'

Davy looked down, scuffing at the dust with the toe of his boot. On the triangle of grass between the White Hart and the school, the brass band launched into a jaunty tune, at odds with the lassitude of the day.

'Did you dress up?' Jem asked. He knew not to expect a reply from Davy himself but didn't want to talk about him as if he wasn't there.

'He did,' Mrs Wells said proudly. 'You were the Grand Old Duke of York, weren't you, Davy? I dug out his father's old coachman's livery and trimmed it up with a bit of braid and he led the parade right out of the church door, smiling all over his face. Twelve, he was—always tall for his age. Oh, it was a smashing day, that was!' The memory lit up her lined face. 'You weren't so shy then, were you, Davy? He was a regular little chatterbox back in those days.'

Jem was surprised; he'd assumed Davy had always been mute. Davy's head was bent, but Jem could make out the scowl on his face. He wanted to ask Mrs Wells what had happened to silence that smiling, chattering boy, but she was hitching her basket up her arm and looking past him. 'Oh—there's Mrs Crawford. I must go and have a word . . . Come along, Davy; say goodbye to—'

'Jem.'

She nodded, already pulling Davy away with her. He turned to look at Jem with dark, mistrustful eyes.

The band was playing a military march now. Jem began to walk, following the general direction everyone else was taking. In the schoolyard, the children were being marshalled into lines by a short-tempered schoolmaster, while a photographer assembled his equipment and the vicar took coronation mugs out of a tea chest full of packing straw. A table had been set up by the door, with cups and saucers laid out in rows. Without meaning to, Jem found himself in the queue for refreshments, and only realised how thirsty he was when the purposeful woman serving asked what he wanted. She reached beneath the table and pulled a bottle of lemonade from a bucket of water and handed it to him.

'You're another one not from round here, aren't you?'

She was hatless, with faded red hair piled up on top of her head, coming loose a little at the sides. Her eyes, pale green like the marble stopper on the lemonade bottle, moved over him with quick curiosity. 'We were just saying—there's a lot of new faces around today. City folk, here for the celebrations. Are you Manchester or Sheffield?'

'Neither.' He pushed the marble into the bottle. 'I work at the hall.'

'Coldwell?' Her expression changed and she gave a short, harsh laugh. 'Hear that, Mrs Mullins? Definitely not from round here, then.'

He took a mouthful of lemonade. 'What makes you say that?'

Her green glass eyes were almost scornful. 'Think about it. No one local works there, do they?'

She looked past him, greeting the man behind by name, asking what she could get for him, leaving Jem little choice but to move aside. He looked at the other woman behind the table, but she was pouring tea from a vast, dented metal pot, listening to the woman for whom it was intended telling her about her husband's toothache.

He walked away, taking another long draught of lemonade. The heat made a pulse beat in his neck: heat and anger. With every step he thought about going back, demanding to know what she meant.

Because she was right, he realised. Apart from the laundrywomen and the girls who provided extra help in the kitchen occasionally, no one from the neighbouring villages worked at the house. Johnny Farrow's thick Geordie accent marked him out as being a long way from home, and he'd heard the Twigg lads speak about their sprawling family in Warwickshire, and their Gypsy roots. Jem had grown up on an estate where families could trace their service back for generations; garden lads marrying housemaids, dairymaids settling in tied cottages with herdsmen from the home farm, each union tightening the warp and weft of the community, providing the estate's future labour.

What had happened at Coldwell to disrupt that natural order?

He walked on, sweat soaking the back of his shirt, despair thickening in his throat, weighting his limbs. He was weary. Tired of watching his words and always being on guard. Tired of being an outsider. Tired of being alone with his demons and the corrosive hatred that coloured everything. Tired of scrabbling around for the most meagre crumbs of evidence to lead him to a truth that everyone seemed determined to obscure and erase. He had come to Coldwell for answers but found himself surrounded by walls of secrets and suspicion and silence. The harder he tried to break them down, the more he felt them close in on him.

The music of the brass band faded as he left the festivities behind and made his way back to Coldwell alone.

—∞∞∞—

It was not a good day for making jam.

Kate had stoked up the stove in the stillroom, but the thick walls held in the heat and made stirring the simmering pan unbearably uncomfortable. She broke off frequently to run cold water over her wrists and hold a damp cloth to her cheeks, but her back ached from standing, her belly ached from cramping, and every inch of her felt sticky with sugar and sweat.

The silence was as thick and sticky as the jam. A wasp ricocheted around the walls, maddened by the sweetness, its buzzing loud in the empty basement. Kate's thoughts bounced around inside her head, as jerky and agitated as the wasp, rebounding between the celebrations currently underway in London and Howden Bridge, the present coronation and the last one.

For all these years she had trained herself not to think of that time, but over the past couple of weeks, the mounting excitement, both below stairs at Coldwell and in the wider world, had stirred the embers of memory.

In Bristol, King Edward's coronation had been marked by a parade during the day and a grand dinner at the Merchant Venturers' Hall in the evening. Alec had been invited, of course; he always managed to insinuate himself into the right places, to rub shoulders with the right people (often by paying wedges of cash to very much the wrong people) in his perpetual quest to secure his reputation amongst the city's respectable businessmen. He expected—*required*—her to be at his side, to squash any unsavoury rumours and banish any lingering suspicions about his past. As the daughter of the Haven Master of Bristol Docks, she had been the decorative seal of respectability on his new-minted good character.

She had been a gullible little fool.

And on that occasion, she had not been able to fulfil her obligation, because she had not been pretty or pleasing or an object of pride. With her black eye and his finger marks on her neck, she had been a blemish on his reputation. A walking reproach.

He hadn't even been sorry that time. She had crossed a line, and for a moment, when his hand had closed around her throat, she thought he meant to kill her. Afterwards, there had been a new coldness in the way he'd looked at her, even as he was reminding her that he loved her.

Too much to ever let her go.

She poured jam into the jars, her aching back protesting at the weight of the pan. Her hands were shaky, and it slipped in her grasp, knocking over one of the jars, so jam spread in a dark, glistening puddle over the table.

She gritted her teeth and swiped damp hair back from her face. The swooning silence of the house carried an echo of that day: the brass-band, flag-fluttering clamour of it, muted and muffled by the closed blinds and thick carpets in her luxurious prison. That day, the seconds had been marked by the throb of pain in the side of her head where his fist had struck her, all of them leading up to the moment in the evening when he had come downstairs, dressed for the dinner, and paused in the hallway to check his reflection and straighten his white tie.

Don't do anything foolish like try to leave, will you? I'd find you, and it would be difficult to forgive such . . . disloyalty.

A wave of nausea broke over her at the memory.

He had gripped her chin as he'd bent to kiss her goodbye, his fingers hard on her bruised jaw.

For better, for worse, remember? Till death do us part.

⸺⸺∞⸺⸺

By the time she had cleared up the spilled jam she was hotter than ever, and the stickiness seemed to have coated every inch of her skin. She had set water to boil for washing the pans, but she had a sudden urge to be clean—to sluice away the sweat and cloying sugar; the memories that crept and seeped and stained her mind like the strawberry juice on her fingers.

In her parlour she rolled back the rug and dragged the slipper bath out from beneath the table in the corner. Fetching water was heavy work, usually done by Joseph or one of the girls; and by the time she had hauled two cans from the scullery and a kettle of hot water from the kitchen she almost groaned out loud with the relief of finally unbuttoning her blouse, unhooking her corset, letting her skirt and petticoat fall to the floor. She unclipped her stockings and slipped out of her chemise, peeling back layers of decency, constraint, and bloodstained femininity until she was naked.

And then, from the kitchen passage, the jarring jangle of a bell.

Alarm crackled through her. She recognised the sound immediately as the front doorbell, though couldn't think why anyone should be ringing in the late afternoon when no one was at home. It was coronation day—surely any visitors would know that the servants would be at the celebrations in the village?

For a second she couldn't move. Then, stumbling through to the bedroom, she grasped the housecoat hanging on the back of the door and thrust her arms into it. Her fingers tangled in ribbon and caught on a lace cuff as she went out into the passageway. The bell had stopped ringing, but the sound still bounced around her head, making it impossible to hear anything else. She waited, feeling the knock of her heart against her hand as she clutched the front of the housecoat together.

Another jolt of panic as the bell was pulled a second time.

Her legs were shaking as she went up the steps to the hall, her bare feet soundless on the stone. She slipped through the green baize door and edged forwards, shrinking into the shadows of the staircase as she peered through the ornate banisters. Terror tore through her as a face suddenly loomed at the window, hands cupped against the glass, and she darted backwards, pressing herself against the wall.

Her heartbeat echoed through the stillness. Panic swelled and shrank with every rasping breath. From beyond the heavy front door, she heard the scuffle of movement, and then—after what seemed like an eternity—footsteps retreating. Over the drumming of her own blood, she could just make out voices on the gravel below.

She slid down the wall until she was crouching on the cold floor. The tiger stared down at her from behind his bared teeth, but for the first time she saw the terror of the prey in his glassy gaze, not the aggression of the predator.

This is what it's like to be hunted, she thought. The second baronet's heavy-lidded eyes gleamed dully in the afternoon light, his red lips parted in that secretive smirk, as if he was enjoying her fear. Excited by it.

Tucking her knees up against her chest, she tried to recall the face at the window. It wasn't familiar, but that was scant comfort. Her husband didn't need to dirty his own hands with the more unsavoury aspects of his business, as she'd discovered. He knew people who would do anything and keep quiet about it if you paid them enough.

She pushed the heels of her palms into her eyes until patterns danced in the blackness. The grandfather clock ticked away the seconds. She waited, trying to steady her breathing to its rhythm, and then—when she was sure the man wasn't returning—got unsteadily to her feet. Going back downstairs slowly, she clung to the stair rail, like an invalid out of bed for the first time after a long illness, and was almost at the bottom when a noise made her freeze.

The back door.

The servants' entrance from the kitchen yard, left unbolted and opening, then closing. She felt light-headed with horror. Whoever had rung the bell hadn't gone away but had come round and let himself in. In a moment, he would take the few paces along the passage, and see her, pressed against the wall on the staircase. Hiding. Helpless.

She heard him exhale. Closing her eyes, she clamped her lips together, biting back the whimper that almost escaped her as his footsteps advanced.

'*Jesus*—'

Jem's voice. She opened her eyes as the breath she had been holding escaped her in a rush.

A sob.

In a second, he had crossed the little space between them and taken hold of her upper arms, gentle but firm. 'What's wrong? Did something happen?'

She couldn't speak. She wanted to laugh and say no, that the ring of the doorbell had just caught her by surprise, but the words were stuck in her throat and she could only shake her head as tears brimmed and coursed down her cheeks.

He held her then. Slowly, carefully, as if it was the most natural thing in the world, he folded her into his arms, so she was cradled against his chest as she shuddered and gasped and her tears soaked his shirt. All the pent-up fear and fury of the last nine years came spilling out, and he rested his cheek against her hair and told her that she was safe.

Bit by painful bit, the panic ebbed and reality reasserted itself. She couldn't look at him as she pulled away, scrubbing her cheeks with the flat of her hand, clutching her flimsy gown around herself, horrified at her state of undress. Not only her clothes but her mask. The professional carapace she had created, stripped away and shattered.

'Oh God, I'm so sorry,' she croaked. 'I was just going to bathe, and then the door—'

He stood back, turning tactfully away so he wasn't looking at her.

'You don't have to explain. As long as you're all right.'

'Someone rang the bell. I thought—'

'It was tourists, on bicycles. I met them on the drive. They wanted to see round the house.' He smiled wryly. 'The housekeeper of Chatsworth was most obliging in giving them a tour there the other day, apparently.'

'Tourists? You're sure?' Doubt lingered. If it was one of Alec's men looking for her, would he ask for her directly? Or would he spin a story to gain access to the house?

Jem shrugged. 'I sent them up to look at the church. Told them about the tiger's grave. Come on—I'll show you.'

She should go back to her room and get dressed, but if she didn't see for herself the seed of disquiet would remain and grow. He didn't look round as she followed him up the back stairs, and she took advantage of the gloom to fasten the ties of her gown securely, as if that could make up for her lack of corset, her unstockinged legs and bare feet. On the second floor he led her along the ladies' corridor, where the rooms looked out towards the church on the hill. Going into the Jaipur Suite he crossed to the window.

'See. There they are.'

She could just make out bicycles propped by the gate and the figure of a woman moving amongst the gravestones. A moment later, in the shade of the yew tree, she spotted the man she had seen at the window. He looked harmless. Not frightening at all.

Just tourists.

She let out a breath. Jem had moved away, and she leaned her forehead on the cool glass, closing her eyes, wondering how she was ever going to come back from this.

'So . . .' His voice came from somewhere behind her. 'Did you get a chance to bathe?'

She gave an awkward laugh. 'No.'

A second later, she heard the sound of cascading water and spun round, her mouth falling open. He had gone into the dressing room and turned on the taps in the cast-iron bath. The soon-to-be Lady Hyde's brand-new, never-used cast-iron bath.

'What are you doing?'

'It makes sense to try it out, don't you think?'

He had to raise his voice over the splash of water. There was something exhilarating about it—the instant, effortless achievement of something that had previously required such arduous labour—and it was as if he had conjured it himself, through some power of his own.

She gave a gasp of incredulous laughter. 'You can't . . . ! *I* can't. These are Lady Hyde's rooms—'

'Not yet.' He shrugged. 'There is no Lady Hyde yet. There isn't even anyone else here. This huge house is all yours. No one will disturb you. No one will know.'

The water flowing into the bath took on a golden hue as it deepened against the pristine white. In the oppressive heat, it looked irresistibly enticing. She was suddenly aware of the musky scent of her skin; the damp heat coming off it. He turned the taps off and the surface of the water shivered and glittered. The room suddenly seemed very quiet.

'I'll leave you to it,' he said softly. With his eyes downcast, he walked past her to the door, but paused with his hand on it. 'If you'll allow me, I'll bring up a towel and leave it outside. If it's all right for me to go into your room . . . ?'

Their eyes met.

'Jem . . .'

It wasn't too late to stop this madness. To assert her authority and take back control.

'If you'd rather I didn't, I understand,' he said. 'But you looked after me when I needed it, and I'd like to do the same for you.'

She wanted to say that she didn't need looking after. That's what Mrs Furniss would have said, had she been standing there in her black silk, with her keys at her waist. But there was only Kate, unlaced, unlocked, undone, her eyes still hot from crying.

'Thank you,' she whispered.

—⊶⧁⊷—

Her room smelled of roses.

The chipped enamel slipper bath stood in front of the fireplace, the few inches of water it contained looking cold and unappealing compared to the crystal depths he'd run for her upstairs. Her discarded clothes were laid over the back of the chair by her desk, along with the towel she had set out, ready to use.

His heart stuttered in his chest.

He tried not to look at them. Tried not to notice the lace-trimmed straps of her chemise, the delicately boned satin corset, or to remember how it had felt to hold her against him. The delicate bones of her. The satin hair.

He'd failed before he'd started.

The girls he had known—had been with—were mostly servants like himself and the corsets he unhooked were made of rough cotton canvas. There had occasionally been women upstairs who had sought to alleviate the boredom of their privileged lives, or subvert the rules by instigating a dalliance with a footman. Those women had corsets like this: satin-smooth and shell pink, like the flesh they contained.

He wondered again who she was, the woman beneath the austere housekeeper's black. She'd been shaking as he'd held her, all her armour fallen away. Where had she come from? What was she so afraid of?

In front of him stood the desk, with its little locked drawer at the back, where all the household keys were kept. Her housekeeper's ledger lay on the blotter and beside it, in a puddle of silver, her chatelaine. He picked it up and let it trickle between his hands, so the key to the drawer swung like a stage hypnotist's watch on its chain.

It would be the work of a second to unlock the drawer and find the library key. To find any key he wanted—they were all labelled. It was the kind of opportunity he had dreamed of: the whole house silent and empty above him . . . his to explore. He would never get another chance like this.

In his mind he pictured the chessboard, the carved figure of the queen.

There was a mirror on the wall between the room's two windows. The man who stared back at him from its murky depths was hollow-cheeked and remote, his face shadowed by fading bruises. For a long moment he held his own gaze, regarding his image as if it were a stranger's and finding it was one he didn't warm to.

He'd used that face like the key on the chain, to open doors and gain access to privileges (and pleasures) unavailable to others. He'd used it to get work and women. He'd used it to turn Annie Harris's head and steal her from under the nose of the stable lad who'd been patiently courting her for months. He'd used it to attract Kate Furniss's attention and to win her trust.

He looked down at the chatelaine in his hand and felt a flash of self-disgust. Opening his fingers, he tipped it back onto the desk.

The stranger in the glass looked at him with a mixture of pity and disdain. *You idiot*, he sneered silently. *If she's the queen, you're a pawn. You'll never be worthy of her anyway.*

Abruptly he turned away and set about emptying the bath.

He did it for no other reason than to save her the trouble, throwing himself into the laborious task with a sort of perverse satisfaction. When he'd finished, he took the towel from the back of the chair and carried it up to the Jaipur Suite, where he left it outside the bathroom door and retreated.

Chapter 13

Mr Goddard returned at teatime.

Kate heard the wagon rattle into the stable yard, and Mrs Gatley's voice (she always spoke at a volume that could carry across a kitchen and above the clash of pans) reminding him about the cheese and onion flan in the larder, calling Jem to assist. Kate knew that she should go out and welcome Mr Goddard, enquire about the day, and give him a chance to enjoy his moment of celebrity, but she kept to her room.

Much to her relief, there had been no sign of Jem when she came downstairs, flushed and damp from the bath. When she went back to her parlour, she discovered that the laborious tasks of emptying the tin tub, rolling back the rug, and restoring the room to order had been done. It was almost as if none of it had ever happened.

Except it had, and she would have to face him again sometime.

In the aftermath of her terror and the weeping that followed, she felt bruised and fragile, as if a hard shell had cracked and peeled away, leaving her exposed. Once again he had seen her, and this time it had changed everything.

Eventually the sounds of activity died away and the basement was quiet again. The light changed: the shadows slid down the walls and the heat subsided into a stuffy, enveloping warmth. Kate was hungry but couldn't gather the courage to go to the kitchen for food. She was acutely aware of the presence of the others—Mr Goddard and Jem—as if she could hear them breathing through the walls. But still, the soft knock at her door was completely unexpected.

She opened it to find Jem standing there. She was so used to seeing him in uniform that in his own clothes he seemed like a different person from the inscrutable, impeccably mannered footman. This was the man who had sheltered from the rain beneath Black Tor and walked back with her across the steaming heath. The man who had gathered her into his arms and held her while she cried.

His hands were in his pockets and he was standing a little way back, appearing utterly at ease. Except for the faint flicker of a muscle in his jaw and the slight hoarseness in his voice. 'There's going to be fireworks,' he said, then paused and cleared his throat. 'This evening. They're setting them off up on the hill before they light the bonfire. I wondered if you'd like to watch them?'

The bonfire had been the subject of some discussion in the servants' hall in the preceding weeks. It was part of a national network of 'celebration bonfires' that were to form a chain the length and breadth of the land, and a local committee had apparently been formed to oversee its construction, on the highest part of Howden moor.

'Watch them?' She was thrown, picturing a walk to the village to join a clumsy jostle of beer-sodden revellers, the effort of assembling her professional mask and keeping it in place amid the merriment. The journey back with him in the dark. 'I—I don't know, I—'

'Not from the village,' he said, as if he'd read her mind. 'From here. You won't even have to leave the house. I know the perfect place.'

'Where?'

She had wondered how she would broach what had happened before, and thank him for what he had done, but somehow, he had made it unnecessary. She'd thought it would be impossibly embarrassing to face him, but as he smiled at her in the fading light, embarrassment was the last thing she felt.

'Come with me. I'll show you.'

It was a different world. One she hadn't known existed.

She had followed him through the servants' basement, waiting outside the footmen's wardrobe while he went in and picked up a cloth-covered crate from the table, taking care not to make a sound as they went up the back stairs. At the door to the footman's attic she hesitated, suddenly doubtful.

'Where are we going?'

'Just to the corridor,' he said. 'There's a way out onto the roof. I'd imagine there must be one in the maids' attic too, though obviously I wouldn't know anything about that.'

His smile was deliberately charming, as if he was trying to persuade her of his honourable character. It worked. Her heart was beating too fast, but she had come too far to go back downstairs to her quiet room and another evening spent poring over invoices or stitching frayed seams. His hands were full, so she opened the door herself and let him go ahead of her up the stairs.

It looked the same as the girls' attic but smelled unmistakably male. It was twilight up here, and they both trod softly on the creaking boards as she followed him to the low window at the end of the landing. The sash had been raised to its fullest extent and beyond it the park was spread out, softened by the evening. A breath of warm air blew a curl across her cheek.

He leaned through the open window and put down the crate, then stood to the side. Placing one hand at the small of his back, as he would do when attending the family, he held out his other, and bowed slightly.

'After you . . .'

She laughed, to cover up a lurch of nervousness and misgiving. 'Is it safe?'

'Completely.' His face, with its mottling of faded bruises, was grave in the half-light, his voice low. 'Have you never been out there?'

She shook her head, trying to remember if the window on the girls' side was the same. Did it open wide like this one? She thought she knew the house well, but she couldn't think. Couldn't focus.

'Then let me show you.'

It was easier than she thought, climbing through, especially with his hand to steady her. She felt a brief rush of vertigo as she got her bearings, and found herself in a new landscape, one of sloping slate, lead-lined gulleys and rows of chimneys as tall and solid as terraced houses. Pressing herself back against the reassuring solidity of the wall, she took in the dizzying panorama of the park: the folds of land where the shadows pooled, the dark copses of trees. The sky was marbled with fine veins of cloud, stained pink and apricot by the sun, which had sunk to rest on the smoky line of the distant hills. It looked like the painted ceiling of some grand rococo ballroom.

'Oh! It's . . . astonishing! Familiar, but so different.'

'I thought you would have discovered it long ago. There's a wall dividing this half of the house from the other so you can't get round to the maids' side, but I assumed they'd go out on their half.'

'There is a window on the maids' landing . . .' Without the distraction of his touch her memory clarified. 'It's got bars across it though, so you couldn't climb out.'

'How unfair.'

And how unsurprising that the girls should be the ones to have their freedom restricted. She followed him round the corner, to the north-facing side of the house, where the temple was disappearing into the darkness of the trees behind it, somewhere between magical and menacing. Setting down the crate in the lea of a dormer window, Jem pointed out the silhouette of the coronation bonfire on the hill.

'The fireworks are being set off just outside the village, but we should be able to see them from here.'

'What's in the box?'

He moved the cloth aside, to reveal half of Mrs Gatley's cheese and onion flan and two bottles of beer. 'I thought you must be hungry. I took some of this to Mr Goddard earlier and I could see you hadn't had any. Between you and me, it's wasted on him this evening. The hospitality in the lounge of the White Hart must have been pretty generous. Very decent of him to condescend to accept it really, given how he feels about the village.'

His tone was grave, but his eyes gleamed with amusement as he unstoppered one of the thick glass beer bottles. Kate smiled.

'Very noble indeed. Mr Goddard has long held that the White Hart is a den of the utmost iniquity. A couple of years ago he dismissed two footmen when he discovered they'd been seen in there. Two footmen, gone at a stroke! Poor Thomas had to do the work of three men until we eventually managed to find a replacement.'

'Big houses usually have no trouble in filling places,' Jem remarked idly, holding out a bottle. 'They're the jobs we all want, aren't they? Why is it so different here?'

'Because it's not like other houses, is it? Too cut off and stuck in the past. Until now, anyway, with all Sir Randolph's modernisations.' Taking the bottle, she shook her head in wonder. 'You've thought of everything.'

'If I'm honest, I didn't really think at all.' He cut the flan, dividing it into small pieces, easy to eat with their fingers. 'If I had, I would never have come to find you. I would have talked myself out of it and come up here alone.'

The parapet that ran around the edge of the roof was high enough to ensure that the attic windows couldn't be seen from below, wide enough to sit on. She leaned her hip against it and half turned to look at the undulating outline of the ancient hills. Silence stretched for the length of one sighing breath, and then she said quietly, 'Perhaps that would have been better.'

'For you?'

'For us both.' She hesitated, summoning courage. 'Jem, about what happened earlier—'

'You don't have to say anything.'

Her laugh was harsh in the soft evening. 'We can pretend it never happened?'

'If that's what you want. You don't owe me anything—no explanations—nothing. You don't have to tell me where you came from or how you ended up in this place, or what happened to make you scared to be alone here on a summer's afternoon.' He tipped the bottle to his bruised lips and added, almost absently, 'I don't need to know any of those things to know that you were made for a better life than this.'

'This isn't such a bad life. There are worse places to live.'

'There are better ones too.'

'Such as?'

'A home of your own. Filled with fine things, and a housekeeper to look after them. A husband to love you.'

'I don't want those things.' She took a cautious mouthful of beer, the bottle feeling unfamiliar against her lips. There was no point in pretending, not now he had seen her with the mask ripped off. 'I had them before—or most of them. I had a fine house and expensive furnishings. I had a cook-housekeeper and a between maid.' She hesitated, realising she was about to cross a line. 'I had a husband too. But he didn't love me.'

His voice was rough. 'Then he was a fool.'

She sighed, perhaps as much with the relief of speaking the truth as the pain of confronting the past. 'He was ambitious. Clever. He'd come from humble beginnings, in Glasgow, and worked his way up—by skill and determination, he used to say, though that was only half the story. He was no fool. But he was also . . . not a good man.'

'Why did you marry him?'

A moth flitted palely through the dusk. She watched its progress until it was swallowed by the blue.

'Because *I* was the fool.'

And bit by bit, the light drained from the pastel sky as she told him about a naïve eighteen-year-old girl, desperate for romance and excitement, who had fallen for the charming stranger who had crossed the Assembly Ballroom to seize her dance card and tear it up so he could have her to himself all evening. Darkness spread across the park like ink bleeding into a blotter as she described his artful show of amazement when, at the evening's end, she'd told him her name, and he'd pretended to be horrified at having been so bold with the Haven Master's daughter, as if he hadn't known who she was all along. As if he hadn't planned everything.

There was only a pale strip of gold left above the hills as she admitted how easily she had fallen for his lies and charm and flattery.

'He was the most exciting thing to happen in my sheltered life. My father saw through him, of course. He knew his stories didn't add up. He tried to stop me, but it was too late; I had already . . . *compromised* myself. I believed that he'd fallen in love with me.' Her voice hardened with self-mockery. 'He told me he wanted to marry me—that he couldn't wait. I was too infatuated to spot the warning signs. I didn't even think it strange that he didn't invite any family or friends to the wedding. He told me his parents were dead, and he was so far from home . . . I felt sorry for him, being so alone in the world. He said I was all that he needed.'

'What happened?'

Jem's face was impossible to read in the velvet dusk. They had moved, so they were both sitting on the stone parapet now, their backs to the dusk-veiled park, their knees almost touching. Only crumbs remained of Mrs Gatley's flan. Kate took another mouthful of beer before carrying on.

'It was harder for him to maintain the pretence once we were married. It became clear that my father was right—his business was built on illegal trade and gambling big amounts of money with ruthless men. He took back the diamonds he'd bought me as a wedding present the week after we returned from honeymoon, and the piano he wanted me to play at his business soirées was removed by the bailiff. He wanted to entertain and impress the right people, but he would go into a rage about me spending too much. The first time he hit me was because I had borrowed money from my mother to pay the dressmaker's bill for the fine clothes he expected me to have. After that it happened more often, and more easily.'

She heard Jem's soft exhalation of disgust.

'He was always sorry afterwards, but only because he regretted the loss of control. He wanted to think of himself as better than that, and he hated that I saw him for what he was. I knew what he was capable of, and in the end that became dangerous.'

'Dangerous?'

She rolled the bottle-stopper between her fingers. 'Something happened . . .' She swallowed. 'A body was found in the harbour. It was so b-badly beaten they couldn't confirm his identity, but I knew as soon as I heard. Alec had gone off to meet this . . . *person* a few days earlier—someone who'd sold him short in one of his illegal deals. The next morning two men turned up at the back door—rough men—and I heard enough of their conversation to piece it together when I read the report in the newspaper. That was the day before the coronation. I confronted him . . . I wanted him to realise he'd gone too far—to encourage him to tell the police everything in the hope of being treated leniently because he'd been cheated, but he—'

A muted crack, like the sound of a gunshot, made her start and jump to her feet, her head whipping round in panic. Jem stood up too, closing the gap between them and taking hold of her shoulders.

'It's all right. It's only the fireworks starting. See?'

Very gently, he turned her around. Across the shadowy park, above the dark treetops, a starburst of white lit up the sky, quickly followed by another and another.

The sense of alarm dissipated, and she was left with the tingling awareness of his touch, the warm solidity of his body at her back. It was cooler now, and she longed to lean into him, but the irony of recounting the disaster that had blighted her past while stumbling into one that would jeopardise her future wasn't lost on her. She forced herself to step away.

'Go on. What did he do?'

'He hit me, of course . . .' She heard his low curse as she sat on the edge of the parapet again, watching scarlet splash the sky. 'But it was different that time. Before, it had always been a flash of temper, but that night I thought he was going to kill me.' She gave a choked laugh. 'Perhaps he would have if he hadn't realised already how hard it is to dispose of the dead. He pulled himself back, made the usual excuses, promised me it wouldn't happen again. I promised myself the same thing. I knew if it did, it might well be the last.'

'And so you left . . .'

'Yes.' It was almost a whisper. 'In the evening of coronation day, when he was at the dinner I was supposed to have attended with him. I knew the city would be crowded and I wouldn't get another chance like that. The maid was out at the celebrations; I'm not proud of myself, but I went up to the attic and put on her clothes. A well-dressed lady with a blacked eye would attract concern and attention, but a poorly clothed woman would be overlooked. No one would notice her in the crush of the station, nor remark which train she boarded.' She met his eye with a small smile. 'A female servant is an invisible creature.'

The fireworks were like shooting stars, trailing light over the inky sky and exploding into constellations of brilliance. They both watched in silence as red, white, and blue glittered across the darkness, and then he said softly, 'Where did you go?'

'London. Where everyone goes to disappear. I'd asked my parents for help before, but they didn't want to know. They'd never really forgiven me for marrying him in the first place. As far as they were concerned, I had made my choice, which was shaming enough. They certainly didn't want me back under their roof when it all went wrong. And what could they have done anyway? He would have found a way to get me back, or shut me up for good.'

The fact that her options were so limited had made it easier to decide what to do. With only the small amount of jewellery not yet reclaimed by Alec to sell, she had to find a means of supporting herself quickly. Entering domestic service was more favourable than the other path available.

'I went to a servants' registry on Tottenham Court Road. I needed somewhere cheap to stay and they had a boarding house where you could lodge while seeking employment. I made up a story about my previous employer making inappropriate advances, which was why I'd had to leave without a character. They made one up for me.' She attempted a smile. 'To go with the name I had made up.'

She had been Katherine before, sometimes Kitty to her parents and friends, but never Kate. Her new surname had come from an enamel sign advertising biscuits on the wall of the refreshment room at Bristol station. *Furniss's Original Cornish Fairings.* She remembered staring at it from her seat in the third-class carriage in the endless minutes before the train pulled away, hardly daring to breathe; keeping her eyes fixed to it as the engine gave a hiss and heaved into motion.

'Kate Furniss,' he murmured, and on his lips, it sounded like a caress.

Her sudden shiver was only partly caused by the evening chill. She stood up, so their eyes were almost level, and wrapped her arms around herself. 'I'm sorry. I don't know why I'm telling you this—all my dark secrets. I've never spoken about it before.'

'Why shouldn't you?' The eyes that held hers were like spilled ink. 'They aren't so dark. Any shame belongs to him. You've done nothing wrong.'

'And yet it's as if I'm serving a prison sentence,' she said with quiet bitterness. 'I'm not free of him, am I? I'll never be free.'

The fireworks had stopped, and it seemed much darker with nothing but the empty sky above them. In the quiet she heard the rasp of stubble as he dragged a hand over his face.

'Do you think he's still looking for you?'

'I can't afford to assume he's not. Alec Ross is not the sort of man to let things go—not wives nor grudges. That's why I was so unsettled by the idea of someone watching the house, breaking in . . .'

'You thought it might be him, or people sent by him?'

She nodded, swaying a little, and wondered how strong the beer had been. She wasn't used to it anymore.

Afterwards she would go over it in her mind, replaying the moment when he had put his hand to her waist to steady her, then gently taken her face between his palms and stroked his thumbs across her cheeks.

'I'm glad you told me. You've carried it all yourself, all this time. You don't have to do that anymore.'

A hesitation. A breath. A heartbeat. And then his lips on hers, warm and full of tenderness, kissing her in a way she had only been kissed in her most secret imaginings.

He pulled away almost immediately, shaking his head.

'Oh, God, Kate, I'm sorry. I shouldn't—'

But it was too late.

It had been too late when she'd circled her arms around his chest in the servants' hall the other morning. When she'd touched his cheek on his first night at Coldwell, when she'd seen him washing in the kitchen yard. It had been too late from the moment their eyes had met as he'd stood at the top of the hill.

She couldn't be sure if her unravelling had been sudden, or slow and gradual; if it had happened in an instant, or in increments. She just knew that it had happened, and she couldn't go back to how she had been before.

As she raised her chin to kiss him back, she didn't want to.

Chapter 14

Jem was cleaning Mr Goddard's shoes in the footmen's wardrobe when he saw her crossing the yard to the laundry the next morning. He had barely slept and had moved through the day's tasks with limbs of lead, a head fogged with self-recrimination. But that glimpse of her made his blood surge and infused him with a strange sort of energy.

Dropping Goddard's narrow black oxford, he wiped his hands on a cloth and ran nervous fingers through his hair. The others were leaving London this morning; by teatime the basement would be full of people and noise and activity. He had to talk to her, now. He just wasn't sure what to say.

Not the truth, obviously.

He'd thought she might be useful in his search for answers, with her keys and her authority to move through the house. He'd seen her as a chess piece. And now he'd discovered that she was warm flesh and soft lips: a woman with a battered heart and bruised past and more courage than he could properly comprehend. A girl who had been hungry for life and eager for love, who had been manipulated by a man who had only thought of how useful she could be to him too.

The shaving mirror on the bench showed a face that was grey tinged with fatigue. The bruising around his eye was a jaundiced yellow; he looked as seedy as he felt. He'd known he wasn't worthy of her. He just hadn't appreciated how much.

Outside a silvery dawn had hardened into another hot, overcast day. The yard was quiet as he crossed it and went through the open door of the laundry. It was a bit like stepping into the coolness of a church, and he hesitated. This was a female domain. On Mondays it billowed with steam and rang with the raucous voices of the village women, but now it was stopped and still and smelled of damp stone and soap flakes.

A sound from the adjoining room told him Kate was there. He trod quietly over the uneven floor, past the huge copper by the chimney breast and the long wooden trough where the clothes were soaked, and into the dry laundry.

'Kate?'

He spoke softly. The room was high and hung with linen. It was Friday, and normally Eliza and Abigail would have taken it down ready for ironing by now, but nothing about this week was normal. Sheets were still draped over the drying racks suspended from the ceiling, like the elaborate sails of some Napoleonic galleon and, as he stood in the doorway, they shivered, as if caught by a gust of wind. He went forward, ducking through them, until he saw her.

'Here—let me help with that.'

She had her back towards him and was unwinding the rope for the pulley from its hook. She didn't turn round. Jem felt a beat of unease.

'I can manage.'

'I know you can.' He squashed down the flutter of nerves in his stomach and went closer, lowering his voice. 'I thought we should probably—'

'Mind your head.'

She unhooked the last loop and the rope slid through her hands. With a creak, the rack above him plunged downwards, just missing his shoulder.

'*Jesus*—'

'Sorry,' she said tonelessly and turned to move past him. Her face was as pale and expressionless as her voice. 'We should probably what?'

'Talk.' His throat was full of sand. 'Before the others get back. About what happened last night.'

She kept her eyes downcast as she pulled a sheet from the rack, but a faint flush appeared on her cheeks. 'I don't think there's much to say. Except that it can't happen again.'

Jem wasn't sure what he had expected, only that it wasn't this. She was as brittle as spun sugar, as cool as the stone beneath his feet. It disorientated him. It felt as if last night had never happened; as if he'd fallen asleep beneath Black Tor, waiting for the rain to pass, and everything since—her shuddering body in his arms, her mouth against his in the midsummer twilight—had been part of some mad, brilliant, inappropriate dream.

'I'm sorry,' he said hoarsely. 'I didn't mean for it to happen at all. I didn't set out to—'

'No.' She cut him off impatiently. 'It's my fault. I shouldn't have gone up there with you. I wasn't thinking.' She gave her head a little shake. 'I'd be grateful if you didn't speak of it. To anyone.'

'I won't.' He struggled to keep his voice even, as frustration and despair beat discordantly inside him. '*Of course* I won't, Kate. Do you think I—'

'*Any* of it.' Her chatelaine clinked as she hoisted the rack up again. 'The things I told you about my past, my . . . my marriage, as well as what . . . took place between us.'

'Kate—'

Briskly she picked up the sheet and held it high to fold it. He went forward, catching the corners at the other end, like he used to do when he helped his mother. It seemed like the only way to step into the orbit of her attention. They worked together without speaking, as if following the familiar steps of a dance. He let her lead, and they folded the linen along its length and pulled it taut, then came together to fold it in half. Their fingers touched on the edge of the sheet, and in the sudden stillness he felt a tremor go through her.

'*Please*, Jem . . .' For the first time she looked at him properly, with eyes that were shadowed with anguish. 'I'd lose my job . . . my home . . . I'd have nothing. Less than nothing if word got out and my reputation was ruined. I'd have to start afresh, and I'm not sure I can do that again.'

'Jesus, Kate . . .' He wanted to be angry that she could think he would betray her, but his conscience wouldn't let him. What he'd considered doing was just as bad. 'I understand, and you have my word. I won't ever speak of what you told me, and no one will ever know what happened, I swear.' His hands moved to cover hers. 'I could tell you that I wish it hadn't happened, but that wouldn't be true. All I can do is assure you that it won't happen again. I can promise to stay away from you, if that's what you want. I'm a footman, you're the housekeeper . . .' From the depths of his self-loathing he summoned a broken smile. 'I know my place.'

She gave an odd laugh, which caught in her throat and became a sob. Taking the sheet from him, she bundled it roughly and set it aside. 'Since when has it mattered what we want?'

'It matters to me. What you want *matters to me*.' He caught her by the shoulders and held her firmly. 'Look at me, Kate . . . Do you want me to leave? Because if you do, just say the word . . . I'll go.'

He hadn't planned to say it. As soon as the words were out, he felt light-headed. Panicky. Everything he'd worked towards . . . everything he'd been through . . . in her hands now. Her eyes were huge and haunted as they held his, searching them. The moment quivered into an eternity. He heard her exhale and felt her rigid body yield so their faces were inches apart. And then she was tearing her gaze from his and pulling away. Shaking out her skirts and smoothing the chains of her chatelaine, squaring her shoulders.

'Don't be ridiculous. I'm sure that won't be necessary.' She moved so the table was a barrier between them, and her voice became clipped and frosty again. 'You know how difficult it is to replace staff, and we can't afford to be a footman down with a wedding celebration to organise. I hope we can both conduct ourselves in a professional manner.'

His legs felt weak. He wanted to stagger outside and take in great gulps of air, but he stayed where he was and said nothing as, with precise, practiced movements she finished folding the sheet and held it against her body like a shield. 'You're very charming, Jem, but I'm not some . . . swoony housemaid.' Her smile was withering. 'I'm sure I'll be able to resist you.'

And then she left, slipping out of his sight behind the curtains of linen, so he could only hear the tap of her footsteps and the musical chime of her keys.

It had been a dangerous gamble. He was lucky to have got away with it. So why did it feel like he'd lost?

⸾⸾⸾

Kate had dreaded the return of the servants. Everything in her shrank from the prospect of brisk normality resuming, of having to reassemble the shattered fragments of her professional mask and take up the reins of responsibility again. She wanted nothing more than to keep to the solitude of her parlour and wait for the fit of madness that had seized her to pass. She still felt shaky and fragile, and the ten days they had been away felt like ten years.

But in the end, she felt relief when the cart came clattering under the archway as the heat began to subside on another oppressive day. Voices rang around the kitchen yard as they all jumped down from the wagon, hauling boxes and dragging wicker hampers across the cobbles.

'Home sweet home,' said Eliza sourly, setting her box down in the kitchen passage and looking around with an air of disdain. 'I swear it's got even dingier since we've been away.'

'It looks the same to me.' Thomas beamed, coming in behind her. 'Sounds the same too. Listen—'

He rested the box he was carrying on top of the one she had just put down and cupped a hand round his ear. Eliza gave an impatient shrug. 'I can't hear anything.'

'*Exactly*. No traffic. No bells. No racket from the street. No Mr-blessed-Dewhurst on my case. Heaven.'

The strange, suspended time was over, the spell broken.

Keen for any comparisons with the London cook to be favourable, Mrs Gatley had spent the day preparing what was, by Coldwell standards, an extravagant tea of pork pie, cold roast chicken, and a strawberry tart. When the luggage had been unloaded and carried upstairs, they took their usual places at the table in the servants' hall with Mr Goddard at its head saying grace and carving the meat.

Although he'd been cynical about it, his role in the village coronation festivities seemed to have revived the old butler's spirits somewhat. He wasn't convivial exactly, but he responded to Thomas's polite enquiry about the tree-planting ceremony with a (rather too detailed) description of the event and didn't reprimand the girls when their voices tumbled over one another, describing the mob of servants in the Portman Square basement, the airless attic bedrooms, the excitement of getting out for an hour on the morning of coronation day to catch a glimpse of the procession and the spectacle of the flag-festooned streets.

'The kitchen is half the size of ours, but they've got a fancy stove, heated by gas,' Susan said excitedly. 'You can adjust the temperature as easy as anything—Mrs Gatley would give her right arm for something like that. They've got no stillroom though,' she added loyally.

'Why would they need one?' Eliza snapped. 'All the things we spend our lives slaving to make, they can have delivered, and a lot more besides. Walter says—'

'Here we go,' muttered Abigail. '*Walter says . . .*'

Eliza threw her a look and went on doggedly. 'Walter says that Sir Randolph's looking to hire a foreign chef from one of the big hotels, so he can have all those fancy continental pastries and the like here.'

'Yes, well, you don't want to believe half of what *Walter* says,' Thomas grunted, helping himself to another slice of pork pie. 'Why would Sir Randolph want to do that? Nowt wrong with Mrs Gatley's English pastries if you ask me.'

Kate let the conversation swirl around her. The food on her plate was untouched, and she felt that if she tried to swallow she would choke. She was painfully aware of Jem to her right, half-hidden by Joseph (who seemed to have filled out and grown two inches). She watched his hands as he buttered a piece of bread but noticed he didn't eat much either.

'I don't see why a foreign chef wouldn't come here,' Abigail was saying. 'Sir Henry wasn't one for modern ways, but Sir Randolph's a different kettle of fish . . .'

Was he finding it as difficult as she was? This pretence that everything was as it had been? She'd tried to be firm earlier, to leave no room for doubt, but was he still feeling the same pull towards her as she was to him? The same sensation that, although the room was full again, the voices of the others were somehow muted and distant and they were alone together.

'. . . I heard Mr Dewhurst talking to Mrs Bryant about interviewing chauffeurs, so he must have bought a motorcar. And I never thought I'd see the day when there were bathrooms at Coldwell, neither,' Susan was saying. 'Are they finished?'

It took Kate a moment to realise the question was directed at her.

'Oh—yes. Almost.' Jolted out of her thoughts, she felt the creep of colour into her cheeks. 'Lady Hyde's is almost ready. The bath has been installed and—'

Abigail gave a moan of envy. 'I couldn't half do with trying it out. I'm that hot and sticky after the journey . . . Just imagine, lying back in water right up to your chin . . .'

At the head of the table, Mr Goddard sucked in a sharp breath and peered at Abigail as if she'd just committed some indecency. 'I'll thank you not to imagine anything of the sort.'

Kate's face was numb with the effort of keeping her expression blank. Sweat prickled beneath her corset and she reached for her glass of water. As she picked it up her eyes met Jem's. His smile was so brief, so slight that she wondered if she'd imagined it.

Thomas—always the one to smooth over any awkwardness—summoned a bright smile and directed it down the table: 'So—what's gone on here then, Mrs Furniss?'

'Nothing,' she said curtly, brushing fallen crumbs into her hand. 'Really, nothing at all.'

Eliza huffed out a dissatisfied sigh. 'Nothing ever does.'

In fact, there was plenty happening at Coldwell that summer.

Too much for Abigail's liking. After London she would have preferred things to be as quiet as they had been in Sir Henry's time, to give her poor feet a chance to recover, but no sooner had Mr Kendall and his men completed the installation of the bathrooms (and she and Eliza had finished clearing up the mess they'd left) than the decorators arrived to paint and wallpaper, leaving dusty boot prints along the upstairs corridors and the smell of turpentine hanging in the hot air.

Sir Randolph's wedding date had been set for mid-September, so there was a rush to get everything finished. Mr Goddard was very miserly in the details he shared, but then the wedding itself sounded like a pretty miserly affair. Abigail had got most of her information from Margaret, one of the parlourmaids in Portman Square, with whom she'd struck up a friendship while Eliza was busy making eyes at Walter Cox. Apparently Miss Addison had wanted the wedding to be held at Coldwell and include local villagers and tenants, but Sir Randolph had flatly refused. Instead, it was to take place in London—a private ceremony at St George's in Hanover Square with a small wedding breakfast afterwards at the Savoy.

Discussing it up in the sewing attic (where they couldn't be overheard by Mr Goddard), Susan said Miss Addison deserved a much more extravagant celebration than that, to make up for marrying an old windbag like Sir Randolph. Eliza pointed out that marrying an old windbag like Sir Randolph was no cause for any celebration at all.

Beggars couldn't be choosers, Abigail thought, though honestly—Miss Addison might have improved her prospects with the help of a lady's maid who was a bit more proficient at hair styling than that Miss Dunn.

The old windbag himself had remained in London to squeeze the last drops of pleasure out of the Season, but as the city emptied at the end of July he returned to Coldwell for a few nights, before travelling up to Scotland for the start of the shooting season. Instead of being collected from the station by Johnny Farrow, Mr Goddard received a letter from Mr Dewhurst to say that Sir Randolph would be arriving in his brand-new motorcar, driven by his brand-new chauffeur.

'Stanley Twigg showed me the room that's been made for him above the new motor house,' Thomas said the afternoon before their arrival, as he polished the dining room candelabra in the servants' hall. Glancing furtively round to make sure Mr Goddard wasn't in earshot, he let out a low whistle. 'Very cushy. I reckon he'll be thinking he's a cut above the likes of us, this "shuvver" chap.'

'Well, if he is, he won't last long out here,' Eliza sniffed, half-heartedly rubbing silver polish off a coffeepot. 'Why would anyone want to leave London for a place like this?'

Even so, Abigail noticed her checking her reflection in the silver surface and practising the smile that showed her dimples. She'd been in a foul mood ever since they'd left London, where she'd flirted herself silly with Walter Cox. Trust her to perk up at the prospect of a new man at Coldwell.

If the motorcar symbolised the modern age, it turned out they were quite unprepared for it. Davy Wells would have had to sprout wings to be fast enough to get down to the church in time to warn them when it turned through the gates, and so the first they knew of Sir Randolph's arrival was the crunch of tyres on gravel and the blast of a horn, which sent Thomas sprinting upstairs to fling open the doors to receive him while Mr Goddard was still struggling out of his post-lunch snooze and into his tailcoat.

Eliza dragged a chair across to the servants' hall window to peer out.

Standing behind her on tiptoe, Abigail saw a man in a sleek uniform (quite unlike the footmen's ancient livery) get out from the shiny green motorcar and walk round to open the rear door. His face was shadowed by the peak of his large cap, but a strip of neck, as thick as a rolled gammon joint, showed above the collar of the tunic stretched wide across his broad shoulders. His arms swung slightly as he moved, giving an impression of swagger, like a fighter entering the ring.

'Crikey, look at that.'

Eliza sounded dismayed, and no wonder. The uniform might be fancy, but even she wouldn't waste her dimples on a man with a neck like a Sunday joint. (Mind you, Abigail would have thought she wouldn't waste them on loudmouth Walter Cox either. It seemed there was no accounting for taste.)

'I wonder where on earth Sir Randolph found *him*?' Abigail said.

'Not from a respectable servants' registry, I'll bet,' Eliza muttered, swiping the mist of her breath from the glass.

Sir Randolph got out of the motor, his dog bounding in his wake. His white flannel trousers were creased from the journey and he had loosened his striped tie, which gave him the appearance of an overgrown schoolboy, home for the holidays. His braying voice reached them through the inch of open window.

'Ah—there you are, Goddard! Caught you napping, eh? So what do you think? Rolls-Royce! Quite a beauty, isn't she?'

Pausing to light a cigarette, he waved it in the general direction of the chauffeur, standing by the car's shiny flank. Abigail just about made out 'This is Robson' (at least she thought it was Robson) before Eliza suddenly ducked down and scrambled off the chair.

'Bloody Henderson's seen me,' she hissed.

Abigail had been too taken up with the spectacle of the motorcar to notice the figure in the front seat. Sir Randolph's valet was just a shadow behind the glinting glass, but in five minutes he'd be a very solid presence in the servants' hall, and the atmosphere would feel entirely different.

Another of the changes at Coldwell that summer. And this one was definitely for the worse.

The kitchen passage was empty when Kate went downstairs after seeing that Sir Randolph was settled in the library. Everyone had gone out to the stable yard to admire the new motorcar, and she couldn't begrudge the girls their curiosity. Going to the stillroom, she checked that water had been set to boil for Sir Randolph's tea and the trays were laid, then retreated to the sanctuary of the housekeeper's parlour.

She smelled his hair oil before she saw him.

'Good afternoon, Mrs Furniss.'

'Mr Henderson! What are you doing in here?'

He was standing by the fireplace with his hands in his pockets, looking entirely at ease. With a shrug of his shoulders, he rocked on his shiny heels. 'It's been a long journey. Very trying, travelling in this heat. I was just thinking how nice it would be to have somewhere to relax at the end of a journey like that—a nice armchair in which to take tea—and I remembered how comfortable you'd made it in here. I hope you don't mind . . . ?'

She did. She very much did.

He looked nothing like the man she had been married to. Alec Ross was taller and less stockily built, but still—something in the speculative way his gaze moved over her reminded her of her husband.

'Shouldn't you be seeing to Sir Randolph's luggage?'

Her eyes darted around the room, wondering if he'd touched anything. He couldn't have been there long—a few minutes at most—but that didn't bring her much reassurance. He was here now, in her space, and something told her that he intended to be there more in the future. That it wasn't really her space at all anymore.

Sliding a hand out of his pocket, he picked up the china dog from the mantelpiece. 'One of the footmen can do it. Thomas or—' He pursed his lips and pressed his fingers to his forehead in a pantomime of forgetfulness. 'What's the other one called? The good-looking one?'

'Jem. Jem Arden.'

'Of course.'

Those eyes. Narrowed and noticing. She made herself meet them and willed her cheeks not to redden.

'Well then, Mr Henderson. Was there something you wanted?'

'Not at all, Mrs Furniss. I wouldn't presume to ask anything of you. Quite the reverse, in fact. I've been thinking . . .'

'About?' she enquired, though she would have greatly preferred not to be privy to Frederick Henderson's thoughts.

'We seem to have got off on rather the wrong foot.' Carefully he replaced the dog. 'I understand that you and Mr Goddard have your particular ways of managing things here and you might feel a certain amount of . . . resentment at the intrusion of a new figure of authority, so I wanted to reassure you that my increased presence at Coldwell need not be a threat to you. Indeed, I hope you'll come to consider it a change for the better. An opportunity, for us both.'

'I'm not sure I follow your meaning, Mr Henderson.'

If he heard the impatience in her voice, he didn't let it trouble him. Unhurriedly he removed his hat, unleashing a further waft of pomade. 'Only that change is on its way, Mrs Furniss. Indeed, it's already arrived—and Mr Fortescue informs me that you've managed the renovations magnificently so far, which is no less than I'd expect. But the fact is, bathrooms and motorcars are just the start. Without putting too fine a point on it, Mr Goddard is advancing in years, and Sir Randolph will be seeking a replacement soon. Someone younger, with more energy for all that the job entails . . .'

'And you want to be the replacement?'

He smiled indulgently, as if she'd said something foolish. 'My dear Mrs Furniss, I may nominally be Sir Randolph's valet, but in reality my role is rather more than that. My background is professional, not in service. I began working for Mr Hyde as an administrative assistant in his Bombay office, you see; we were both with the East India Company. After all these years he has come to . . . rely on me somewhat. Not just for organising his wardrobe and seeing to his personal care but in more important ways. Put it this way, I don't see myself in the dining room, supervising the passing of the port.'

'I'm not sure what this has to do with me, Mr Henderson.'

He regarded her thoughtfully, his head on one side.

'I admire your resilience, but the changes will be unsettling for everyone—you most of all. You've worked alongside Mr Goddard for a long time; it won't be easy adjusting to a new man in the house.' He set his hat down carefully on the table where she usually put her tea tray. 'I just wanted to make it clear from the outset that you can rely on me, Mrs Furniss. You have . . . my *full* support. Regardless of who takes the position of butler, I believe we could make a powerful alliance, you and I.'

A powerful alliance.

Kate snapped open her watch. She wasn't sure what Henderson was suggesting, but she didn't need to understand to know she wanted no part in it. With the air of someone who had other things to get on with, she let the watch fall back against her skirts.

'Well . . . I'm sure that we will work alongside each other as courteously as we always have, Mr Henderson, though of course as housekeeper and valet our roles are quite separate. Except for at mealtimes, we probably won't see much of each other at all.'

There was a pause. The heavy air seemed to shift and settle, as if a door had closed somewhere. She got the impression he was making some mental recalibration, as if she had given him the wrong answer.

'I wouldn't be so sure about that . . .' His voice retained its reasonable tone, but his bearded jaw had hardened. 'I know you don't have much previous experience in service, so perhaps you're not aware that the housekeeper's parlour is generally used as a sitting room by all the upper servants?'

'I *am* aware of that, Mr Henderson. Perhaps we're unusual at Coldwell in that Mrs Gatley returns to the gardener's cottage at the end of the day and Mr Goddard prefers to keep his own company in his room. It's the way it's always been here.'

His smile was as smooth as butter. 'It's the way it's always been, *up until now*. But things are changing, and we must change along with them. The new Baronet Bradfield will be doing a lot more entertaining than the old one, and the way the servants' hall is managed says a lot about a house.' His gaze skimmed the room again, more critically now. 'We'll need another armchair, of course . . . and I'll ask Goddard to supply us with a drinks tray and some ashtrays . . . If that wouldn't offend you, Mrs Furniss?'

It would.

It did.

The whole idea offended her, but she wasn't going to give Frederick Henderson the satisfaction of knowing that.

'I'm afraid it's impossible, Mr Henderson. With both Mrs Gatley and Mr Goddard preferring to spend their leisure hours elsewhere you must see it would be entirely inappropriate for only us to share this room. It would set a very unfortunate example to my girls.' She managed a cool smile. 'I'm sorry, but I simply can't allow it.'

He nodded slowly. 'Very well. I understand. However, in a few weeks' time Sir Randolph will be married, and the new Lady Hyde's maid will join our ranks. I'm sure Miss Dunn will appreciate having a nice sitting room, away from the lower servants. Presumably her presence will reassure you?'

It would do nothing of the sort, but Kate was outmanoeuvred. After a moment's hesitation she managed a nod of acquiescence.

'Excellent.' Retrieving his hat, Henderson sauntered to the door, spinning it rakishly on one hand, like a variety show performer. 'Oh, and a tip, Mrs Furniss. You'll find that I make a far nicer ally than adversary. Bear that in mind.'

He winked. He actually winked. And when he left the room, his smile seemed to hang, Cheshire Cat–like, in the cloud of hair oil he left in his wake.

<hr>

June 28th

The weather is making us all restless. In spite of the rain it's stiflingly hot, and the air is heavy, so you feel you can't breathe. We haven't seen the sun for days.

One of the men said that he couldn't remember a summer like it.

But I can.

Chapter 15

It was a summer like no other.

In the cool of the marble-floored hallway the barometer's needle had edged round to *fair* and remained stuck there, unmoving, despite Mr Goddard's daily tap on the glass. As the long August days passed and still no rain came, Coldwell's park shimmered in the heat and the surrounding hills changed from green and purple to brown as the heather and bracken crisped into premature autumn.

In the kitchen garden, the dipping pond was reduced to a few inches of brackish water, and the river that twisted along the western edge of the park dried up to a brown trickle over baked stones. Gatley, fretting over his wilting lettuces, sent the garden boys to fill their pails from its shallows, and Johnny Farrow took the cart down to the ford by the home farm and pushed it in up to its axles, to soak its shrunken wheels.

The newspaper boy still toiled up the drive on his bicycle every morning with *The Times*, though Sir Randolph had left for Scotland (taking his valet and chauffeur with him, thank goodness) and wasn't there to read it. Along with letters from Mrs Bryant in Portman Square and Miss Addison in Shropshire, it provided Kate with a link to the world beyond the parched hills. Mr Goddard commandeered it first, so the news was a day old by the time it reached the servants' hall, but in that slow, sweltering summer it hardly mattered. The hot days melted together, separated by sultry, sleepless nights.

While Sir Randolph slaughtered grouse on a Scottish moor, in Shropshire Miss Addison busied herself with wedding preparations and her new role as mistress of Coldwell. Mr Fortescue had authorised her request for new livery for the footmen; and one afternoon a cart appeared over the crest of the drive (unannounced by Davy Wells, who had abandoned his lookout post for the shade of the woods). Dust ballooned in its wake and coated the carrier, so when he pulled up in the stable yard and wiped the sweat from his face, his handkerchief left smears of dirt.

Kate signed the receipt, running her eyes down the list of items: braided cutaway coats, striped waistcoats, moleskin knee breeches, silk stockings, and neckties.

'It's all right for some,' Abigail remarked sourly as she stood in the doorway of the footmen's wardrobe and watched Jem and Thomas unpack it all. 'You lads get kitted out in livery costing a king's ransom, and what do we get? A bolt of cheap cotton as a Christmas box and the job of making it up ourselves.'

'Yes, well, now the house is being smartened up the new Lady Hyde isn't going to want a pair of scruffs in the dining room, is she?' Thomas said, picking at the knotted string on one of the parcels. 'We footmen have to look the part. Doesn't look like there are any wigs. I think I'm going to get on with the new her ladyship.'

Kate stood at the table with the invoice, waiting to mark off the items as they were unpacked. The cupboards had been thrown open and Jem was sorting through the old uniforms, making space for the new ones. Joseph perched on a stool in the corner, eating the stale end of yesterday's loaf (since he returned from London he'd been perpetually starving), and Abigail shuffled a little farther into the small room to make way for Eliza and Susan, who crowded into the doorway to watch.

Kate bit her tongue against the urge to snap at them to go away. With Sir Randolph absent there wasn't much for them to do in the afternoons, but their chatter and clumsy flirtation grated on her taut nerves.

It was hardly their fault. *Everything* grated on her taut nerves.

'Look at that,' breathed Susan, as Thomas folded back brown paper and held up a livery coat. 'Those cuffs . . .'

The coat was the same dark green used by the Hyde family to mark ownership of their carriages and menservants since the creation of their baronetcy. The deep cuffs were crimson velvet, banded with gold braid top and bottom, finished with a row of four crested buttons. In the dingy basement, the brass gleamed with the incongruous opulence of a miser's hoard.

Jem moved behind Kate, leaning past her to lay the old uniforms on the table. The gap between the table and the countertop behind was narrow, and his nearness was like a static electrical charge. It took all her concentration to keep her face neutral and to resist the invisible, instinctive forces pulling her towards him. The lines of elaborately looped handwriting on the invoice swam meaninglessly before her eyes.

It was almost unbearable, sometimes.

She thought their conversation in the laundry had settled the matter. If neither of them spoke of what had happened—if she made it absolutely clear that it had been a moment of madness—it would be possible to return to how things had been. Outwardly she supposed they had: they each moved through the days as they always had, going about their work in their respective parts of the house, sitting at the servants' hall table at mealtimes, addressing each other only when necessary, and in the most impersonal terms.

Outwardly, it was all perfectly respectable and correct.

No one would guess that her blood raced when she passed him and that the incidental touch of his fingers when she took a tray from him in the scullery sent sparks up her arm. No one would suspect that she went over every glance, every word, every casual touch as she grated sugar or stared at columns of figures in her ledger. And relived his kiss as she lay in her tangled sheets at night.

She might have made it clear to him that it had been a regrettable mistake. It seemed she had yet to convince herself.

Abigail picked up one of the old garments from the table. Against the opulence of the new ones, it looked shabby and threadbare, its colour faded. 'You'd hardly know them for the same livery,' she said, examining it disdainfully. 'I wonder how old these are.'

'Almost as old as Mr Goddard, I'd wager,' Eliza muttered. She was leaning against the doorframe with her arms crossed over her chest, her face sallow and shiny with sweat. Kate should have reprimanded her, but she let it go. The weather was getting to them all.

'What's that?' Susan said, taking hold of the faded lapel and folding it back. 'Look—a label with someone's name on it. William? Williams?'

Abigail peered at the scrap of embroidered tape stitched into the yellowed lining. 'Oh yes . . . Looks like *Williams* to me. Funny to think that there were once enough footmen here that they had to name their uniforms.'

Thomas unfolded a new pair of breeches. (Kate mustered her focus to find them on the list.) 'You can see from the photographs out there in the kitchen passage there were five or six, at least. Probably wearing these very coats.'

Susan rummaged through the pile of old uniforms and held up another jacket. 'This one's different from the others. Smaller too.'

'Part of a tiger's uniform, isn't it? For a young lad.' Eliza pushed herself away from the doorframe and burrowed in the mound of clothing. 'I saw the waistcoat in here somewhere—a gold striped one . . . Here.'

She put it on top of the pile. Its black velvet was balding, and the bars of gold braid that formed the distinctive stripes were worn to a dull grey in places. She opened it to look in the lining.

'Here we are . . . Mullins? Is that what it says?'

Out of the corner of her eye, Kate saw Jem look round.

'Yes,' Abigail said, looking inside the tiger's coat. 'There's one in here too. *A. Mullins.*'

'I wonder what A. Mullins is doing now?' Susan spoke in a tone of awe, as if it were possible that the lad who had once been a tiger at Coldwell might now be conducting the orchestra at the Queen's Hall or leading an expedition across the Antarctic.

'Working as a footman somewhere else, likely,' Eliza retorted. 'That label looks recent. Mullins is probably the same age as us. That uniform'll fit you, Joseph.'

Jem had turned back to the empty cupboards, but he wasn't moving. He didn't seem to hear Susan either, urging Thomas to try on the new coat, and Abigail joining in. 'Ooh yes, go on; show us your fancy finery. After all, we'd better get used to it so we're not completely giddy when we see you on duty.'

Thomas's ears were bright pink as he took the new coat down from the peg rail. 'I'll put this on, just to see if it fits'—he grinned—'but I'll be trying them britches on later, without company, if you don't mind.' Slipping the coat on, he glanced round at the others. 'Come on, Joseph—and you, Jem—don't leave me on my own here.'

As Abigail helped Joseph into the old tiger's livery, Thomas handed the other new coat to Kate to pass to Jem. Hidden by the open door of the cupboard, their gazes held as he slid his arms into it. The heat seemed to intensify, spreading upwards into her cheeks, downwards into her pelvis. Unfurling itself.

She could barely look at him, and yet . . . she couldn't not look. The top two buttons of his collarless shirt were open, and there was something incongruous about his golden skin and the hollow at the base of his throat against the braided lapels. He looked like he'd stepped out of the past or from the pages of one of Miss Austen's novels. As he dropped his arms to his sides again his hand brushed hers.

An accidental touch, but the rush of want it unleashed made her head spin. Only vaguely was she aware of Thomas strutting around, flicking his coattails and tugging at his scarlet cuffs, while the girls broke into a chorus of appreciative whoops. Her heart was beating so hard it was making her whole body throb.

Secretly, in the folds of her skirt, his fingers caught hers.

She looked up and met his gaze. The others vanished, their voices drowned out by the crash of her pulse. There was only Jem. His eyes— intense and fathomlessly dark—full of despair and hunger.

'Come on then, Jem, let's have a look at you!'

Thomas's voice broke the spell. Kate jerked her hand away and turned round. The girls must have noticed the expression on her face, or sensed the change of atmosphere, because their exuberant shouts faltered into silence.

Finding her voice, Kate iced it with her chilliest disapproval, to counter the heat that was searing through her. 'This is a respectable house, not a music hall. Girls, it's time you got back to work. Thomas, make sure everything is unpacked and hung up properly to get the creases out. Jem, you can finish checking the invoice. Bring it to me when it's done.'

She swept past them, curling her tingling fingers into a fist.

Standing outside the housekeeper's room, Jem knocked and stood back. He pushed a hand through his hair and listened for her voice over the drumbeat of his heart.

'Come in.'

She was sitting at her desk in front of the open window, her head bent over the letter she was writing. The blinds were half-drawn to keep out the heat; the room smelled of potpourri and fine white soap, but he could just detect beneath it a trace of her own scent.

Vanilla. Nutmeg. Roses.

She had made her wishes quite clear. He had given his word, and he had kept it, though it had required ruthless self-control. He hadn't let his guard slip.

Until this afternoon, when he had sensed the longing rising from her like heat.

'The invoice, Mrs Furniss. From the tailor.'

She laid down her pen and stood up to take it from him. He could see the sheen of sweat on her upper lip, in the little hollow of her Cupid's bow.

'Thank you. Was everything there?'

'It seems so.' His throat went dry as his eyes found hers. 'Nothing missing.'

'Good.'

He should have stepped away then, before he heard the little hitch of her breath and saw the darkness spread in her eyes. The heat made it impossible to do anything in haste, which was why it felt like they were moving through honey as he lifted his hand to cup her cheek and their bodies came together, her face tipping up to his, lips parting.

He'd promised not to compromise her, and anyone passing in the corridor outside would have heard nothing untoward or inappropriate. They might perhaps have been puzzled by the long spell of silence, unbroken by conversation. They would likely have noticed that his cheeks were flushed when he came out of the room a few minutes later, his breathing uneven. They would have probably thought it odd that he hesitated for a second after he shut the door behind him, and leaned against it, collecting himself.

Luckily the passage was empty.

The heat was relentless.

Eliza had never known anything like it. It dragged at her: a physical thing, like weights sewn into her petticoat hem. It made everything move more slowly, from the stupefied flies in the stillroom to the hands of the clocks that ticked through the house.

The days crawled by.

In the evenings Thomas read aloud from the newspapers. In London the intense heat had been interrupted by a sudden freak storm one afternoon, with hailstones as big as golf balls bouncing off the pavements in the Strand. The dockers' strike was still going on, so the shop shelves were empty while cargoes of fruit, meat, and vegetables rotted in ships' holds at Rotherhithe. It reminded Eliza that London was a real place; one that still existed. It hadn't just been the setting of a bizarre dream that had vanished with the coming of daylight.

Even though she was beginning to wish that were true.

He'd promised to write. Well, maybe not promised exactly, but he'd said he would, and the daily hope that a letter might come was the only thing that helped her drag herself out of bed. But it was starting to look like writing was just another one of Walter Cox's extravagant claims that turned out to be nothing but hot air.

Like when he'd told her she was beautiful. And when he'd said if she left Coldwell and came to London, she could be his girl.

For some reason she kept thinking of those ships' holds full of spoilt produce, everything blackening and turning to rot. The thought made her stomach heave.

It felt like the whole summer had turned bad.

The work was finally finished in Lady Hyde's rooms.

For weeks Susan had listened to Eliza and Abigail talking about the furnishings—the eau-de-Nil silk curtains and rose-pink eiderdown, the deep, wide bath standing on lion's feet—but as a kitchen maid she had no business beyond the servants' basement and hadn't seen them herself. One hot afternoon, with Mrs Furniss's permission, she scurried up the back stairs to have a look.

The light was different upstairs, and the air smelled of potpourri undercut with fresh paint, which was a lot nicer than the mutton fat and boiled cabbage she'd been breathing all day. She followed the sound of Eliza's voice to a room halfway along the corridor and stood on the threshold, folding her arms across her chest and tucking her chapped hands into her armpits as she looked around.

'Why are you hovering there with a face like that?' Eliza demanded, appearing in the doorway of the adjoining room. 'Come in properly, for goodness sake! Feast your eyes on this bath, and be glad you don't have to clean it. I might have known all her ladyship's luxuries would mean *more* work for us, not less.'

Susan advanced doubtfully. Her feet sunk into the plush carpet and her eyes swept over the walls, where blossoms bloomed on trees that looked nothing like the ones in Derbyshire, and peacocks perched, trailing their extravagant tails.

'Very nice, I'm sure.'

'*Nice?*' Eliza sounded affronted, as if she'd chosen the fancy fittings herself. 'Is that all you can say? *Nice?*'

'Well, it's not what I would have chose.'

Eliza gave a short laugh. 'Hark at you! Lady Hyde must be kicking herself for letting her housekeeper furnish her new suite of rooms, instead of the kitchen skivvy!'

Misery twisted in Susan's stomach. Eliza's sharp tongue had been a match for Mrs Gatley's filleting knife lately. Susan wished she didn't feel its cuts so deeply.

'I'm not saying that,' she mumbled. 'It's just . . . peacocks.' She shuddered, her gaze shifting uneasily from one painted bird to another. 'They're bad luck, aren't they?'

Eliza's eyes flicked skywards. 'I thought that was owls? Or was it crows?'

'It is . . .' Susan wished she'd held her tongue. 'Owls and crows can be bad omens, but peacocks are too. Or at least their tail feathers. You shouldn't have 'em in the house, not even as images. They have eyes, see?' She flapped a hand at the rich plumage of the nearest bird. 'The devil's eye.' She tucked her arms tight into her body again. 'Still, I suppose it's all right for Miss Addison. Only a few weeks before she's safely wed, and if the rest of us die old maids . . . Well, that'll suit them nicely, won't it?'

She could tell Eliza was about to make some stinging retort, but she stopped short, her mouth open.

'Wait—what do you mean, die as old maids?'

It always surprised Susan that Eliza and Abigail didn't know these things. But Eliza had grown up in a town, not a village like the one Susan had left, where half the stones in the churchyard had her surname on them and the seasons flowed to the rhythm of ancient sayings and superstitions.

'It's like a curse,' she explained. 'If you bring peacock feathers into a house, it's said that any unmarried women there will stay that way. Old maids, on the shelf forever.'

Eliza's mouth snapped shut. There was a pause.

'What a load of nonsense,' she said, but before she turned away Susan saw the fear on her face.

⸺◦◦◦◦⸺

On the last night of August, it rained.

Kate was woken by the sound of rushing water and cool air moving across her body. For weeks she'd slept with the sheets pushed back and the window by her bed open. Now, as the black heavens unleashed their pent-up fury, the gutters filled and overflowed and a waterfall cascaded onto her windowsill. Instantly awake, she wrestled with the window, trying to shut out the deluge, but the wood must have warped in the warm weather. Giving it a frantic pull, the metal latch came away in her hand.

She lit the candle and stared at it stupidly. At the same moment, as if engineered by some unkind deity, the rain doubled in strength and the pool on the windowsill began to fall in a steady stream onto the corner of the bed.

She yanked the bed away from the wall and snatched her wash jug to catch the flow. Still it came. In desperation she ran out into the corridor and through the summer dark to the back door.

Outside the night was loud with water. Dawn was close enough for the sky to have lightened to gunmetal grey, against which the rain was a silvery cascade. The air smelled green and teeming, and within seconds she was drenched. High above her bedroom window a broken gutter channelled the rain down with particular force, and attempting to ram the window shut from outside, as she had intended, meant standing directly beneath it. She hesitated, then—taking in a breath—stepped into the stream of water and pushed at the jammed window.

'Here—let me.'

Jem was there, his hand beside hers on the stuck window frame. 'I heard you go out,' he said, close to her ear. Her strength had been inadequate to shift it more than a fraction, but with two sharp shoves he closed the gap. Shielding her from the onslaught with his body, they ran together back to the door.

He shut it quietly, sliding the bolts back across, then turned to look at her. They were soaked through, though he was wearing trousers and a shirt and could still make some claim to decency.

Unlike Kate. Her wet nightdress stuck to her like a second, transparent skin and rain dripped from the end of her plait. After the weeks of stifling heat, the change in temperature was dramatic, but it wasn't just the cold that made her shiver.

'We do seem to be unlucky with the weather,' he murmured, turning his head away, trying not to look at her.

'Come with me,' she whispered. 'I'll get you a towel.'

They slipped through the shadows to her parlour as silently as ghosts. She shut the door softly, carefully, and went into the bedroom to pick up her keys from the bedside table. The candle still burned, but its glow didn't reach Jem, standing in the shadows by the parlour door. She sensed him, though. Awareness of his presence shimmered through every cell in her body as she unlocked the linen cupboard.

He took the towel she held out and shook out its folds, but he didn't use it for himself. His gaze was soft as he took her face between his hands, drying her gently, squeezing the water from her hair, the towel a caress against her neck, her cheek.

'I'll go. You need to take that wet nightdress off before you freeze.'

That was what did it, what snapped the last gossamer thread of her resistance. His tenderness. The way he looked after her, like no one else did or had ever done. The way he made her feel as if she mattered.

'Don't go.'

She rose onto her toes to press her lips to his, lightly at first. Hesitantly. She had no right, she knew that, not after the way she had spoken to him on that morning in the laundry. His mouth was motionless beneath hers, and then he pulled back, his sigh fanning her cheek.

'We said this mustn't happen . . .'

'I know.'

He took the towel and wrapped it around her, drawing her to him with its edges, close enough to rest his forehead against hers.

'We can't, Kate—'

'But we can't not, can we?'

She had tried. All these weeks, she had tried, and it had taken so much effort that she feared it would break her. Turn her mad.

'It's dangerous . . . You could lose your place—'

He was repeating her own argument back to her. Their mouths were so close together their words were little more than exhalations of breath. She took his face between her hands, and water dripped from his hair onto her skin.

'I know, and it scares me. But what scares me more is the thought of still being here as an old woman with an empty life behind me. A life of service . . . Being invisible.'

He shook his head, helplessly. 'You're not invisible. You're all I can see . . . But I'm not good enough for you, Kate; I'm not worth the risk. There are so many things you don't know about me—' His eyes flickered closed. 'I should never have dared come within a mile of you. I'm a *footman*, for Christ's sake—that's the most I can ever hope to be—'

'None of that matters.'

His insecurity touched her, just as his tenderness had, but his lack of certainty only made hers grow stronger. She cupped the back of his head and kissed him slowly and with a sort of reverence, marvelling at the presence of him . . . the living manifestation of her solitary dreams. And then she twisted herself free of the towel and went to blow out the candle, so they were folded into secretive shadows.

She found his hand and led him to the narrow bedroom.

'You're sure?'

She didn't want to think of all the reasons why she shouldn't be.

'You said what I want matters to you.'

'It does.'

'I want this.'

Gathering up handfuls of wet cotton, she lifted her nightgown upwards, over her head. In the silence she heard his shaky exhalation and stepped into his arms.

It was the hour between night and dawn, where the old day was spent and the new one not yet minted. The still hour, when those late to bed were sleeping and the early risers weren't yet stirring. Around them the vast old house was silent as he peeled off his damp clothes and lay down beside her in the narrow bed, and the world shrank to the scent of his skin, the touch of his fingers—brushing her collarbone, trailing across her ribs, stroking her hair—the warmth of his mouth and the hard planes of his body against hers.

Outside the rain still came down steadily, a murmured lullaby. It puddled on the baked ground, soaking down to the roots of the scorched grass, running off the hills in rivulets that swelled into streams, that gushed into waterfalls. It splashed on the dusty leaves of trees in the park—crisping and turning prematurely brown—washing them clean, bringing them back to life. It fell on the wilting lilies in Gatley's garden, and they tipped their faces up to the heavens and opened their parched throats to the deluge.

July 2nd 1916
France

He comes to with a jolt, levering himself upright, his veins singing with panic. For a moment the pain in his head makes the sky blacken and the figures moving around him fade to phantoms. He thinks he might be sick.

His face is tight and hot, his lips parched to stiffness. As his surroundings swim back into focus, he understands that he is at an Advanced Dressing Station and is one of many men laid out on stretchers on the baked earth.

He searches his mind but has no recollection of how he got there. Was it Henderson again? His memory gapes, then he remembers the advance. He remembers Joseph falling, and the blood on his hands. He remembers his promise to go back.

Staggering to his feet, he sways drunkenly and almost falls on the man lying next to him, who has a blood-soaked bandage wrapped around his face, and recoils, whimpering in alarm. Jem feels like he's standing on the deck of a listing ship and raises his hands to his own head, but can find no dressing or any wound that would account for the feeling of a sledgehammer beating at the inside of his skull. Carefully, stopping frequently to steady himself, clutching his head with both hands to contain the ache, he picks his way through the stretchers.

A Regimental Medical Officer standing at the door of a sandbagged dugout breaks off his conversation and looks round as Jem approaches. His neat moustache has lost its definition in several days of stubble and the red cross on his white armband is almost obliterated by bloodstains. 'I'll try to get you on the next convoy,' he says wearily, through the roar inside Jem's head. 'The ambulances can't keep up. Those with bleeding wounds take precedence I'm afraid.'

'I don't need it, sir.' His tongue is thick inside his mouth. 'I have to get back.'

Beneath his tin helmet the RMO's face registers surprise. 'Lance Corporal, you were in a trench mortar attack. You were brought in unconscious and suffering from a severe concussion—'

'I'm all right. I have to get back. Sir.'

Has he said that already? He senses that the RMO is torn between professional duty and the prospect of lightening his burden of responsibility. To sway the balance, Jem makes an effort to lift his head and meet the man's eye, though his face blurs out of focus and there seems to be a curtain across one side of his vision.

'I need to return to my battalion, sir. I have to collect the wounded.'

The RMO's face seems to be coming close and then moving away, looming and retreating, looming and retreating. Jem tries to swallow but his mouth is too dry. The need to be sick is building inside him and his face feels clammy, but just as he's not sure he can hold it much longer, the RMO looks past him.

'Thank bloody God,' he says with jubilant relief.

Three ambulances are snaking towards them in a plume of dust. Patting Jem absently on the arm, the RMO goes to meet them, and the other man comes out of the dugout to follow. As he passes Jem, he says, 'I wouldn't bother, pal. Going back for the wounded. It's been almost thirty-six hours. There'll be no one left out there alive.'

Thirty-six hours? More than a whole day?

Jem's legs take him forward. He makes it a hundred yards and is sick into the long grass beside a heap of stinking dressings.

Brighton

When she next goes to Lewes Crescent on Tuesday afternoon, the first convoys of wounded men have arrived.

They were greeted at the station that morning by crowds of cheering well-wishers. (She knows this, because Mrs Van de Berg was one of them, having gone with one of the ladies from the bridge club, to distribute chocolate and cigarettes to the Poor Brave Boys.) At Lewes Crescent, she finds stretchers leaning against the railings, drying in the sun after being scrubbed clean. The elegant hall is cluttered with trolleys and screens, and a laundry hamper has been left at the foot of the stairs. The space is filled with male voices; and through the doorway to the inner hall, she sees a queue of men, dirty and bedraggled. Upstairs, on the gallery, Corporal Maloney is talking to one of the doctors, too grimly focused to give her a second glance. The front of his white tunic is smeared with blood.

The smell is overwhelming. The tang of disinfectant has been swamped by the stench of the slaughterhouse, of meat gone bad. It makes her gag.

She finds Sister Pinkney at Matron's desk, writing rapidly in a ledger. She waits, not wanting to intrude in this place of purpose and protocol. When Sister Pinkney glances up, she finds herself apologising. 'Mrs Van de Berg has provided postcards, with stamps attached, for the men to send word home, but I'm sure now isn't the time—'

'On the contrary, Miss Simmons.' Nurse Pinkney's face is drawn, and she removes her wire-framed glasses to rub at the red welts they have left on the bridge of her nose. 'Now is the perfect time. A lot of families will be waiting for news.' She lowers her voice. 'But, please, prepare yourself. If you're shocked, do not show it, and if you're upset, do not cry. I hope you don't faint at the sight of blood?'

A flash of memory. A white shirt splashed with red, scarlet drops on the stone flags.

She shakes her head.

'Good.' Sister Pinkney's expression softens. 'These men are soldiers, Miss Simmons, but they are also sons, brothers, husbands. Without nursing experience it's quite natural to be daunted by their injuries, but you must look past them and see the man. Think of him as someone you might know yourself.'

'Of course, Sister Pinkney.'

But as she goes into the ward, where the smell of the charnel house is stronger than ever and the pristine beds she made up are occupied, it is exactly that possibility that makes her heart falter.

Autumn

Chapter 16

The thin, metallic note of the church bell started up as Eliza leaned over the washbowl and splashed her face with cold water. Behind her, Abigail had unpinned her hair and turned her head upside down to brush it vigorously. On hearing the bell, she flipped it back, so that it settled around her shoulders like an expensive sable cape.

'Oh Lord, that must be Davy telling us he's here! I'm not ready. I wanted to try that new style I saw in the magazine.'

'He won't be here yet; Davy will have just seen him. And anyway, even when he does get here it's going to take him ages to set up all his fancy equipment, isn't it? You've got plenty of time.'

Even to Eliza's own ears her voice sounded weary and snappish. Not so long ago she would have shared Abigail's excitement about a photographer coming to take staff portraits to hang alongside the others on the kitchen passage wall, but she couldn't seem to muster much enthusiasm for anything these days.

Yesterday evening Abigail had carried up cans of water to wash her hair and Eliza had intended to use it once she'd finished, but in the end the effort had seemed overwhelming. It had been a long day; Sir Randolph was back from Scotland and as demanding as ever, and with the additional work for the wedding celebrations and the couple's permanent return to Coldwell, everyone was rushed off their feet. By the time tea was cleared Eliza had been done in and decided to make do with sponging the roots with a bit of cider vinegar. The smell wafted about her now, and in the mirror, her hair hung lankly around her pasty face, a stark contrast with the silken swathe Abigail was pinning into a shiny pompadour. Eliza regretted not taking the trouble.

She found she was regretting quite a few things, these days.

She buried her face in the towel to smother her envy, and the nausea that rolled through her. Abigail had already changed her morning print dress for the smarter afternoon black, but Eliza was putting off undressing until Abigail had gone downstairs.

'I wish we didn't have to wear these stupid caps,' Abigail grumbled. 'I'm going to pin mine right on the back of my head so's you can't see it. I hope the photographer doesn't want us to do that ridiculous thing of holding something to show what job we do. The one we had at my last place did that. So embarrassing. I was standing there holding a dustpan and brush like a right lemon. I looked like a crossing sweeper.'

In spite of herself, Eliza laughed.

'That's more like it,' Abigail said, securing the last pin in her cap and letting her arms fall to her sides. 'Haven't seen you crack a smile in weeks. Not since London.' There was a little pause, and she sighed. 'You really fell for him, didn't you?'

Eliza picked up the hairbrush from the washstand and pulled the dead hair from its bristles. Acid-tasting saliva pricked at the back of her throat and with difficulty she swallowed it down, shaking her head. That was the most galling thing about this—she hadn't been that keen on Walter Cox at all, but if she opened her mouth to say that, she feared she would succumb to the tide of sickness that was slowly rising inside her again.

Abigail turned away, clearly hurt that her attempt to bridge the new distance between them had been rebuffed. 'Well anyway . . . I'll go down.' She nodded to the two folded aprons that were laid on her bed; the ones for best, with lace edging and pintucks. 'Which one do you want? Square neck or round?'

'Either. You choose.'

She didn't look to see which one Abigail took. Fixing her eyes on the garlands of roses circling the china wash jug, she focused on breathing in through her nose and releasing the air in a steady stream, without parting her lips too much. At the door Abigail paused. 'I could help you with your hair if you like?'

'Don't worry, it's fine,' Eliza said, in a strangled voice. 'You go down—I won't be a minute.'

Sweat broke out across her forehead and she breathed in again, holding it until Abigail's footsteps had reached the bottom of the stairs and she could fumble under the bed for the chamber pot. Crouching on the floor with her arms wrapped around her body, she gave herself up to the paroxysms of nausea, though she had long since brought up her breakfast and there was nothing left to spit out but bitter-tasting bile.

The photographer was a twitchy little man in a dapper suit who reminded Kate of a music hall turn. He set his camera up on the gravel in front of the house and got the gardeners' boys, who were first to arrive, to stand on the steps while he buried his head beneath his black cloth, then emerged again to dart around, adjusting the position of his tripod and mopping his forehead with a spotted silk handkerchief.

It was a crisp morning of blue skies and cool, damp air. The end of the summer heat wave had brought a sense of renewed energy and purpose, heightened by the imminent wedding. Yet another troop of men had arrived that morning to begin setting up a large tent on the stretch of grass to the west of the house for the dance that was to be held for local people—tenants and villagers as well as staff—to celebrate the return of Sir Randolph and the new Lady Hyde to Coldwell. Standing at the top of the steps, Kate watched them unfolding the huge canvas and hammering in poles. Behind them, the trees were already wearing their autumn colours, the hills painted in shades of brown and khaki. Change was in the air.

'Mrs Furniss?'

She turned, smothering the smile that spread inside her at the sound of Jem's voice. He was coming up the steps, his tone businesslike, his expression serious. He was wearing formal livery for the photograph, and the high collar accentuated the slant of his cheekbones, the clean line of his jaw. She felt her chest constrict. Stopping a few respectable feet from her, he lowered his voice so that only she could hear.

'Can I tell you how beautiful you look?'

'Absolutely not,' she murmured, making sure to keep the intimate warmth in her tone from showing on her face. 'That would be unforgivably forward.'

'It seems I never learn . . .'

'And in fact, get worse.' She risked a sideways glance at him. 'It's just as well I'm not some swoony housemaid and can easily resist you.' It was so hard not to smile. 'Was there anything else you wanted?'

'There was, actually.' The spark went out of his eyes. 'I asked Goddard if I could take my half day on Monday instead of tomorrow. He said no.'

On the gravel the photographer was waving his arms, directing the garden lads into a tighter group. Kate realised they were in the way and moved along the steps, to the other side of the stone pillar. Thomas, standing where Jem had been a moment before, glanced round.

'Never mind. There's far too much to do, with the wedding celebration,' she said in her brisk, public voice, loud enough to be heard.

'I do mind,' he said softly, moving to stand beside her. 'You're going to Hatherford on Monday, for the bank. I could have met you there.'

Beneath the portico, behind the group of garden boys (who had been joined by Gatley), one of the front doors opened. Susan and Abigail scurried out, followed a moment later by Joseph.

The photographer's face turned puce with frustration. 'Please, please . . . out of the way!' he spluttered, gesticulating frantically.

'There'll be other times,' Kate said quietly. 'Sir Randolph's leaving for London tomorrow. It'll be easier when he's gone.'

Sir Randolph himself wasn't the problem, but when he was out of the way, his valet was too.

For a moment, neither of them spoke as they watched the garden lads relax their stiff poses and disperse, to make way for Johnny Farrow and the Twigg boys in their faded coachman's coats. They were joined—after some uncertainty—by Robson the chauffeur in his flashy livery, which was, Kate thought absently, like watching the past meet the future. The old give way to the new.

'I wish everyone was leaving for London,' Jem said softly, 'and we could have that time again.'

She took a breath, trying to appear indifferent. When she spoke, it was almost without moving her lips.

'What would you do with it?'

'Not waste it trying to resist you. Spend it getting to know you properly.'

She thought about his hands on her breasts, his mouth on her thighs. Reaching for her chatelaine, she snapped open her watch to distract from the heat that was creeping into her cheeks.

'I'd say you know me quite well already.'

'I want to know more,' he murmured. 'And there are things I want to tell you, things I need to'—he broke off abruptly and cleared his throat—'take down to the gamekeeper's cottage, like you asked,' he finished loudly.

Kate's head snapped round, and she saw a shadow move behind the pillar.

'Joseph?'

The hallboy emerged, cowering a little as he always did, though no one at Coldwell had ever raised a hand to him. It was a hard habit to break, as she understood well. The workhouse authorities had warned her that the boy had witnessed significant violence in his short life, and that it was likely to have marked his character. His mother had died at his father's hand—which was why Joseph had ended up in the care of the parish—and it was thought that he'd witnessed the event, though he claimed not to remember it. This was never far from her mind. It made it hard to be angry with him.

'Yes, Mrs Furniss.'

Joseph's eyes were blue and imploring, his face slightly grimy with coal smuts and jam from breakfast.

'What are you doing there? You're not even ready! Go and wash your face—quickly. You can't be in the photograph looking like that.'

He scampered off, down the steps towards the stable yard as Mr Goddard appeared through the front doors, little more than a shadow in his worn tailcoat and striped trousers. Down on the gravel, the photographer pleaded querulously for the footmen since they didn't seem to have a full complement of housemaids. Eliza was missing, Kate realised. Trust her to take ages getting ready.

Mrs Gatley came out, apron crackling with starch. 'D'you think we could be next? Upper servants?' she called, with an aggrieved air. 'Only I haven't got time to hang about—not if Sir Randolph's going to be having his luncheon this side of teatime.'

Mr Goddard craned his tortoise neck around. 'Unfortunately, Mr Henderson has yet to join us. Perhaps by the time the footmen have had their portraits taken he'll be here . . .'

Mrs Gatley threw up her plump arms and muttered that she couldn't be blamed if the venison was half-raw, and Jem went to take his place in the centre of the steps. Kate looked around with a twinge of unease.

Henderson was like one of those giant house spiders that crouched in dark corners, or hid in the folds of a linen pillowcase, setting her nerves jangling when it darted out. She could cope with it if she had some warning, though it made her shudder. She'd rather know one was there than be caught unawares by its sudden scuttle.

But she'd much rather it wasn't there at all.

Joseph ran, skidding a little on the gravel as he turned the corner to the stable yard, his footsteps echoing as he passed under the brick archway.

The front door was open, and it would have been quicker to go that way. It was allowed today, with everyone coming and going for the photographs, but still, it didn't feel right. On the day he arrived at Coldwell he'd been told that the front door was for family and guests only, and Joseph preferred to stick to the rules. He liked knowing what was expected of him: what was permitted and what was likely to get him a hiding. Not that he'd ever had a beating here, but the fear of it was stamped into him, like a bruise that wouldn't heal. It came roaring back sometimes, catching him out, making his heart jump and his mind go black.

The back door was open too. He plunged into the dimness, barely slowing his pace, so he had to put out a hand to steady himself as he turned the corner into the kitchen passage. After the brightness of the day, the shadows swamped his vision. He didn't see the figure emerge from the footmen's wardrobe until it was too late.

A hand, heavy on his shoulder. The smell of hair oil.

'And where are you going in such a hurry, young man?'

———⊸∞∞⊷———

June 29th
France

The rain has stopped and the clouds have lifted. I think that means all this wait-ing will soon be over, whatever we're waiting for.

Joseph is in a bad way. I asked the captain if he could be moved out of the line because of his nerves being gone, but apparently it would be considered a dereliction of duty. He'd be arrested. That might possibly be worse for him— being imprisoned on his own. He has nightmares about what happened back then, and when he was a kid. Lately they've been so bad that he has them when he isn't even asleep.

He never spoke to me about his life before Coldwell. I suppose I never asked. Perhaps things would have been different if I had.

Chapter 17

On the day that Sir Randolph Hyde was taking Miss Leonora Addison to become his lawful wedded wife in a small, private ceremony in London, Kate made her fortnightly visit to Hatherford, to settle the accounts and place orders in the shops.

Johnny Farrow was even more taciturn than usual, barely acknowledging her 'good morning' as she climbed up onto the wagon in the stable yard. They had just begun their swaying progress up the drive when a shout from behind made them both look round. Jem had emerged from the arch and was running easily after them.

'Can I join you? Mr Goddard's asked me to go to the brewery, to check the beer order for the dance.'

Kate's heart soared.

It wasn't fair to slow the horses on the hill, so he had to jump up onto the moving wagon. 'Forgive me, Mrs Furniss,' he said, with a convincing mixture of humility and regret. 'There's not much room.'

She was struck by what a good actor he was. But, as servants, weren't they all? Used to keeping their feelings hidden behind expressionless faces.

Autumn had gilded the parkland and the circling hills, and clouds trailed languidly across a sky of blameless blue. (Mrs Gatley had pronounced it perfect weather for a wedding, though Susan had swiftly soured that sentiment by informing them that rain on a wedding day was a sign of good luck.) This was the gently glowing tail of summer's searing comet, and it bathed everything in its golden light. Kate relaxed back on the wooden seat and felt a burst of quiet joy at the sensation of the sun on her cheeks and Jem's hip hard against hers, his arm resting on the back of the seat behind her.

Hatherford seemed busier than usual. The change of season carried a crackle of energy as people began to make their preparations for the winter ahead. Johnny Farrow set Kate down, as he always did, outside the bank. The brewery was behind the Bull's Head, where he hitched the horses, so there was no reason for Jem to get down with her. She caught his wistful smile as he handed her basket down.

'Midday, same as usual,' Johnny Farrow called, flicking the horses on, and Jem's eyes held hers as the wagon moved away.

Inside the bank, she slid Mr Fortescue's cheque beneath the glass partition at the counter, watching the teller's bony fingers as he counted out the money for her to settle the household accounts. She could still feel the warmth of Jem's hand on her shoulder. With the money folded in her bag, she crossed the road and went into the spice-and-soap-scented interior of Pearson's the grocers.

Kate took her place in the queue and idly watched the other women waiting. They were mostly farmer's wives or countrywomen, in clogs and hats that were functional rather than fashionable, but a woman at the counter wearing a coat of moss green velvet caught her eye. It was not new nor particularly smart, but somehow . . . stylish. The kind of thing Kate would have chosen for herself, had she been able to choose.

She found herself thinking a lot lately about the things she would choose, if she were able: the kind of house she would live in, the way she would furnish it, the life she would have. It was idle dreaming, she knew that, but there was a grain of something more behind it too, an element of self-discovery, perhaps. Her life so far had been dictated by her roles, as daughter, wife, housekeeper, but Jem had uncovered the person she had never had the chance to be. Someone who surprised her. Who laughed, and made love. Who wanted a cottage in the countryside, with fruit trees in the garden, and roses . . . where the skills she had acquired would be used for her own benefit instead of someone else's. Who wished for a life of simple domesticity, in tune with the seasons.

With Jem, of course.

'Mrs Furniss. What can I get for you today?'

The woman in the green coat had moved away and Mr Pearson was looking at her over the top of the Fry's Chocolate cabinet. He had sandy hair, a thick moustache like a fox's brush, and an air of permanent harassment, as if the queue of customers in his shop was something of a trial to him. Kate pushed her dreams aside and placed her list on the counter.

'There's quite a lot this week, I'm afraid.'

Mr Pearson picked it up and adjusted his half-moon spectacles as he studied it, glancing up at her with an expression that lay somewhere between incredulity and outrage. '*Three* cones of sugar, Mrs Furniss? Six pounds of tea?'

'It's this week Sir Randolph returns to Coldwell, isn't it?' Mrs Pearson, serving another customer, bustled behind her husband, nudging him out of the way none too gently as she reached for a tin of treacle. 'Bringing his new wife. My sister lives in Howden Bridge—she says there's a dance on Friday, to welcome home the happy couple.' Kate heard the cynicism in her tone. 'It'll be quite a change for you, I daresay?'

'A new era for Coldwell Hall,' Kate said smoothly. 'Speaking of which, perhaps you might be able to help . . . ? With Sir Randolph and Lady Hyde in residence we're going to need more staff. I'm looking for girls— kitchen maid, scullery maid, and housemaid—I wondered if you might know of anyone looking for a place. I don't mind if they're young—full training will be given, and a good wage—'

There was a muffled snort to Kate's right. She looked round and saw that it had come from the customer Mrs Pearson was serving; a solidly built woman, with iron-grey hair escaping in wisps from beneath her battered hat and an expression of undisguised hostility. 'You could pay a king's ransom and you still wouldn't get any takers for that place, girl *or* boy,' she muttered, just loud enough to be heard. 'Not now *he's* back. People hereabouts aren't daft. And they've got long memories.'

Kate felt the colour creep up her cheeks as embarrassment burned down inside her. The criticism felt personal, though she didn't know what had prompted it. She was aware of eyes on her—Mr Pearson's, the woman who'd spoken, the other customers behind her. The hum of conversation had stopped, and there was a moment of frozen silence before Mrs Pearson stepped in to fill it.

'Perhaps you could write to the matron of the Barnardo's Home in Sheffield? Their girls are always grateful for a place,' she said, addressing Kate with soothing courtesy. 'Now, leave that order with Mr Pearson and we'll get the lad to deliver it tomorrow, as usual. Won't we, Mr Pearson?'

'*If* we've got it all,' her husband muttered dubiously as he hurried round to open the shop door for her. 'But I'll always do my best for you, Mrs Furniss, as you know.' He lowered his voice, as if admitting something shameful. 'The Coldwell account is very valuable to us and we're grateful for your business. Good day to you.'

The brewery was at the scrag end of town by the river, where the neat streets of shops and houses gave way to sheds and workshops and privies and the cobbles were slick with mud. Once Jem had got down from the wagon at the back of the Bull's Head it was easy to find. He just had to head towards the tall brick chimney and the smell of yeast and roasting hops.

Mr Goddard might have refused his request for a day off, but it hadn't been hard to find an excuse for the trip. The old man was so vague these days, he could barely remember what year it was, never mind whether the beer he'd ordered for Sir Randolph's homecoming dance was adequate. Jem had casually sown the seeds of doubt and seen the relief on the butler's face when he'd offered to go to the brewery himself, reassuring Goddard that, with his experience from the Station Hotel, he was well-placed to make sure they had secured the best deal for the best ale, and enough of it.

He'd planned his strategy carefully, using his last Sunday half day to go to church in Howden Bridge. He'd positioned himself at the back and spent the tedious service studying the congregation, looking for the woman he had spoken to on coronation day. It was easy to spot her red hair, especially as she had a brood of children with the same striking colouring. Slipping out quickly at the end, Jem had lit a cigarette and waited by the door to catch her.

'Is there a Mullins here?' he asked the foreman now, raising his voice above the hiss of steam and the mechanical clank of the great pumps.

The man barely glanced at him. 'Why d'you ask?'

'Just curious. If it's the Mullins I'm thinking of, I might have found something that belongs to him.'

He was as certain as he could be that it *was* the Mullins he was thinking of. The woman with the red hair had eventually confirmed that Mrs Mullins, who'd helped her with the teas at the coronation fete, had a lad who'd once worked at Coldwell. She too had asked why he wanted to know, and he'd told the same lie.

He followed the foreman across the dusty floor of the brewery, past the gleaming, steaming coppers to the wide mouth of the cavernous space. 'What kind of something?' the man said.

'Personal.' Jem shrugged. 'Something that might have sentimental value, if it's his. It might not be, but I found it in an old coat that had his name in it. Heard he worked here so I thought I'd ask. Of course, if he's not—'

'*Mullins!*'

The foreman pushed his cap back and bellowed across the yard. Having done that, he gave Jem a cursory nod and disappeared inside.

A head appeared over a stable door; a broad, blank face with the mouth hanging open. Jem went unhurriedly over, sliding his hands into his pockets and closing his fingers around a small fold of paper so he could feel the hard disc inside it. It was his own St Christopher medallion, the only thing he had that had belonged to his mother. He didn't want to lose it, but he hoped it wouldn't come to that.

'Are you Mullins?'

'Who wants to know?'

Jem had thought about this. It was likely that for the duration of his brief stay at Coldwell Jack would only have been known by the name of his employer, as was the custom for visiting servants. However, he couldn't be sure, and couldn't risk revealing too much at this stage. 'I work at Coldwell Hall,' he said, watching the lad's face. 'I think you used to have a place there? We were going through the old uniforms and came across a coat with the name Mullins in it. Tiger's livery.'

Mullins's eyes narrowed and his slack mouth closed like a trap. 'Yeah, well, it's a common enough name round these parts, ain't it?'

He was half-hidden by the stable door, but his agitation was obvious. Behind him, the heavy horse seemed to sense it and shifted its hooves, scraping them on the stone floor. Jem patted his pockets absently, making a show of looking for something. Eventually he pulled out the square of folded paper.

'This isn't yours, then? Belongs to some other Mullins?'

'What is it?'

'Found it in the pocket of the tiger's coat. But if you weren't at Coldwell—'

'I never said I wasn't. I don't like talking about it, that's all. It was a long time ago—I was glad to get away. So . . . you going to give it back then?'

The hand he stuck out over the door was deeply ingrained with dirt. Playing for time, Jem took a half-smoked cigarette out of his waistcoat pocket and relit it, pausing to inhale deeply.

'How long ago were you there?'

'I dunno—a few years. Like you said, I was a tiger. Just a kid.' He thrust his hand forwards. 'Now, if you'd give me what's mine, I'll get back to work.'

Frowning, Jem exhaled a column of smoke. 'The thing is, I'm not sure now that it *is* yours. It seems like a sentimental thing; if you'd lost it, you'd probably know . . .' He began to unfold the paper. 'You don't remember misplacing anything?'

Mullins's eyes were fixed on the paper. Opening the last fold, Jem slid the St Christopher into his other hand and flipped it in the air. It glinted and flashed for a second before he caught it. 'If you can tell me what it is, it's yours.'

'A sovereign.' Mullins's voice cracked. He gripped the top of the stable door, his ruddy face suddenly waxy. 'It's a bloody sovereign, isn't it? That bastard—'

Backing away, he gave a bitter and broken sort of laugh, and rubbed his black-nailed fingers across his forehead. 'You can keep it. I don't want it.'

'What makes you think it's a sovereign?'

A pulse had begun to throb uncomfortably in Jem's temples. Inside the stable Mullins spun round, grasping the fork he'd been using to muck out the stall. 'I said I don't *want* it, whatever it is. And I don't want to talk about it, neither. Now bugger off and leave me alone.'

For a long moment they stared at each other, then Jem nodded. 'All right,' he said softly. 'All right. But if you change your mind, you know where to find me. My name's Jem Arden. I think you know who I am.'

It was a gamble, and one that he'd lost before. But he'd never been this close to the truth; he'd never found himself face to face with someone he was pretty sure had the answers he was looking for. Mullins held all the aces.

Jem walked back across the cobbles with his head bent, his hand closed around the St Christopher in his pocket, the curse Mullins called out after him ringing in his ears.

The church clock was striking the half hour when Kate came out of the chemist with her packages of tooth powder, witch hazel, and oil of cloves. Usually she would be glad to have finished her errands and have time to browse the shops for her own pleasure, but the exchange in Pearson's had unsettled her.

There was a cool nip in the air, a bite that hadn't been there the last time she was in town, but that wasn't what made her pull the collar of her coat up around her face. All this time she had been afraid of being discovered and exposed, had thought she was safe in this small, cut-off town in the Derbyshire Peaks. The people here knew her as Mrs Furniss, respectable housekeeper of Coldwell Hall, but it seemed she was just as ignorant of their lives as they were of hers. She felt self-conscious, tainted by a secret that everyone seemed to know but her.

She walked slowly, aware of her own ghost in step beside her, slipping in and out of the corner of her vision in the shop windows. She passed the tea shop where, when the weather was cold, she sometimes ordered a pot of Darjeeling to sip while she watched the passers-by on the street, savouring her aloneness and anonymity.

Little did she know that she hadn't been anonymous and unremarkable at all, and that people must have been talking, *whispering*, about who she was and where she was from. It wasn't her past associations that tainted her here but her present one, with Coldwell.

She stopped in front of Holdsworth's Pawnbrokers, hitching her basket onto the other arm as she peered in through the window's small panes. Some shopkeepers favoured a methodical approach to showing off their wares—symmetrical towers of tins and packets, serried rows of produce, but here everything was piled into the dusty window space without design or forethought. Kate's gaze moved over china jugs, children's shoes, smelling salts bottles, and pocket watches, until a small box in the far corner of the window caught her eye.

A dragonfly nestled on folds of blue satin, its enamelled wings delicately veined in gold. She stared at it wistfully, thinking back to the day of the fair, and the walk back to Coldwell over the steaming moor.

It took a moment to notice that someone had come to stand beside her, and another to realise that it was Jem. Neither spoke, but she felt the comfort of his presence; a loosening of the tension in her shoulders, as if she had stepped out of the teeth of a gale into shelter.

She heard his soft outward breath, like a sigh, and felt him move fractionally closer. The effervescent joy she had felt when he had jumped up onto the wagon had dissipated, leaving a quieter, more wistful longing in its wake. Almost like sadness.

After a while he said in a low voice, 'I wanted to come and find you, but—' He glanced round, over his shoulder. 'There's nowhere we can go, is there? Nowhere that we won't be seen, and people won't talk.'

The reflections of people on the street behind them slid across the window. The inside of the shop was dark and murky, but Mr Holdsworth would be lurking somewhere in its depths. He would be watching them.

Someone was always watching them.

Jem turned away from the window. With an impressive show of nonchalance, he leaned against the wall, flipping a silver coin from one hand to the other.

'It's the way it is,' she said quietly. 'The way it has to be.'

Since the night of the downpour, they had survived on snatched moments and stolen kisses, furtive glances and fleeting smiles. It was harder than she'd imagined, but she sometimes wondered how she had got through the days before—the blank, flat years without him. She had only been half-alive. Frozen, like a fly trapped inside one of the blocks of ice hauled up from the icehouse. He had quickened her blood again. He had brought her back to life, and however difficult it was, she couldn't regret it.

He put the coin back into his pocket and turned to look up the street. A muscle flickered in the hollow of his cheek, and inside her gloves her fingers ached to touch him.

'I wish I could court you properly,' he said softly. 'I wish I could hold your hand and sit across a table from you in a tea shop, like any other man with his sweetheart . . .'

He made it sound so ordinary. So blissfully commonplace. She couldn't help smiling.

'You want to buy me tea?'

His head was bowed, but he cast her a sidelong glance from beneath his dark lashes. A half-smile.

'Yes. I want to buy you tea. And when the waitress isn't looking, I want to peel your glove back and kiss the inside of your wrist.' His voice was a husky growl. 'I want to take your arm as we walk down the street and put my hand on your waist. I want to take you home to a place where we can shut the door and be alone. Where we can . . . I don't know. Just *be*.'

Just *be*. Together. No guilt or fear or weighing up risk. No lies or excuses. No elaborate code system, and notes left in the Chinese vase on the scullery shelf.

'I like the sound of that,' she whispered, moving away from the window to stand beside him. 'A home, where we can shut the door and be alone.'

'A bedroom with a big brass bed, where I can fall asleep with you in my arms . . .'

In her head she saw the cottage, with the apple trees and roses in the garden, and found she couldn't speak anymore.

She had known from the first time she touched him that there was no future for them. It was the nature of service. Occasionally you came across a married couple in the roles of housekeeper and butler, but aside from that, relations between staff were simply not tolerated. As a female servant you either lived a half life in someone else's home, a shadow in the wings of their three-act play, or you left to get married.

She was married already.

There was no way out. No happy ever after awaiting. It was scraps and crumbs and compromises. That was the deal she had made for her freedom, and she had considered it a good bargain. She had no right to want more.

But she did.

Oh . . . she did.

———∞∞∞———

We're all tired. The guns make it difficult to sleep and they are always there, even in your dreams. I'm tired of the waiting too, though I'm not finished writing yet. I have yet to make my confession.

Before I left Coldwell for the last time I went into Goddard's room and found the photographs that were taken that day on the steps. The one showing the whole staff was hung on the wall, but the others were in a pile of old newspapers and unanswered correspondence on his desk.

There was one of you with Goddard, Mrs Gatley, and Henderson. In it you look beautiful and composed, and only someone who knew you well would spot how you were turning away from Henderson and your mouth was set tight. I cut you out from the rest of the group, so it looks like you're standing on the steps alone. Your expression seemed softer then. I've carried that scrap of photograph with me ever since and looked at it a thousand times. I'm looking at it now.

I left the half with Goddard and Mrs Gatley on the desk amongst the others. I threw Henderson into the fire.

Chapter 18

The photograph, marked with the year and framed in black, had been delivered and hung on the wall of the kitchen passage, alongside the others. It appeared on the day before Sir Randolph was due to return to Coldwell with his new bride; and although everyone was rushed off their feet with preparations for the wedding dance, they still found time to go and look.

Beside the faded faces in the other frames along the wall, they looked sharper and infinitely more modern. Jem stood back while the girls wailed over unflattering angles and unfortunate expressions, instead studying the previous photographs. The last one had been taken in 1900, and his eyes skimmed over footmen with oiled-down hair, grooms and gardeners with fulsome moustaches and muttonchop whiskers, over Mr Goddard and Gatley (the former a little more solid and substantial, the latter with a fuller head of hair) until they came to rest on the boy in the tiger's livery at the edge of the group.

Mullins must have been about thirteen then; the same age as Jack, but bigger built. His jacket strained over his shoulders and you could see his shirt between the bulging buttons of his waistcoat. Jem studied his face, blurred by time and furred by dust on the glass. It was rounder then, more open. He was smiling, his chin tilted up, as if he was proud of his smart uniform (even if it was too small).

What had happened to change that? To make him leave and want to forget his time at Coldwell?

Mrs Gatley's sharp voice summoned Susan, and the girls moved away. Jem found himself standing beside Thomas in front of this year's photograph, life mirroring art.

'Binking 'eck,' Thomas said, leaning forward to study himself. 'We scrub up all right, don't we? Mind you, the new livery helps.'

Jem made a noncommittal noise. He wasn't looking at Thomas or himself, or their livery. He was looking at Kate.

Standing in the centre of the group, beside Mr Goddard, she looked as she had when he'd glimpsed her in the window on the day he'd arrived, her face pale and inscrutable, her gaze direct and slightly challenging. Her slim figure was upright, her chatelaine gleaming against the black silk of her skirt as she took her place in the procession of Coldwell housekeepers, preserved for posterity on the kitchen passage wall. Those who came after—generations of servants not yet born—would remark on how young she was for the role, and how beautiful, and they might be curious about who she was and where she'd come from.

No one would know her like he did.

No one would know her story. No one would know that she'd taken her surname from an advertising sign, or that she slept with her hand curled under her chin and was frightened of spiders, or that she had a small birthmark on her hip and smelled of vanilla and nutmeg and roses and that the second footman, standing a few places to her left, was in love with her.

His heart gave a lurch that made his blood feel hot.

'The group photograph of us footmen is in Mr Goddard's room,' Thomas said. 'Reckon my old mum will be very happy when she gets one of those for the parlour. Are you going to send one home?'

'Oh. No.'

He felt winded, like he had in the second after Henderson punched him.

Love.

For all these years he had focused only on hate. He hadn't seen it coming; hadn't recognised the signs. And now it was too late.

The atmosphere in the kitchen was like a pot coming up to the simmer. The weather might be cooler (and the Lord be thanked for that), but with only one day left until Sir Randolph and Lady Hyde's homecoming, the range was roaring from dawn to dusk and the list of tasks—sauces to make, steak to mince, fish to fillet—never seemed to get any shorter. No wonder, with only two of them to manage it all. Clarys Gatley had trained as a cook, not a ruddy magician.

Which was why she wasn't in the best of tempers when Mrs Furniss appeared in the kitchen doorway and asked, in that la-di-da way she had, if she might have a word.

Mrs Gatley peered through the briny steam above the fish kettle. 'A *word*?'

'When you can spare a moment.'

She couldn't help but laugh, though the housekeeper didn't appear to be joking. 'I can't see that I'll be able to "spare a moment" until hell freezes and pigs fly over the park,' she snapped, prodding the salmon poaching in the kettle, then clanging the lid down. 'Not without another pair of hands to take on some of the work. Have you found anyone?'

'That was what I wanted to talk to you about.' Mrs Furniss glanced at Susan, who was forcing rabbit liver through a fine sieve for pâté. 'Shall we go to my room?'

Mrs Gatley certainly couldn't spare the time, but the thought of the housekeeper's parlour with its little velvet armchair (a bit *too* little for Mrs Gatley's frame, but welcome nonetheless) was too tempting to resist. Following the swish of Mrs Furniss's silk skirts along the passage, she wiped her hands on her apron and, stepping into the rose-scented cool of the parlour, subsided into the armchair with a huff of relief.

'So—you've found someone?' Her feet throbbed painfully, and she strained forward to ease a finger under one shoe strap. 'I hope whoever she is, she can start soon, because with Sir Randolph and a new her ladyship—'

'I'm afraid not.'

She was an odd one, Kate Furniss. In all the years they'd worked together Mrs Gatley felt she'd never quite got the measure of her. She'd come to Coldwell as a stillroom maid, though you wouldn't know that to look at her now. Sitting there at her neat desk, the cook was suddenly reminded of the interviews she used to have with the last Lady Hyde, up in the Yellow Parlour, discussing menus and dining arrangements. There was definitely something of the upstairs about Kate Furniss, with her elegant hands and porcelain complexion. The way she kept to herself, in her pretty parlour, and never talked about where she'd been before she pitched up at Coldwell. Where she'd come from.

Everyone had the right to a bit of privacy, Gatley said; nothing odd about wanting to keep your business to yourself. But that was men for you—no curiosity. Women were different. They talked. Unless they had something to hide.

The housekeeper straightened the silver chains of her chatelaine, not meeting Mrs Gatley's eye. 'You know what it's like, trying to get staff here ... Especially these days, when the girls would rather work in a shop or serve in a tearoom. I always thought it was the location that put a lot of young ones off—being so cut off and not having much to do on half days and so on—but yesterday I mentioned in Pearson's that we were looking, and I got the distinct impression that there was something else.'

She lifted her head and looked at Mrs Gatley directly. Very blue eyes, she had—like one of the china dolls up in the nursery. Unblinking.

Mrs Gatley felt her own eyes narrow, her lips tighten.

'Well, if there is, I wouldn't know it,' she said shortly, gripping the arms of the chair in preparation for hauling herself out of it. 'If that's all, I'll be getting along—'

'There was a woman—another customer—who implied that something had happened here in the past. Something involving Sir Randolph, and that's why no one local wants to come here now. *People round here have long memories.* That's what she said.'

Mrs Gatley was a great one for trusting her gut on all matters, from boiling an egg to seasoning a steak pie. Right now it was giving her the same sense of misgiving as a rabbit that had been hanging too long and smelt wrong. She tugged her rucked-up apron smooth. 'People round here love a gossip, more like,' she said tartly. 'That's all it is—gossip. Nothing was ever proved. Folk like to sit in judgement, especially of them that are better off and—'

'What was never proved?'

Oh, she was a sharp one, and no mistake. Mrs Gatley could have bitten her own tongue for letting that slip, but Mrs Furniss wasn't the only one who could play her cards close to her chest.

'Nothing,' she said. 'It was a bad business with a visiting servant, that's all. In them days there was parties all the time, strangers trooping through the servants' hall—not surprising one of them turned out to be a wrong 'un. The police came up, gave the place a good going over, and found nothing amiss. But folk don't care about that, do they? They're more interested in a fanciful story, like that daft ghost nonsense, than facts. I'd have thought you'd know better than to listen.' She threw the housekeeper a withering look. 'Now, if you're quite finished, some of us have got work to do, and not enough hands to do it.'

Mrs Gatley's poor arches protested as she marched back to the kitchen, but her conscience needled her just as sharply. The lad's face swam into her mind. Skinny thing, he'd been, like Joseph ... Nice enough manners from what she'd seen and she certainly hadn't pegged him as a thief. But what did anyone know of the folk that passed through a house like this? It had been an unfortunate business and it had left its mark on them all, none more than old Sir Henry. There was nothing to be gained by raking it all up now.

And the fact was, she didn't know what had happened that night all those years ago, at the Indian banquet in the temple. It could very well have been just as Mr Henderson had said, exactly what he'd told her to say to Sergeant Timmis. Whatever the truth of it, they'd all agreed not to speak of it again. Given their word, and been paid a bit extra to keep it.

Loyalty, she thought with a sniff, was a fine quality in a servant. Mrs Furniss, for all her airs and graces, would do well to remember that.

In the scullery Susan was peeling apples at the sink, and the autumnal sweet-sharp scent of them made Eliza's mouth prickle with saliva. She had no business to be in there really; she was supposed to be sweeping the main staircase but was using the excuse of fetching more damp tea leaves to have a rest. She was so tired she could sleep on a clothesline these days.

'I wonder if Sir Randolph will carry his new wife over the threshold when they arrive,' Susan said with a giggle. 'Can you imagine?' She threw a quick glance over her shoulder, making sure Mr Goddard wasn't nearby before performing an impression of someone staggering under a great weight. 'He'd never manage it.'

'Sir Randolph never carries anything himself,' Eliza remarked. 'He'd get Thomas or Jem to do it.'

This sent Susan into gales of laughter, though Eliza felt a sharp kick of envy at the image of Jem, effortlessly scooping Lady Hyde into his arms and striding into the hall with her. Her mind was playing these tricks a lot lately: sudden flashes of longing or terror or despair that could set her heart at a gallop. Dreams too, so startlingly vivid that she woke up gasping or with tears streaming into her hair.

'In my village it's supposed to be lucky to throw shoes after the bride and groom's carriage when they leave for their honeymoon,' Susan went on, picking up another apple. 'I don't know what you're supposed to do when they're coming back *after* the wedding though . . . I'm sure there must be something.'

Eliza reached over to catch a bit of apple peel as it dropped from Susan's knife. 'Plenty of old shoes in the boot room—you could hurl a few at the happy couple when they get out of their fancy motorcar tomorrow, just to be sure.'

Laughing, Susan twisted away as Eliza went to grab another bit of apple. The curl of peel fell onto the cracked tiles. 'Ooh, look—a letter *C*!' Susan exclaimed, bending to study it. 'It's supposed to show the initial of the person you're going to marry. I don't know anyone whose name begins with *C*, do you?'

'Maybe you'll meet a handsome Charles or Cedric at the wedding dance,' Eliza said. 'Here—let me have a go.'

Susan shaved off another sliver of peel. Closing her eyes, Eliza tossed it gently over her shoulder and turned round to look.

'*S*,' pronounced Susan with a crow of laughter. 'Stanley Twigg!'

'Ugh, I'd rather die an old maid.'

It probably wasn't even possible to form a *W* for Walter out of apple peel, but bending to pick it up, Eliza's heart gave a little skip. It was more like a letter *J* than an *S*. Jem, not Stanley.

It was just a stupid superstition, but as she collected her jar of tea leaves and trailed back up to the hall, she hoped there was something in it. Almost three months had passed since the London visit. Two lots of courses hadn't appeared. There was no point in kidding herself that if she ignored it the problem would go away. She wasn't stupid. She knew that this kind of problem only got bigger.

Too big to hide.

She didn't have much time, and she didn't have many options. In fact, during the nights she lay awake staring at the attic ceiling, she could only think of two; one was illegal and dangerous, the other simply unlikely.

But still, she thought grimly, nothing ventured, nothing gained. *Faint heart never won fair maiden*, as her mother would say; nor would it win a handsome footman and a last chance of respectability before it was too late.

Tonight she was going to make the effort to wash her ruddy hair.

Chapter 19

The day of Sir Randolph and the new Lady Hyde's homecoming dawned damp and misty, with a distinct chill in the air. The previous week had been marked by sudden downpours that stripped the dry leaves from the trees and turned the parched grass green again, but it looked like fate was smiling on the newlyweds and the weather would be dry for the celebrations.

Up early; washed, corseted, and dressed in her plainest black, Kate went out onto the front steps. She checked that the garlands of twined leaves and flowers that Gatley's men had hung between the great pillars of the portico were still in place and the sweep of gravel was raked smooth; and she looked out over the park to where the tents stood, like some medieval ghost village, with the temple emerging from the mist behind.

In the house, Abigail and Eliza were opening shutters as they carried their boxes of dusters and polish from room to room, laying fires, plumping cushions, and sweeping up fallen petals from the flower arrangements Kate had put together the previous afternoon. In the dining room the table had been laid for luncheon with cut crystal, the second baronet's looted Indian silver, and the flower-twined Rockingham service. Miss Addison (or Lady Hyde, as Kate must get used to thinking of her) had kindly said that she and Sir Randolph would have supper on trays, so once luncheon had been served and cleared, the servants would be free to join the festivities outside.

The park was quiet, but in a few hours, people would begin to arrive: curious, cynical, or just keen to take advantage of free ale and food. It was hard to imagine Coldwell's spell of solitude being so completely broken, hard to take in the fact that, by the end of the day, this bubble of shimmering seclusion would have burst. The park would be crowded with strangers, upstairs properly occupied, and the household on duty once more.

And Frederick Henderson would be there.

The thought was like a stain on the pristine morning. Taking in a lungful of crisp air, Kate tried to turn her mind away from it, and all it meant. On the rise of the hill, the trees that sheltered the walled gardens were smudges of rust in the pearly morning, their autumn colours glowing like hot coals through ashes. The grass was silvered with dew; and as she watched, a male pheasant—richly plumed in copper and bronze—broke cover from the woods and flew low, landing clumsily in a tumble of feathers on the slope in front of the house.

These birds were the distant descendants of the ones raised by the last Coldwell keeper, before Kate had arrived. Like the red deer that drifted down from the hills, they had grown plump and complacent, never having known the threat of guns. She watched the pheasant pick himself up and look around, comically imperious and indignant.

He was safe enough for the time being: as far as she knew, no one had yet been found to take the gamekeeper's post. At the start of the month, they had worked hard to clear out the little cottage in the wood and get it ready for a new man, but in a recent letter Mr Fortescue had admitted that no applicants of suitable quality or experience had replied to the advertisement in either *Country Life* or the *Yorkshire Post*. The cottage still stood empty, its sagging brass bed unslept in, its fires unlit.

Turning to go back inside, she stopped. Blinked. Looked round in the direction of the temple and the mist-shrouded woods beyond, where the gamekeeper's cottage was hidden.

And she wondered why she hadn't thought of it before.

'There.' Thomas settled his new livery jacket over his shoulders and smoothed down the facings as he stood in front of the long mirror in the footmen's wardrobe. 'That's me ready. Or as ready as I'll ever be.'

Jem, who'd just finished helping Joseph replenish the kitchen coal store, was using Thomas's soap-scummed water to shave. He looked round, lathering soap onto his jaw with a brush. 'Very nice,' he deadpanned. 'I might ask you to dance later.'

In the second before he realised Jem was joking, terror flickered across Thomas's open face, then he blushed furiously and laughed. 'Two left feet, me. I'll be staying far away from that dance floor they've set up and sticking to the tent where the ale is. We might not be able to go into the pubs round here, but Mr Goddard can hardly ban us from entering a tent in the park, can he? They're kitting it out now, the men from the brewery. You should see it—barrels and barrels of the stuff.'

Jem had seen it, and the men who had brought it. To his surprise, Mullins was amongst them. Jem had assumed, from the lad's reaction the other day, that wild horses couldn't have dragged him within a mile of this place. It was possible that he hadn't been given a choice, but watching him as he stood on the dray and rolled the barrels down, Jem had wondered if there was another reason; if Mullins had decided it was time to confront whatever had happened here. As soon as his duties were finished this afternoon, Jem intended to find out.

There was a perfunctory knock on the door, which immediately opened.

'Eliza—come in, why don't you?' said Thomas, with a sarcasm that was quite bold, for him.

'Mr Goddard wants you,' Eliza said. 'In the dining room. It's about the wines for luncheon—you'd better hurry.'

She stood aside to let Thomas pass, but didn't follow him out of the room. Instead, she came further in and leant against the table, crossing her arms. 'Shouldn't you be ready by now?' she said, looking at Jem's undershirt, and his braces hanging down; watching as he ran the razor along his cheek, cutting a clean path through the soap.

'Mm-hmm.'

'Anything I can do to help?'

He glanced at her. She'd changed into a black afternoon dress and best apron, with lace-edged flounces. She also seemed to have gone to some trouble with her overall appearance, though he couldn't say how exactly (her hair, perhaps?), and the sour mood that had followed her around lately like bad weather seemed to have lifted.

'Don't think so, thanks.'

He expected her to leave then, but she didn't. Nor did she take her eyes off him. There was something unsettling about it, as cloying as the cloud of lavender water that hung around her.

'People are arriving already,' she said. 'In the park—have you seen? It's strange, seeing them wandering about, laying out picnic blankets and what have you. Gatley's sent Bert Oakley up from the garden to stand by the gravel, making sure no one messes it up before Sir Randolph and Lady Hyde get here.' When Jem didn't respond, she said, 'The band's arrived too. They're tuning up. I can't quite believe all this is right on our doorstep, can you? A hot supper and a real dance—usually we're miles away from any goings-on.'

Jem wiped the blade clean and lifted his chin to shave beneath it. Out of the corner of his eye he saw Eliza's teeth catch at her bottom lip as she watched.

'Do you like dancing?' she said, her voice lower.

He shrugged. 'In the right place, with the right music.'

And the right person.

'Will you dance with me this evening?'

The words held a pleading note. He picked up a towel to wipe the soap residue away and was trying to formulate a polite answer that didn't encourage her when a brisk knock at the door saved him the trouble.

'Ah, Jem—' Kate's professional façade always made his blood surge. 'The matches you asked for.'

He kept his face perfectly straight as she put a Bryant & May box on the table. It was their code. Bringing an item, pretending the other had asked for it, meant a message had been left in the Chinese vase on the scullery shelf.

Kate turned to Eliza. 'I can't think of any reason for you to be in here,' she said with the cool hauteur that was so at odds with the private Kate he knew. 'Sir Randolph and Lady Hyde will be arriving soon. Get back to where you should be and don't give me any further cause to ban you from this afternoon's celebrations.'

She left before Eliza could stutter an excuse, in a rustle of silk and a musical shimmer of silver. Eliza rolled her eyes sulkily as she went to the door. 'So, will you? Dance with me?' she prompted.

Jem reached for the shirt hanging on the cupboard door.

'Ask me later.'

Eliza sighed. 'I was hoping you'd ask me.'

After she'd gone, he felt a moment's guilt at his lack of chivalry, but it dissolved even as he registered it. Fastening his shirt studs, he slipped out into the corridor and along to the scullery. The Chinese vase was on the shelf of the battered old dresser, placed unobtrusively amongst the other jugs, vases, and vessels for flower arrangements.

He paused, listening for footsteps and making sure no one was nearby before reaching inside. He should have taken the note to the relative safety of the footmen's wardrobe, but he was too impatient. Turning his back to the door he read the pencilled writing, in capital letters that no one would recognise as hers, and smiled.

GAMEKEEPER'S COTTAGE. 9 O'CLOCK.

The newlyweds made their stately arrival in the motorcar at midday (greeted by the decidedly lacklustre cheers of the gathered locals), and by the time they had been served the five elaborate courses of Mrs Gatley's luncheon, and the dishes had been cleared, the afternoon had advanced into a smoky autumn evening.

Downstairs Kate had supervised the washing and drying of china in the scullery, making sure that the maids weren't too careless in their haste to join the festivities. Once every piece of Rockingham had been returned, clean and intact, to the china cupboard, she took pity on them and told them she would see to the coffee things from the drawing room herself.

She was in no hurry to join the crowds gathering in the park. According to Thomas, they had been arriving steadily all afternoon, but when Kate went up to Lady Hyde's room with a jug of barley water at six o'clock, she was still surprised by the scene that greeted her through the window on the stairs: people milling about between the tents, chatting in groups, sitting on the ground around the temple. She could hear the thin notes of a fiddle drifting like smoke on the breeze.

She was in no hurry to join them at all, but still, her stomach gave a twist of anticipation at the evening ahead.

Lady Hyde had gone up half an hour ago to change. Soon Coldwell's new mistress would accompany her husband as he went out to welcome everyone and get the evening's celebrations officially underway, but when she knocked, Kate found the room in disarray. The rose-pink eiderdown was buried beneath heaps of garments, the floor littered with drifts of tissue paper from the open trunk at the foot of the bed.

'Oh! It's you—' Miss Dunn stiffened. 'I was expecting one of the maids.'

It was the first time Kate had seen her since her return. It had been so busy downstairs that she hadn't thought it strange that Miss Dunn had gone straight up without so much as a greeting, but now she wondered if there was something wrong. As Miss Dunn stood back to let her in, her eyes slid away from Kate's, and a tide of dull colour crept into her cheeks.

'I let them go and get ready.' Kate looked round for somewhere to set down the tray. 'Is everything all right?'

The bathroom door was slightly ajar, and the sound of splashing water could be heard from within. Miss Dunn began moving around, collecting up sheets of tissue and discarded petticoats; anything, it seemed, to avoid meeting Kate's eye.

'Yes, thank you.' Miss Dunn snatched up a pile of gloves from the table by the fireplace. As soon as Kate had set the tray down, she sprang to the door and held it open.

'Do ring if there's—' Kate began, but Miss Dunn spoke at the same time.

'I was wondering if I—'

There was a beat of awkward silence. Miss Dunn's blush deepened, and she clamped her mouth shut.

Kate gave an apologetic laugh as she went out into the corridor. 'Sorry. You were saying?'

'It doesn't matter.' Miss Dunn spoke distractedly through the narrowing gap between door and frame. 'I should—her ladyship will—'

The door shut.

As Kate went back along the corridor she was torn between amusement and annoyance. What was it about the woman that unsettled her? Or, more to the point, what was it about *her* that so obviously unsettled Miss Dunn? She remembered the day Miss Addison had first come to Coldwell: that unblinking stare from inside the carriage, the sense Kate had of being watched—

The thought stalled as a shadow detached itself from one of the doorways along the passage. Jem stepped forward, looking swiftly left and right, then held out his hand with a wicked smile.

Her fingers twined with his and she bit her cheeks to stifle laughter. The room he pulled her into was one of the smaller bedrooms, which hadn't been used for years. The shutters were half-closed, the furniture draped in dust sheets, and they fell against the faded roses on the wall, their mouths coming together.

'You got my note?'

'Mm-hmm . . .' he murmured against her lips. 'The gamekeeper's cottage. You're not just a *very* pretty face, Mrs Furniss . . .'

He smelled of lime shaving soap and tasted of Sir Randolph's brandy. 'You remember where the key is, if you get there first?' She flexed her neck as his mouth moved down, exposing her throat to his kisses. 'On the ledge in the porch . . .'

'I remember . . .'

The tip of his tongue found her earlobe. Shivers of bliss ran down her neck, echoing through her whole body as his teeth gently grazed the tender flesh. She moaned softly. 'Nine o'clock seems a very long time away . . .'

'Three hours . . .' The words were a whispered exhalation, and his breath caressed her ear, quickening the shivers into something more urgent. Her back was pressed against the wall and she could feel the beat of his heart, strong and quick beneath her palm as her hands moved up the facings of his livery jacket. Her hips rose up to his. Three hours might as well have been three centuries.

'I'm not sure I can wait . . .'

His mouth returned to hers. The only sound was the rasp and sigh of their breath, the rustle of her silk skirts and the silvery chime of her chatelaine. She felt his hand move down, and, without letting his lips leave hers, he unclipped the clasp so the chain slipped from her waist into his hand.

'Are you . . . *undressing* me, Jem Arden?'

'Well . . . I *was* making sure no one heard this . . . It's quite a distinctive sound.' He turned and put the fistful of silver carefully on top of the shrouded piece of furniture beside them. 'But now you've put the idea in my head . . .'

His hands slipped over her hips, cupping the curve of her bottom.

'We can't!' she squeaked.

'Maybe not undress . . . but that won't be necessary.'

In one swift movement he hitched her up so her legs were round his waist, pressing his mouth to hers to capture her little cry of surprise. She hooked her arms around his neck as he carried her to the bed, pushing back the dusty velvet hangings and laying her on its bare mattress. Before she could muster a token protest (she wasn't sure she was capable) his hand had found the hem of her skirt and was moving up her leg, skimming over the thin lawn of her drawers, his fingers pausing at the top of her stockings, stroking the place where black lisle met bare flesh.

He lifted his head to look at her, his languid smile fading into something more intense. He was so beautiful. In the velvet gloom of the old bed there was just enough light for her to make out the deep shadows beneath his cheekbones, the molten darkness of his eyes. She read the unspoken question in them and knew he was giving her the chance to tell him to stop.

She opened her mouth, but his thumb was tracing circles on her thigh, dissolving all sense of duty and decency. All that came out was a ragged breath, a soft whimper.

She was weak with longing, liquid with want.

Unlocked. Undone.

His fingers slid upwards, expert and gentle. His movements were delicate and unhurried, in sharp contrast to the savage waves of sensation that were building inside her, and the swiftness with which they overwhelmed her. He knew just when to gather her against him with his free hand and hold her as the storm gathered and broke, so she could gasp her shivering ecstasy into his chest.

For several long moments he cradled her against him, rocking her as her breathing steadied. When she could form words, she raised her head to look at him.

'My God, Jem—' It was a croak. 'How do you—where did you learn—?'

'Shh . . .'

He kissed her into silence again. They were both laughing softly, incredulous at their own audacity. They had been bold before, in snatching moments and taking risks, but not like this. She felt shaken, exhilarated, disorientated. Frightened by the speed with which she had abandoned herself and the ease with which he could unravel her. Already he was getting up, straightening his clothing, preparing to return to respectability.

'You're going?'

'I have to.' He was whispering, but still she caught the rueful note. 'You know that.'

Of course she did. Briefly she had slipped outside of reality, but it was still there waiting for her. The knowledge that every second was stolen, and every passing minute increased the danger of discovery. Time was a luxury reserved for those who inhabited the upstairs rooms, not those who crept into them illicitly.

'It's not for long.' His hair was ruffled from her fingers. He smoothed it down, swooping to press a kiss on her forehead, hovering his mouth next to her ear as he said, 'We can do it again later. And I'll undress you slowly, bit by beautiful bit, with all the care you deserve.'

With one last lingering kiss he was gone, closing the door softly behind him, leaving her washed up on the retreating tide of sensation, broken open and hollowed out.

It took great effort to get up. Her legs felt too weak to carry her along the empty corridor and down the stairs. Before she left, she twitched aside a dust sheet to check her reflection in the looking glass, leaning in to scrutinise her face through the last of the light, reassuring herself that she might still pass as Coldwell's capable housekeeper.

Jem would have gone down the back stairs, so she took the main staircase. Halfway down her heart gave a stutter of dismay as Frederick Henderson appeared from the library corridor. As he crossed the hallway he looked up, and his eyes moved down her body, coming to a halt at her waist. His brows rose a fraction.

'Everything all right, Mrs Furniss?'

With a jolt of horror, she remembered her chatelaine, lying where Jem had left it in the shuttered bedroom.

To admit error or show any sign of weakness would be a mistake. She would have to return for it later. She forced herself to keep going, down the stairs towards him.

'Perfectly, thank you, Mr Henderson. I hope you enjoy the evening.'

She was satisfied with how assured she sounded, though without her chatelaine she felt oddly undressed. Or maybe it was the way he was looking at her that made her feel that way. Exposed.

'Oh, I intend to, Mrs Furniss.' His eyes followed her as she passed and turned towards the baize door to the basement. 'I intend to enjoy it very much indeed.'

Chapter 20

The sky had darkened into bruised twilight, but strings of lights, powered by a throbbing generator, had been hung between the tents and around the wooden platform that had been set up for dancing. They shone on the faces of the couples circling the rough boards—flushed with drink, smiling, or glassy-eyed—and those clustered at its edges, tapping their feet and swaying as they watched.

Jem stood outside the ale tent with a half-empty pewter mug, and impatiently searched the crowd of drinkers and dancers. The two beers he'd drunk already had done nothing to calm the restless pulse inside him or slow the whirr of his thoughts, which circled between Mullins and Kate. His senses were on high alert, ears straining to hear the stable yard clock above the music.

'What time is it, do you think?'

'About ten minutes later than last time you asked.' Thomas drained his tankard of ale. 'And time for another of these. Drink up, I'll get more, before they run out.'

'It's all right, I'll go.'

He didn't want more beer, and Thomas certainly didn't need it, but it was an excuse to have another scout round for Mullins. He'd looked earlier, but hadn't been able to find him in any of the tents where beef stew was be-ing dished out from great vats by the staff of the Bull's Head, nor amongst the crowd around the wooden dance floor. It was past eight o'clock. Time was running out.

There was no sign of Kate either. He was torn between willing the time to fly by so he could be with her, and wanting to stop the clock and search for Mullins. Frustration sluiced through him as he ducked beneath a flap of canvas to join the crush around the beer table. He considered asking the man in the grimy neckerchief who served him if he knew of Mullins or his whereabouts, but the tent was noisy and if he shouted to be heard he risked drawing unwelcome attention. He carried the brimming tankards back to where Thomas stood, swaying out of time to the music.

'Did the lasses find you?' The three pints had gone to Thomas's head and his words were beginning to run into each other. 'They were here a minute ago—Eliza's looking for you. Said you promised her a dance.' He nudged Jem's arm, splashing ale onto his sleeve. 'She likes you, you know.'

Jem didn't answer. Through the slow-circling carousel of dancers he'd caught a glimpse of Kate. Mullins dissolved from his thoughts.

'Look—there she is,' Thomas grunted, then turned to Jem, blinking stupidly. 'Ha—you like her too! You do, I can tell!'

Jem hadn't even noticed Eliza. It was Kate his eyes were fixed on as she wove her way through the crowd. Her eyes melted into his, making heat build in the pit of his stomach as she approached.

She was with Miss Addison's maid, who fluttered nervily at her elbow, her head darting every which way. They were a few feet away when Thomas noticed them.

'Watch it, there's Mrs Furniss,' he remarked, loudly. 'And what's 'er name—'

The band were playing a lively folk tune and the dancers' feet thudded on the wooden boards, but even above the noise it was clear that they'd heard him. 'Miss Dunn,' Jem said, smoothing over Thomas's oafishness as they reached them. 'Mrs Furniss. Are you enjoying the evening?'

'We've only just come out,' Kate said. The dark green dress she was wearing was less formal, a little more bohemian than her housekeeper's uniform, and her hair was loosely pinned, with soft curls framing her face.

'It took longer than I thought, tidying up, though Miss Dunn very kindly offered to help.'

Her eyes telegraphed a message: exasperation and an appeal for assistance. Jem smothered a smile. 'Could I perhaps get you both a drink?'

'*No, thank you,*' Miss Dunn said vehemently, pressing a hand to her chest where her temperance ribbon was pinned. 'Lady Hyde assured me there would be a tent where tea would be served? Perhaps, Mrs Furniss, you and I might—'

Jem became aware of Eliza and Abigail approaching, drawn by Thomas's clumsy waving. He could see the direction the evening was in danger of taking; him stuck in a four with the other servants, Kate condemned to hours of tea and polite conversation with Miss Dunn. As the tune ended and the dancing couples fell apart, hot and exhilarated, he seized his chance and extended his hand to Miss Dunn.

'Plenty of time for tea later,' he said. 'For now, might I possibly have the pleasure?'

'Oh no, I—'

'Oh, you must!' Kate had clearly read his mind and understood the exit route he was preparing. 'Please, don't feel you have to stay and keep me company. In fact, I might go and . . .'

Already backing away, she trailed off vaguely, but Jem caught the gleam of her eyes in the second before her lashes swept down. His stomach tightened with anticipation and want; just as well he'd changed out of his flat-fronted livery breeches, he thought, as Miss Dunn put a hand in the crook of his arm and reluctantly allowed him to lead her to the dance floor.

She assumed it was some sort of private joke; Coldwell's handsome footman asking the new mistress's plain maid to dance, the housekeeper insisting she accept. If not jest, then charity. They thought they were doing her a kindness, assuming she would be grateful, when really she would far rather be left alone.

There was plenty to be getting on with in the house, unpacking the trunks of garments Lady Hyde (it still felt strange to think of her as that) had gone mad ordering for her trousseau. Miss Dunn had only come out because she wanted to speak to Mrs Furniss. *Needed* to. Anguish made her stomach gripe as the footman steered her through the circling couples. She held herself stiffly, straining to see past the people gathered at the edge of the dance floor and beyond the strings of lights, trying to keep track of her.

But it was impossible. The dusk had deepened, blotting out anything outside the golden lamp glow, and the housekeeper's slim figure was quickly swallowed up by the crowd. The strangers' faces around the platform blurred as the steps of the dance spun her round, but she picked out the other Coldwell servants (the stillroom girl scowling as she followed their progress). Miss Dunn felt giddy, her head still thick and throbbing, and was almost glad of the footman's light hand on her back, supporting her.

'How was the wedding?'

If he was playing a joke on her, he didn't seem to be finding it very amusing. His expression was grave, his tone as respectful as if he were addressing Lady Hyde herself.

Sarah Dunn bit her lip, not knowing how to answer. Her experience of nuptials was limited, but it had been a strained and cynical affair by anyone's standards. Sir Randolph had been firm about keeping the celebrations small and private, depriving Miss Addison of the support of her Shropshire friends, yet it was amazing how many of his acquaintances just happened to be passing through the Savoy Grill that afternoon, all keen to partake of a celebratory drink with the bridegroom. No wonder he had insisted on holding the wedding in London rather than out here at Coldwell.

'It went well enough,' she said tersely. 'That said, it would have been nice for my lady to have had more say in the arrangements and more of her own people present.'

'She had you there. I'm sure that was enough.'

He meant to be kind, not twist the knife of her guilt—how could he know that she had abandoned her mistress and retired to bed halfway through the afternoon? She pressed her lips together and turned her head away, willing herself not to cry.

The need to find Mrs Furniss swelled on a tide of panicky shame. For the hundredth time she cursed herself for her earlier cowardice in not asking the housekeeper if they might talk. She had hoped that an opportunity might present itself naturally, but Mrs Furniss seemed distracted and not her usual professional self: she had ignored all Miss Dunn's hints about the unfortunate events at the wedding. Blinking back tears, she peered past the twirling couples, through the milling crowd. The music went on and on, the scrape of the violin sawing on her raw nerves, until her gaze suddenly snagged on a figure standing in the mouth of the beer tent.

Frederick Henderson's eyes met hers. Before she could look away, he smirked and raised his tankard to her in a sort of mocking salute.

Revulsion rose in her throat. Wrenching her hand from the footman's she pulled away, cannoning into the couple behind them and almost causing a pileup.

'Miss Dunn? Are you all right?'

'I think I'll go back to the house now.'

'Of course.'

At the edge of the wooden platform, the blonde stillroom girl was slipping the shawl from her shoulders and handing it to the other maid, readying herself to take Miss Dunn's place in the footman's arms. Even so, he offered to walk her back to the house. She should say no and leave him free to enjoy the rest of his evening, but just knowing *that man* was nearby made her feel shaky and ill at ease. Swallowing her pride, she gave a quick nod.

'That would be kind, if you don't mind.'

'Not at all.'

She had to admit, he was very professional. He even made it sound like he meant it.

After all these years, Kate thought that she was familiar with the Coldwell parkland, but everything looked different in the dark.

Earlier a harvest moon had hung low in the sky, its creamy light as bright as the lantern in the stable yard, but it had been muffled by cloud as it rose, and now there was nothing to be seen of it except a silvery marbling across the heavens. The way through the woods to the gamekeeper's cottage seemed farther at night, but at last she made out the outline of the chimney, the glimmer of the white-painted porch, and her breath came a little more easily.

She'd spent the day trying to temper her anticipation, but what had happened earlier had tipped anticipation over into need: uncomfortable, urgent, impossible to ignore. When Miss Dunn had come to the housekeeper's parlour as Kate was getting ready, it was all she could do to be civil. She was in no mood to encourage the woman's clumsy attempts at conversation.

For a woman who'd barely spoken two words previously, Miss Dunn suddenly seemed very keen to talk, and had kept up a disjointed monologue as they went out to join the festivities. Kate had barely listened. She was aware of Miss Dunn darting odd, furtive glances at her as they walked, as if there was something she wanted to get off her chest. Whatever it was—if there was some issue with Lady Hyde's new rooms or a grievance about household management—it could wait until tomorrow.

Tonight belonged to her and Jem.

There was a smell of leaf mould and damp stone by the squat little cottage. As she felt for the key, the back of her neck prickled with the sensation of being watched, but she shrugged it off and refused to give in to the urge to look behind her.

The door was warped and scraped loudly on the tiled floor as she pushed it open. Despite the effort they'd made to scrub and freshen the place, the air inside the low-ceilinged kitchen smelled mossy and stale. The doubt that had stalked her since she'd left the lights and music and dancing edged closer, curling its tendrils around her excitement. On stiff legs she went across to the sink and leaned over to tug the curtain (stitched by her own hand, from a piece of worn, mangled cloth) across the window. As she did, she caught a movement outside.

Relief coursed through her, warm and reviving, like brandy. She'd seen Eliza, taut with eagerness at the edge of the dance floor, and feared that it might be a long time before Jem could safely make his escape, so the scrape of the door made her heart soar and her stomach twist with anticipation. She turned towards it, her smile already spreading as a shadow slipped in.

'Thank God you're here.'

'Oi! *Oi*—you!'

Jem heard the shout from behind him but kept walking with his head down. He had tried to avoid the places where the crowds were thickest and the lights brightest and skirted around the back of the tents, but the evening was taking on a nightmarish quality—like one of those dreams when you try to run and can't move. The stable clock had struck nine as he'd left Miss Dunn at the back door. He was late already—he couldn't spare the time to give someone a light or directions to the latrines.

'Oi—*wait!*'

This time the voice was more insistent. In spite of himself, he looked round and saw a figure lurching towards him. In the dark, with the strings of lights behind casting a bright aura that left the man's face shadowed, it took a moment to recognise him.

'I've been looking for you,' Mullins slurred.

———✂———

June 30th

Kate, I think this is the last chance I'll get to write. Today we have had kit inspection and this evening we have been visited by the chaplain and the general (both looking very smart and very clean, unlike us). The attack is set for tomorrow morning at half past seven. The general told us that we should be proud to play a part in the decisive battle of our time, one that could bring this war to its end. He assures us that the bombardment has obliterated enemy defences and our advance has every chance of being unchallenged. I hope to God he's right.

We'll be moving into position soon, so I don't have long left. I still need to explain what happened that night, at the wedding dance. I tried to meet you—I was on my way to the gamekeeper's cottage when I was stopped by a lad who had worked at Coldwell years before, who had been there when Jack was. I'd got his name from the tigers' uniform in the footmen's wardrobe and tracked him down to the brewery in Hatherford. He wouldn't tell me anything at first, but he sought me out that night when he was steaming drunk. He was ready to talk then, and it all came spilling out.

I'd waited so long to find out what happened to Jack. I'd always blamed myself for letting him down, you see. I just wanted the truth, but I didn't realise that getting it would mean letting you down too.

More than I could have imagined.

Chapter 21

'Well, well . . . what have we here?'

Frederick Henderson's shoes clicked on the stone flags as he walked slowly across to the table. He removed his hat, as if he were paying an ordinary social call. As if it wasn't dark, and they weren't alone in an empty cottage in the woods.

'Mr Henderson . . . What are you doing here?'

Dread solidified in Kate's throat, making her voice hoarse. As soon as the choked words were out, she regretted them, because she knew exactly what he was going to say in reply.

'Funny. I was going to ask you the very same thing.'

'I overheard people talking about this place . . . about whether it was empty. I didn't . . . I didn't like the sound of it. I thought I should come and make sure that the door was locked.'

The clouds must have parted enough for the moon to reappear because suddenly she could see his face and read the amusement there. He knew she was lying and was deciding how far to play along with her.

'As always, Mrs Furniss, your dedication to duty is . . . *exemplary*.' He trailed a finger over the scarred surface of the table. 'If a little unwise. You should have sent someone else to check, or at least to accompany you. And brought a lantern. A place like this—dark and isolated—isn't safe for a respectable woman alone at night, when any of the local drunks might be wandering about. What were you *thinking*?'

At some point his tone had changed, losing its silky, cajoling note and turning flinty. Her whole body felt hot and light, like a paper lantern. Fear glowed inside her. For a second everything was still and suspended, and the air seemed to quiver with malice. She was still standing by the low stone sink, but she swivelled her eyes to the door, mentally calculating the distance.

A mistake.

He saw, and read her intention. When she moved, he was ready to dart in front of her, blocking her way.

'I swore I'd never say anything. They made me promise. And I never did—all these years. I put it out of my head until you came poking around . . . digging it all up again.'

Jem had steered Mullins round the back of the ale tent, where he dropped to the ground amongst piled-up crates of empty lemonade bottles, like a puppet with cut strings. After a few moments of floundering to get his balance, he settled with his head in his hands, elbows resting on his knees.

Jem couldn't see his face. Mullins had reached the pitch of drunkenness when logic was jumbled and speech punctuated by long spells of silence, so it was difficult to tell if he'd fallen asleep. Jem shoved his hands in his pockets and prayed for patience, trying to drown the urge to take hold of him and shake the truth out.

'It was a game. A laugh.' The words came grudgingly. 'That's how it started. Hyde didn't live here all the time in them days. He worked in India, but he'd come back for a few months and invited his friends up here. House was fuller than it had been in years. They had a shoot, but it wasn't up to much—the old keeper had let the bird stocks go down. It showed him up, that did . . . Made him look a fool in front of his fancy mates. I reckon he felt he had to make up for it. Impress them.'

'That sounds like Hyde,' Jem muttered. His reputation in London had been as a bragger and a show-off. Amongst other things.

'They had dinner in the tower that night. The temple, they called it. I don't know whose idea it was, but it had never happened before while I'd been there. Foreign food it was, like they have in India. Made the inside of your mouth burn something shocking. Sir Henry didn't join them. He went to bed and left them to it, and they didn't want old Goddard hanging about, but the footmen—Wilf Williams and what's-'is-name, the other one—stayed downstairs in the tower. Wilf kept having to come back for more wine, more port, more brandy and whisky—Goddard looked like he was going to have a turn at all the booze they were going through.'

Mullins had hit his stride now, his initial reluctance disappearing as the events of that night caught him in their current. 'Wilf kept us informed about what they were getting up to—gambling games and the like. We thought the whole thing was a laugh. There were plenty of bottles around for us to help ourselves to on the sly, and that other lad—Viscount Frensham's tiger—he was all right. A bit quiet, but we hit it off. The older footmen always treated me like a dog. It was good to have someone the same age to joke around with . . .'

He trailed off. On the other side of the tent, the country dance tune the band were playing was accompanied by stamping feet and whoops of merriment. Jem had to lean in closer to hear Mullins speak. Close enough to smell ale and sweat and bad teeth.

'It was a laugh.' Defensiveness bristled in his tone. 'It felt like no one was in charge anymore . . . like there were no rules. We were having a fine time, drinking the dregs in all the bottles, telling ghost stories; then Wilf comes back and says they want us to go over there—me and the other lad. Some game they want to play.'

In spite of the warmth of the evening, Jem realised he was shivering.

'I didn't think nothing of it. I'd sat up keeping score for their billiards and that plenty times, and there's always the chance for a bob or two from the toffs when they're pissed.' He squinted at Jem with a frown. 'I was a bit pissed myself, if I'm honest . . . so we went up there, me and him. Up to the room at the top of the tower.'

His head dropped heavily, his stubby fingers sliding into his hair to support it.

'I'd never been up there before. There were these carvings all around the walls and the candles made them look like they were moving. We'd been telling the story of the Indian lad—Samuel—about how his ghost haunts the woods, and *there's* his portrait, right there above the fireplace. And they've got his clothes—his actual bloody *tunic* and the silk thing what wrapped around his head and his britches and what have you—and they wanted us to put them on.'

There was a long pause. Jem clamped his jaw shut and looked across at the tower, silhouetted against the blue dark. He felt light-headed, slightly sick. After all these years he was about to find out what had happened to his brother, but for the first time it struck him that he might be better off not knowing. He felt a sudden compulsion to leave Mullins, alone with his ghosts and demons and guilt. To leave the past where it belonged and go to Kate. The future, if only he could find a way—

'It wasn't funny no more.' Mullins's voice was thick with emotion. 'There was something wild about them—like you wouldn't expect of the gentry. Savages, they were. None of them things was ever going to fit me, but they got the other lad and were pulling his jacket off, then his shirt, winding this silk about his head, and Hyde was going on about his stupid ancestor. There was this silver hunting horn on the wall and Hyde took it down and was blowing it. They made Frensham's lad stand up on the table in front of the painting and they were all cheering and shouting . . . baying like animals—'

He broke off with a wet, snivelling sound and dragged his arm across his face.

'I don't know how it happened. I don't remember. Someone made a joke about the tiger hunter, and said they didn't need to go to India when they had their own tigers to hunt. It was . . . out of control. One minute we were up there, in the temple, the next they were shoving us down the stairs, starting to count. I can still hear their voices, all of them together, counting, before they came after us. Frensham's lad tried to follow me, but I knew he'd be easier to spot in that stupid bloody get-up. I told him to bugger off and make his own way—every man for himself.'

Jesus.

'I went back to the house. I'm not ashamed to admit it.' Mullins's tone was one of aggressive defiance, at odds with the claim. 'I hid in the privy for a bit and I could hear that bloody horn . . . I was going to go back and give myself up, I was, but . . . I was feeling proper rough by then. I took myself off to the silver cupboard. That was where I slept.'

'What happened to Jack?' Somehow Jem was on his feet, though he hadn't been aware of moving. He looked down at Mullins, slumped amongst the crates. When he didn't answer, Jem nudged him with his boot. '*What happened?* Did you see him again?'

'I don't know what happened, I swear! I went out like a light, slept in my boots, and woke up with a splitting head, a good bit later than I should have. There was no sign of him and damned if I was going to do all the coal myself, so I went looking, up to the nursery corridor where the visiting servants kipped. His clothes were there—the ones he'd arrived in. I was going to tell Goddard he hadn't come back, but he wasn't up. The place was still in a state from the night before, but Hyde's valet was buzzing around.'

'Henderson?'

'*Bastard.*' Mullins turned his head to spit viciously onto the grass. 'He didn't seem that bothered then, but later he came to find me. Twisted my arm right up behind my back and told me that I wasn't to breathe a word about no tiger hunt. All that had happened was the boy had been dressed up to wait on the dinner. He said that if I told a soul, my family would be turfed off their farm. He said if anything ever came out, they'd know it was me who'd blabbed, and my pa would be finished. Fat lot of good it did them—everyone round here knows what the Hydes are like, any road—'

He made an attempt to stand, fuelled by rage but sabotaged by drink. Collapsing back into the crates, his voice was raw. 'There's something rotten about this place. Always has been. That bastard nearly broke my arm, and then he tossed a sovereign on the floor, *to buy my silence.*'

Jem was pacing in front of where Mullins sat. It was beginning to dawn on him that the answer he had come so far to find was no answer at all and he had only stumbled upon another question.

'So that's it—he'd just *vanished*?'

'I don't know, all right?' Gripping the crates, Mullins made another attempt to get to his feet. 'I've told you everything I know and that's a lot more than I should have said. I'm sick of keeping their secrets.' Upright, he took a few staggering paces towards Jem and grabbed the front of his shirt. 'Ask that fucking bastard Henderson if you want to know what happened. Or Hyde himself. I've told you all I know—now leave me alone.'

He gave Jem's chest a shove and let go, swearing as he stumbled backwards. And then he swung round and lurched away, leaving Jem standing alone in the dark, blood pounding, fists clenched against an enemy that somehow managed to stay ahead of him, always beyond his reach.

———————⬚⬚⬚———————

'Now, now, my dear Mrs Furniss, there's no need to be so unfriendly. Since the two of us find ourselves here together, there's no need to hurry back.'

Kate heard the click and rasp of a lighter flint, and Henderson held the small flame aloft. 'I must say, you've got this place looking better. One can't make a silk purse out of a sow's ear, but it's cleaned up nicely. I daresay it could be quite homely with a fire in the grate and some lamps lit. For an unmarried woman, it seems you have a knack for creating a home.'

'I must be getting back.'

Henderson went on, as if she hadn't spoken. 'Marriage has been on my mind rather a lot of late, understandably. A wedding gives one pause for thought, doesn't it? Were you never tempted to take the path of matrimony, Mrs Furniss? A woman with your . . . *advantages* must have had plenty of offers.'

'I'm perfectly satisfied with my life as it is, thank you, Mr Henderson.'

'I can understand that. You have your independence—the Pankhurst woman would applaud you. But the life of a housekeeper is essentially solitary, is it not? This is the closest you'll get'—he swung the wavering flame around—'to making a home. The warmth of the hearth and the blessing of children . . . The companionship of marriage. You must once have hoped for those things?'

A fleeting vision of the cottage she had imagined flashed into her mind, and she shoved it away. She would not allow Henderson to insinuate himself into her dream and sully it.

'If you'll excuse me—'

'The thing is, I sense that you're a woman who needs that sort of companionship, Mrs Furniss. The . . . *physical* sort, if you get my meaning.' His voice thickened. 'You and I—'

'I need to go.'

She forced her legs to carry her towards the door, groping for her chatelaine and clutching helplessly at the empty folds of her skirt.

'Not yet.' His hand shot out, his fingers closing around her arm. 'You haven't shown me upstairs yet.'

'Mr Henderson, *please*—'

She heard the rising panic in her voice in the moment before his body slammed against hers, knocking the breath from her, pushing her back against the door. He wasn't tall, but he was solid, strong. Though she twisted and thrashed she couldn't shift him, and the scuffle of feet was loud in the small room, his hot breath gusting across her face.

'You can pretend you don't want it,' he rasped, close to her ear, 'but I know you do. I can smell it on you. This is what you came here for, isn't it?'

His knee drove into her crotch, forcing her legs apart. His arm was across her neck. And then suddenly there was a juddering blow and they were knocked sideways. It took her a moment to realise that someone had rammed the door open, catapulting them away from it.

Henderson's laugh was cruel and jagged. 'Well, look who's here. The village idiot. What do you want, boy?'

The moon had cast off its veils of cloud. Davy Wells was clearly visible as he stood by the table, shoulders hunched, face screwed up so that he looked like he might be about to cry. He was carrying a stick—one of the sturdy branches he collected on his wanderings through the woods and stripped of its bark, honing it to a sort of staff. Breathing hard, he raised it, preparing to strike.

Henderson swung round to face him properly, smoothing his hair and straightening his clothing. Kate stumbled past him, moving to the other side of the room with the table between them.

'I know you're not very bright,' Henderson growled through clenched teeth, all traces of laughter gone. 'But even I didn't think you were this stupid.'

Davy's chest was rising and falling quickly, the stick still held aloft. His face was a mask of anguish and rage.

'It's all right, Davy.' Kate straightened her dress and cleared her aching throat. 'Good boy—you can put the stick down. Mr Henderson was just leaving.'

Slowly, his eyes darting between Kate and Henderson, Davy lowered his arm, though his fingers remained tightly clenched around the stick. His whole body bristled, like an animal facing a predator.

'*Are* you a good boy, Davy?' Henderson queried softly. 'Or are you a liability, to Coldwell and to your poor old mother? Where will she go, I wonder, when she loses the home that she's been living in all these years on Sir Randolph's generosity? So hard for a widow to manage . . . especially with an idiot son. Luckily there are places . . . *institutions* . . . that take people like you, Davy. That lock them up, so their violent rages aren't a danger to the rest of us.'

'Leave him alone!'

A flare of protective fury fizzed through Kate's body. Davy shrank back and hissed in a breath as Henderson took a step towards him, but he made no move to touch him.

'Let's just check, shall we? Open your mouth,' he said softly. 'Say *ahh* . . .'

It was how a doctor might speak to a child. Kate was confused, but Davy did as he was told, his eyes wide with terror.

'Still there, I see,' Henderson murmured. 'For now.'

He clapped Davy on the shoulder, almost avuncular, and without so much as a glance at Kate, slipped out into the dark.

Jem walked quickly, stumbling on the uneven ground, his head full of the rasp of his own breath and the swarm-like buzz of his thoughts.

Plunging into the woods, he didn't look behind him, to where the windows of Coldwell Hall glittered gold in the dusk. But in his mind a different version of himself turned round and went back, slipping along the garden corridor to the gun room, where Randolph Hyde kept the collection of weapons essential to any country gentleman for the slaughter of wildlife, selecting the first that came to hand.

No one would remark on the sound of a gunshot once the fireworks started. And with the park full of so many people, no one would think to point the finger at Jem. How could they? Doing so would mean acknowledging what had happened to Jack. What Hyde had done.

They had their own tigers to hunt.

He stopped walking and looked around in bewilderment, realising he had lost his bearings. The darkness was thicker here, the sounds of the celebrations more distant. Above his head the trees stretched towards the sky, blotting out the stars. He swung round, breath burning in his chest, trying to orientate himself. What time was it? Panic pumped through him at the thought of Kate, waiting for him in the gamekeeper's cottage. It was closely followed by guilt and a brutal sideswipe of longing that made his knees buckle. Longing to hold her and breathe her in and let the goodness of her drive away the rottenness of everything else.

Pushing himself forward, he was shocked to feel a stinging sensation at the back of his eyes, which he didn't immediately recognise as tears.

She was all he cared about now. She was the only one who was on his side, who saw him for who he was. And still he had kept a part of himself hidden from her.

If he told her, would she understand? Would she despise him?

She had been brave enough to lower her guard and confide in him. She had trusted him enough to share her secret.

Now it was his turn.

In her room Kate locked the door and poured boiling water into the bowl on her washstand. She pulled off her stockings with shaking hands and struggled out of her dress with a shudder of disgust. She would never wear any of those items again.

She had maintained a veneer of calm as she had walked back with Davy, instinctively seeking to minimise what they had just experienced by chattering distractedly about stupid, inconsequential things. As if remarking on the moon, or the strains of a country jig drifting over the trees, could make either of them forget the dark cottage and what had happened there.

And what would have happened next, if Davy hadn't appeared.

It wasn't so easy to avoid thinking about it now that she was alone, or about where Jem had got to and why he hadn't come. In a far corner of her mind there lodged a painful shard of worry that Henderson had somehow prevented him, but he would have been keen to taunt her with that, if it had been true. Instead, her thoughts cycled through other possibilities. That he hadn't been able to shake off the others, and had eventually given up trying. That he'd got drunk and lost track of time, or been swept up in the dancing and found he'd rather stay at the party, rationalising that he had satisfied her once already and would apologise later. She pictured him circling the floor with one of the pretty village girls, their eyes fixed intently on each other in the glow of the lights. In the mirror above the washstand her own image swam in the darkness—hollow-eyed and haggard.

The water was so hot it made her wince. She set her jaw hard and rubbed the soap onto a flannel, concentrating on the rose scent of it, splashing water onto her body and scrubbing her skin.

Still she could smell it. Hair oil. Meat. Sweat.

It could have been worse, she told herself. She had been lucky that Davy was there.

But the thought brought her no comfort.

As she pulled on her nightdress, she heard a tentative knock on the parlour door. She froze, torn between hope and dread, her head signalling a warning that it might be Henderson, wanting to smooth things over or finish what he'd started, her heart spiralling with yearning for Jem.

'Who is it?'

She closed her eyes. The answer came quietly, in a voice she hadn't expected.

'It's me, Sarah Dunn ...'

An expectant silence spooled from the words as Kate's hope was snuffed out. Which was exactly what she needed to do to Miss Dunn's sudden odd need to seek her company. Kate opened the door a crack. The corridor outside was lit only by moonlight and the dim glow of the lamp at the far end by the basement stairs, so the figure of Lady Hyde's maid merged with the shadows. Only the white ribbon pinned to her dress stood out in the gloom.

'Was there something you wanted, Miss Dunn? Only I'm rather tired ...'

In the silvered dark she saw the gleam of Miss Dunn's eyes as she took in Kate's loosened hair, her nightdress.

'Forgive me. It—it can wait. Sorry to have disturbed you.'

Kate was vaguely aware of guilt, but it was a pale, colourless emotion compared to the lurid flashes going off inside her head. Insipid, like Miss Dunn. Easily pushed aside.

She closed the door and turned the key in the lock. Then, as an afterthought, she dragged the velvet armchair across the room and pushed it hard against the door.

———⚬⚬⚬———

I came to your room that night.

I hoped that you would have left the door unlocked, as you so often did. When it wasn't, I assumed you must be angry that I hadn't come to the cottage. I didn't blame you. I was angry with myself for having been so single-minded that I'd left you waiting there, as if you didn't matter, or as if I didn't care. I had allowed myself to be so focused on getting revenge for my brother's wasted life that I didn't notice I was throwing my own away.

I'd hoped I could make it up to you, but when I saw you the next day, I realised that was impossible. You never said exactly what happened in the game-keeper's cottage, but you didn't have to. I knew from the outset that you were too good for me, but I thought I could make myself worthy of you. All I did was drag you down. I compromised you, in every way.

Sorry isn't adequate, but I need to say it anyway. I don't have any right to comfort myself that you would forgive me—hell, I don't even have any hope that you'll read this—but dawn is only a few hours away and I want to confront my own conscience. I lost my faith a long time ago, but I have some superstitious need to confess my sins before meeting my maker, as I am very likely to do.

God knows, there are enough of them. I'm an ex-felon, after all. I wasn't guilty of the crime they laid on me, but I have plenty more charges to my name—deception, dishonesty, breaking and entering, failing those I love. All of them pale into insignificance compared to what I did to you.

It's not God's forgiveness I want, Kate, it's your understanding.

I loved you, but I betrayed you. I want you to at least know why.

———⚬⚬⚬———

Date unknown
Somewhere in France

'I say—you, soldier! Stop, man!'

The voice seems to come from a great distance away and it penetrates the strange ringing in his ears. Jem turns. The figure approaching rapidly from behind him on the road is nothing more than a dark shadow against the glare of the sun. It has an aura of gold around it.

'What on earth are you doing, man? Where's your tunic?'

Jem looks down and feels a stutter of surprise. His shirt is stained with blood—properly soaked—though he appears to be standing upright and he has a feeling he's been walking for a while.

'I don't know. Sir.'

'What's your name? What regiment are you with?'

Jem wants to answer. He can't quite bring the figure into focus enough to see how many stripes he has on his shoulder, but you can tell from his tone he's an officer, and if you ignore an officer, you get put on a charge. He opens his mouth, but the pain in his head makes him wince and the ground is suddenly tilting and the man (who is probably an officer) is getting farther away, the aura of gold around him becoming dazzling, too bright to look at.

It is a relief to realise he is lying down, though his mouth is full of dust.

He closes his eyes.

———⊶⊷———

July 7th
Brighton

As the days go by the tone of the reports in the newspapers grows less triumphant, more sombre. After almost a week, the decisive success that seemed so certain on the first day has failed to materialise, though the convoys of wounded arrive with dreadful regularity at the station and guns go on and on, their muted boom rolling across the ocean, an incongruous backdrop to the golden July weather.

She is more used to the wounded now. There are so very many, and while all of their faces are dirty and exhausted, unshaven and seamed with pain, none of them are familiar. No one recognises her. After that first day, and the shock of going into the ward for the first time, the sheer number of men becomes perversely reassuring. She writes their stoic platitudes on postcards and sends them to addresses across the British Isles from Inverness to Ipswich, Cardiff to Carlisle and any number of towns, villages, and hamlets in between. But not Coldwell. Not Howden Bridge or Hatherford. Not yet.

'What would you like me to write?' she asks a Scots Guard, whose head is swathed in bandages, his right ear torn off by a bullet. His brown eyes stare out from his swaddled face, his pupils pinpricks from the morphine. They seem to look straight through her.

'Dear Mother . . .' he says eventually. 'I wanted to let you know . . . I am . . . well . . .'

She puts it down. (Who is she to call out a lie?)

As she finishes the card and writes the address he mumbles, she notices Nurse Frankland hovering by the door. She gets up, promising to put the card in the post that afternoon.

'Miss Simmons . . .'

Nurse Frankland is twitchy with urgency, glancing behind her to check if Sister Pinkney is on her tail.

'What is it?'

She suspects a housekeeping crisis. Since Nurse Frankland discovered her background, she has furtively sought her help with bed making and dealing with soldiers' soiled clothing (*honestly, anything like that I'm just hopeless . . .*) which will land them both in trouble if Sister Pinkney or Matron find out. But as she reaches the door Nurse Frankland takes her hand and holds it gently, drawing her aside. Her eyes—the same colour as her blue chambray uniform—are full of compassion.

'I must be quick, but I wanted to let you know . . . I've just come from Rodney Ward. I think someone you know may have been brought in this morning.'

It's a hot day. They are struggling to keep the wards cool as the sun streams through the house's wide windows, but in that instant the heat seems to gather inside her, sweeping down through her body with an intense, searing flame.

'I don't—' Her voice has dried to a husk. Her heart seems to have ballooned and is booming inside her chest. 'I mean, how do you—?'

'I haven't got time to explain—Sister will skin me alive if she catches me here. His name is Joseph Jones, Fifteenth Battalion, Sherwood Foresters—I undressed him when he came in, and in his tunic pocket I found this.'

From the pocket beneath her apron, she produces a letter, and shoves it towards her. On the grimy envelope it says *Miss Eliza Simmons*.

The handwriting. . . .

She knows it immediately. Stars burst like fireworks inside her. The words shimmer and blur in front of her eyes as the blood beats hotly in her head.

'That's you, isn't it? I'm not wrong, am I? Nurse Williams said we should hand everything over to Matron to go through, but—well, if it *is* you, and not another Eliza Simmons, I was quite sure you wouldn't want Matron reading your business, and it would be jolly annoying if this got posted on to'—she glances at the envelope—'Little Langley in Nottinghamshire, when you're right here.' There are spots of colour on Nurse Frankland's china doll cheeks, suggesting that there had been some disagreement over this decision. 'And if you don't know Private Jones, and it's just a coincidence, I'll slip it back with his other things.' She shoots another glance over her shoulder, and turns back expectantly. 'So, do you? Know him?'

Joseph Jones. Skinny Joseph from the Sheffield Union Workhouse with his bony knees and birds'-wing shoulder blades. Surely he isn't old enough to be fighting in France?

'Yes, I know him.'

Her voice is little more than a whisper, but Nurse Frankland's face breaks into a beaming smile and she gives her hands an excited little clap. 'Oh, phew—thank goodness for that! Thought I'd made a chump of myself for nothing for a minute. Wouldn't be the first time. Anyway—I'd better dash—'

'How is he?'

'Oh—you know . . .' A shadow passes over her face. 'Bullet wound to the thigh, and he was out in no man's land for an awfully long time. Heatstroke and sunburn haven't helped. He was brought in by a friend, apparently . . . a few more hours and he wouldn't have made it. Come and see for yourself before you go.'

'Yes,' she says faintly. 'Thank you.'

She wants to, but she can't.

Of course she can't.

228 · Iona Grey

Because Joseph knows that she is not Eliza Simmons, and the letter is not intended for her. He will recognise her and name her for who she is: Mrs Kate Furniss, disgraced housekeeper of Coldwell Hall.

He will say she is a murderess.

Winter

Chapter 22

'I'll need currants and beef suet. Candied peel . . .' Mrs Gatley crashed pans in the kitchen, raising her voice over the cacophony of her own racket. 'Mixed spice, I daresay—I'll have to look out a recipe. It's been a good while since I've had to bother with fancy festive folderols, but if her ladyship wants a traditional Christmas with all the trimmings, what does it matter what *I* think?'

She slammed a roasting tin down on the range, conveying her thoughts on Lady Hyde's tentative Christmas plans very clearly indeed. 'Seven guests for five days? Who on earth is she thinking will trail out here for that long in the depths of December?'

Kate picked at a crusted spill at the edge of the table, missed by Susan's cloth. 'Well . . . Lord and Lady Etchingham, of course . . . And Lady Hyde's father and an aunt, I think . . .'

She trailed off. She had only just left the Yellow Parlour, which Lady Hyde had chosen as her sitting room and the place where she conducted daily meetings with Kate to discuss household matters, but already the details of what they had discussed escaped her. As Lady Hyde had chattered on about plans for Christmas—still almost two months away—Kate's attention had wandered as it so often did lately; her head as light as a balloon, only loosely tethered to the body in which she went through the days.

Outside, the park was a blur of brown, the outlines of trees and hedges smudged by the rain running down the window. The year had entered the tunnel of winter, with all the extra labour and inconvenience that entailed. The servants rose in frozen darkness to clean grates and lay fires, and the days were a race to complete the household tasks before the light faded again. That morning, writing the date in her ledger—*November 1st*—Kate had thought back to the syrupy heat of summer, but it felt improbable now, impossible to recapture. It was hard to believe she hadn't imagined it.

Along with everything else.

'Yes,' Lady Hyde had said, with a brave attempt at conviction, 'I think that will be just what we all need, don't you? A lovely festive celebration, with the house lit up and decorated with as much greenery as Gatley can supply. Singing and games by the drawing room fire, and dear Papa and Aunt Ethel here.' Her eyes had grown suddenly bright and damp then, and she'd rummaged in her sleeve for her handkerchief. 'I wonder if we might be able to organise a group of carol singers to come from the village? We could give them sherry and mince pies for their trouble. I'm sure Mrs Gatley will be up to the challenge, won't she? I know it'll mean more work for her, but she can begin preparations now. The Christmas cake can be made and set aside, and of course, the pudding should be made on Stir-up Sunday, in the last week of November. It's a tradition I've kept since childhood. We must all take a turn in the stirring—all the servants too—and make a wish for the year ahead.'

Kate had pressed her lips together, holding back the sour torrent of cynicism that threatened to spill out over Lady Hyde's determined optimism. It would take more than wishes or childhood rituals to rid Coldwell of the misery that weighted the air in its upstairs rooms and seeped through the basement like smog.

'Well, we'll see what Sir Randolph has to say about it when he gets back,' Mrs Gatley said knowingly now, bustling past Kate to collect a bowl of eggs from the dresser. In the weeks since the wedding, unspecified business had taken Sir Randolph away from Coldwell on several occasions, accompanied by his valet and chauffeur. These periods of absence were a relief to everyone, though the inevitability of their return, the knowledge that the reprieve was temporary, cast its own shadow.

Mrs Gatley plucked off a feather that had stuck to one of the eggshells. 'I can't see him agreeing to spending Christmas out here with his sister and some old maiden aunt of her ladyship's. That's if his sister even agrees to come ... Anyone who'd willingly leave Whittam Park for this draughty old place should be spending Christmas in the county asylum, if you ask me. Place the orders at Pearson's by all means, but I won't get myself worked up about a Christmas house party just yet. My guess is it'll come to nothing, like all of Madam's other grand plans.' She cracked an egg into a bowl and gave a scornful laugh. 'A sewing circle in the village—wasn't that one of them? I could have told her that was a non-starter. As if most of us have got time to sit around doing fancy embroidery on church kneelers.'

Kate watched the feather drift on one of the icy draughts that curled through the downstairs rooms. She couldn't argue. It was true that Sir Randolph's bride had come to Coldwell with an abundance of rather childlike enthusiasm for the role of lady of the manor. In the weeks immediately following the wedding, there had been an air of brisk purpose about the meetings in the Yellow Parlour, which had provided a welcome distraction for Kate. Noting down her ladyship's plans and requirements—when she would need the carriage and what to put in the baskets of provisions she took on her visits to the elderly and sick in the village—had given her something other than the gulf between her and Jem to think about.

For a little while, at least.

But, as autumn hardened into winter, Lady Hyde's cheerful determination had faltered. Her baskets of Gatley's apples and plums had been accepted without grace or gratitude at cottage doorways through which she was never invited, and her suggestions for a sewing circle and a Mothers' Union were met with stony cynicism by harried women to whom sewing and motherhood were part of the tough warp and weft of their lives rather than a pretty embellishment upon it.

'You can't blame her for trying.' There was a low note of weariness in Kate's voice. 'She's just trying to make the best of things, like all of us.'

Mrs Gatley snorted. 'Things would be a lot more pleasant round here if folks weren't going around with faces like a wet weekend in Blackpool. I don't know what's come over everyone lately, I really don't.'

She wouldn't, Kate thought.

Mrs Gatley didn't eat her meals in the servants' hall. She returned to the cottage in the kitchen garden at the end of the day, and remained unaware of the undercurrents that swirled through the basement, as icy as the draughts. Inconceivable as it seemed, the cook probably hadn't noticed that Kate went to elaborate lengths to avoid Frederick Henderson—leaving a room if he entered it, making any necessary communications with him via a third party. When she was there, Mrs Gatley moved in a whirlwind of her own preoccupations, too caught up to notice the chasm of silence that had opened up between Kate and Jem, too busy to listen to the whispered reports about what went on upstairs or register the tight set of Miss Dunn's mouth when she came down from her mistress's rooms.

The sharp jangle of the bell at the back door saved Kate from having to think up a reply. 'That'll be the post,' Eliza said, appearing in the kitchen doorway so quickly that she could only have been hovering outside. 'Thomas is cleaning the silver—shall I get it?'

Usually the girls were discouraged from opening the door to the postman, who fancied himself a ladies' man, and kept them talking too long and in a way that was too familiar for Kate's liking.

'Where's Jem?'

'Day off!' Eliza called, already halfway down the passage to the door. 'Left just after breakfast.'

Kate's heart twisted. Not so long ago she would have known when he was taking his day off and what he planned to do with it. She might have contrived a reason to absent herself from the house at the same time. But since That Night (which was how she had come to think of it), the closeness they had shared had dissolved, corroded by the acid of her bitterness.

She didn't blame him for what Henderson had done. It had been her idea to go to the gamekeeper's cottage that night; she had chosen to risk her reputation and her safety for a few forbidden hours of pleasure. Jem had sought her out the next day to apologise for leaving her there alone. He wanted to explain; but when he touched her, she had flinched away, and a new distance yawned between them. *Alone?* she hadn't been able to stop herself from echoing scornfully. *I wouldn't have been afraid to be* alone.

It would have been better not to say anything. She couldn't bring herself to tell him what had happened, but he had worked it out, near enough. And then his anger had filled the space between them, impenetrable, like fog. Directed at Henderson, but chilling and choking her too. Closing her off.

High up on the kitchen window ledge, a hollowed-out turnip with a crudely cut gargoyle's face leered down, giving off a sulphurous, rotting smell. Susan had insisted on carving several of them the previous day, for All-Hallows' Eve, and placed them throughout the basement. To ward off evil, she'd said.

Kate thought about Henderson, on his way back from wherever Sir Randolph's 'business' had taken them. She pictured him, sitting in the front seat beside the shadowy chauffeur, his eyes flicking over the passing landscape as the motorcar ate up the miles.

'Susan, get rid of those turnips,' she snapped. 'They're starting to smell.'

It would take more than a few decaying turnips to drive out the malevolence that lurked in the basement passages at Coldwell, thickening the air with cigar smoke, leaving the whiff of hair oil in its wake.

———— ⟋⟍⟋⟍ ————

Jem's coat was a threadbare jacket, its fabric worn to a shine about the pockets and thinned at the shoulder seams. Before he had passed the church, he could feel the rain seeping through it, wicking into his shirt and chilling his skin.

The discomfort was of his own choosing. There were several heavy livery coats in the footmen's wardrobe, available for anyone's use. These had seen decades of service, protecting Coldwell men from the savage Derbyshire weather as they rode on top of the carriage, but some private sense of defiance had prevented him from taking one. It was his day off. He didn't have to be one of Baronet Bradfield's men today. He didn't want to wear his colours or bear his crest on the buttons of his coat. He would rather be soaked to the skin and shivering than be marked as the property of Randolph Hyde.

He kept his eyes downcast as he walked. There was nothing much to see anyway: the trees were stark and skeletal, stripped of their autumn colour, and clouds cloaked the surrounding hills, drawing the horizon closer so that the world was shrunk to the confines of the Coldwell's park.

Jem's thoughts felt similarly muffled. His perspective was altered and he had lost sight of the way ahead. He had arrived at Coldwell with nothing more than a few sketchy facts to hang his suspicion on. But now that he had uncovered the truth, and lost Kate in the process, he didn't know what to do.

The wind buffeted about him, making his face ache with cold. Turning up the collar of his jacket he saw the gate lodge just ahead, a smudged shape huddled against the high wall of the park. Even from a distance it had a forlorn appearance, its windows dark, water falling in a steady stream from its leaf-choked gutters. As he got closer Jem could see that the apples Mrs Wells usually made into pies and chutneys had fallen from the tree and were rotting in the long grass. Weeds had already clambered over the path, as if the house had been empty for a year, rather than a month.

He'd been there on the mellow October day when Mrs Wells and Davy had moved out. He had helped to load their meagre possessions onto the cart, ready to travel the short distance to the damp cottage she had arranged to rent at the back of the White Hart in the village.

Mrs Wells had endured the upheaval with a sort of numb bewilderment, pausing to dab her eyes with a handkerchief as she took teacups down from her kitchen dresser and wrapped them in dish towels. The terse letter from Mr Fortescue had given no reason for their eviction, beyond the terms of their tenancy having expired, since neither she nor Davy were official employees of the estate. *I don't understand,* she'd protested. *It's twelve years since my Harry passed away. Why now?*

Davy was nowhere to be seen. When the cart was ready to leave, two of Gatley's garden lads were summoned to comb the woods. They had found him, they told Jem later, right in the heart of one of the giant rhododendron bushes, crouched on the damp earth. 'Never would have seen 'im in a million years,' Bert Oakley had said. 'Never would have found 'im if he hadn't been making a noise. Sort of whimpering. Like a wounded animal.'

Jem stopped by the fence and looked at the forlorn cottage.

Henderson had come up on the afternoon of the move not on foot but in the passenger seat of the motorcar, driven by that shady bastard, Robson. He had watched as Jem and Stanley Twigg manhandled bedsteads and pot cupboards, crates of china and linen onto the cart, and finally the kitchen dresser itself. He had watched as Davy was escorted across the rough grass, the garden lads on either side of him, gripping his arms as if he were a felon they had apprehended. The valet had watched as Mrs Wells hurried up the path of the place that had been her home for more than thirty years and fussed over her boy, reaching up to brush leaves from his hair and wipe away the tracks his tears had made in the grime on his face, and then he had got out of the motor and walked over to take the key from her. As he tucked it into the pocket of his waistcoat, he had looked straight at Jem and smiled.

Jem was in no doubt who was behind the eviction. That smile had been a warning: a reminder of who held the power at Coldwell.

He had got rid of Davy, and he could get rid of Jem too, if he wanted. When he wanted.

And there was nothing Jem could do about it.

'Morning.'

'Morning.'

'Bit of a filthy one.' The postman looked up at the sky, tipping his head back so that water ran off the flat top of his hat and splashed onto the shoulders of his oilskin cape. His cheeks, beneath straggly whiskers, were mottled red by the rain. He winked. 'All right for some though, warm and dry inside.'

His gaze skimmed down Eliza's body, making her pull her shawl more securely around her. They all pitied the postman for the long ride out to Coldwell, and he was often given a mug of tea and leftovers from breakfast, which he paid for with local gossip as he gathered his strength for the return journey. But today Eliza was in no mood for idle chatter and flirtation.

'Sir Randolph's on his way back today—we're rushed, getting ready for him,' she said shortly. 'I presume you must have post, as you've come all this way?'

Beneath the dripping peak of his hat, the postman's face hardened. He reached into the bag at his hip. 'A few letters,' he said. 'For Mrs Furniss and Lady Hyde. And this'—he pulled out a small package—'for Miss E. Simmons . . .'

He gave it a little shake, making the contents rattle. Eliza felt colour flood her cheeks as she snatched it from him. 'I'll take those, thank you, and let you get on. I wouldn't like to keep you out in this weather.'

She caught a glimpse of his startled expression in the second before she closed the door. Going back along the passage, she left the letters on the table outside Mr Goddard's room. It was the butler's responsibility to distribute any correspondence, which meant that he could monitor it, and withhold it, if he chose. He could call you into his pantry to open it in front of him, which was exactly why Eliza had made sure, for the past week, that she was by the back door when the postman came, and she was the one to receive the package with her name on it.

Tucking it beneath her shawl, she glanced over her shoulder and slipped through the door to the back stairs. When she reached her attic room, she closed the door and stood against it as she tore open the paper with shaking fingers.

A small brown cardboard box rattled into her hand.

Dr Octavius Pink's Female Pills it said in scrolling writing on the label. *For the Treatment of Menstrual Irregularity, and to Restore Feminine Vitality and Well-being. Safe, Fast-Acting, and Effective. A Boon to Womankind.*

Eliza felt a rush of relief so powerful that it brought tears to her eyes. She had found the advertisement for Dr Octavius Pink's pills in one of Lady Hyde's magazines when she had been tidying the Yellow Parlour, and had hastily torn out the page. *The Lady* was a respectable publication, for respectable people. They wouldn't allow advertisements for anything dangerous, would they?

Dr Octavius Pink offered two choices of pill—'ordinary' at 2/9, and 'special' at 4/6—which, for some reason, further reassured her. 'Ordinary' sounded like they were made for girls just like her, and so she had sent her coins (carefully wrapped in an old piece of flannel and parcelled in blue paper torn from a sugar bag) to the Hygienic Stores on Charing Cross Road. And she had waited, hardly daring to let herself hope that this might bring an end to her trouble.

There was a leaflet enclosed in the package, which she unfolded and skimmed quickly. *Formulated from a Patented Combination of Specialist Ingredients inc. Pennyroyal, Rue, Bitter Aloes, and Slippery Elm, these Pills offer Immediate Relief from all Female Ailments . . . Universally Efficacious in Removing Obstructions, Regulating the Natural Cycle, and Restoring Health. Two Pills to be taken Three Times a Day, After Meals.*

Eliza pried off the flimsy lid. The pills were small and greenish in colour, and the box smelled faintly of liniment. She took two out and dropped them onto her tongue. Her mouth was dry and swallowing was difficult. The pills stuck in her throat and she retched, eyes watering, before gulping them down.

Dr Octavius Pink was right, the relief really was immediate. She tucked the box into her pillowcase, and as she closed the door and went back down the stairs, she felt calmer than she had for weeks.

———— ∞∞ ————

The police house in Howden Bridge was situated on the edge of the village, at the junction of the High Street and the road to Hatherford. Built in the middle of the last century and constructed of smart red brick under a steeply gabled roof, it was a good deal taller and more imposing than the straggle of stone cottages that lay beyond it. In the summer, the front garden was a riot of colour, but in dreary November it had a bleak and forbidding aspect.

Jem walked past the gate once, his hands bunched into fists in his pockets, his mind still at war about whether to go in. Bitter experience had taught him that the law was not there to serve the likes of him, but some innate sense of justice had brought him here anyway. The fact was, his brother had been at Coldwell and had disappeared without a trace. Surely the constable couldn't dismiss Jem's theory out of hand without supplying an alternative explanation?

The sudden memory of Jack—quick and skinny and smiling, *alive*— was like a kick to the stomach. He turned abruptly and walked through the gate of the police house.

The front door was painted dark blue. On either side, the large-paned windows were blank and unlit, though there was a bicycle covered with an oilskin propped against the wall, which suggested the officer was in.

Jem knocked.

The door was opened by a stern-faced woman in a red-smeared apron. She'd obviously been cooking and was wreathed with an air of impatience and the smell of frying onions.

'What's it about?' she said when he asked to see Constable Hollinshead, looking disapprovingly at the drips falling from the hem of his jacket.

He didn't know how to answer. The word *murder* seemed too melodramatic, but wasn't that what it was when a fourteen-year-old boy was sent out into the night to be hunted by a pack of men, fired up on fine wine and brandy?

'A disappearance,' he said gruffly.

She went ahead of him up the tiled hallway, wiping her hands on her apron before knocking on a door and gesturing to him to enter.

The room he stepped into had an impersonal, institutional look. The walls were painted shiny brown and yellow, and the bookcase by the fireplace was untidily stuffed with piles of paper and bulging folders. A large map hung on the wall and a board to which newspaper cuttings, flyers, and handbills were pinned.

'What can I do for you, lad?'

The man behind the desk leaned back in his chair and folded his hands over the paper he'd been reading.

Jem had seen Constable Hollinshead at a distance before; a tall man, well built, with a florid complexion and fulsome grey-flecked beard. He'd always been wearing his helmet, and looked incomplete without it now, the top of his bald head appearing naked and vulnerable.

'I've come from Coldwell,' Jem said. 'I work there. I want to report something that happened a while ago—nine years. A boy went missing.' He hardened his tone. 'I believe he was killed.'

Constable Hollinshead's eyebrows climbed up his smooth, pink forehead. Keeping his eyes downcast, he shut the pamphlet he'd been reading (a seed catalogue; that colourful garden obviously didn't take care of itself) and lined up the pencil and fountain pen at the edge of the blotter. His movements were precise and unhurried.

'Is that so?' He folded his arms and looked at Jem thoughtfully across the desk. 'A murder investigation, then?'

'Yes.'

'In that case, lad, you'd better sit down.'

Chapter 23

By half past four the day's gloom had thickened into dusk. In the hour when she would usually have been sitting in the housekeeper's parlour catching up on mending, Kate made her way slowly upstairs to take fresh towels to Lady Hyde's rooms.

It was a job she could have given to one of the girls, but they were in the stillroom, where the stove was warm, the lamp burned cheerfully, and the smell of proving bread ripened the air. Kate was glad to find something to do upstairs, in a part of the house where Frederick Henderson had no business.

He and Sir Randolph had been back for two hours at the most, but already she was wondering how she would bear it. He had claimed the housekeeper's parlour with the same entitlement as he had tried to claim her that night in the gamekeeper's cottage. The same casual assumption that what was there was his, to take and use.

He made sure that she was never able to forget that. Even when he wasn't in the parlour, he left his stamp on the room. She couldn't go in there without finding his coat thrown over the back of her chair, a coffee cup and a plate of crumbs left on her desk. The smell of him. *Hair oil. Meat. Sweat.* It made her stomach rise.

Lady Hyde's room smelled comfortingly feminine, of Floris soap and rose potpourri. Kate took the towels through to the bathroom and went to the window to lower the blinds. She paused briefly beside the bath, resting her fingers against the cold enamel and remembering . . . silken water, her body warm and loose and thrumming. The way Jem had made everything seem simple and possible, quietly pushing back the boundaries that had narrowed her world, loosening her laces so she could breathe. The way he had brought her briefly to life.

Like a dragonfly. A short spell in the sunlight before the darkness closed in.

At the window she looked out over the parkland, raking the winter twilight for the shape of him or the glow of his cigarette as he walked. But the gloom was unbroken, and the church on the hill had already been swallowed by the encroaching night. And anyway, it was no business of hers where he was or when he would be back. Whether he was all right.

She left Lady Hyde's room and went back along the dimly lit corridor. Her footsteps slowed as she came to the bedroom he had pulled her into on that sweet autumn afternoon. She watched her hand reach out, as if to touch the brass handle.

But she withdrew it, leaving the room closed up, its stillness and shrouded furniture and memories undisturbed.

The night smelled of sheep and sodden earth, with an iron tang of frost. The cold stung inside Jem's nose and made his eyes water, though he didn't particularly notice. The track was uneven and difficult to walk in the dark, even if he'd been sober. Which he wasn't.

He very much wasn't.

He had no idea what time it was but suspected he would find the back door locked when he reached the house. Goddard barely emerged from his room these days, but even he was likely to notice a footman coming in drunk, and after the curfew. For one misdemeanour he might get away with a reprimand and docked wages, but two . . .

He swore softly and walked faster.

It was probably time to leave anyway. At least now he knew the circumstances of his brother's disappearance, though he might never discover exactly what had happened after Mullins had parted company from Jack that night. Constable Hollinshead certainly had no interest in finding out.

'I remember the incident, as it happens . . .' the policeman had said with mild curiosity, leaning back and folding his arms across his straining shirtfront. 'I was stationed at Glossop at the time. Sergeant Timmis put a call out for men to go over and help with the search. Quite a team of us, there was . . . Weather was bloody awful—about this time of year, as I recall.'

Jem had listened with his jaws clamped tightly shut against a rising tide of frustration at the man's casual indifference. He might have been leaning against the bar in the White Hart, relaying an amusing anecdote about a lost dog over a pint of ale.

'We had a good look, of course . . .' Hollinshead had stroked his beard thoughtfully. 'Big place, Coldwell, as you know. We combed the woods and checked all the outbuildings, but no sign of the lad. Someone found a length of red silk, which it turned out had been wrapped around his head in the manner of a turban. The gentlemen had been enjoying an Indian banquet, you see, in homage to an ancestor of Mr Hyde's, and the young man had been dressed up in the costume of an Indian servant boy. So, the silk was found, but not the jewel it was fastened with, which, it turned out, was a very ancient and valuable emerald, fashioned to look like a tiger's eye, brought back from India by a previous Baronet Bradfield. The clothes the lad was wearing when he'd arrived the day before were gone as well, while the Indian get-up he'd worn to serve at dinner was left in their place . . .'

With that, the policeman had opened his large hands, as if presenting the shining truth. 'So, there we are. It's true the lad was never found, but that's because Mr Hyde and Sir Henry were good enough not to press charges. Information was circulated to jewellers' shops, but likely he would have sold the gem in an alehouse somewhere for a fraction of its worth. Most servants are honest—I'm sure you are yourself—but there's always a few bad apples who'll take advantage. I hope that puts your mind at rest . . .'

It had not.

Jem's mind had been very far from at rest as he stumbled out into the street again. It churned and seethed and swarmed with dark thoughts. With the rest of his day off ahead of him, he only knew that he wasn't going back to Coldwell before he had to, and so had walked, away from Howden Bridge on the road to Hatherford, where he had wandered from one public house to another, finding a seat in the farthest corners, speaking little, drinking a lot.

When he emerged, blinking, from the warm beer fug of the town's least salubrious alehouse, he was surprised to discover that it was dark and a watery moon was spinning above the rooftops, bouncing between chimney pots. He had hitched a lift on a farmer's cart as far as Howden Bridge and had fallen into a jolting, uncomfortable doze propped up against the milk churns until he was prodded awake at the crossroads.

The effects of the beer were wearing off now, and the cold air brought a certain clarity to his senses. Since he had left the police house his thoughts had been in a dark spiral, sucked down and inwards by the force of his bitterness. For the first few pints of ale, Hyde and Henderson had been at the forefront of his mind, the centre of the vortex; but as the afternoon wore on, hatred had burned down into maudlin sorrow and he had found himself thinking of Jack, swiping away tears with his shirtsleeve as he sifted through his memories of the boy that everyone else seemed determined to pretend had never existed.

But now, lurching over the rough ground and jolted back towards relative sobriety, he could think only of Kate. He passed Black Tor, a silhouette against the pewter night with ghost sheep huddled beneath it, and felt himself falling helplessly back through time to the day of the fair.

The cold stung his lungs. He tipped his head up to the stars and felt despair scour his insides. He remembered how she'd looked that day, her blouse sticking to her wet skin, her hair slipping from its pins. And how guarded she'd been, how spiky, and how unexpectedly protective it had made him feel. As well as other, less noble, things.

She was perfection. His foolish heart stuttered, and his drunken head reeled, wondering how he had ever had the luck and the nerve to touch her. She was as far above him as the spinning stars, the marbled moon, and yet for a little while she had been his.

Until he let her down and fucked it up, like he fucked up everything.

It was Kate that kept him here, even though she'd made it clear that she wanted nothing more to do with him. He didn't blame her. It was his fault that she'd been at the gamekeeper's cottage alone, and that Henderson had been able to—

His mind shut like a steel trap on what Henderson might have been able to do.

The reason she wanted nothing more to do with him was the very reason he couldn't leave. At least while he was at Coldwell there was someone to look out for her, to keep an eye on that bastard. He couldn't change what had happened, but he could do his best to make sure it didn't happen again.

In his pocket his fingers closed around the dragonfly brooch he'd spotted in the window of the pawnbrokers in Hatherford all those weeks ago. This afternoon, he had gone in and emptied the coins from his pocket onto the counter. The shopkeeper, a crabbed old man with thistledown hair and small, moist eyes, had been in his trade long enough to know that when young men bought jewellery it was usually a transaction of the heart rather than the head. He had counted the coins with yellowed fingers like crows' claws and pronounced them insufficient for such a pretty piece.

Jem left the shop with the dragonfly brooch in his pocket. He watched from outside as the man's crab-like arm extended into the window space to drop his St Christopher in its place, amongst his hoard of mouldering treasures.

Afterwards, slumped in a corner of the Red Lion, Jem turned the dragonfly between his fingers, and realised what a stupid impulse it had been. A pitiful gesture—utterly inadequate. She had been married to a man who bought her diamonds.

She was still married to him.

Jem could offer her nothing. He had a shameful past and an unpromising future: no money, no prospects, no power. He couldn't marry her. He couldn't support her. He couldn't even protect her. In fact, it was he who had put her in danger.

The night air had sobered him up a bit, but his self-disgust cut deeper than the cold.

He was late, he was drunk, he was trouble.

She'd be better off without him. Better still if she'd never met him at all.

'Ah—Mrs Furniss. There you are. I was beginning to think you were avoiding me.'

Kate put the Derby coffee service, brought down from the drawing room only half an hour ago, back into the china cupboard in the housekeeper's parlour.

'Not at all, Mr Henderson,' she said coolly. Without turning to look at him she locked the cupboard again, keeping hold of her chatelaine and closing her fingers around the scissors. 'Just busy, as I'm sure you are too.'

'Not particularly.'

Henderson yawned, not bothering to cover his mouth. He was sprawled in the velvet armchair by the fire, one ankle resting on the other knee and the newspaper spread out across his lap. 'Sir Randolph is in the library, and I imagine it'll be a while before he goes up to bed. Poor sod. You'd think after being away for a week a man would be hurrying up to join his new wife, wouldn't you?' His eyes went to the door in the corner. 'Are you turning in yourself? Please—don't let me stop you . . .'

'I won't.' Her voice was flint and ice. 'My bedroom is upstairs now, in the maid's attic.'

Nothing had been said about what had happened. How could she call him to account for what he had done in the empty cottage in the woods when that would raise the question of why she had been there in the first place? However, the following day she had moved her things from the room adjoining the housekeeper's parlour, up the stairs to a slant-ceilinged room across the landing from where Abigail, Eliza, and Susan slept.

She went to the door, holding herself rigid against a shudder of loathing. As she touched the handle Henderson spoke again.

'I've been hearing about her ladyship's plans for Christmas. It's quite the extravagant programme of festivity you two have come up with. Carol singers and charades and musical entertainments—a full week of enforced merriment. Apparently she even wants to revive the tradition of the servants' ball on Boxing Day.'

His voice was a sneering drawl. Kate wanted to turn on him and snap that Lady Hyde's plans were of her own making—did he really think that she would have been instrumental in the creation of all that extra work when they still hadn't managed to secure more help? Did he honestly imagine that she felt any enthusiasm for the ordeal of a *servants' ball*? Instead, she kept her tone neutral. 'Christmas is traditionally a time for entertaining. It's hardly unusual to spend the season with family.'

'It is for Sir Randolph. He loathes all that sentimental nonsense, as *his wife* should have known.' He got to his feet and stretched expansively, then slid the gold watch out of his waistcoat pocket. 'Looks like it's time to lock up. Is that footman back yet?'

He always referred to Jem like that. As if Jem wasn't significant enough to remember his name.

'I wouldn't know,' Kate said tightly. 'The male staff are Mr Goddard's responsibility. As is locking the back door.'

Panic squeezed her lungs as Henderson came towards her. His hands were in his pockets and he stopped a foot away, moustache twitching upwards in a small smile of amusement as she shrank back.

'Not anymore.' He produced a bunch of keys and dangled them in front of her. 'Not while Sir Randolph is in residence, anyway. Getting on a bit, is Mr Goddard. It's nice to give the old boy a break, ease the burden a bit.' He flipped the keys around his finger and captured them in his fist. 'Don't worry, I'll deal with the footman when he comes in. *If* he comes in. Who knows where he is, or what state he'll be in?'

The skin between her shoulder blades crawled as she walked ahead of him along the corridor. She went through the door to the back stairs and let it swing shut behind her before allowing her shoulders to slump and her breath to escape in a rush. For a moment, she leaned against the wall, her heartbeat reverberating through her body as visceral panic subsided and a colder fear crystallised.

Who knows what state he'll be in?

She remembered the dark glisten of blood on Jem's ashen face. The bloom of bruises on his chest. Wherever he was now, she knew what state he was likely to end up in if Henderson stayed up alone to 'deal' with him.

Grasping her skirt, she raced up the stairs and slipped soundlessly along the ladies' corridor, where the lamp burned low outside Lady Hyde's rooms. She held her keys to hush their jangle as she unlocked the door to the nursery wing, and shut it carefully behind her, feeling her way through the dark to the stairs. Her hands shook as she turned the key in the door that led outside.

The wind was as sharp as a blade and the night was full of noise. The house was a blank black slab above her, blotting out the moon-marbled clouds. Keeping close to the wall, she put her head down and hurried through the shadows to find somewhere to wait.

———— ∞∞∞ ————

Eliza lay under her blanket, listening to the glass rattle in the window frame.

The giant fist squeezing her guts had loosened a little, but she didn't dare move in case she disturbed it again. In the bed a few feet away, Abigail sighed and turned over, altering the rhythm of her soft snores. Wide-eyed, tensed against the waves of nausea that battered her body like the wind battering the house, Eliza had never envied her more.

She had taken two more pills, as the leaflet instructed, after lunch and tea, and had begun to wonder if Octavius Pink was no more than a charlatan. She had asked Mrs Furniss for rags, ready to express confusion and dismay that it was only a little over a fortnight since she'd last requested them (she'd been careful to maintain the fiction of needing them), but Mrs Furniss, who seemed vague and distracted these days, had handed them over without challenge.

Nothing had happened.

Until they had been clearing up after dinner upstairs, when the sickness hit her like a fist in the stomach. She'd made it to the privy at the back of the stable yard and thrown up the bread and cheese they'd had for tea, and then the dinnertime mutton stew. In the reeking darkness of the earth closet, her hair wet with icy sweat, helplessly tumbled in wave after wave of retching, she had felt a glimmer of relief. This must be what the leaflet meant by 'obstructions removed.' She had sent a silent apology to Octavius Pink, for doubting him.

She had felt better after that. The nausea had abated and she felt lighter. Freer. It wasn't until they had washed up the coffee service and were preparing the early morning tea trays—always the last job before turning in at night—that she had felt a twist in her guts and the sensation of her stomach turning to water and fled back across the yard.

'It must have been that mutton,' she muttered when she finally came upstairs, to find Abigail waiting up for her. The candle stub showed shadows of concern on Abigail's face.

'Really?' she said doubtfully. 'I feel right as rain.'

'You wait—everyone'll be the same by the morning.'

But morning seemed like a lifetime away. Abigail was asleep within minutes of blowing out the candle, while Eliza lay rigid, the blankets bunched in her fists. Outside, the treetops heaved, and clouds churned across the moon, and it felt like her insides were performing much the same movements. Hauling herself up and clutching her stomach, she grabbed her shawl and shoes and slipped out.

At first, it seemed pitch black on the back stairs, but it wasn't really, not when her eyes adjusted. Besides, she'd toiled up and down them enough to know every step blindfolded. The kitchen passage was dark too. The shapes of familiar things—the table outside the scullery, the staff photographs on the wall, the row of silent bells—loomed dimly as she passed them, bent double against the griping in her stomach. There used to be a spare key for the back door, kept for emergency purposes under the mat (the old baronet had been paranoid about fire), and she prayed it was still there. As she groped for it, she felt the burn of acid in her throat and, shoving back the bolts, threw herself outside, coughing a stream of vomit onto the cobbles as she ran to the privy.

Slumped on the wooden seat, she listened to the wheeze of her breath. It was like being wrung out from the inside, she thought, and an image of the laundrywomen's mottled arms, twisting and pulling wet sheets, swam into her head. Oh God . . . She leaned against the wall and closed her eyes.

Perhaps she dozed. The next thing she knew there were voices, though she couldn't tell if they were just a trick of the wind. Shivering violently, she pulled her shawl around her and listened.

Nothing. Only the muted roar of the night. And then, unmistakably, footsteps scuffling on the cobbles of the yard.

'Gimme a second.'

It was Jem's voice, slurred. In the icy darkness, Eliza felt her eyes widen and she started violently as the door to the adjacent privy slammed hard against the dividing wall, making it judder. She heard the sound of liquid splattering on the soil in the trench below. And then another voice, close at hand, low and soft.

'It's past eleven. Are you in trouble? What happened?'

Eliza's mouth fell open.

Mrs Furniss?

'What happened?' Jem repeated with a strange sort of laugh. '*What happened?* Such a simple question, so bloody impossible to get an answer.'

'What do you mean?'

Mrs Furniss was good at controlling herself. Eliza had never heard her lose her temper—not properly—but you could tell when she was angry because her voice went all clipped and cold. It wasn't like that now.

It wasn't like that at all.

'Nothing,' Jem mumbled. 'You shouldn't have waited up. I would have slept in the stables and faced Goddard in the morning.'

'It's not Mr Goddard I'm worried about. Henderson's onto you. He's waiting.'

'*Bastard*—I'll fucking *kill* him—'

'No! Jem—*no*. Shhhh . . .' There was another scuffle of feet and the huff of heavy breathing. Cowering in the dark, Eliza could tell that Mrs Furniss was restraining him, that they were grappling together. 'Don't give him the satisfaction. This is what he wants—an opportunity to pin something on you. An excuse to give you another battering. Stay out of his way. I've unlocked the door to the nursery stairs—go to bed quietly. Make him wait for nothing and find that you were where you should be all along.'

Another thud against the wall. The breathing settled to a steady, sawing rasp. Eliza couldn't see them, but she had a mental picture of them clasped together. (Surely not?) And then Jem spoke again, in a tone of such desolation it sent a chill through her.

'I'm sorry, Kate. *Jesus*, I'm so sorry. You shouldn't have to do any of this for me. I don't deserve it, and I don't have any right to—'

'Jem, don't. *Please*—'

'I want to explain . . .' His voice was raw. 'All of it, from the beginning. I wish we could go back. I'd do it so differently—I'd tell you everything from the start—'

'It wouldn't change anything.' The words contained an ocean of sorrow. 'It's too late—it's over, and it should never have happened. Now, get yourself to bed without waking the whole house.'

The privy door slammed shut and footsteps retreated across the cobbles. Eliza's chest heaved out air, and she wrapped her arms around her scoured-out stomach, feeling utterly empty.

When I said I'd tell you everything, I meant about Jack, and my past. Secrets like that are dangerous. They usually come out in the end, often from the mouths of those who don't wish us well, who use them for their own purposes. But looking back, there's something else I wish I'd said. Something far more important.

I wish I'd told you that I loved you.

Maybe that wouldn't have changed anything either, but I'll never know for sure.

Chapter 24

Stir up, we beseech thee, O Lord, the wills of thy faithful people; that they, plenteously bringing forth the fruit of good works, may of thee be plenteously rewarded; through Jesus Christ our Lord. Amen.

The little church on the hill, in use on the last Sunday in November for the first time since Sir Henry's funeral, was as cold as an icehouse. Reverend Moore's breath formed a ghostly aura about him which merged with his wispy grey hair, and the frayed cuffs of his cardigan protruded from the sleeves of his surplice. Beside Kate, Mrs Gatley eased herself awkwardly on the kneeler, her thoughts probably on the great quantities of currants, candied peel, sweet almonds, and beef suet she had measured out and left on the kitchen table, the mixing together of which was to be ceremonially undertaken after the service, led by Lady Hyde.

Everyone was to take a turn. ('*Very nice, I must say, having every Tom, Dick, and Harry traipsing through my kitchen,*' Mrs Gatley had grumbled.) Lady Hyde had assembled everyone in the marble hall last week to go over the plans for Christmas. She took great pains to make it sound like marvellous fun for everyone, beginning with Stir-up Sunday and ending with the servants' ball on Boxing Day, and glossing over the enormous amount of extra work in between. She had explained the ritual of stirring the pudding at some length—the spoon was to move in the direction from east to west to represent the journey of the Wise Men to Bethlehem; and a sixpence would be added to the mixture, representing the promise of wealth in the year ahead to whoever found it in their helping on Christmas Day. She had also been most insistent that, while stirring, everyone was to make a wish.

The candle flames bent in currents of cold air, casting flickering shadows on the walls. Through the diamond panes of glass, the sky was losing its light; and beyond the quavering, plaintive tones of Reverend Moore, Kate heard the crows calling as they circled the treetops, ready to roost.

What should she wish for?

As the reverend invited them to join him in the Lord's Prayer, Kate turned to look along the pew. The maids' folded hands showed cracked, reddened knuckles; and at the end, the new scullery maid sniffed and wiped her nose on her sleeve. The first wish that sprang into her mind was that the girl (whose name was Doris) would pull herself together and apply herself to her work, instead of bursting into tears every time she was asked to do anything.

Thy kingdom come; thy will be done; on earth as it is in heaven.

Give us this day our daily bread . . .

Kate's lips murmured the words, but her mind was on wishes, not prayers. She wished to regain the peace she had once found at Coldwell; the security she had once felt in the quiet house, when the year had passed gently, marked only by the changing seasons and the different demands of each. When her heart had been quiet inside her, like a stopped clock.

And forgive us our trespasses,

as we forgive those who trespass against us.

She would not allow herself the foolish luxury of wishing for that little cottage in the country, with the fruit trees in the garden and the brass bed beneath the eaves to share with Jem. Instead, she wished she could stop longing for him. She wished she could escape the memories that unfurled themselves without warning, taking her unawares and making her breath catch. She wished she could hush the need to know what he'd meant when he said he could explain. She wished she had given him the chance.

And lead us not into temptation,

but deliver us from evil.

All at once she was aware of Henderson's voice, rising above the bass rumble on the other side of the church where the male servants stood. Her eyes flickered across, to find that he was looking at her.

He smiled and nodded, as if registering some private victory. Hatred flared inside her, and she wished she could be rid of him: the smell of hair oil and his prying, probing eyes. His hints and insinuations.

In that moment, more than anything, she wished him gone.

The kitchen passage was warm in the lamp glow, loud with the voices of the outdoor servants, who pulled off caps and loosened mufflers as they shuffled in a slow-moving line to the kitchen.

Miss Dunn felt stiff with embarrassment as Lady Hyde held out the spoon, encouraging her to go first and 'show everyone how it's done. East to west, remember—that's the spirit! And don't forget to make a wish!'

In the moment before Miss Dunn shut her eyes, she saw Mrs Furniss's face. It remained imprinted on the darkness—a pale reproach—and she found herself wishing she'd never remembered where she'd seen Coldwell's housekeeper before.

It was barmy, in Eliza's opinion.

All this performance for a fanciful childish notion. But that was how it was, she supposed: if you were a lady, married to a baronet, you could indulge your fanciful, childish notions, and get other people to indulge them too. Lady Hyde stood beside Mrs Gatley, pink-cheeked with her own importance as Mr Goddard stood by to announce each member of staff.

Standing in the doorway, Eliza watched Mrs Furniss take her turn to stir and felt her insides curdle with resentment. The housekeeper's expression was perfectly composed, as if butter wouldn't melt. As if she was every inch the respectable senior servant that everyone believed her to be.

What did you wish for, Eliza wondered bitterly, when you had your cake and could eat it too?

A little voice inside her head whispered the answer.

Not to be discovered. And she felt a little beat of satisfaction at the knowledge that she had the power to grant that wish or shatter it.

Jem's broad back and bent head entered Eliza's view and she averted her eyes. At least now she knew not to waste her effort on him. Of course, she wished she'd realised earlier and not made such a display of herself, but it was too late for that.

If wishes were horses, beggars would ride, her ma used to say. Eliza had spent the last three weeks wishing that Dr Octavius Pink's Female Pills had done what they were supposed to; wishing she'd saved her 2/6; wishing she'd never been stupid enough to fall for Walter Cox's flattery, nor even set foot in London at all.

A ripple went through her belly, as if a shoal of little fishes were swimming there.

A fat lot of good wishing had done her.

What she needed now was a bloody miracle.

On the first day of December, Kate woke to ice on the inside of the window and a thick furring of hoarfrost on the branches outside.

In the days that followed, the cold only deepened and the earth hardened to iron, like in the Christmas carol. The needle of the barometer in the marble hall swung round to the left and stayed there. The world was bleached of all its colours, iced white like the trays of spiced currant cakes Mrs Gatley turned out in preparation for the Christmas guests. The final descent of the drive glistened treacherously, and Mr Pearson's lad, bringing the fortnightly order with all the festive treats Lady Hyde had requested, refused to risk his horse by bringing the cart down, so the Twigg boys had to unload packages of tea and tapioca, paper-swathed sugar loaves and crates of fragrant oranges, and bring them to the house in barrows.

Gatley came in from the kitchen garden with potatoes and swedes, too heavy for Mrs Gatley to carry. He lingered in the kitchen, blowing steam from a mug of tea and grumbling about Lady Hyde's request for a Christmas tree. 'Seems folly to cut a fine old tree for a week or two of decoration. Sir Randolph won't like it, I'm sure.'

A new keeper had finally been found and had moved into the cottage in the woods. Arthur Platt brought neither wife nor children with him, only a retriever with a rosy golden coat and a far friendlier disposition than its master. Kate had had no involvement in Platt's recruitment, and aside from the Sunday when they had all had to play their part in the stirring of the Christmas pudding, had barely seen him; but when she crossed the yard to the laundry, she heard the distant crack of gunshots. They ricocheted between the bare trees and echoed over the frozen park.

The hapless Doris was given the unpopular task of plucking the pheasants that duly arrived in the game larder. She sat on a stool in the yard, red-eyed with crying and red-nosed from the cold, tearing soft feathers from limp bodies, until the air was a swirl of white; a forewarning of the snow that already lay on the distant hills. With Sir Randolph back at Coldwell, Frederick Henderson haunted the gun room at the end of the passage beyond the butler's pantry, rubbing dubbin into Sir Randolph's shooting brogues, cleaning his Purdey sidelocks, and oiling his Holland & Holland 12-bores. One afternoon, going to collect cream from the dairy for Lady Hyde's scones, Kate passed the lighted window and saw him in there, bent over the table as he polished. When she came back, he was standing up, testing the weight of a shotgun against his shoulder, adjusting the balance. As she watched, he closed one eye and looked down the gleaming barrel, as if taking aim.

That evening, in her lamplit attic room, Kate opened each of her drawers in turn and surveyed the contents.

When she had taken a tea tray up to the Jaipur Bedroom that afternoon, Lady Hyde and Miss Dunn had been unpacking boxes that had been delivered from Kendal Milne department store in Manchester. The bed was heaped with garments, and snowy drifts of tissue paper had settled on the carpet.

'So nice to have something to dress up for, at long last,' Lady Hyde said, holding an evening dress of emerald silk against herself. 'I think I might wear this for the servants' ball . . .' She had looked up at Kate, who was setting the tray down on the table by the fire. 'Have you chosen what you're wearing, Mrs Furniss? You always look so elegant, I'm sure you'll put us all to shame.'

'Oh, I—' It seemed rude to confess that she hadn't given it a moment's thought. 'You're very kind, madam, but I don't really have anything special . . . I must think about it though. Thank you for the reminder.'

She pulled open the lowest drawer and peered in without hope. Folded at the bottom was her best silk dress; black, of course. She shook it out and squinted at it in the dim light, but there was nothing much to see. All that could be said of it was that it was serviceable, which was all it had ever been required to be.

She should seek only to look neat, professional, presentable. Why would she want to appear attractive?

A knock at the door made her heart jolt, providing the unwelcome answer to that unspoken question. Of course, it wasn't Jem who came in, but Miss Dunn, mumbling an apology and carrying something draped over her arm.

'I brought you this—I hope you don't mind.' She spoke quickly, darting across to the bed and laying a dress out on it. 'It's an old one of Lady Hyde's which I remodelled. I thought it was too pretty to get rid of, but I doubt she'll fit into it again. It's not exactly the latest fashion and it might not be to your taste, but . . .' She hurried back to the door. 'Well. It's there, if you want it.'

In the lamplight, Kate could see the glitter of sequins, and a chiffon sleeve fluttered in the draught. The dress was midnight blue, with a square neckline and a high waist; it was so far removed from the items that made up Lady Hyde's current wardrobe that Kate could only imagine the amount of remodelling it had undergone. She was a little lost for words.

'Thank you,' she managed. 'How very kind . . .'

Through the long, flat weeks of early winter, when Lady Hyde had been struggling to get to grips with the huge changes her marriage had brought, Miss Dunn had been kept busy, altering dresses to suit her mistress's new role (and to fit her expanding figure—which was, as far as Kate could make out, due to the comfort she found in afternoon tea and Mrs Gatley's puddings rather than anything more significant). The night of the wedding dance, when Miss Dunn had knocked on Kate's door so late, had never been mentioned, and certainly never repeated. Sometimes Kate wondered what had brought her there, and felt mildly guilty for not being more welcoming.

But only mildly. For years she had gone out of her way to avoid friend-ships and familiarity, the swapping of stories and sharing of secrets. She had protected her solitude. She had no wish to change that now, especially for Lady Hyde's rather serious maid.

Miss Dunn shrugged. 'Not at all. I just think we women should stick together . . . Especially—' she faltered, her heavy brows pulling together in a frown. 'Especially in a house like this.'

The comment took Kate by surprise. Had something happened to Miss Dunn? Had Henderson—? She opened her mouth to ask, but found she didn't know how to frame the question without revealing her own experi-ence, which was a confidence she couldn't afford to give away.

Miss Dunn hovered at the door, picking at a flake of paint at its edge. The moment stretched and quivered, and then she glanced up with a swift, unconvincing smile. 'Well. I should let you get on.'

Kate didn't argue. 'Thank you—for the dress.'

'You're welcome. It's the least I can do.'

She seemed to regret the words before she'd even finished speaking them. Flustered, her fingers went to the white ribbon on her dress, and she gave Kate a curt nod, almost trapping her skirts in the door in her haste to close it firmly behind her.

Chapter 25

The air smelled of iron and stung like splinters. The ground Jem had walked over from the house was hard, each blade of grass edged with frost. Early afternoon and the sky had an odd yellow tinge. The bare trees were a scribble of black against it.

It was going to snow.

The hills were already blanked out. Day by day he had watched the snow thicken on the tops, until it was hard to make out where the icy horizon met the hard white sky. As the temperature dropped, he had the uncomfortable feeling that the outside world was disappearing; that they were being sealed off.

In the servants' basement, Susan listed signs and portents—a halo around the moon, the sheep huddling together under the trees—and Mrs Gatley talked about previous winters when Coldwell had been cut off for weeks, inaccessible to the grocer's cart, the postman's bicycle, visitors. Her tone was one of I-told-you-so warning: Lady Hyde had been daft to make all those grand Christmas plans. If the weather closed in, no one would be coming to Coldwell.

Nor leaving neither.

Those words had haunted Jem these past few days. The thought of them all being trapped together, beyond reach of the outside world, filled him with an unease he couldn't shake off.

His patience was as brittle as the twigs underfoot. He didn't trust himself not to snap at the slightest provocation from Henderson, so he avoided him as much as possible. Still, he was always aware of him, watching, like he had that day at the gate lodge, never letting Jem forget he was on borrowed time. And so, as the days darkened and the weather closed in, Jem had the sense of something gathering to a head. The atmosphere shifting, as if some sort of reckoning was coming.

Instinct told him to leave while he still could, but the next quarter day, when wages would be paid, was at Christmas, and it pained him to leave without what he was owed. And, of course, there was Kate. If he had his way, he would leave with her, but, having forfeited that chance, he wouldn't go without her blessing at least.

The wicker hamper he carried bumped painfully against his leg and he shifted it to the other hand, so it bashed the other shin. It was less of a weight now, returning to the house, than it had been when he'd brought it out, laden with hot soup, game pie, jars of chutney, bottles of claret and port. The novelty of the new gamekeeper hadn't yet worn off, and Hyde went out to play with his guns most days, picking off the game birds that had been allowed to breed undisturbed during the years when there had been no ritual of annual slaughter at Coldwell. Today he had demanded a picnic lunch, a table and canvas chair at which to eat it, and a man to serve it. As first footman that dubious honour went to Thomas, thank Christ. Jem had only to trail back and forth, burdened with cushions, china crockery, silver cutlery, and rugs to bring indoor comfort to Hyde's outdoor whimsy.

Thomas, poor sod, had looked frozen to the bone when Jem had unloaded the hamper. He was wearing one of the old coachmen's coats, but even so, his ears were scarlet, his lips almost blue, and he had seized the jar of soup and clutched it against his body to absorb the warmth for a few moments. Jem had promised to bring two small jars of hot water to slip into his pockets when he came back with Hyde's plum crumble and coffee.

Leaving the cover of the woods, he paused and set down the hamper, flexing his stiff hand. It took a moment for him to notice that it had begun to snow: fine white flakes, barely there. Not heavy enough to fall properly, they blew on the wind, like ash.

He was bending to pick up the hamper when he became aware of movement between the trees to his left. He didn't look round immediately, but busied himself unfastening the hamper and making a show of looking inside, unhurried.

'It's cold out, Davy,' he called out casually. 'Starting to snow too. You'd better get yourself off home.'

He stood up as he finished speaking, and caught a glimpse of Davy Wells's scowling face before he darted clumsily behind a tree, leaving half of himself still visible.

Abandoning the hamper, Jem trudged towards the tree, and the shoulder and arm that stuck out from behind it.

'It'll take you a good while to walk back to the village from here, Davy. Set off now and go quickly and you'll be back in the warmth before your mum starts to worry. She won't want you being out in the snow, will she?'

Davy didn't move. Keeping his head bent, he didn't look at Jem either. It was as if he was hoping to make himself invisible so Jem would leave him alone.

Jem sighed, at a loss. Already the snow was falling faster, more decisively. The flakes were still fine, but they had lost their timidity and the air was a mass of swirling white, softening the great solid shape of the house, almost obliterating the dark tower at the top of the hill. Jem thought of the walk across the park and the time it would take, and the ever-present uneasiness quickened. The hamper stood where he'd left it, waiting to be carried back to the kitchen and refilled. He couldn't offer to take Davy back himself, though something told him he ought to.

He tried again.

'You're not supposed to be here anymore, Davy. Remember?' Pausing, he lowered his voice, his eyes darting back towards the woods. 'Look, if Henderson sees you, you'll be in trouble. He's out shooting with Sir Randolph—'

The name had a dramatic effect. Davy cowered away and clapped his hands to his ears, his face screwed up in anguish.

'Davy—it's all right—'

Alarmed, Jem reached out to reassure him, but Davy twisted away and stumbled a few paces backwards. With a panicked glance at Jem, he turned and began to run.

'Davy!'

But he didn't look back.

It was a good thing, Jem told himself. At least Davy was on his way home now, even if he'd had to frighten him into going. Battling guilt, he watched him run across the stretch of open ground, tripping every now and then on tussocks hidden beneath the gathering snow, leaving a trail of messy footprints on the thickening white.

<hr />

'Well, that's that, then.'

Mrs Gatley's chest was puffed up with self-importance, her tone almost pleased as she took her apron off after dinner and sent Joseph to fetch her coat. 'I told you it was a fool's mission to make those plans for Christmas. There'll be no visitors making their way out here for a good while, that's for sure. At least we've plenty of supplies in for the household. As long as someone can get down to the farm for butter and milk, we shouldn't want for anything.'

'I'll send the lads over with the old sledge,' Gatley muttered gruffly. He had come in from the walled garden to escort his wife home and stood in the doorway of the servants' hall, clutching his cap between his callused hands, looking out of place in this domestic setting.

But then, there was a sense of reality being suspended and the normal order of things disrupted. The windows were dark, but there was a strange glow to the sky and Gatley had brought with him the metallic scent of frost. The servants' hall seemed very full, with the Twigg boys standing by the fire to get warm (it was perishing in the grooms' loft, they said) and Johnny Farrow planted firmly in Kate's chair at the far end of the table, while outside the snow kept falling, cutting the great house adrift from the rest of the world.

'Bert Oakley's lad came to pick him up on the pony trap. Didn't fancy his chances of making it back to the village in this,' Gatley said. 'Brought the news that Mary Wells has been taken bad. Nellie Crawford from the White Hart found her collapsed in the yard, frozen to the bone. Her heart, they reckon.'

A current of consternation went around the room. Mrs Gatley put a hand to her own ample chest in alarm.

'Is she all right?'

Gatley shrugged. 'Nellie's taken her in for the time being,' Oakley said.'

Kate imagined a room above the pub; the noise coming up from the saloon bar below, the smell of ale and tobacco smoke. But Mrs Wells was lucky to have that. She wouldn't be able to afford Dr Seymour or the subscription for the cottage hospital in Hatherford, and she wouldn't want to leave Davy to go to the infirmary at Sheffield Union Workhouse.

'I hope they've taken Davy in too,' she said. 'Or someone has. He won't manage on his own.'

Gatley turned his cap between his hands, frowning. 'That's the thing. Lad's disappeared,' Oakley said. Asked if I'd seen him up here. He checked the gate lodge on his way down—no sign of him there, and we've given the woods a quick going over.'

'I saw him.'

Jem spoke from the shadows. He had been leaning against the dresser at the far end of the room, but he straightened up, suddenly tense. 'He was out in the woods earlier, when I took the hamper out. I spoke to him. Told him to go home before the snow came properly. He was—'

He stopped abruptly.

'He was what?' George Twigg prompted.

'I don't know. Upset. Agitated.'

'I'm sure someone will have notified the constable in the village,' Kate said, with a conviction she didn't feel. 'He'll have organised a search, I'm sure.'

'Not in this weather,' Johnny Farrow said.

Thrusting a hand through his hair, Jem squeezed past Johnny Farrow's chair. The Twigg boys moved aside to let him through.

'Where are you off to?' Stanley asked.

'Going to look for him,' Jem said grimly.

Kate felt a ripple of fear at the thought of the bitter cold, the silent woods; the snow that muffled sound and covered things up. She was standing by the door, and without thinking put her hand out to stop him. She wanted to tell him not to go but didn't know how to without giving herself away.

'Don't be daft, lad.'

Gatley, not troubled by appearances nor hampered by a forbidden, ill-advised love, beat her to it. 'You wouldn't last five minutes out there in this weather—it closes in fast up here, mark my words. Davy Wells knows this estate like the back of his own hand. Folk might write him off as simple, but he can look out for himself in the woods, no doubt about that. Chances are he's safely back in the village long since, but if he isn't—if he *is* up here—he'll have found himself somewhere safe, like he has many a time before. Got an animal's instinct, has Davy.'

Mrs Gatley gave a grunt of assent. 'That's true. We always used to say he was part boy, part fox, that one. Mary could never keep him indoors; even as a little 'un he'd let himself out at night and wander. He knows this park better than anyone, so wherever he is, I reckon he'll be all right. Which is more than could be said for you, Jem Arden, if you go out there looking for him.'

Kate realised that her hand was still on Jem's arm. She withdrew it, but not before she'd noticed Eliza looking at her from the other side of the table, her jaw set hard and her eyes flinty in the glow of the lamp. Beside her, Susan shrugged her shoulders in an exaggerated shiver.

'You'll be like poor Samuel, wandering the Coldwell woods for all eternity. Or the souls of the lost travellers on the road to Hatherford, with the coachman whipping his ghostly horses . . .'

Eliza gave a snort of disdain and rolled her eyes. Kate was suddenly struck by how much she'd changed these past few months. She'd always had a cynical streak, but it had been tempered with a quickness of wit and sweetened with a sense of fun. Now, above the shawl she was permanently huddled into, her face looked puffy and sallow. Sour. Kate wondered what had taken the bloom off her. Or who.

'You can sneer all you like, Eliza Simmons, but it's true,' Susan retorted, craning forward to look down the table. 'Johnny Farrow's seen them— haven't you, Johnny? Tell the story.'

The old coachman nodded slowly and sucked on his pipe. Around the room an expectant silence stretched. Huddled on his hard chair by the door, Joseph's eyes were as round as saucers. Mrs Gatley, who had sunk into Mr Goddard's chair, made no attempt to get up, her coat spread across her lap, her hands folded comfortably on top of it.

'Winter of ninety-seven, it was . . .' Johnny Farrow began ponderously, around the stem of his pipe. 'Bitter cold, hard frost for days. Sir Henry was

coming home from a stay at Whittam Park, but the train was delayed . . .
black as pitch by the time we set off from Sheffield. Well . . . the snow
started as we reached Hope End Farm. By the time we got up to the top
by Gallowstree Heath it was fair coming down. That was when I saw it . . .'

All eyes were on the coachman at the far end of the table, just beyond
the circle of lamplight. All except Jem's. His head was turned towards the
window, and he watched the white flakes tumbling through the glowing
dark.

Johnny Farrow told his well-worn tale of the ghostly coach with its
phantom horses galloping hell-for-leather through the blizzard, but it was
Jem—a few feet away from Kate and a thousand miles beyond her reach—
who looked haunted.

<hr />

Outside, the snow had changed everything. The landscape of the park was
unrecognisable, and even the sky looked different, lit by a yellow glow, like a
lamp burning low behind a shaded window. Only the dark silhouette of the
tower remained as a fixed point of familiarity. It cast a long blue shadow on
the snow, like an accusing finger pointing towards the house.

Sir Randolph's spaniel dashed around in circles, burying his nose in the
snow and snorting, not knowing what to investigate first. Joseph hunched
his shoulders and watched, dully aware that last winter he would probably
have run about with the same excitement.

But he'd grown up a lot since last winter.

'Boy!'

His voice cracked and the shout came out deeper than he'd expected,
as if a stranger had spoken. The dog took no notice, rushing up the slope
towards the woods. There was no way Joseph was going after him if he
went in there. Not after all that talk of ghosts in the servants' hall.

'Must be six inches deep already,' Jem said absently. He had offered
to come with Joseph when he took the dog for its last run of the day, and
stood now, his body taut as he scanned the line of the trees. Joseph had
been grateful for the offer; he thought Jem must have noticed that he was
afraid. With a thud of disappointment, he realised now that Jem hadn't
come for his sake at all, but to look for Davy Wells.

'It's so white,' Joseph muttered. 'I've not seen owt like it before. In town it always melts and turns dirty as soon as it touches the ground. Everything looks so . . . clean.'

It was as if the world had been made pure and new. The spaniel let out a couple of high, excited barks and bounded joyfully forward, sending up sprays of powder as white as the sugar cones in the stillroom. It was deceptive, the purity. Beneath the pristine snow was mud and stones, secrets and lies.

This whole beautiful place was rotten with them.

'Jem?' he said tentatively, but the footman had begun to move away, following the furrows the dog had left in the snow. Joseph dug his hands deep into the pockets of his fustian jacket and set off after him. His footsteps faltered as his cold fingers closed around a sixpence.

At first, he had been happy about the coins Mr Henderson gave him. It was something . . . to be noticed and singled out for praise. Joseph was as invisible as Samuel's ghost to Mr Goddard, and treated much the same as Boy the spaniel by Thomas and the girls. It had given him a glow of pride when Mr Henderson called him a bright lad, and said he was shaping up to be a useful servant.

He didn't have to like Sir Randolph's valet to recognise that as a good thing. You had to toady up to all sorts of rum characters if you wanted to get on, and he didn't want to be a workhouse nobody, scraping mud off boots and carrying coal for the rest of his days. Mr Henderson had promised him his own uniform—a proper tiger's livery—and a special job waiting on at the house parties Sir Randolph was going to have for his gentlemen friends. The sixpences were just the start, Henderson said—rewards for the scraps of servants' hall gossip Joseph gave him. He'd get proper money from the toffs, for being loyal and discreet and a *good sport* (whatever that meant).

Too late he'd realised the trap Henderson had set for him.

He'd seen the growing collection of coins as a means of washing off the stain of his early life; of distancing himself from the snivelling kid who had cowered from his father's fists, and becoming the man he wanted to be—a man like Jem. But in earning those coins, he had proved himself the opposite. In trying to make himself worthy of Jem's friendship, he'd been required to betray it. Just as Henderson must have planned.

He trudged up the hill in Jem's wake. It had started to snow again, and flakes brushed his cheeks and caught in his lashes. He had decided that the only thing to do was to talk to Jem . . . carefully. Sound him out for advice without quite letting on what he'd done.

'Jem . . .' he tried again, quickening his pace to catch up. 'Wait! There was summat I wanted to ask you . . . About—'

He paused. Jem turned and walked backwards for a couple of paces. 'About what?'

A volley of barks echoed like gunshots through the frozen night, making them both jump. Boy was standing at the edge of the wood, staring into its darkness, the fur standing up in a ridge along his back.

Fear turned Joseph's mind blank and made his voice quaver. 'What's he seen?' Animals were supposed to be able to sense spirits, weren't they? Johnny Farrow said the carriage horses had squealed and skidded and refused to go forward when the phantom coach appeared. But it was clear Jem's mind wasn't on ghosts. He started to run, feet sliding on the snow as he scrambled up the slope towards the trees.

'Davy! Davy Wells—is that you?'

With his heart rattling against his ribs, Joseph followed. He would rather have turned and run back to the light and warmth of the servants' hall, but he didn't dare go back without the dog. As the shadow of the trees fell over him, he saw Jem stop, his hands going to his head, his shoulders slumping.

'Deer,' he said flatly, as Joseph caught up. 'They must have come down from the hills to shelter from the cold.'

Joseph looked past him and saw a pale shape move between the trees. He laughed uneasily, relief loosening his insides. 'I thought it was the ghost lad. Susan said it were a winter's night like this when he tried to run away. Should've waited until it were warmer, the daft sod . . .'

He said it to make a joke of his own embarrassing fear, but Jem didn't laugh. He carried on staring into the trees, his whole body tense, like he was listening intently. But not to Joseph. He gave no sign of having heard him at all.

'I don't know why you're shouting 'im, any road.' Joseph muttered, kicking up a plume of snow. 'Not going to answer, is he? Never speaks. Come on, let's go in. I'm half froze to death.'

Reluctantly Jem tore his eyes from the trees and turned away. Joseph felt a flare of anger towards stupid Davy Wells as they trudged down the hill, the spaniel bounding ahead, Jem glancing back towards the wood every few paces. Joseph hoped he might remember the conversation that had been interrupted, and pick it up again, but he didn't, and pride prevented Joseph from trying himself.

They walked in silence.

When he was younger Joseph used to wish he was invisible, to avoid the force of his father's fury. Now it felt that he might be. That he had faded into the nothing his father had always said he was, like the trail of their footsteps, fast disappearing in the freshly falling snow.

Chapter 26

While the snow fell it was like they were under some sort of enchantment; a spell of silence, where everything was altered. Folding back the drawing room shutters on the third day Eliza saw that the flakes had stopped and there was a pink dawn spreading across the sky, making the white world blush.

She stood looking out, watching the crows rise raggedly from the wood, before briskly turning away, picking up her box of dusters, brushes, and black lead. As she passed a wide mirror, she caught sight of a figure in the glass and felt a judder of shock.

It was her. The stout woman with the pudding face and the hair scraped back under her cap was *her*.

The foxed glass above the washstand in the maids' attic only showed small bits of her at any one time, so she had been spared the impact of the whole. With a soft moan, she faced her reflection fully, setting down the box and twisting left and right, checking to see if the swelling in her belly, which felt like she'd eaten a tray of underbaked currant buns, was visible.

She'd had to let out her corset laces, of course, but she couldn't risk loosening it as much as she'd like, so the roundness she felt at night, beneath her nightgown, was concealed a bit. Miserably, she tugged at her apron. She looked like the laundrywoman who sometimes came up on Monday with a snivelling infant strapped to her back.

'*Eliza . . .*'

She spun round and felt her heavy stomach drop.

Mrs Furniss had come into the room and stopped short. For a moment they stared at each other, and Eliza watched the colour drain from the housekeeper's face as her eyes moved from Eliza's stomach to her face and back, realisation dawning like the sun rising over the snow outside.

'I think . . .' Her voice sounded like someone had her by the throat. 'I think you'd better come to my room.'

⚬⚬⚬

Kate had always prided herself on her attention to detail.

At twenty-five, she had been inordinately young to take over the post of housekeeper in a house this size, and relatively inexperienced in matters pertaining to cleaning and household maintenance. However, those were things that could be learned from *Cassell's Household Guide* and Mrs Beeton. The qualities that were so notably absent in Mrs Walton—understanding of the girls whose labour she relied on, awareness of their lives, their alliances, their squabbles, their worries, and their pleasures—came naturally to Kate, and she believed that these things (along with a head for figures and a methodical approach to accounts) were what made a good housekeeper.

And that's what she had thought herself—a good housekeeper, up until that moment in the drawing room, with the low winter sun stretching its rosy rays across the faded carpet and giving Eliza an aura of gold. Kate's first thought was that she looked like a figure from an old painting—a shepherd girl, or Demeter perhaps—womanly and voluptuous. It took her a second to understand why.

It was her fault.

Self-recrimination beat inside her as she went down to the basement, where Frederick Henderson had collared a miserable-looking Joseph in the gloom beneath the stairs. Any other time she would have stepped in to rescue him, but her head was too full of her own responsibilities—if she had kept her focus, none of this would have happened. Sending Eliza to wash her hands, Kate went into the housekeeper's parlour and sat down at her desk. She let out a shaky exhalation.

She had never held with the idea that servants should—or could—be controlled by intimidation. Kate had tried to lead her girls by example . . . to show that it was possible to find satisfaction in work well done, to establish a valuable life for oneself as an independent woman.

And then Jem Arden had come to Coldwell and she had stopped trying to do those things. She had lost sight of everything but him.

Eliza came in quietly, without knocking. She stood beside the armchair, leaning against it as her eyes moved around the room, eventually fixing themselves on the window.

'How did it happen?' Kate asked in a low voice. She suspected she already knew and could hardly bear to hear it, but she owed Eliza the chance to share the burden of her secret.

'I should think you know that, Mrs Furniss.'

Eliza's tone was sardonic. Defiant almost; a sharp contrast with the shame Kate had expected. She felt herself instantly disconcerted, as if she had opened a door and found quite a different vista from the one she'd anticipated. Distress affected people differently, she reminded herself. She must be patient.

'I mean, was it—were you—assaulted? Did he force himself on you?' As she said it, she felt her throat close in a gag, remembering the smell of hair oil and the hardness of fingers digging into her flesh. 'If so, you must tell me, and I will deal with it. I will see to it that the man who did this is not allowed to remain in this house and does not go unpunished . . .'

There was the silver lining to all this. She would never forgive herself for this happening to one of the girls in her care, but at least now she could openly confront Frederick Henderson and make sure it didn't happen again.

'No, Mrs Furniss.'

'*No?*'

'I wasn't assaulted. Or forced.' Eliza shrugged, sounding almost bored. Her eyes slid from the window to rest on Kate, faintly challenging. 'I suppose I wanted a bit of excitement. I reckon *you'll* understand that.'

Kate moved her leather-bound ledger a fraction, lining it up precisely with the inkstand. Words swirled in her head, but it would be a mistake to snatch at the first ones that came to her. It was important to hang on to her temper. She inhaled, then paused for a beat.

'Eliza, do you know what you're saying?' It was the tone of voice she used to talk to Davy Wells. 'Are you protecting this man because you're afraid of him? Has he threatened you? Because I can promise—'

Eliza gave a tut of impatience and shifted her weight to the other hip, so the swell of her belly seemed more obvious. 'He hasn't threatened me, and if he did, I'd take no notice—Walter Cox is full of big talk that comes to nowt. He doesn't know anything about it, and I daresay he never will. There's nowt to be done about it now.'

Walter Cox?

Dear God. Eliza had spoiled her chances for *Walter Cox*?

Kate rubbed her fingers across her forehead, as if that would help assimilate this unexpected information.

'Well . . . I'm afraid something will have to be done. You can't leave immediately because of the weather, and Christmas . . . But you can't stay here—you know that, don't you? I'd let you if I could, but Mr Goddard and Mr Fortescue simply wouldn't countenance it. Have you made any plans?'

'Not as such. I had hopes, but they came to nothing.' The words were edged with steel, sharpened with blame. 'I don't know where I'll go for the . . . Well, anyway, I'm not keeping it. I can't. Afterwards I'll get back to work as soon as I can.'

Eliza's tone was offhand, as if she'd barely given it a second thought. As if bearing an illegitimate child and handing it over to the parish was a mild inconvenience, and finding another position afterwards would be a simple matter. Kate saw behind the bravado and understood that Eliza hadn't thought about it because it didn't bear thinking about. She hadn't decided what to do because she had little choice.

She sighed. 'I'll do what I can to help. You won't be alone in this, Eliza. I'll give you a good character reference. The truth will no doubt come out sooner or later, but for now your secret is safe.'

Eliza nodded and turned her head away. Her mask of nonchalant defiance had slipped, and her throat worked against tears. When she looked back at Kate, it was with swimming eyes and a grudging smile.

'In that case, so is yours.'

In spite of everything, Christmas still had to be got through, somehow. Neither the weather nor the tension that crackled through the house could alter the fact of it. Instead of the days of amusement and diversion Lady Hyde had envisaged, it now felt more like a series of trials to be endured.

For two days, while the snow fell, Miss Dunn had hurried up and downstairs with trays for Lady Hyde, who had taken the disappointment of the cancelled visits very badly. But by Christmas Eve the sense of being suspended in the glass dome of a snow globe was shattered and brisk purpose returned. The outdoor staff shovelled paths through the snow and scattered soil to make them safer underfoot. Mrs Gatley swung into action in the kitchen, ordering Susan and Doris (who was more tearful than ever at the prospect of Christmas cut off from her family) to make bread sauce and scrub the mud off parsnips. The monster Christmas tree was brought into the entrance hall and it took Gatley and five men to hoist it into place, while the second baronet smirked at their exertions.

Jem too felt galvanised, although reluctantly. Those stopped days, when leaving was impossible, had made him realise it was what he had to do. When he'd stood with Joseph at the edge of the wood, disjointed fragments of information had slotted themselves together in his brain; Mrs Gatley's words—*even as a little 'un he'd let himself out at night and wander*— merging with what Mrs Wells had said about Davy being *a regular little chatterbox* at the time of the last coronation, a few months before Jack came to Coldwell. It suddenly struck Jem that he had been looking for answers in the wrong places, asking the wrong people, when the one person who could have helped him had been there in plain sight.

Until he wasn't.

And so, he decided. He would wait until after Boxing Day, when their wages had been paid and the servants' ball was over, and then he would go to Goddard and ask for a character. He would leave as soon as he could and find Davy.

In the meantime, he would try to speak to Kate one more time. She had said it was over, but he couldn't leave without being sure. He had to tell her that he loved her, and once he'd heard her say she didn't feel the same, he would move on.

After lunch on Christmas Eve, he and Thomas were sent up to the storage attics to find the box of glass decorations Sir Randolph's mother had collected from Germany, to hang on the tree. Following his afternoon in the woods serving Sir Randolph's shooting picnic, Thomas had started a head cold, and plodded disconsolately up the stairs ahead of Jem, trailing self-pity.

'Mrs Furniss said they should be in the first room on the left'—he paused to blow his nose extravagantly—'in a packing crate.'

The storage attics were on the other side of the house to the ones the servants slept in, though the layout was the same: a corridor with doors leading off both sides and one at the end. In the glory days of Coldwell there must have been enough servants to fill this half of the attics too. Curious, Jem walked to the end of the corridor and tried the door. It was unlocked, and led to another landing, disconcertingly similar to the one he was standing in, so it was like looking in a dingy mirror.

'Back in them days this must have been the men's side of the house and ours was the lasses, or t'other way round.' Thomas sniffed. 'So few of us now we can fit in one wing, with room to spare.'

Logically, Jem had known how close the female quarters were to theirs, but it was another thing seeing it like that. After Kate had removed her personal things from the room off the housekeeper's parlour, it had felt like she was miles away from him, as far beyond his reach as the moon. It was a surprise to see the opposite was true. Only a few feet separated them.

A locked door.

'Come on—it's bloody freezing up here. Let's find these blooming decorations and get downstairs.'

Thomas's cold had made him tetchy. 'Bloody hell,' he grumbled, going into the first room at the top of the stairs. 'There are loads of crates. They could be anywhere. Old Sir Henry never bothered with Christmas after his missis died so they'll likely be buried at the back somewhere.'

'Don't worry, we'll find them,' Jem said absently, stopping to look out of the window on the landing.

The sun was already sinking, staining the sky pink and casting long blue shadows on the snow-covered park. Jem's eyes raked the trees. He had taken every opportunity he could to look for Davy and had found no trace, but the new keeper had come to the kitchen door yesterday to report that the best part of a loaf and a wedge of cheese had gone missing from his cottage. Mrs Gatley took this as hard evidence that Davy had, as she predicted, found somewhere safe and warm and was fending for himself just fine.

Jem wished he shared her confidence.

'Are you going to help or not?' Thomas grumbled, sticking his head round the door. 'What are you playing at?'

Jem turned away from the window. 'Just looking. It's been three days since Davy Wells went missing. No one seems bothered.'

Thomas shrugged irritably. 'It's not that. It's just you're the only one who thinks he's missing. A law unto 'imself, is Davy. Now it's stopped snowing he can make his way back to the village if he hasn't already, or come to the kitchen door if he needs owt.' He blew his nose, shoulders sagging. 'God, I feel rotten. I ache all over. Never slept a wink last night.'

Jem, who had lain awake listening to his snoring, didn't argue. He was glad to be swapping places with Joseph tonight and taking his turn in the silver cupboard. He nodded at a lumpy old chaise longue shoved against the wall, its faded upholstery nibbled by mice and spewing stuffing. 'Sit down for a bit if you like. I'll find the decorations.'

It didn't take long, for all the fuss Thomas had made. They carried the wooden crate down to the entrance hall, where the fire had been lit in a futile attempt to warm the frozen air, and Lady Hyde was overseeing the arrangement of trailing ivy and branches of holly on the great marble mantelpiece and the console tables on either side of the door. The stepladders from the garden had been brought in, so the top section of the tree could be reached. While Lady Hyde busied herself unearthing delicate glass baubles from their nest of packing straw (making exclamations of delight over each one), she ordered Thomas up the ladders to hang them on the branches, apparently oblivious to his ostentatious suffering.

'Dear God,' Sir Randolph drawled, passing through on his way to the library.

'I didn't realise quite how large it was.' Lady Hyde gave a shaky laugh. 'But still, it's here now and rather splendid, don't you think?'

'Splendid? It's damned ridiculous. This is a country house, not some provincial ruddy town hall. What the hell d'you mean by getting Gatley to hack down a fine specimen tree from the park and bring it in here for some vulgar foreign decoration fad?'

Lady Hyde's smile slipped, like a broken paper chain. Reaching up to pass Thomas a pink glass bauble she withdrew her hand too soon, and it fell to the floor, shattering in a silvery explosion of shards.

'Oh!'

'There,' Sir Randolph said harshly. 'A bloody fool's mission to prettify a tree like that.' He glared at Jem. 'Well, go on then—fetch a brush! Quick about it!'

Jem went, hatred curdling in his stomach like something spoiled.

He was determined not to hurry. Downstairs it was the quiet hour of the afternoon when the maids were in the stillroom preparing the tea trays and Susan and the new girl had gone upstairs to snatch a few moments' peace before starting on dinner. In the scullery he found the brush and pan, and—making sure no one was approaching—took out a torn square of paper from his pocket and the pencil stub they kept in the dresser drawer.

This was his only chance. He weighed the words carefully before writing them down, then dropped the paper into the Chinese vase. He was so preoccupied with the task that he didn't notice Joseph standing in the doorway until he turned to leave.

Jem's first reaction was one of irritation, but it was quickly replaced by guilt. In all his plans, he'd only considered Kate's feelings, but his leaving would hit Joseph hard too. Jem ruffled Joseph's hair (not so easy now he'd grown two inches) and said, as cheerfully as he could, 'What's up, Joe? Did you want me?'

Joseph ducked away, scowling.

'Doesn't matter,' he muttered.

Christmas Eve was supposed to have been the start of Lady Hyde's programme of festivities. If the snow hadn't spoiled everything, the house would have been glowing with lamplight, fires burning in its guest rooms, the basement busy with visiting servants and everyone already fed up with hearing from Lady Etchingham's maid how things were done at Whittam Park. There should have been carolers crossing the park at twilight to sing on the front steps as the family and guests gathered in the drawing room. But the crisp snow remained unspoiled, and the frozen landscape was blue and silent in the moonlight.

They pressed ahead half-heartedly, preparing to convey salmon vol-au-vents, lemon sorbet, stuffed roast partridge, and potatoes dauphinois up to the echoing dining room. Gatley had appeared with a bunch of mistletoe earlier, to hang in the servants' hall 'for a bit of festivity, like,' but Susan had shrieked that it was unlucky to bring mistletoe in before New Year's Eve and Eliza had snapped that it would take more than a bit of greenery to tempt her to kiss any of the Coldwell lads, thank you very much. (Looking at Thomas, with his red nose and streaming eyes, that was understandable.) Mrs Gatley, hurling parsley sprigs in the general direction of the soup, complained that the youth of today were a miserable lot and wouldn't know fun if it stood in front of them waving a flag.

Peace and goodwill were in very short supply.

Kate would have liked to retreat to the housekeeper's parlour, but Henderson, having dressed Sir Randolph for dinner, had ensconced himself in there with a bottle of claret, so she hovered listlessly in the kitchen. Jem appeared from the footmen's wardrobe, dressed in his formal livery, which Lady Hyde had specifically requested (*scarlet cuffs and gold braid are simply made for Christmas . . .*). His hair was freshly slicked back and, catching the scent of lime shaving soap, Kate had to grip the edge of the table to steady herself against an avalanche of longing.

'Excuse me, Mrs Furniss, but here's the clothes brush you asked for.'

She looked at it, confused. She found it hard to remember things these days, but surely she would recall asking for a—

And then she realised; the code they had devised in the summer. She lifted her gaze to meet his and her heart stuttered as she took the brush from him.

'Of course. Thank you.'

'What d'you want a clothes brush for?' Mrs Gatley demanded, sloshing juices over the crisped partridges in their roasting tin.

It was a good question.

'Oh—my best coat, for church. I noticed some dried mud on the hem.'

'I thought church was cancelled tomorrow, on account of Reverend Moore not being able to get through on the trap?' Mrs Gatley bent to shove the birds into the oven, slamming the door shut with a clang. 'He'd be daft to try it, with it being so icy. Or am I the last to be told what's going on, as always?'

'No. I mean, yes, it has been cancelled . . .' Kate said blandly, not looking at Jem. 'My coat needs cleaning, that's all.'

Distraction came, mercifully, in the form of a volley of violent sneezes, echoing along the passage, followed by Mr Goddard's outraged voice.

'For pity's sake, Thomas—what's the *matter* with you?'

'A cold, Mr Goddard, sir. A real stinker.'

'You're not fit to be seen. You'll have to manage as best you can in the dining room—we can't be a man down, but Jem will take over upstairs as soon as dinner is over. I won't have you snivelling into Sir Randolph's evening brandy.'

Jem's eyes met Kate's and skimmed upwards in silent exasperation. She moved swiftly past him, taking the clothes brush with her, and went straight to the scullery, where she took the Chinese vase down from the shelf, tucking the little fold of paper she found inside into her sleeve.

She couldn't wait to read it, and she couldn't risk being seen, so she went up the back stairs to her room and lit a candle with a shaking hand. His handwriting leapt off the page in the flickering flame.

I know I have no right to ask anything of you but there are things I need to say. If you unlock the dividing door between the attics, I'll come to you tonight.

If the door is locked, I'll know it's too late, and I'll understand.

If I'd known then what would happen, I would have put so much more in that note. I would have written it there—I love you—so at least through everything that came after you would know that was true. I would have left the present I'd

bought you, and I wouldn't still have it with me now—a reminder of everything that remained unfinished between us.

There's a saying, isn't there—ignorance is bliss. Perhaps it's better not to know what lies ahead. There's no blissful ignorance here. I'm so aware of last times—last sunrise, last mug of tea, last glimpse of the moon—in a way I wasn't then. Even over the noise of the guns I can hear the sand running through the glass.

That's why I have to write this. It's now or never. There won't be another chance.

Chapter 27

The evening seemed to go on forever.

The six-course dinner Lady Hyde had devised for her guests was eaten largely in silence (or not eaten, in Lady Hyde's case), and every course felt like an eternity.

At the end of each, removing the wine that had been served with it, Jem had paused in the darkness of the hallway and drunk from the bottles, swallowing down Riesling, Burgundy, Sauterne, and champagne with grim defiance. Now, with the house finally quiet and the alcohol warming his blood, he stood outside the back door, dragging on a cigarette and thinking of his first night there. That fool Cox, showing off and getting a dressing-down from Kate for swigging champagne. It made his breath catch to remember how she'd appeared to him then—beautiful and disapproving, intimidatingly remote. Until the moment she touched him.

He inhaled deeply, making the tip of the cigarette glow, then expelled a slow breath which turned to silver in the frozen air. He couldn't afford to think about her touch. Not yet, not with Hyde still in the library with the drinks tray and his filthy French lithographs spread out over the desk. Earlier, Kate had taken a tray of dirty crockery from Jem and her eyes had met his, a brief inclination of her head acknowledging that she'd got the note. That the door would be unlocked, and she would be waiting.

But for how long?

He'd thought it wasn't possible to hate Randolph Hyde more than he did already, but it turned out he was wrong. Why didn't the bastard just go to bed?

At that moment, the bell in the passageway behind him shattered the silence. Usually he hated to jump to a summons upstairs, but tonight he wasn't going to let anything delay him from getting to Kate. He ground out his cigarette and ran along the passage, taking the stairs two at a time.

The hallway was as cold and dark as the kitchen yard. The huge Christmas tree gave off the resinous scent of the forest, which made him think of Davy again. As he passed, he looked up at the portrait of the second baronet; the man who had taken a boy from his family in India and brought him here to hunt like an animal. A surge of rage washed through him, mingling dangerously with the wine.

Steady . . . he told himself. He couldn't afford to do anything stupid. Not until he'd seen Kate. Not until he'd got the last quarter's wages in his hand.

The library was warm and bright compared to the draughty darkness of the rest of the house. Hyde was slumped in the chair behind the desk, which was littered with the debris of his evening: teetering piles of books, smeared glasses, and a decanter, drained to the dregs. The lithographs were scattered everywhere, some stained with sticky rings of port. Hyde was peering through a large magnifying glass at a cluster of diamonds clutched in his hand. He didn't look up when Jem came in.

'Ah, Thomas—' He grunted. 'More coal on the fire. Blasted perishing in here.'

God, he was *steaming* drunk. So that was why he hadn't gone to bed. He probably couldn't stand up.

'It's not Thomas,' Jem said coolly, deciding he could afford to dispense with the 'sir.' Hyde was in no fit state to do anything about it.

Hyde raised his head stupidly and blinked his small, bloodshot eyes. 'It's Thomas if I say it is,' he snarled. 'You're all bloody Thomas to me. Now get that bloody fire going.'

Jem added coal from the box on the hearth and poked the embers to rouse a flame. Straightening up, he looked back towards Hyde and noticed that the safe, built into the panelling by the window, was open. On the pretext of gathering up the empty glasses and removing the decanter, he went across to the desk and stooped to pick up one of the lithographs that had slid onto the floor. A shudder of revulsion went through him as he glanced at the scene of graphic depravity it depicted. He was about to place it on the desk when Hyde dropped the magnifying glass and made a lunge for it.

'How dare you touch those papers, boy? How bloody *dare* you? Know your place!'

The diamond necklace he'd been holding slithered onto the desk, and another jewel that must have been taken from the safe skidded across the scattered papers and fell to the floor, lost to the darkness. Hyde's face was puce as he spluttered helplessly, dropping to his knees and floundering around on the carpet.

'You bloody fool—look what you've done! You'd be horsewhipped for this in my father's day. You'd have your bloody marching orders, man . . .'

From where he stood, Jem could see a glint of gold on the carpet. Calmly, he went forward to pick it up, enjoying Hyde's disadvantage and the spectacle of his impotent, port-soaked rage.

'Quite so,' he said blandly. The jewel was set in a heavy gold surround, and he placed it on the desk, beneath the lamp. It cast a pool of clear green light with a dark shadow at its centre. Almost like a . . .

Realisation slammed him in the stomach.

A very ancient and valuable emerald, fashioned to look like a tiger's eye . . .

He stared at the jewel and felt his mouth open. Drunk as he was, perhaps Hyde felt the shift in the atmosphere, or perhaps some spark of memory ignited a subconscious recognition.

'Get out,' he slurred, his face darkening. 'Get out of my bloody sight and don't come back.'

'Very good, *sir*.' Jem's hatred rose from him, like heat. 'I'll say good night.'

Up in the attic, the frost crept in curlicues across the black windowpane and the candle flame stuttered in the icy drafts. Hours after the house had settled and the girls' muted voices across the landing had fallen silent, Kate waited, pacing the floor to keep warm and to work off her agitation.

Her indecision.

She had vowed never again. What had happened in the summer was the kind of madness that led to nothing but trouble. She had allowed her judgement to be impaired, her professionalism compromised. She had rediscovered something in herself, but lost sight of her responsibilities. She should count herself lucky that she had come to her senses before anything truly disastrous happened. What was she doing, unlocking the door and opening herself up to that risk again?

The creased scrap of paper was on the desk, but she didn't need to read it again to remember what it said; the words had been echoing around her head all evening. *There are things I need to say.* He may not actually have added *before I leave*, but still she heard it, and it chilled her.

It was inevitable, really. He'd never belonged at Coldwell. He wasn't like Thomas, or the Twigg boys: someone who would keep his head down and plod on, accepting what he was given without question. He would never settle in this out-of-the-way old house, nor have his will bent to the tyrannical rule of Sir Randolph and Henderson. He didn't have to explain that to her.

Perhaps it would be better if he didn't.

The key to the dividing door between the attics was on the desk, beside his note. She imagined herself picking it up, tiptoeing out into the corridor, and sliding it silently into the lock. In less than a minute, she would be back in her room and could undress and slip between the cold sheets, and leave it all behind: the summer of madness they had shared, the thrill of secret glances in the servants' hall, brushed fingertips when passing a cup or a laden tray. She could forget, in time, that a handsome footman called Jem Arden had ever been at Coldwell and had brought her briefly back to herself. After a while, the pleasure and exhilaration and sense of possibility she had felt with him would become a faded dream.

The candle flame swayed in a sudden current of air. Her taut nerves hummed. She stood up, reaching for the key, but a soft step on the landing told her she was too late.

Swiftly she crossed the room and opened the door. It need not be too late: she could tell him to go back—he wasn't like Henderson, he would do as she asked. But every sound seemed vastly magnified in the listening house; the creak of the old floorboards as he slipped into the room, the squeak of hinges and the click of the latch as he closed the door behind him. She pictured Eliza and Abigail, Susan and Doris lying a few feet away, heaped beneath their eiderdowns, and couldn't trust herself to speak.

And besides, she couldn't think of the words. Not when he was standing only inches away, half-hidden by the shadows, the gold of the candle glinting in his eyes, gilding the ridge of his cheekbone, the edge of his upper lip.

'It's so late . . . I thought he'd never go to bed.' His voice was a breath. 'You're shivering . . .'

In one fluid movement, he slipped off his jacket and came closer, putting it around her shoulders so she was enveloped in his warmth. Neither of them moved, and their eyes held as the silence pooled around them, the ripples of sound spreading outwards and dying away.

'Kate—'

She knew what he was going to say. She wasn't sure what form his goodbye would take, only that she didn't want to hear it. Perhaps it was pride as much as anything that made her press her finger to his lips; the fact that she would be left here, in this stagnant backwater, while he rejoined the current of life and was carried away from her. Perhaps it was some perverse instinct for self-preservation that made her want to put off the moment of parting, not just from him but from the woman she had been when she was with him. Or maybe it was simply a childish refusal to accept reality that made her take his face between her hands as she kissed him, the need to snatch a few more moments in her blissful fool's paradise before it was lost to her forever.

With a soft moan he kissed her back, grasping the lapels of the jacket and pulling her against him, where she fitted the contours of his body.

It was as if she was watching from outside herself. Marvelling at the abandonment of the woman in black, who fumbled at the buttons of his shirt and slid her hands inside and pushed it off his shoulders, so his bare skin gleamed like burnished ivory in the candle glow. Envying her as he worked free the small buttons of her dress and unhooked her corset, bending his head to brush his lips along her collarbone, to press them against the swell of her breast above her chemise. Storing up the images, the memory, to feed on later, when he was gone.

But then the watching part of her was pulled back into her pulsing, shivering, arching body, and there was nothing but that moment, stretched and exquisite, and the darkness beyond the circle of candlelight.

Outside the window the silent stars went by.

Eliza woke.

At night, the baby—freed from its tight-laced restraints—rolled and flipped inside her like a fish in a barrel. And yet it wasn't that, nor the burn of acid at the base of her throat that had jolted her from sleep, but a noise. A cry.

An owl perhaps. Or a fox? Something high and primal, quickly hushed.

She lay in the darkness, listening, as the child inside her arched and stretched, nudging her bladder and pushing the air from her lungs, but the noise didn't come again.

The silence settled, like snow.

Jem watched the stars, and the shadows flickering on the walls as the candle burned itself down.

He should get up and blow it out, but he couldn't move. Kate's cheek rested against his chest and her body was tucked into the crook of his arm, one leg across his thigh, pinning him down. He hadn't meant for her to fall asleep, but in the aftermath of what had happened between them, he'd felt spent and scoured out, and he couldn't find the words.

He hadn't meant for any of it to be like this.

All the things he had intended to say were scattered now. They made no sense. The restless purpose that had driven him before had dissolved and it seemed like a miracle to find himself there in the early hours of Christmas morning, with her hair like silk across his chest and her skin warm against his. A shiver of reflexive pleasure convulsed him as he remembered her mouth on his flesh, the expression of abstracted intensity on her face as she'd looked up at him.

How could he leave?

But then he thought of the jewel that he had picked up from the library floor. The same jewel that the policeman had described; the one that Jack was supposed to have stolen but was securely hidden away in Sir Randolph's safe.

How could he stay?

The candle was almost burned out. The last of its light glinted on the chatelaine beside it, a puddle of silver. His eyes came to rest on it, and he examined the idea that was forming in his mind; tentatively, like someone probing an aching tooth. The prospect of getting up, of leaving the warmth of the bed and relinquishing her delicious body, was unappealing in the extreme, but this was his last chance to prove Jack wasn't a thief, that he hadn't disappeared voluntarily. If Jem had the jewel, Henderson's story would be proved a lie and Hollinshead would have to investigate what had really happened that night, wouldn't he?

Love was a physical ache in his chest. With infinite care, he drew the blanket more securely over Kate and slid out of bed, dropping a kiss on her pearly shoulder. The cold wrapped around him as he dressed in the clothes that had been so quickly, so eagerly discarded. It made his fingers stiff as he picked up her chatelaine and unclipped the ring of keys from its chain.

He blew out the guttering candle and paused to look back at Kate. She slept on, her inky hair spilling over the pillow, her face softened by sleep. In the cold, clear, Christmas sky, the moon was bright enough to cast sooty shadows on her cheeks beneath the sweep of her lashes. He had to grit his teeth and steel himself not to slip back into the bed beside her, to make the most of the precious, secret hours they had before dawn. It was only the thought of being with her properly once this was all over that allowed him to tiptoe from the room.

He would ask her tomorrow. Somehow, he would find the time, even if he had to request, in front of the others, to talk to her alone in the housekeeper's parlour. He was so tired of the petty rules and invisible barriers of the servants' hall. He was so tired of all the things that he knew and felt and wanted being obliterated by duty, and of having to surrender everything that mattered for twenty-eight pounds a year. Once he had the jewel he would go to Scotland Yard, where the officers weren't in the pocket of Randolph Hyde at the big house, and he would say what Mullins had told him and hand over the emerald Jack was supposed to have stolen. And then he would set about finding work somewhere he and Kate could be together, where no one knew them. He could go back to working with horses, on an estate where they'd have a cottage of their own. She could have his name, even if they couldn't marry. He would keep her safe and devote his life to making her happy. If only she would come with him.

Dear God, he would move heaven and earth to make her happy, if he was lucky enough to have the chance.

He hadn't dared risk putting shoes on and his bare feet made no sound on the icy flags of the basement passage. The moonlight spilled across the floor like thin blue buttermilk, making it easy to see what he was doing. It was only the cold, and the burden of his own guilt that hampered him. It felt wrong to be unlocking the housekeeper's parlour with Kate's keys and slipping into the room that was her domain. Like a violation.

He pushed the uncomfortable thought away, avoiding his own spectral reflection in the mirror as he stole across to the desk and lit the lamp. Unwillingly, he recalled that midsummer afternoon when he had stood in the same place and some latent sense of honour had made him dismiss the idea of doing exactly what he was doing now. He had wanted to be better than this. To be worthy of her.

He still wanted that.

Once he was done, he would go back to his room and collect the dragon-fly brooch he'd hidden in his pack. A Christmas present. The thought offered a faint glow of consolation as he unlocked the drawer of her desk. There were so many keys, but each one had a small ivory tag bearing the name of the room, or a paper one for the cupboards, trunks, and chests. It didn't take him long to find the one for the library, and he had just shut the drawer and locked it when a noise set his heart hammering.

He didn't have to turn round. In the mirror above the desk, he watched the door open, letting in moonlight.

And Frederick Henderson.

Chapter 28

'I have to hand it to you, Arden. You're very persistent.'

Henderson came forward, his movements unhurried. 'Or should that be, *very stupid*? You don't know when to stop, do you? You just can't see that you're beaten.'

'That's because I'm not.'

Jem spoke through a clenched jaw, surprised at how steady his voice was. Despite the biting cold, he was sweating.

Henderson laughed softly. 'I've known for months who you are. I worked it out soon after you arrived. Do you really think I'd have let you stay all this time if I suspected there was the slightest chance that you could do any damage? It's been quite entertaining watching you scramble for crumbs, but I would have had you sent on your way if I'd thought you'd find anything. Or done a proper job on you that night, back in the summer. I admit, I was tempted . . . I almost got carried away.'

Jem remembered. His ribs still ached with remembering.

'Just as well you managed to stop yourself. You were lucky enough to get away with one dead servant at Coldwell. Another one might be harder to cover up.'

He put it out there to test Henderson's reaction. The way his face hardened, his eyes narrowing and lower jaw jutting, told Jem everything he didn't want to know.

'Watch your mouth, Arden. I wouldn't go throwing baseless accusations around if I were you. Your brother was a grubby little nobody. A common thief. The constabulary conducted a search of the house and park and came to the obvious conclusion that he'd made off with a very valuable jewel, which he had been trusted to wear for a special occasion.' He shook his head with exaggerated regret. 'So difficult to find honest servants. They're the criminal class, aren't they? Boys like him—they can't help themselves. They learn it at their mother's knee.'

Jem's fists shook, his clenched fingers burning and pulsing with the urge to throw a punch. He heard, in some distant part of his mind, Kate's voice. *Don't give him the satisfaction.*

'Except'—his voice was hoarse—'except the jewel he's supposed to have stolen is here, isn't it? Upstairs, in the safe.'

Henderson wasn't expecting that. Jem saw it on his face, the flash of surprise and a split-second of uncertainty. He recovered quickly, changing tack with a nonchalant shrug.

'Do you really think anyone will believe you if you say that? Especially as you appear to be cut from the same coarse cloth as your brother.' He nodded at Kate's keys lying on the desk, and triumph glinted in his eyes. 'Unless, of course, the lovely Mrs Furniss handed those over herself?'

And there it was.

Henderson's checkmate.

'She didn't.' It felt like he'd swallowed broken glass. 'This has nothing to do with her.'

'Of course not. I won't ask how you managed to procure them.'

Smirking, Henderson went across to the fireplace and picked up an Indian silver box from the table beside it. He removed a cigarette and tapped it on the mantelpiece. The flame of his lighter briefly illuminated his face: leering and hard, like Mr Punch. Or the devil himself, with his black pointed beard.

'I imagine . . .' he went on thoughtfully, 'that she still thinks it's pure chance a handsome footman appeared at Coldwell from nowhere and . . . just *happened* to fall for the housekeeper . . .' His laugh was a sneer. 'And fell so completely that he was willing to flout all the rules and risk his position for a thrilling fumble in the linen cupboard . . .'

Henderson took a leisurely drag of his cigarette, leaning a shoulder against the mantelpiece with exaggerated ease. Jem felt sick. Stunned into immobility, like a rabbit cornered by a dog.

'You've played a good hand, Arden, I'll give you that. Got yourself a nice place here, haven't you? Decent job, and a piece of skirt that's a real cut above the scullery skivvies you must be used to. Older, of course,' he qualified, with a wave of his cigarette, 'but that means she knows what she's doing. Those grasping young girls are always such a disappointment. I bet she's quite the wildcat beneath that stern housekeeper's dress. I assume you know that she's married?'

The question came from nowhere and caught Jem off guard. Just in time he recognised it as a test. A trap to incriminate Kate.

'All housekeepers are called Mrs,' he said gruffly. 'It's a courtesy title.'

'So you didn't know?' Henderson looked smug. 'I must say I was rather stunned myself when Miss Dunn let that gem of information slip.' He laughed, almost fondly. 'It's surprising how quickly a drop of vodka in the fruit cup loosens the tongue of a lifelong abstainer. Anyway, small world, isn't it? I mean, it's not so remarkable that so many friends and associates of Sir Randolph just *happened* to be dining at the Savoy on the day of the wedding—between you and me, he did put the word about that a bit of male company would be welcome. But for one of those associates to be the erstwhile husband of our own Mrs Furniss, *and* for Miss Dunn to recognise him . . . !' He shook his head in a great show of amazement. 'A small world indeed.'

Jem was barely listening. His brain, stalled by shock, was now whirring, trying to catch up. From along the passage he heard the kitchen clock strike—four times? Five? It wouldn't be too long before Susan came down to put the water on. The night was slipping away, spinning out of his control. He needed to work out what to do. What his options were.

Did he still have options?

'So, it seems our mysterious Mrs Furniss has a past,' Henderson was saying. 'And a husband. Who is still very much present.'

Jem wasn't sure what Henderson was planning. He couldn't tell which direction the decisive blow was going to come from, or what form it would take. He only knew that it would come.

'Alec Ross—that's the fellow's name.' Henderson flicked ash into the fireplace. 'With a bit of lubrication, Miss Dunn had a lot to say about him and his unsavoury past. He and Sir Randolph have a mutual interest in gaming—cards and so on, and frequent the same . . . sporting clubs in London.'

He paused to pull on his cigarette. The bastard was enjoying himself, Jem thought. Loving the power he held. 'Ross has a reputation for being a fearless adversary,' he continued. 'A ruthless man, not to be crossed. Loss can do that to a person, can't it? He plays for high stakes, and the rumour is that he has some rather unsavoury connections. Friends in low places, you might say. I suspect he'd be very grateful to the man who could give him information that would reunite him with his estranged wife.'

Jem remembered the summer night, upstairs in the garden passage. The punch that had come from nowhere, hard enough to knock him off balance.

He felt like that now.

'You wouldn't,' he croaked.

Henderson laughed. 'If it suited me, why not?' Frowning slightly, he picked a strand of tobacco off his tongue, which glistened pinkly against his beard. 'But, unlike some, I take the responsibilities of my position very seriously. My duty is to Sir Randolph, and I put his interests first. Which is why I'm going to make you a deal, Arden.'

Placing the cigarette carefully between his lips he inhaled, then blew a column of smoke out of the side of his mouth. Jem waited, fighting nausea.

'I'll keep the secret. The lovely Mrs Furniss will be safe here. I will take personal responsibility for her protection and do all I can to ensure Ross is never invited to Coldwell . . . *if* you leave, tonight. *Now.* Without a word.'

Jem's head reeled. He thought of Kate, asleep in the bed where he had left her; waking up and realising he wasn't there. He thought of her pressed against the wall of the basement stairs on the day of the coronation, trembling and sobbing in his arms. *He's not the sort of man to let things go . . .*

'And, to be perfectly clear, you *stay away*,' Henderson went on, his tone hardening as he jabbed his cigarette in Jem's direction. 'Disappear, and keep your sordid accusations and ridiculous theories to yourself, and Mrs Furniss can remain here in the peace and security she has always enjoyed; the respectable housekeeper of a respectable house. Do you understand?'

Jem wanted to tell him exactly what to do with his deal. He wanted to push past him and run upstairs to the attic where Kate was sleeping, and gather her up and take her with him. He didn't give a toss about leaving this miserable house, but it killed him to go without her. Yet how could he ask her to come with him when he had nowhere to go? No future to offer her, not even the last quarter's pay.

'You bastard,' he whispered.

Henderson laughed. 'I'll take that as your charming way of saying, "Yes, Mr Henderson, sir, I do understand. Thank you for being so . . . gentlemanly."'

There was a noise in Jem's head. A sort of muffled roar. Above it his own voice sounded distant.

'I'll get my things.'

'Nice try, but I don't think so.' Henderson looked down at Jem's bare feet with a sneer. 'Wait by the back door. Tempting as it is to send you out there like that, I'll do you the kindness of going up to the attic to get you some shoes myself. It is Christmas, after all.'

Joseph wasn't sure what woke him.

There was no loud noise, no obvious disturbance, no intruder standing over him with a cosh and a crowbar to break into the silver cupboard. And yet, his heart was beating a rapid warning and his scalp prickled with fear, just as it used to all those years ago, on the nights when his father came in from the alehouse.

He squeezed his eyes shut and pushed his fists against them to try and halt the jerky picture reel that had started up in his head. In the daytime he kept it shut away, but at night the door swung open, and he couldn't make it stop. There it was, flickering across the darkness of his memory.

He moved his hands to his ears to shut out the sound, but it echoed across the years and bounced around inside his skull. (The baby's frantic cry, the rhythmic thud of his father's fist . . . his mother's head against the wall . . .) Scrabbling at the blanket, he sat up and groped for the chamber pot. He hadn't wet the bed for ages, and the very real fear of doing it now was enough to bring him back to himself.

Just in time.

He let out a pent-up breath and was just yanking up his trousers when a pale glimmer of movement in the passage caught his eye. The ghost boy, passing silently through the dark basement where he had once lived and slept—

Blood roared in Joseph's ears and the night closed in on him. And then, through the woozy panic he heard another noise—the chink of china from the scullery and the scrape of things being moved on the shelf. He stumbled to the door and peered into the dark corridor, one way, then the other.

The scullery door was open, as always. The cold from the icy floor came through his socks as he crept towards it, pressing his eye to the gap by the door's hinges.

Relief tumbled through him.

It was Jem. Just Jem, replacing the vase that Joseph had seen him drop something into earlier—the one with the Chinese scenes painted on it. Joseph was about to ask what he was doing when a noise along the passage set his heart clanging again. Footsteps on the stairs. He made it back to the butler's pantry just as the door creaked open.

The footsteps advanced along the corridor. He recognised them even before he caught the waft of hair oil and cigar smoke. Frederick Henderson had his shoes handmade in London—Joseph had cleaned them often enough to be able to picture the horseshoe of tiny silver nails around the heels, which made that thin metallic tapping sound when he walked.

Dread sloshed in his stomach. Stifling a whimper, he pressed himself against the wall, praying that the footsteps would pass.

A bar of lamplight fell briefly across the floor and slid away. He heard voices; Henderson's low, harsh laugh and Jem's bitter retort, the scuffle of movement. This time they went in the other direction, towards the back door. Joseph felt a draft of frozen air billow along the passageway as it opened, then shut.

The kitchen clock ticked into the silence.

It wasn't right—none of it. Jem had never actually said he hated Mr Henderson, but he didn't have to; just as Mr Henderson didn't need to spell out what he thought of Jem. So what were they doing, going out into the snow together in the middle of the night?

Joseph had to clamp his teeth together to stop them rattling. Supposing Frederick Henderson had somehow tricked Jem, or blackmailed him?

Supposing Jem had left a note in the vase, hoping Joseph would think to look there after seeing him with it earlier? Supposing he was relying on Joseph to help . . . ?

On trembling legs, he darted into the scullery, where the moonlight silvered the stone flags and gleamed on the jars of salt and sand on the windowsill, the rows of vases on the dresser shelf. The vase with the Chinese figures was high enough that he had to stand on an apple crate to reach it. Putting his hand inside, he let out a grunt of triumph as his fingers closed around a square of paper.

He jumped down from the crate. His fingers were shaking, making it hard to unfold the paper, and the gloom was too thick to make out the lettering on it. He was squinting at it closely when a beam of lamplight fell across the page. It threw the words into sharp relief and catapulted his heart into his throat.

'Thank you, Joseph. I'll take that.'

Henderson held out his hand. The lamp lit his face from below, casting shadows that made it look like a carved wooden mask, with dark slits for eyes and a strange, cruel smile.

Joseph's guts turned to water. He handed over the note and watched it vanish into the pocket of the valet's waistcoat.

And he took the silver sixpence that appeared in its place.

———— ✺ ————

Kate woke slowly.

It was a gradual coming back to consciousness, putting off the moment of opening her eyes, savouring the suspended time between sleeping and waking; between the secret, sensual night and the brisk business of daytime. Stretching her body, she felt its pleasurable ache, and was aware that she was smiling.

For the first time in months, she had slept long and deeply. It wasn't a surprise to find herself alone in the narrow bed; thank goodness Jem had been more alert than she and got himself back to where he should be before the house awoke. Through the frosty window the sky was lightening. The girls would have been up for an hour already, rising in the dark to get the day's work underway.

Christmas Day, she remembered, sitting up drowsily and shaking her hair from her face (no plait last night ...). Getting out of bed she looked for her chatelaine to check the time.

It was where she had left it on the table in the corner. The silver was cold on her bed-warm skin as she unclipped the watchcase (*a quarter before seven!*) and it took her a moment to realise that there was something wrong. Something missing.

One of the chains that hung from the Indian silver clasp swung down, its clip empty. She blinked blankly for a second, wondering when she'd removed the scissors, the buttonhook, the pencil ... and then realised that they were all still there.

The keys.

The keys were gone.

A soft knock sounded on the door. She darted forward to open it—had Jem taken the keys for some purpose and was hurrying to return them? He was taking a risk, coming up here now—

'Morning, Mrs Furniss. Sorry I'm late.'

Abigail came in with the tea tray. She set it down and struck a match to light the candle. 'The fact is, we're in a bit of a state downstairs ...'

Kate was suddenly wide awake. 'What's happened?'

'It's Jem Arden.'

'What about him?'

Abigail looked at her with a sort of bewildered consternation, shaking her head a little. Twin candle flames glinted in the dark pools of her eyes.

'He's ... gone.'

Chapter 29

It was the least merry of Christmases at Coldwell.

Upstairs in the marble hallway the branches of the great pine tree drooped, its needles falling, its candles unlit. Lady Hyde usually had breakfast on a tray in her room, but Sir Randolph stayed in bed until past midday too, throwing the day's routine into disarray. Mr Henderson had Susan mix up a concoction of raw eggs and Worcestershire sauce to take up to him, while Mr Goddard came down from the library carrying a tray of decanters to be refilled, several smeared glasses, and an empty port bottle.

'I don't know why I bother,' Mrs Gatley grumbled, sticking a fork (with rather too much relish) into the goose that was drying out in the roasting pan. 'All this work, and I may as well serve up pease pudding and tapioca for all anyone notices.'

The shock of Jem's sudden departure was felt by everybody. It was like, Eliza thought, when a crow swooped down on a brood of ducklings and snatched one: the fluster of stunned confusion that followed amongst the others. For a long time, she'd felt cut off from her fellow maids, but that morning they all huddled in the scullery, where Susan and Doris were working their way through a mountain of potatoes, carrots, and parsnips, to speculate about what had happened.

A girl somewhere, Abigail reckoned; a wife, even, whom he'd sneaked off to spend Christmas with. Susan fretted that he'd taken it upon himself to go out and look for Davy Wells and met an accident—fallen through the ice on the lake or something. Thomas, slipping in from the butler's pantry with the silver fruit plate he was polishing, put paid to that theory by announcing that Jem had taken all his things, and reported that Stanley Twigg said you could see his footsteps in the snow, cutting across the park in the direction of the road.

Eliza said nothing.

There was a time, not so long ago, that she would have been bursting to add her two penn'orth. To produce, like a conjuror drawing a rabbit from a hat, the identity of Jem's actual romantic interest, which was far more jaw-droppingly scandalous than a common or garden spouse (even a hidden one).

But a lot had changed since that time.

She had a bit more respect for secrets now, and those who kept them. She found herself in the strange position of being more aligned with Mrs Furniss these days than with Abigail, Susan, and Drippy Doris. It occurred to her that Mrs Furniss might know more about Jem's departure than she was letting on, and it might be part of some plan, cooked up between them, so they could get away from Coldwell and make a new start together.

It was going dark outside by the time they had cleared the barely picked-at goose from the dining room, scraped untouched sweetbreads, game chips, and cod in oyster sauce into the pigswill, and sat down to their own Christmas dinner in the servants' hall. In spite of the room being more crowded than usual, and the space around the table a squeeze of elbows, shoulders, and knees, Jem's absence was as noticeable as if they'd left a seat empty for him. At the end of the table, Mrs Furniss looked like she'd been turned to marble. In the low lamplight she was white as a sheet, her skin stretched tight over her cheekbones, her lips bloodless.

So there was no plan, Eliza thought. The housekeeper was as much in the dark about Jem's departure as the rest of them.

The outdoor servants kept the conversation going, heaping praise on Mrs Gatley for the succulence of the birds she had roasted (chickens for the staff) and the crispness of her potatoes, making up for the personal slight she'd felt from upstairs. But once the pudding had been brought in, and ceremonially set alight in its pool of brandy by Mr Goddard, Henderson spoke up.

'You'll have noticed by now that we are one footman down. I'm sure you're all wondering why.'

'Didn't like to ask,' muttered George Twigg.

'I see no reason why it should be a secret. Jem Arden was a habitual liar and a convicted criminal. I discovered him last night, two hours before dawn, in the housekeeper's parlour with the key to the library. He'd attended to Sir Randolph during the evening and had seen him taking Lady Hyde's Christmas gift—a diamond choker—out of the safe. He must have suspected Sir Randolph would leave it out to give to her this morning.'

Eliza felt the babe inside her lurch, as if it too felt the shock. A gasp went around the table. One of the Twiggs swore quietly, without reprimand. Mrs Gatley shook her head, chins wobbling, and Miss Dunn's fingers flew to the temperance badge on her chest, touching it like a talisman. Joseph half stood, his eyes like holes in the snow outside, mouth opening as if to argue.

Eliza looked at Mrs Furniss. In that moment, she reminded her of a stone angel in the churchyard back home, head bent, face carved into an expression of exquisite suffering. Her eyes flickered closed, and Eliza, seeing what it cost her to bear the news of this betrayal in silence, looked away.

Around the table, the initial impact of Henderson's bombshell was wearing off. Spoons were taken up and the clatter of cutlery resumed.

'I always thought there was something shifty about him,' Stanley Twigg said. 'His face never quite fit, if you ask me.'

'Which no one did,' snapped Thomas.

'Well, I never saw it,' Susan said tearfully. 'I've got an instinct when it comes to reading a person's character, and I never suspected a thing.'

'I'm afraid that says more about your instinct than Mr Arden's character,' Henderson drawled. 'I imagine the judge who sentenced him to six months in Norwich Gaol with hard labour was going on his instinct too ... and the evidence of four silver serving spoons, stolen from Ward Abbey and found in Arden's room. Of course, the young housemaid who let him into the house and fell for his charm and that handsome face probably felt she *had an instinct* for character too. Who can blame her? He was a very plausible fellow.'

Mrs Furniss pressed her napkin to her mouth and kept it there.

'I had my suspicions about him too,' Henderson went on. 'Which was why I did a little research . . . asked a few questions. Ward Abbey may be a long way from Coldwell, but it's one of Lord Halewood's properties. Sir Randolph is a good friend of Viscount Frensham, Lord Halewood's eldest son, so I am well acquainted with his valet. Arden would have perhaps been wise to change his name on his release from prison.'

'How?'

Everyone looked round in surprise. You tended to forget Miss Dunn was there, since she hardly ever troubled herself to speak. Her tone was almost accusing, and she was staring at Henderson with a mixture of challenge and dislike.

'How did he get the key to the library?'

Henderson, who was about to lift a spoonful of plum pudding to his mouth, paused. 'My dear Miss Dunn, a fellow like that'—his eyes slid along the table, towards Mrs Furniss—'will always find a way.'

Returning his gaze to the bowl in front of him, he frowned, then carefully extracted something from his pudding. 'Ah, the sixpence . . .' He held it aloft. 'It seems I'm the one fortune has favoured.'

As bloody always, thought Eliza bitterly.

The bothy was in an advanced state of dereliction, its doorway a gaping hole of tumbled stone beneath a tilting lintel, its roof a tattered patchwork of slipped slates and broken rafters. Through a hole above the gable, Jem could see a torn scrap of indigo sky, pinned with a single star.

The moors were dotted with structures like this, built at intervals along the ancient packhorse trails, their crumbling ruins used these days by sheep to shelter in. This one had the remnants of a fireplace, in which Jem had been able to get a small blaze going, using one of his precious matches and dried leaves from the floor, along with an old bird's nest. A person could easily perish out on the exposed moorland in weather like this (perhaps that was what Henderson had hoped), so he was glad of the meagre fire and the sheltering walls, despite the reek of sheep.

He had managed to sleep for a few hours, once dawn had unfurled its pink streamers across the sky. Huddled into his jacket, wearing all the clothes he had, it seemed he had slept the short day away and woke to the sky drained of light, the star hovering above the broken-down barn. The symbolism wasn't lost on him on that Christmas night, though he had never been able to muster much in the way of faith. If anything, his current predicament—frozen, aching, hungry—made him less inclined to believe. Surely no labouring woman or her newborn would survive conditions like this? Maybe it was a good deal warmer in Bethlehem.

He crouched by the smouldering fire and blew on his hands. It was only for a few more hours. Just before first light he would head back to Coldwell and find shelter in the park, close to the church. With any luck, they would think he was far away by now, and not coming back, and the snow would have melted enough for his footsteps to be lost.

He wondered if Kate had got his note. If, in all the commotion around his departure (and he could only begin to imagine *that*), she had thought to look in the Chinese vase, and knew that whatever Henderson said, he hadn't abandoned her; that he would be waiting for her in the church at three o'clock on Boxing Day. *Only a few more hours.* By this time tomorrow, he would have had a chance to see her and explain and—please God—persuade her to go with him. Or have arranged for her to join him very soon.

Please God.

Staring up at the distant star he mouthed the words, so that they formed themselves into wisps of white breath against the deepening blue.

It was funny how the most cynical nonbeliever could muster a flicker of faith if he was desperate enough.

———⊗———

I will get through this.

Kate repeated the words inside her head as she went through the motions of overseeing the clearing up after Christmas dinner.

It won't always feel this bad.

But on that dark afternoon in the dying of the year, it was hard to imagine a time when she would be happy again, or even anything approaching content. The future seemed as dreary as the December day. A restless despair pulsed inside her. She wanted to go upstairs to the footmen's attic and search Jem's room for a clue, or any trace of him left behind. She wanted to leave the oppressive house and go out into the fading light to follow his footsteps for as far as they would lead her. She wanted to stand on the top of the hill and scream out her rage until her lungs were scoured out, or fling herself onto her bed, burying her face in sheets that might yet bear some faint scent of his skin.

But she could do none of those things. And so, she moved mechanically through the familiar tasks, like a tinplate automaton.

When she was collecting the red ironstone serving dishes from the scullery to put away for another year, she remembered the Chinese vase.

She didn't care that Susan and Doris were standing at the sink, elbows-deep in greasy water, or that Eliza and Abigail were whisking in and out, still bringing in dirty dishes from the servants' hall. Now that she had thought of it, she couldn't wait until the scullery was empty to see if Jem had left a message—some word of reassurance that Henderson was lying.

Seizing the vase, she thrust her hand into it, turning it upside down and shaking it.

There was nothing there.

'Something wrong, Mrs Furniss?'

Susan's abrupt question made her jump. The vase slipped through her fingers and shattered on the tiled floor.

Joseph was coming out of the housekeeper's parlour as she took the ironstone china back. He held the door open for her but kept his head down and didn't meet her eye as she muttered a thank-you. She was unsurprised to find Henderson in there (in fact, she should really stop thinking of it as the housekeeper's parlour, since it clearly wasn't her territory at all anymore). Breathing in the smell of hair oil, she had to force herself not to recoil and retreat.

She had to face him sometime.

Except, facing him was something she couldn't bring herself to do. If she had to look at him directly, she wasn't sure that she could keep it in— the loathing and contempt, the *blame*—and she was afraid of what she might say. But even without looking, she was aware of him, reclining in the velvet armchair where she used to drink tea in the quiet afternoons, his feet up on the coal box, his newspaper raised. Without thinking, her hand went to the chains at her waist, reaching for her keys. She remembered that they weren't there as his laconic voice came from behind the newspaper.

'You'll be needing these, I daresay.'

The newspaper was lowered. He held out his hand, the ring containing her keys suspended from a soft white finger.

Hatred burned in her gullet, like something hot, swallowed too quickly. Reluctantly she went towards him, half expecting him to snatch the keys away as she reached for them. The fact that he didn't was somehow unsettling.

'You didn't know, did you?' Uncrossing his legs, he set the newspaper aside. 'That he had form for this sort of thing? That he'd spent time in prison?'

She was glad to turn away from him and busy herself with unlocking the china cupboard, lifting out the Rockingham serving plates to put the servants' hall ironstone beneath it.

'None of us did.'

Her throat felt like it was filled with gravel. Behind her, she heard him sigh.

'My dear Mrs Furniss . . . you don't have to pretend with me. It's rather pointless trying to maintain the fiction that there was nothing between you. I assumed he would have told you about his criminal past—if only to paint himself as an innocent man, wrongly convicted. When I began to suspect he wasn't quite the model servant he claimed to be, I feared he might have charmed you into joining his little deception . . . I even wondered if you'd given your keys into his hand yourself. But I see now that he tricked you, along with everyone else.' Another little sigh. 'I'm sorry.'

Kate's eyes were hot with the tears she couldn't shed. This . . . *kindness* was disorienting and disturbing. A trick, she guessed, to compromise her, or trap her into some sort of confession.

'Save your sympathy,' she said coldly. 'I don't need it.'

She shut the cupboard and locked it. As she turned towards the door, Henderson stood up, making her stiffen with alarm. However, he made no move to block her way. His movements were slow and deliberately casual as he slid his hands into his pockets and stood in front of the fire's glow.

'My offer still stands, you know, in spite of this . . . unfortunate lapse of judgement.'

'Offer?'

'I know what it is to be given a second chance. I understand—perhaps more than you realise. A servant's life can be a lonely one, especially for those of us above the rabble of the lower ranks, but it doesn't have to be like that. An alliance could benefit us both. I could offer you protection, respectability, and you could—'

Oh God, was he talking about marriage? Was that the *offer*?

She'd had an uneasy suspicion of what he was hinting at when he'd spoken of an alliance back in the summer. Now he was talking about a united front . . . *a powerful team* . . . though his words sounded distorted, as if she had slipped underwater. The room tilted a little, as if she were in the cabin of an old galleon, pitching on rough seas. She groped behind her and found the handle of the linen cupboard to hold on to.

'I think we could come to an arrangement that would suit us both, don't you, Mrs Furniss?' The silkiness of his tone filled her with queasy dread, and he started to advance towards her, with the predatory menace of a cat closing in on a bird. 'Especially if—'

The door opened, stopping him quite literally in his tracks.

Miss Dunn came in, looking dismissively at Henderson before turning her attention to Kate.

'I've made Lady Hyde some chamomile tea and there's some left over, if you want it. I know you weren't feeling too well, and I always find it works wonders for a headache.'

Kate hadn't said anything of the sort, though she certainly wasn't going to argue. The thank-you she mumbled as she walked stiffly to the door was wholly inadequate to convey her gratitude.

She didn't look at Henderson. She didn't have to. She could just imagine the flinty fury on his face at being thwarted like that—and by Miss Dunn, of all people: mousy, colourless, *female*. Of course, it wasn't over. As she wearily went up the back stairs to her room, she knew she would have to deal with him sometime, and make it quite clear that hell would freeze over before she would make any kind of alliance with him. Though she supposed she ought to say it more neutrally than that.

But she was glad not to have to think about it now, when it felt like something inside her was about to snap and the grief and bewilderment and rage were rising in her chest, threatening to choke her. Inside her room she sat on the edge of the bed and unclipped her chatelaine, letting it slither to the floor. Then she lay down, tucking her feet—shoes still on—under her, clutching at the sheet that still smelled of their mingled bodies, laying her cheek on the pillow where Jem's head had rested only a few hours earlier and a whole lifetime ago.

And she cried.

I know he must have told you that I used you. That it was all a pretence and I never felt anything for you. I wish I'd done enough to make you certain that wasn't true.

I didn't use you, Kate, you have to believe that. I fell in love with you, and though the time we had together only amounts to a few snatched, secret hours, they were the best of my life. They made me believe that happiness was a possibility. They gave me hope. I never pretended any of it—every moment was real.

I don't know if that makes any difference though, because what I did in the end was even worse.

Chapter 30

On Boxing Day, a fat pink sun rose into a clear sky full of fading stars, and a gentle thaw began. The quilted snow slid down the roof of the laundry, the trees shed their armfuls of white, and the slope of the drive lost its treacherous sheen. The roads beyond Coldwell must have become passable too, because in the middle of the afternoon a spluttering motor appeared on the hill and made a careful descent to the stable yard, where it disgorged four men and what appeared to be enough luggage for a week's stay.

They took everyone by surprise (particularly since there was no Davy to give notice of their sudden appearance), but introduced themselves as the string quartet, booked by Lady Hyde at the beginning of November. The luggage, it turned out, was an assortment of valises, violins, violas, and a cello which took up most of the back seat. Once they had unloaded it all onto the slush-covered cobbles of the stable yard it seemed that the servants' ball—which everyone had somehow assumed would be cancelled—was going ahead.

Mrs Gatley was the only one with any enthusiasm for the evening. 'Heaven knows, I work hard enough every other day of the blessed year, I'm not going to miss the chance to put on my best frock and dancing shoes,' she said to Susan and Doris, who were grumbling about having to prepare a cold buffet at such short notice. 'What's the matter with you young things? Slice the ham thinly for the sandwiches, and we can use up the leftover salmon from luncheon on Christmas Eve. We're too late for jellies—they won't set in time, but we can do meringues. I've plenty eggs.'

Mr Goddard dispatched Eliza and Abigail upstairs, to remove small items of value from the hallway and dining room, in case they proved too much of a temptation for the less civilised outdoor servants.

It seemed, after Jem's defection, no one was to be trusted.

⸺⦵⸺

From his hiding place in the church, Jem saw the motorcar arrive. He had heard its puttering engine and climbed onto a pew to look out of a tiny diamond windowpane to watch its careful progress along the drive, sending up plumes of slush as it lurched through the puddles, and finally disappearing beneath the stable arch.

He felt slow with hunger, light-headed with lack of sleep, but his hollow stomach clenched. Had Henderson summoned the police, with another concocted story about a missing servant stealing something? He looked around for some means of escape, but there was only a small door to one side of the altar, which proved to be locked, and another in the porch that led only to the dark bell tower.

But it couldn't be long until three o'clock.

When he'd arrived at the church, the dawn was only a faint hint of pink above the dark blue hills to the east. He'd left his pack in the porch and crept round to the garden bothies by the orchard to steal a couple of apples.

Hollinshead could collar him for that, as well as whatever Henderson was going to pin on him.

He'd dozed a little, propped up on the Hyde family pew (cushioned in red velvet and twice as deep as the narrow shelves the servants perched on), slipping in and out of uneasy dreams but not managing to escape the bone-deep ache in his shoulders, his neck. He'd thought he was back in a cell waiting to be brought into the Norwich Assizes, and heard his own voice saying *not guilty*. It jolted him awake, and he suspected he had spoken it out loud.

He didn't dare sleep after that.

The church was small, surprisingly simple in style, its edges softened with age. He paced around, killing time, eventually picking up one of the Bibles from the shelf by the door. Lying on his back on the velvet cushion, his head propped on his pack, he flicked through the tissue-thin pages, idly noting how many times he spotted the word *servant* (*We are unworthy servants . . . Blessed are those servants, whom the lord when he cometh shall find watching . . . Well done, thou good and faithful servant . . .*) until the light started to fade and he had to strain his eyes to read.

A noise, out in the porch, made him sit upright. He got to his feet—too fast, making his head swim—and stumbled into the aisle. The afternoon gloom tented the little church, and he blinked to see into the shadows as the heavy door creaked open, his lips parting to say her name.

But it wasn't Kate whose slow footsteps tapped on the stone floor; who came forward to stand, arms folded, beside the ancient stone font.

Henderson sighed deeply. 'You just won't be told, will you?'

There was something wearily unsurprising about it. Jem had no idea how Henderson had found out about the meeting place, but he'd known somehow that it wasn't going to be as easy as he'd hoped. That didn't mean he had any intention of letting Henderson stand in his way. He was tired and he was hungry, but a quick mental calculation told him that he had the advantage of height and strength. And rage. He had a lot of rage.

'You didn't think I'd just give up and go quietly, did you?'

Jem's aching shoulders squared, and his hands balled themselves into fists. By contrast, Henderson appeared completely at ease as he leaned against the font. In his neatly buttoned overcoat and expensive leather gloves, he looked unprepared for a fight.

'No, I suspected you'd be foolish enough to push your luck,' he drawled. 'That's your trouble, Arden. You don't know when to accept that you're beaten. You think you're on some noble quest for justice? You're a fool. Your purpose—the purpose of all the staff here, and in every great house—is to serve your betters. To represent the family. Don't you realise that the good name of a man like Sir Randolph and the reputation of a house like Coldwell are far more important than the petty grievances of a nobody like you?'

Jem let his hands go limp at his sides. There was no point in arguing;

nothing to be gained by taking him on, this tin-pot downstairs despot, who wouldn't survive for five minutes out in the real world without Randolph Hyde's name to hide behind. Shaking his head, he leaned across to pick up his pack, then walked up the aisle towards Henderson, confident that if he tried to stop him on the way out that he could take him down.

The judge in the Norwich Assizes had instructed him to learn from his poor choices, and he had. One of several valuable things he'd learned in Norwich Gaol was how to stand up for himself. How to punch hard and clean.

But Henderson didn't try to stop him. He made no move at all. And Jem, opening the door to step into the darkness of the porch, felt a flash of surprise as he collided with a solid figure, barring his way.

There was no time to think. No chance to speak. He saw the glint of gold epaulettes and the flash of braid on a chauffeur's cap, and felt a meaty hand grab his arm, holding him still in the second before a fist connected with the side of his face.

An explosion of white light inside his head. (Maybe the chauffeur had spent time in gaol too.)

Pain tore through him as the world reeled and turned upside down. Another blow, and his cheek smashed against the stone floor, wetness seeping into his ear, running into his eyes, turning everything dark.

***

The blue silk dress was lovely. Kate could see that, as she smoothed the narrow band beneath the bust, where the little glass beads caught the lamplight. It made her feel acutely uncomfortable.

Her black working dress hung on its hook on the back of the door. As she went through the motions of brushing out her hair, twisting it up, and repinning it (tightly, with no concession to frivolity,) she kept fighting the temptation to exchange it for the unfamiliar blue, which exposed her arms, her neck, her throat, her former self. The woman in the mirror in the silk and chiffon looked like the one who had sat on overstuffed sofas in the Bristol house and sipped Madeira wine from cut crystal. The woman she had tried so hard to outrun.

But she had discovered that you couldn't escape yourself. And she couldn't bring herself to snub Miss Dunn's kindness, either. Even in her state of shocked numbness, with her heart like a stone in her chest, she couldn't do that.

We women should stick together.

The only sound in the attic was the whistle of the wind through the window frame and the hiss of the lamp. Eliza and Abigail, Susan and Doris had finished getting ready a quarter hour ago and clattered downstairs in their best Sunday shoes, leaving a trail of lavender water and excited chatter behind them. Kate supposed that everyone would be assembling in the hall, where the candles had been lit on the tree and the band had set up.

She should go down . . .

She had seen Henderson briefly, after breakfast. Passing the stillroom, he had looked inside and enquired, with guileless courtesy, if she was feeling a little better after her early night? He had appeared pleased to hear that she was (what else could she say?) and said that he was looking forward to continuing their conversation later.

'I don't have anything more to say, Mr Henderson,' she had asserted coolly.

'Perhaps not, Mrs Furniss,' he had replied, dropping his voice confidingly. 'But I do.'

Her ledger lay on the table beside the character reference Eliza had brought from her previous position. Kate had been putting off writing her new one, but even that awkward task was preferable to going downstairs and facing Henderson. She picked up the watch from her chatelaine, lying beside the ledger.

It was half past seven. They would be waiting for her to start the dancing; Mr Goddard with Lady Hyde, herself with Sir Randolph, as was the tradition. If she didn't hurry, they might send someone up to find her. A sudden unpleasant image of Mr Henderson climbing the attic stairs to seek her out was enough to galvanise her into motion.

She put a silk shawl round her shoulders and picked up the lamp, holding it above the bed for a moment as she made her way to the door. It was neatly made, its secrets folded in the smooth linen, as if everything that happened there last night had been nothing but a dream.

───── ⣿ ─────

There was a time, thought Eliza, stifling a yawn, that she would have considered this a proper treat.

A string band, done up in evening suits (though they were cheap ones and had seen better days), and a buffet spread out in the dining room, with candles alight in the crystal chandelier, reflecting in all the mirrors. A huge Christmas tree, and dancing; everyone standing around the floor watching Sir Randolph and Mrs Furniss, Mr Goddard and Lady Hyde, waiting to take their turn.

Now she felt only indifference.

Abigail had finally noticed her altered shape. Getting changed into their best before coming downstairs, she had glanced at Eliza in surprise and asked why she wasn't wearing the velvet skirt she'd made last winter (honestly—this was someone who'd always boasted that she had a good eye for clothes and the fit of them). Eliza, weary of waiting for the penny to drop, had told her, quite bluntly, that it wouldn't do up. And she'd watched Abigail's gaze move downwards and her mouth fall open.

She didn't have to be so superior about it. So horrified. As if Eliza was the first person ever to get caught out after a bit of fun (not much fun, but that hardly mattered now). She was over there now, standing with Susan and Drippy Doris beneath the portrait of the second baronet, and it was obvious from the way they kept looking at Eliza—trying to look as if they weren't—that she'd told them. Susan would probably let on she'd read it in the cabbage leaves or something, but the fact was, none of them had guessed. They fancied themselves modern girls, but they were as silly and sheltered as hens in a coop, with their old country sayings and superstitions. They knew nothing of the real world.

Tapping her foot idly to the music (some dreary waltz), Eliza's attention shifted to the dancers. Mr Goddard looked like a broken umbrella—all spiky elbows and flapping black coattails as he steered Lady Hyde around the floor. (She was wearing the diamond choker Sir Randolph had given her for Christmas—the one Jem was supposed to have had his eye on, though that didn't seem likely to Eliza.) Sir Randolph stumbled on the hem of Mrs Furniss's dress as they passed, and Eliza caught a whiff of whisky and bad digestion. Anyone could see that he was three sheets to the wind, hanging on to Mrs Furniss like a drowning man on a life raft, his eyes heavy, his hands too low on her back (not on her back at all, you might say). Mrs Furniss was stiff in his arms, straining to maintain a space between her body and his, and you could tell from looking at her that his touch made her skin crawl. Eliza didn't envy her.

It was funny to think that she ever had.

Even in her own current predicament, Eliza wouldn't swap places with her now. The mauve silk housecoat and the silver chatelaine and the parlour with the velvet armchair that Eliza had coveted so much hadn't stopped Mrs Furniss from falling for a bit of charm and a nice smile, just like Eliza had. And a housekeeper had that much further to fall.

Around the walls the deer and cattle watched, looking as bored as Eliza felt. She stifled another yawn and wondered when they would be allowed to start on the buffet. People were pairing up, preparing to join the couples on the dance floor: Gatley and Mrs Gatley, Thomas and Susan. Eliza watched George Twigg offer his arm to Drippy Doris (who looked like she might cry from excitement this time. Tragic.) and the new gamekeeper approach Miss Dunn, who shook her head and turned away quickly, as if he were a dog begging for scraps at the table and shouldn't be encouraged. She wondered if Mr Henderson was going to ask Abigail, who was sipping her fruit cup and trying not to look like a spare part, but his narrowed eyes were fixed on Sir Randolph and Mrs Furniss as they made their hobbled progress around the floor.

Eliza was so taken up with watching that she didn't notice Robson the chauffeur until he was almost on top of her. Starting with surprise, she stepped back to let him move past. Except he didn't. He flexed his thick neck and stared at a point past her shoulder as he asked her if she'd like to dance.

There was a mark on the collar of his white shirt, she noticed. A splash of scarlet, which looked like blood. Fancy being so ham-fisted you could cut yourself so badly while shaving that it dripped on your shirt. Fancy being so stupid you would put your clean shirt on *before* you shaved.

A few weeks ago, his request might have been a straw she would have gratefully clutched. Now she couldn't see the point. She'd be leaving any day. It wasn't what she would have chosen, but neither was meaty Robson, with his thick neck and bristly skin like pink pork rind.

'No thanks,' she said, giving him an offhand glance. Then, as an afterthought, she added more kindly, 'Look—Abigail doesn't have a partner. Why don't you ask her?'

—⊶⊷⊶—

Dripping.

Something was dripping, slowly and steadily. The sound reverberated around Jem's throbbing head, echoing in the darkness.

The darkness was . . . total.

Perhaps he was blind.

The thought sent a surge of suffocating panic through him. With difficulty he propped himself against the slimy wall and fumbled at his pockets, pain pulsing through every muscle. His hair was wet, and so were his clothes. The brick floor beneath him was mossy and the air was damp and rank, like the inside of a well. Or a grave.

Moaning with the effort, he tried his pockets again, and this time his stiff fingers found the matchbox. He eased himself back, breathing hard, waiting for the florid pulse of pain inside his head to fade a little before he summoned the energy to strike one.

The first match skittered and fell from his grasp. The second sparked and died. The box was almost empty, so he forced himself to wait, to gather his strength and quell the panic that was rising with every slow drip.

The third match flared into a tiny, leaping flame that dazzled in the dark. He was not blind, nor sealed in a grave, but in a wide tunnel, with brick-lined walls. His own hand, holding the match, was crusted with drying blood.

It was too much to take in before the match went out. But as the blackness closed around him, the images stayed. Slime-slick bricks. His fingernails, rust rimmed. His shirt sleeve, soaked red.

The brief brightness seemed to have burnt itself into his eyes. He could still see it, dancing in front of him, after the match had died. But then he realised it was coming closer, and there were footsteps too, echoing and splashing along the tunnel.

His body responded instantly: a whipcrack of panicky energy that sent him scrambling to stand as pain ripped through his shoulder and exploded in his head like fireworks. He didn't want to give Henderson another go at him while he was on the floor. Bent double, with his arms clamped around his body, he staggered up, tasting blood as he coughed, almost passing out from the spasm of pain it unleashed.

He wanted to square his shoulders, to lift his head, and raise his fists, but he couldn't. And so he waited, every screaming nerve taut, braced for the blow.

The footsteps stopped a few feet away.

'It's all right. Don't be scared,' said a voice he didn't recognise.

He forced his eyes open a crack.

The light swayed, gleaming on the wet walls. On the face of the person who held it. Jem squinted, trying to bring it into focus.

'*Davy?*'

Chapter 31

Once the initial awkwardness wore off, the evening seemed to be a success.

It had been a lean and quiet Christmas for most, cut off in their cottages by the snow, so there was a mood of festivity and an appetite for celebration. And however numerous his faults, it had to be said that Sir Randolph was a generous host. Beneath the blaze of the chandeliers, cheeks grew red with beer and cheer as the evening wore on.

Henderson caught up with Kate in the dining room. She wasn't hungry but had drifted there to give herself a purpose, as if the staff couldn't be trusted to serve themselves from the buffet without her supervision. Lady Hyde came across, to remark kindly upon the marvellous job Miss Dunn had done with the blue dress, and how much better it suited Kate. She chattered (with a trace of wistfulness) about the hunt ball she had worn it to, back home in Shropshire, until Frederick Henderson joined them, apologising to her ladyship, and asking Kate to dance.

As always, he had worked it out carefully and left nothing to chance. By approaching her in front of Lady Hyde, Kate couldn't refuse. Not without appearing rude. She had no choice but to take the arm he offered and go with him into the hallway, where the band were playing the opening bars of 'The Blue Danube.'

'Forgive me for stealing you away like that,' he said, his voice an intimate murmur as he guided Kate round the floor. He was only an inch or so taller than she, so his lips were level with her ear, and his breath fanned her neck. Through her gloves she could feel the heat of his hand and through the thin silk of the blue dress she could feel the heat of his body. The smell of him made her rigid with revulsion.

'You really left me no choice, though; I've been trying to catch up with you for the last hour to ask for a dance. A more cynical man might say you were avoiding me, Mrs Furniss. I must say, you look very lovely. Are you enjoying the evening?'

'Oh yes, Mr Henderson,' she said tersely. 'I'm quite giddy with enjoyment. I can't think of anywhere I'd rather be.'

Above them, the second baronet smirked knowingly, as if he were enjoying her discomfort. Henderson laughed, ignoring her sarcasm, rather like an indulgent parent with an overtired child. 'I'm sure that's not true,' he said mildly. 'A sophisticated woman like yourself, with such a refined background; a woman who has experienced the finer things in life . . . I'm sure there are many places you'd rather be, Mrs Furniss . . .'

He paused, steering her carefully around Platt the gamekeeper and Mrs Gatley.

'Or should that be . . . Mrs *Ross*?'

<hr />

The pain came in waves, like water in a tin bath. Every movement created more, gathering force and momentum until it was impossible to stay afloat and they dragged him under.

Davy hauled him up, hoisting Jem's arm over his solid shoulders. Jem clamped his jaw shut, biting down on the howl that tore through him, aware, through the haze of agony, that it might frighten Davy away if he let it loose.

He couldn't afford to frighten Davy away. Even though, at that moment, being left on the floor in the tunnel seemed preferable to this agonising, uneven progress along it.

His head lolled against Davy's arm. There was an angry buzzing sound inside it. Nausea rolled him in its powerful swell, and there was nothing to do but give himself up to it. He was jolted back to consciousness by his own jagged cry and the searing, white-hot pain in his shoulder as Davy set him down on a bare wooden floor.

Later, when the sawing scrape of his breath had steadied and the agony had subsided a little, he could see they were in a square room, with arched windows on three sides and a fireplace on the fourth. The windows were crowded with stars and let in the silvered light of the moon, enough to faintly illuminate the intricately carved wooden panels around the walls, the murky portrait hanging on the chimney breast. The details of the painting were lost to the shadows, but he could make out the dark oval of a face, the white froth of a lace collar beneath it. The gleam of a jewel fastened to a headdress above.

'Is this the tower?'

Davy nodded. He had retreated to the other side of the room, where there was a blanket on the floor and a little collection of supplies: the stub of a candle, a jam jar, a handful of sweet chestnuts with a scattering of their spiky cases. He picked up one of the chestnuts and began to pick at its shell, scowling with concentration. The lower half of his face was darkened with a scrubby beard, which seemed at odds with his childlike manner.

'Is this where you've been hiding?'

Another nod. Jem knew now that Davy was capable of speaking, but it seemed he'd rather not.

'We were worried about you.'

Tentatively Jem pressed his fingers to his face, around his eye, across his cheekbone, and down past his ear. Robson's fist had struck him at the angle of his jaw; Jem gave a sharp inhalation as his fingers found the place. His tongue felt fat from where he'd bitten it and he could still taste blood. It hurt to open his mouth. To speak.

'It's safe here,' Davy mumbled. His voice was hoarse, his words indistinct, as if he'd fallen out of the habit of forming them.

'How did you get in?'

Davy shuffled over to the fireplace and dropped the chestnuts onto a coal shovel, laying it carefully over the remains of a faintly glowing fire. (*He can look out for himself in the woods, no doubt about that . . .*) 'The tunnel, of course,' he replied, with a hint of scorn. 'From the church. It went to the old house, before this one. No one knows about it except—'

He broke off abruptly, his face closing again like it had in the woods. 'Henderson,' Jem guessed.

Davy was crouching in front of the hearth, his broad back hunched over, his grimy coat blending into the gloom. He had gone very still.

'Henderson makes it his business to know everything at Coldwell, doesn't he?' Jem said, with difficulty. 'And to stop everyone else finding out what it suits him to keep quiet.'

Pain was throbbing in big, florid pulses through his shoulder and down his arm. It was echoing around inside his head. He wanted so much to lie down on the dusty floorboards and sleep.

Not now, he told himself ferociously. *Not yet.*

Davy shuffled the chestnuts on the fire shovel.

'But you know just as much as he does, don't you? More, I bet . . .' It was hard to speak around his swollen tongue and the great tiredness that dragged at him. 'You're like the watchman here, Davy . . .' He made himself pause, balancing his burgeoning sense of urgency with the need for caution, to avoid alarm. 'You saw what happened that night years ago, didn't you? When the gentlemen had an Indian banquet in this very room, and the boy went missing . . .'

Davy set the shovel down with a clatter, so the chestnuts rolled across the hearth. He didn't stand upright, but his hands covered his ears, like they had that day in the snow. He rocked his body, making a high whimpering sound.

'It's all right . . .' With a mammoth effort, Jem hauled himself to his feet and leaned against the wall until the fog of pain cleared and the urge to vomit passed. 'It's all right, I promise. He can't hurt you.'

He reached out to put a hand on Davy's shoulder, but the boy flinched as if he'd landed a blow. 'I never said anything!' he cried, 'I didn't! He made me swear on my mam's life—he said if I ever said *one word* he would cut my tongue out. He said he done it to a boy in India. *One word*, he said . . .'

Dear God.

'He's a *bad man*.'

So that's why Davy the chatterbox had stopped speaking. Wincing, Jem sank down onto the window seat, cradling his left elbow in his right hand as a white shaft of pain speared his shoulder. Closing his eyes, he breathed out through tight lips, concentrating on the whistle of his breath.

Out . . . and in again. Out and in.

'I've said it now, haven't I?' Davy moaned. 'I've said words and now I'm going to get into trouble . . . But what they did was *worse* and nobody told them off, not even the *constable* . . .'

Jem's eyes opened a crack. Davy was rhythmically hitting his fists against his head. It almost seemed that he was talking to himself, letting the words he had held back for so long spill out.

'You won't get into trouble,' Jem prompted hoarsely. 'I promise. What did they do?'

Davy thrashed his head from side to side. 'They took his clothes off!' It was an anguished wail. 'He was wearing . . . clothes like that—' In the glow of the fire he pointed to the portrait. 'But when I found him, he was . . .'

'Naked?'

Davy nodded, his eyes wide, his face a mask of shock. Jem felt his throat close in anguish. And anger.

'He was sleeping. He didn't know the good places to go, like I do. It was too cold to be out without a coat . . . there was a . . . a *sharp frost*—' (Jem heard the voice of Mary Wells in those words.) 'I put my coat over him, and I was going to get my mam, but *he* caught me . . . the bad man. He made me show him where the boy was.'

Through the blue shadows Jem could see the imploring expression on his face. 'He picked the boy up and carried him, but he didn't take him to the house. He took him to the tunnel and left him there, and he told me not to say *one word*. He told the constable that the boy had run away! Everyone believed him, but it wasn't true. He told a *lie.*'

So that was it. The information Jem had chased all these years.

The ending to the story.

Jack, the blond-haired kid who had loved animals and bread pudding—who had been shy and quiet and had no patience for reading and writing but could recognise any bird from its song and any tree from its leaf—had been stripped naked by a pack of baying men and left outside in the woods on a November night. And Henderson had chosen to get rid of him like rubbish to protect his master's name.

He wanted to tell Davy that it was all right. To reassure him he wouldn't be hurt and thank him for trying to help Jack. In a minute he would, when the ache in his throat had subsided and he could speak. But for now, he turned his head away and pressed his cheek to the window, where his tears felt warm against the icy glass.

⸰⸰⸰

The attics felt bitingly cold after the crowded downstairs rooms. Cold and dark. Kate lit the lamp in her room with a shaking hand and stood numbly, holding the spent match, not knowing what to do after that. For the next five minutes, or the next five years.

The flimsy foundations on which she had built her life had collapsed, and she felt like she was falling, with nothing to hold on to.

How did Henderson know?

He had given some sketchy explanation that she had barely heard— Alec turning up at the Savoy, a gaming acquaintance of Sir Randolph's. (*I must say, he's not the sort of man I thought you'd go for, Mrs Furniss, though I daresay that roguish charm might have a certain appeal . . .*) It had been all she could do to keep herself upright and get through the rest of the interminable 'Blue Danube,' because she knew that leaving before it finished would cause a scene. She hadn't trusted herself to speak, and to ask the question that now filled her head, squeezing out all other thoughts.

Did Alec know she was here?

Distractedly, she began to scrabble at the back of her dress, desperately trying to reach the row of little buttons that fastened it. It had been made for a lady who enjoyed the assistance of a maid; Abigail had fastened her into it earlier, but Kate couldn't wait until the festivities had ended and the girls made their way up to bed to take it off. Nowhere felt safe anymore. She was shivering with cold, and her mind felt as frozen as her body in the thin, exposing dress. She pulled at the silk, not caring if it tore, until a knock on the door stilled her.

'Mrs Furniss?'

Miss Dunn's voice from outside was an urgent whisper, close to the door. Had it not been for the stupid dress Kate would have called out to her to go away, said that she was unwell, but she went across to let her in.

It struck her that there was something different about Lady Hyde's maid recently. It was strange to think that she had seemed so timid and insignificant when she had first come to Coldwell, faintly ridiculous with her air of anxious disapproval and her temperance ribbon. But as she came into the small room there was a determined set to her jaw and a steadiness in her gaze, though her hands twisted together and her thin lips were pale.

'He's told you, hasn't he?' she said without preamble. 'About your husband?'

Kate's head reeled.

All this time she'd believed that she had escaped the past. She'd thought that no one knew who she was, or where she came from, but it seemed that illusion was as flimsy as her safety.

'How did you know?'

A thought, like a dark spot on her brain, had begun to spread. Jem was the only person she'd told, and he was gone. Had he betrayed her more completely, more cruelly than she'd begun to comprehend?

'I'm so sorry.' Miss Dunn's voice was low and steady. 'I'm afraid I have played a most regrettable role in this situation, a fact for which I can only beg for your forgiveness and understanding. It was I who identified the . . . *gentleman*' (a slight hesitation over the word, and a faint trace of scorn) 'at the Savoy as your husband. I wasn't thinking straight at the time. I wasn't . . . myself.'

Kate turned round, pushing her fingers into her hair, making it pull at the pins.

'But . . . *how*? How did you *know*?'

She could barely articulate the question, but Miss Dunn, recovering her composure, took charge. With a cursory 'May I?' she pulled out the chair from beneath the table and sat down. 'I should have been honest with you from the start; I see that now. But we pack our pasts away when we enter service, don't we? It never does to ask too many questions in the servants' basement.'

She tucked her skirt carefully about her knees and clasped her hands in her lap as she told Kate that her father was a Methodist minister, who had moved to Bristol when she was a child. She described a household dedicated to the Methodist movement, and how she, from a young age, had joined her father in working for the church, and become an active member of the city's Band of Hope, enthusiastically spreading the word about the benefits of abstinence.

Kate had seen the temperance disciples, of course. A city like

Bristol—with its teeming population of dockers and stevedores; its brisk brewing and import trades and countless taverns, gin palaces, and alehouses—provided fertile ground for those earnest young women distributing pamphlets on street corners, the children singing hymns and carrying banners in Sunday parades (*Buy Bread Not Beer!*). She had never paid them much attention, but Alec hated them with a scornful passion. *Joyless harpies*, he'd called them. *Silly spinsters who should keep their noses out of men's business.*

'It was through my work for the Women's Total Abstinence Union that I crossed paths with Mr Ross ...' Miss Dunn didn't look at Kate as she spoke, instead keeping her eyes downcast and folding the lace edge of her handkerchief over and over. 'I didn't know his name, but he was a regular in some of the places we used to hand out our tracts and periodicals. It wasn't unusual for us to be mocked and jeered, but I remember him because on one occasion he took the pamphlet I offered him and made a great show of reading it out loud, feigning sincerity, only to set his lighter to it and insult me in the ... crudest, *coarsest* terms.'

Kate could imagine. Alec Ross had taken a great deal of trouble to cultivate his cultured persona and polish his thin veneer of charm, but it didn't take much for the mask to slip, especially with drink inside him.

'I went out of my way to avoid him after that. I'm sure he wouldn't have recognised me once he'd sobered up, but I never forgot him. Which I suppose was why I noticed him coming out of the theatre one evening, with his lovely young wife on his arm.'

She raised her eyes and looked at Kate with an apologetic half-smile.

'So, you knew?' Kate croaked. 'From the day you arrived, you knew who I was ...?' She remembered the carriage arriving at the front steps on that bright spring day, when so much change had come to Coldwell. She remembered the figure inside, the glint of her stare in the gloom.

Miss Dunn shook her head. 'No—not straightaway. I had a feeling I recognised you, but I couldn't put my finger on from where. It had been *years* since I'd moved away from Bristol ... Before I worked for Miss Addison, I had a position as a shopgirl in a department store, and of course you see an awful lot of faces in that type of work. It wasn't until I saw him again—Mr Ross—in the hotel that day, that it came back to me. I recognised him immediately. Not so much his face—the years and the drink haven't been kind—but his accent caught my attention. And his attitude. Arrogant ... if you'll forgive me for saying so.'

'And you told Henderson.' Kate sank down onto the edge of the bed, rubbing her fingers over her forehead. 'You told *Henderson* what Alec Ross was to me.'

'I didn't mean to.'

Miss Dunn's tone had changed. Even through her own distress Kate registered the sudden terseness. A shutting down, a drawing inwards. Miss Dunn's lips were pressed together more thinly than ever, and her handkerchief was a tight twist between her fingers. 'I wasn't myself,' she muttered. 'He tricked me. Took advantage.'

Kate's head snapped up. She waited. Miss Dunn's face was composed, but one hand had gone to her breast, to the ribbon badge, and her chin trembled. When she spoke again, her voice was little more than a whisper.

'It was a wedding, so of course there was a lot of imbibing going on. I don't judge anyone for that, but as you know I don't partake of alcohol myself, *ever*, and I never have. Abstinence is the foundation of my faith— it's ... fundamental to my whole being. Lady Hyde had made it clear that I was at the wedding as a guest, not a servant, and had very kindly made sure there was a non-intoxicating fruit cup for me. It was something of a speciality of the hotel, I was told, and though I found it a little bitter for my taste, I appreciated her consideration.'

Kate's mind jumped ahead. She knew what was coming next, without Miss Dunn's faltering explanation, because she knew Frederick Henderson.

'I began to feel a little woozy halfway through the wedding breakfast. It was rather warm, and I ...' Her face started to crumple, but she took a sharp breath in and carried on, her tone laced with bitterness like the fruit cup Henderson had laced with alcohol. 'Well, by the time Mr Ross appeared I was feeling very light-headed indeed. Not quite in command of myself, you might say. I was so surprised to see him there, and I conveyed that astonishment to Mr Henderson, who—as far as I recall—took a great interest. A very great interest indeed.'

Kate was shivering. Now that the initial shock was wearing off, the whole thing had an air of wearying predictability. She could picture all too easily how it had happened: Henderson, the master manipulator, always watching out for weakness to pounce on and exploit.

'I tried to tell you when we got back from London, at the wedding dance, but there was no opportunity.' Miss Dunn sounded weary. 'And then I wondered if I was being selfish, burdening you with it. I wondered if I was just trying to ease my own conscience by confessing. As time went on, I allowed myself to hope that Mr Henderson might have turned out to be more honourable than I gave him credit for.' She gave a short, bitter laugh. 'Of course, that hope was entirely misplaced. He was waiting for his moment, wasn't he?'

Kate stood up, pacing across to the door and back, though it took only three steps to cover the floor. Her thoughts were bouncing around madly, like the glass ball in one of the roulette wheels on which Alec used to lose so much money. This is what she had feared, for years, and yet she hadn't made a single contingency plan.

She thought of the body in the harbour, beaten beyond recognition, and put her hands to her own cheeks. 'He'll kill me if he finds me,' she sobbed. 'What shall I do?'

Miss Dunn's gaze was steady.

'Exactly as I say.'

Chapter 32

Joseph crouched in the darkness under the basement stairs, his knees drawn up against his chest. He had moved the pile of wicker hampers out a little way, so he could hide behind them, but he needn't have gone to the trouble. No one was looking for him. No one had noticed he was missing. He was invisible. A nothing.

He groped for the bottle at his side and lifted it to his lips, wincing as the spirit scorched his throat. Mr Goddard had stopped him from having cider upstairs like everyone else, but he'd remembered Mrs Gatley's bottle of brandy, left out after being used to set the Christmas pudding alight. It tasted worse than cough medicine, but it had slowed his racing mind and made his body feel like it wasn't quite his own, which was (he decided) a good thing.

It hadn't stopped the sound of the baby crying inside his head though. The wet smack of fist on flesh.

Upstairs the band had finished playing and the ball was over. The merriment had moved downstairs to the servants' hall, where Mrs Gatley was trying to teach George Twigg the polka and the band were eating leftover sandwiches before making the journey back to wherever they'd come from. Huddled in the cobwebbed dark, Joseph listened to the laughter. Every time Mrs Gatley's raucous cackle rang out he tensed, though it sounded quite different to the baby, really. Nothing like that urgent, quavering cry.

Earlier he had gone to his bed by the silver cupboard and taken out the old candle box from beneath it, where he kept his sixpences. He didn't count them before shoving them into his pocket—the sum he had amassed was a source of shame, not pride. He was going to give them back to Mr Henderson. Tonight. He was going to tell him that he didn't want any part in his special duties no more and he'd rather earn his money the regular way. And he could get someone else to wear the Indian lad's uniform for Sir Randolph's gentleman's parties.

Currents of frozen air gusted along the passageway as the band members went back and forth to their motorcar, loading up their things, passing a few feet from Joseph's hiding place. Part of him wanted someone to notice him, so he straightened his legs till his feet were sticking out past the hampers, but when he realised that his cheeks were wet and his nose was running, he withdrew them again.

Anger began to uncurl inside him, like an animal waking up and stretching.

Out in the corridor, a bell started to jangle, greeted by a chorus of jeers from the servants' hall. There was a scraping of chairs, a clatter of feet. 'Lady Hyde's room!' he heard Susan call. 'Not our business. Where's Miss Dunn?'

'Haven't seen 'er. Nor Mrs Furniss.'

'Well, I'm not going . . .'

'Someone better had . . .'

Joseph put the bottle to his mouth and tipped his head back, but only a scant drop trickled onto his tongue. His arm suddenly felt incredibly heavy, and he let it fall, so the bottle cracked down onto the tiles and rolled away.

The bell rang again, joining with the clamour of the baby's cry in his head.

He fumbled in his pockets and pulled out the coins. Some of them slipped through his fingers and rolled away too. He scrambled to pick them up, but as he groped in the dirt, he knew he was wasting his time; it was all for nothing anyway.

He could return the money to Henderson, but it wouldn't bring Jem back.

'I've spoken to the violinist chap—he's the driver. He says there's not much room, but they'll take you as far as Sheffield and drop you at the station. Find somewhere to sit tight for a few hours, and you can get the milk train to London.'

Kate had followed Miss Dunn in silence through the nursery wing and down the stairs. Now, in the darkness of the stairwell, they spoke in whispers.

'What reason did you give?'

'Just what we agreed. A telegram arrived earlier saying that your mother is ill. It must have been delayed already because of the weather and you don't want to waste any more time getting to her.'

Kate nodded, fighting uncertainty. The plan was all Miss Dunn's, but she couldn't find fault with it, nor see any alternative. In so many ways, it was similar to the one she had come up with herself on the night she had left Bristol nearly ten years previously. Seizing the moment, not allowing doubts and what-ifs to throw her off course. Forcing herself out into the unknown.

'Thank you. For helping me.'

'How could I not, when this is my fault?'

'Don't say that. It's the fault of men, isn't it? Their demands and their desires and their need to control. I came here to escape one man, and another will use that to manipulate me. If I try to stand up to him, he'll ruin me. And he'll get away with it, won't he? Because they always do.'

She was talking to herself as much as Miss Dunn, going over the things they had already been through upstairs, reminding herself why it was impossible to stay. How there was no reason to, with Jem gone.

'But we're stronger than they think,' Miss Dunn said softly. 'They can use all their power to control us, but they won't break us. We won't let them.' She was holding Kate's chatelaine and it sounded its familiar chime as she slipped it into the little drawstring reticule she carried, then lifted her hand to clasp Kate's. 'Ready? You've got everything?'

'I think so.'

Miss Dunn had taken charge of her packing too, and the case she carried (a small one of Lady Hyde's, more convenient than the box Kate had arrived with all those years ago) contained the bare essentials for a new start: a plain skirt, two blouses, nightclothes, and underthings. While

Miss Dunn had folded and packed, Kate had bundled together the writing case on the table along with some headed paper. She would need it to apply for a new position and start from scratch with a new set of half-truths.

Miss Dunn went ahead of her into the cold night. High above the stable block, the moon was like a mother-of-pearl button in a sky full of sequin stars. Its light silvered the cobbles and the chrome trim of the motorcar that waited with its doors open.

'Here we are,' said Miss Dunn, in a voice that was bolder and more assertive than usual. One of the men from the band straightened up from loading things into the back seat, and turned to Kate with a smile. 'I hope you don't mind being a bit squashed in. We're used to it, but that doesn't always stop the complaints.'

'Not at all. I'm very grateful for your help.'

She climbed into the back seat, with the cello case and a large valise between her and its other occupant, the viola player. Her own case she put on the floor by her feet, bending her legs awkwardly around it and sliding along to make room for the other violinist, who settled in heavily beside her.

'I'll say goodbye then,' Miss Dunn said stiffly. 'Good luck . . . with your . . . mother.'

'Thank you.'

With a curt nod, Miss Dunn shut the door and stood back, as the cellist turned the starter handle and jumped into the passenger seat.

The car circled the yard. Kate kept her eyes fixed on the figure of Miss Dunn, almost indistinguishable from the shadows, except for the pale oval of her face and the temperance ribbon on her dress.

A moment later they passed under the stable arch, as Kate had done a thousand times before, the motorcar gathering speed as it went up the incline of the drive, far quicker than Johnny Farrow's wagon and horses had ever done. Kate could feel the house at her back and knew exactly how it would look; its rows of glowing windows, the four muscular pillars at the top of the steps. The temple on the hill, dark against the stars.

But she didn't turn round.

She didn't look back.

Jem slept. Cold, hungry, and battered by waves of pain. It was a relief to give himself up to the swell of exhaustion and let it take him; carrying him away for a few hours of respite.

It was still dark when he woke, but the luminous dark of near dawn, not the inky blackness of night. The fire was ashes, but there was enough light inside the tower room to see Davy in a huddle of blankets in the corner, and the face of the boy above the fireplace.

Jem's eyes stayed fixed on him as he inched gingerly upright, bracing himself against the pain. Beneath his red headdress, the boy's face was calm and unsmiling. Resigned, almost. He had been taken from his home and family and brought to this cold house in the bleak Derbyshire Peaks by an Englishman who believed the world was his playroom and other people his toys. The painting showed a boy who had learned that his life was simply worth less than the jewel on his turban.

Over a hundred years had passed and nothing had changed.

Davy rolled over and sat up, blinking sleepily, his hair sticking up on one side, his bearded face scrunched into a sleepy scowl. Jem stood, gripping the edge of the panelling and praying not to pass out.

'It's time to go, Davy.' It hurt to talk. 'Now, before everyone's awake.'

'Where?'

'To the house. To find Ka—Mrs Furniss. And after that we'll get you home. Your mum will be very glad to see you and hear how brave you've been. How you saved my life.'

Davy nodded, shaking off his ragged assortment of blankets and shambling to his feet.

Jem found that once he was on his feet the pain settled to a steady thump, bearable if he didn't make any sharp movements. He didn't need Davy's assistance to go down the stairs this time, but was glad of his presence as he followed him through the oily black of the tunnel. He wanted to ask about Jack . . . about what had happened to his body after Henderson had left him down here, but he couldn't let that distract him now.

And there was something inside him that didn't want to think of Jack like that. As a body, not a boy.

The darkness was choking. The tunnel got narrower as the ground slanted upwards, until they were both bent double, and the pain was like a saw, deep in the flesh of Jem's shoulder. It made the breath burn in his throat, but just when he wasn't sure if he could go on any longer, Davy was pushing through a door at the top of some steps.

The dark was softer on the other side, the air cleaner. It held the unmistakable scent of churches. Slumping against the wall, waiting for the pain to loosen its teeth, Jem's heart lurched as the gloom revealed a rope hanging from the ceiling. It was another second before he realised they were in the bell tower, where for so long Davy had carried out his unofficial duty.

It seemed that the prospect of getting home had made Davy impatient. He opened the low door into the porch and waited for Jem, twitching with pent-up energy. Keeping his arm folded close against his body, Jem followed, gathering strength from the thought that he was minutes away from Kate.

Her image burned in his mind like a beacon as he stole through the fading night behind Davy. He pictured her, as he had left her, in her bed, asleep on her front, one hand curled beneath her chin. He imagined himself kneeling beside the bed, stroking her hair back from her face—ever so gently—and kissing her awake.

I didn't mean to let you down a second time. I didn't want to abandon you. I'm here now . . .

The stable yard was sleeping as they passed through it, the horses silent in their stalls. Jem looked nervously up at the chauffeur's loft, but no light showed.

Through the arch, the big kitchen window glowed with lamplight. Susan must be up, seeing to the water. In the yard he came up against the first flaw in his plan. He'd thought to wash in the stone trough; to submerge his head in the water and rub the dried blood from his matted hair and swollen face, but the trough was covered with a crust of ice an inch thick. The laundry house window reflected his image back at him; colourless but still horrifying. He looked like the ghost of someone who'd met a violent end.

He supposed he nearly had.

Behind him the back door opened; a slice of yellow reflected in the glassy black. A second later a little screech echoed around the yard as Susan spotted Davy.

'Oh my lord—*Davy Wells*,' she said in a furious whisper. 'I thought you were a—a *cutthroat* or something. What are you doing hanging around in the dark like that? You nearly frightened me to—'

Jem turned, not knowing if Davy would speak and getting ready to step in and explain. She saw him, crossing the yard towards her.

And this time she began to scream properly.

———⚬⚬⚬———

Eliza heard the noise as she came down the back stairs, tying her apron. She hadn't bothered to put her corset on this morning—since everyone knew about her predicament, or would do soon, she didn't need to endure the discomfort of concealing it anymore. As the scream spiralled through the sleeping house she stopped, hands stilling behind her back, red hot alarm flushing through her, driving her down the rest of the stairs as quickly as she could in her new clumsiness.

Downstairs was still in disarray from last night. The table outside the scullery was piled high with serving dishes and plates, and the floor was smeared and scattered with crumbs. In the wreckage of the usually ordered basement and the wake of the scream, the silence felt sinister, but as she hurried past the kitchen Eliza heard low voices at the back door.

'Susan, it's all right—*please*—don't wake everyone—'

She was standing in the doorway, her hands clamped over her mouth. And someone was outside in the yard, obscured by the lingering dark.

'What the bloody hell's going on?' Eliza went forward. '*Jem?*'

Dear God . . .

She'd thought what had happened that night before the London trip had been bad, but it was nothing to this. His clothes were filthy and his shirt torn, his face swollen on one side. A gash slashed across his forehead, just at his hairline, and had bled like nobody's business, the blood in dried rivulets down his cheek and neck, blackening his collar. He had one arm crossed over his chest, and the curled fingers of his hand were blood crusted too.

'We can't let him in,' Susan said in a shrill whisper. 'He tried to steal—'

'Oh for God's sake, Susan—are you mad? It's *Jem*. I don't give a monkey's what bloody Frederick Henderson said—stop dithering about like a halfwit and get some hot water and a cloth.'

She pushed her briskly back in the direction of the kitchen, then went to Jem, sliding her arm around his waist and drawing him gently forwards. In the passageway he winced at the light.

'It doesn't matter about the water,' he said hoarsely. 'I just need to see Mrs Furniss . . .'

'Oh my life—'

Abigail had appeared, almost colliding with Susan rushing the other way. When she saw Jem, her mouth fell open in horror and she backed away. 'What's happened?'

'Henderson,' Jem said tersely. 'I found out something he didn't want anyone to know. He got Robson to do this, and if he finds me here, he'll finish the job off. I need to—'

'He won't.' Eliza kept her voice calm. 'He won't dare do anything with us here. Isn't that right, Davy?' The lad was hovering as close to Jem's side as he dared, and she guessed that he had made all the difference between Jem quietly bleeding out somewhere and making it back here. 'Let's get you inside and cleaned up. Abigail, go and get Mrs Furniss.'

'No, I'll go—'

Jem made to push past her, but Eliza grabbed the arm that wasn't crossed over his chest.

'No, you won't,' she said firmly, lowering her voice so only he could hear. 'You can't. For her sake, Jem—think about it. Come on . . .' She put his arm over her shoulder. 'Let's have a look at the damage and clean you up.'

She could feel the beat of Jem's heart against her chest as she led him to the servants' hall, and felt a surge of ferocious protectiveness. She tried to steer him into Mr Goddard's chair, where Mrs Furniss had fussed over him last time, but he wouldn't sit. Instead, he paced restlessly, putting his fingers to the cut on his head, his eyes returning every few seconds to the door.

Susan came back, silently leaving a bowl of steaming water on the table, with a clean cloth. Eliza pictured Mrs Furniss dampening the cloth, the tenderness on her face as she'd sponged his skin. (She'd seen it then, but was too naïve to trust her own eyes.) She managed to stop him pacing and pin him against the wall long enough to clean the worst of the dried blood from his forehead and down his cheek. He flinched as she pressed around his jaw, and let out a jagged cry as she applied the cloth to the curve of his neck. Pulling his bloodstained shirt open, she sucked in a breath.

You didn't have to be a nurse to know that the hard lump pushing the bruised skin upwards shouldn't be there. She couldn't be sure what that bone was called, but she was one hundred per cent certain that whatever its name was it was supposed to be straight.

'It's all right . . .' she soothed, and she wondered if he could hear the ache of longing in her voice. 'It's broken, but you'll live . . .'

'Not if Henderson comes down.' He spoke through gritted teeth, his eyes swivelling desperately to the door. 'Look, I just need to see Kate—'

Abigail's footsteps rang along the corridor. Jem started forward as she appeared in the doorway, shaking her head.

'If she won't come down, I understand—' His voice was raw and desperate. 'But *please*—tell her I—'

'It's not that.' Abigail sounded almost afraid. 'She's not there.'

Afterwards Eliza remembered it as if it happened with no sound.

Jem moving past her, brushing her hand away as she tried to stop him. The urgency coming off him, like a physical force. She and Abigail following him out into the corridor. They were a few steps behind him as he ran to the housekeeper's parlour, so she didn't see him knock, or watch him go in.

They only saw him come out again, stumbling, his face milk-white, his hands held out to stop them going further.

And she wished that she'd let him.

That she hadn't seen Henderson, slumped in Mrs Furniss's little velvet armchair, which wasn't pale blue anymore, but crimson. Like his shirt, and his hand hanging down, and his dripping fingers.

Crimson, like Mrs Furniss's chatelaine, lying on the floor beside him in a coil of chains.

Like the scissors, with their sticky blades open.

Chapter 33

A fug of steamy warmth clouded the tea shop windows, obscuring the street outside. After Derbyshire, London seemed oddly warm—there was no sign of any recent snow—and after Coldwell the Lyons Corner House on Tottenham Court Road felt stifling. Kate had unbuttoned her coat but stopped short of taking her gloves off. A woman alone, she felt conspicuous enough as it was.

She sipped her tea and looked without enthusiasm at the dry slice of Madeira cake she had ordered. She had got off the train at St Pancras a little over an hour ago and felt as dazed and disorientated as if she'd landed on some distant foreign shore. It was impossible to comprehend that at the same hour yesterday she'd been making preparations for the servants' ball, moving through the rooms that had been her world for almost ten years, with no inkling that before the day was over she would have left them forever.

But she couldn't allow herself to think of Coldwell, or of Jem. Not now. (An emotional unravelling would draw even more attention than removing her gloves.) She was a servant, skilled at hiding her feelings. Numbly she unfolded the copy of the *Evening Standard* she had bought outside the underground station and pushed aside the unappetizing Madeira cake to make room for it on the table.

The advertisements for employment and accommodation were near the back, but as she went to turn the page a small front headline snagged her attention, one familiar word leaping out as if it had been written in six-inch scarlet letters.

MURDER AT COLDWELL HALL

At the next table the two elderly ladies stopped their conversation and looked round, eyes stretched with alarm at the gasp she made.

'My dear, are you quite well?'

She nodded, unable to find her voice. Folding the newspaper and picking up Lady Hyde's valise, she left the tea and cake and a scattering of coins on the table as she blundered clumsily to the door, to gulp the cool outside air.

It was an hour later, as the train she had hastily boarded slid past the goods yards and engine sheds of Victoria Station and began to gather pace, that she pulled out the paper and read the story properly.

> *Mr Frederick Henderson, valet to Sir Randolph Hyde, Fifth Baronet Bradfield of Coldwell Hall, Derbyshire, was discovered by household staff in the housekeeper's parlour in the early hours of Wednesday, December 27th, having suffered a single stab wound to the neck. The instrument of his misfortune was a pair of sewing scissors, attached to the housekeeper's chatelaine. The housekeeper herself, a Mrs Kate Furniss, had fled the house and remains at large. She is described as being of slim build, with dark hair and of refined appearance, aged approximately thirty years, and is wanted by the police for an interview.*

The train plunged into a tunnel. In the carriage window the ghost of Mrs Kate Furniss stared back at her for a second, all hollows and shadows. And then the train emerged again, into the light of the dreary December afternoon, and she disappeared.

———— ✆ ————

I don't remember much about it.

The police came, and Dr Seymour. I don't know who sent for them—Goddard, I suppose. The doctor must have given me something to knock me out, though I would never have agreed to it if I'd known. I was desperate to find you. I woke up in the cottage hospital at Hatherford with my arm strapped across my chest—a broken collarbone and a fractured jaw, they said.

I was there for a week, paid for by Hyde, so I missed what went on at Cold-well, but Eliza came to visit and told me that the police had spoken to the musicians. They all remarked that you were tense and mostly silent in the motorcar, as if in shock or distress. You wanted to get to the station, even though there were no trains that night. And of course, you left Coldwell with no word to Goddard or Lady Hyde and no forwarding address for your sick mother, no instructions for the running of the household in your absence. The evidence was stacking up, and it all seemed to point to one conclusion.

Except everyone at Coldwell knew it wasn't the truth.

None of us had noticed that Joseph wasn't there when we discovered Hender-son's body, and no one thought to look for him. The gamekeeper found him later, half-naked, none too sober and out of his wits, trying to wash the blood off his clothes in the lake.

The story came out slowly. I'd say there are still bits that haven't come out, about the things he witnessed before he went into the workhouse. Henderson had made a bit of a favourite of him and had been bribing him to spy on us. Joseph didn't realise what he was getting into at first, and I suppose he liked the money. By the time he understood, Henderson had his hooks well and truly into him. Joseph must have been desperate to do what he did.

You'd have thought that Hyde would be devastated to lose his right-hand man, but that wasn't the case. He knew as well as the rest of us what Henderson was like and what he was capable of, but Henderson was privy to Hyde's un-savoury secrets too, and that had given him a hold over his employer. Hyde must have been relieved to be rid of him, though if he believed his secrets were buried alongside Henderson in his pauper's grave, he was mistaken.

I could have told the police what he had done. Perhaps I should have, to try to get justice for my brother, though it would have been an unequal fight—a footman with a criminal record against a baronet—and my appetite for revenge had left me by then. It seemed more important to look to the other boy I should have protected. The one who was still living.

We all closed ranks around Joseph and kept him away from the police as much as possible. They weren't much interested in him anyway. They had their suspect—the housekeeper who had disappeared so suddenly and couldn't speak for herself.

I could have spoken for her.

God knows, Kate—I wanted to, please believe me. But I kept silent, because clearing your name would have meant exposing Joseph's guilt and I couldn't do that to him. Not when I should have seen what was going on and prevented it, or at least listened when he tried to tell me. Besides, I'm almost ashamed to say that I wanted the police to look for you. Finding you was all I could think about, and they had a better chance of success than I did. I would have admitted to the murder myself, then. I would have gone to the gallows without complaint if it meant I could see you again and have the chance to explain.

I never went back to work at Coldwell, only to help close it up. In the new year, the Hydes moved down to the London house, taking Miss Dunn and Thomas with them. Goddard was given a pension and went to live with a niece somewhere, and the rest of us were given generous characters and a sum of money to tide us over. The Gatleys stayed on as caretakers of the estate, and are still there, as far as I know. Lady Hyde didn't stay in London long. She and Miss Dunn returned to Shropshire, with the excuse of nursing her father, who wasn't in good health. You perhaps heard that Hyde suffered a heart attack at the card table in a London gaming club later that year. He wasn't much mourned, except by the fellow who was beating him at cards. When Lady Hyde returned to Coldwell for his funeral, she instructed the solicitors to put it up for sale.

I didn't want to work in service again. What I really wanted to do was scour the country and search until I found you, but I felt a responsibility for Joseph and Eliza. I know you were aware of her situation and were going to help her, and since she looked after me when I was recovering, it seemed only right that I should do the same. Joseph was very troubled after what happened, and I couldn't leave him to make his own way. I managed to get farm work for us on a small estate in Nottinghamshire. It came with a cottage, and I presented Joseph as my half brother and Eliza as my widowed sister.

It would have been kinder to say she was my wife. I know that was what she would have chosen, but I couldn't do it. Just in case word got out and reached you somehow and you believed it was true. Or, by some miracle you came looking for me, asking around, and were told I was married. It was a small hope, but I clung to it. I had nothing else.

I thought the arrangement would just be for the short term, until the child had been born and Eliza had decided what she wanted to do, but it didn't work out like that. The baby—a tiny girl—came too soon, in the coldest part of that winter, and never drew breath. In spite of everything, Eliza took it badly. We all did. Such a little life, but a big loss, on top of everything that had come before. Someone else I hadn't been able to keep from harm.

After that, it was just a case of going on. Long days, hard work, the shifting seasons. In another life, I might have been happy there. I wrote to Miss Dunn from time to time. She was better placed to hear word of you than I was, and though she used her connections in the church and in service, we could find no clue. I knew you must have changed your name and done all you could to disappear again.

Why did you have to do it so well?

The night is almost over, and time is running out. It's beginning to get light now and the chill is starting to ebb away. In any other circumstances I'd say it was going to be a glorious day.

Maybe, wherever you are, you are happy. I hope you are. Maybe you found someone else and fell in love and have a home and children and the life I said should be yours. I hope you have.

I can say that now and truly mean it. More than anything else I want to know that, wherever you are, you are safe and loved and you have a good life.

But I am still selfish enough to wish that it could have been with me.

Chapter 34

Brighton
July 7th 1916

When she leaves Lewes Crescent she finds that she very much doesn't want to go back to Belgrave Place. Since the wounded started to arrive Mrs Van de Berg has demonstrated a vampire-like thirst for information about the Poor Brave Boys which she is in no mood to indulge today. Not with the letter like a burning coal in her pocket.

Her heart is beating an erratic rhythm as she waits to cross Marine Parade, eventually losing patience with the late-afternoon traffic and dodging between an omnibus and a grocer's cart. The beach is emptying now, mothers and nannies corralling children and packing up picnic baskets, and she doesn't have to walk far to find a place that feels safe from the scrutiny of others.

She can feel the warmth of the stones through her skirts as she sits down. All day, as she has gone from bed to bed, writing postcard after postcard; as the VADs have peeled stinking, tattered uniforms away from torn flesh and the orderlies have lifted stretchers from ambulances and Sister Pinkney has cleaned wounds and administered morphine; and across the sea the guns have rumbled, on and on . . . All that time, it has been a dazzling high summer's day and children have played and paddled and begged for ice creams, and Joseph—*Joseph*—has made the final part of his journey from the carnage of trenches, first aid posts, and casualty clearing stations, through a series of randomly assigned trains and boats and ports and stations, and arrived here. With this letter.

She stares at it for a long time. The dirty envelope tells a story of its own, one she can just begin to comprehend, having seen the men and heard them talk of where they have come from. But it's the writing she focuses on. Although she has got used to being called Eliza Simmons, and can almost think of it as her own name sometimes, she cannot hide from the fact that this letter is not intended for her and she has no business opening it.

She never meant to assume Eliza's identity. On the night she fled from Coldwell, as Miss Dunn helped her to bundle up her scant possessions, she had only thought to put enough distance between herself and Henderson that he wouldn't be able to compromise and control her, or give away her whereabouts to Alec. She had scarcely been aware that the character reference from Eliza's previous employer was amongst the papers she shoved into her writing case, much less planned to use it. But after seeing the newspaper report of Henderson's death—his *murder*—what choice did she have but to reinvent herself again?

She strokes her thumb over the address on the envelope. She can still do the right thing. She can affix one of the stamps with which Mrs Van de Berg keeps her generously supplied for the Poor Brave Boys . . . She can get up and walk back to the street, along the seafront and drop it into the post box. It will be in the real Eliza's hands the day after tomorrow.

But she knows very well she is not going to do that.

The envelope contains the answers to questions that have tormented her for four and a half years. It is fat with them. Here is the ending to the story, and she cannot let it go without finding out what happened to the man she fell so foolishly in love with.

And so, she shoves aside the guilt and silences the prim little voice of her better nature. Her hands are trembling as she tears a flimsy corner and slides a finger in to rip it open. The paper she pulls out is creased and marked, as if it has been carried around for a long time, though she is surprised to see that it contains only a few brief lines.

She reads them with her heart in her throat and tears in her eyes.

His writing. His words. His voice.

Dear Eliza, I am writing this quickly before we move up into the line for whatever action is coming. If anything should happen to me, I want you to know that you are the beneficiary of my possessions and effects, such as they are. Look after yourself and live well. You deserve to be happy.

With my love,
Jem.

P.S. If I don't make it through, can I ask you to keep safe the enclosed? In the hope that one day you'll get the chance to pass it on.

She moves the page aside and the air leaves her lungs in a rush as she sees the second envelope that it has been wrapped around.
Mrs Kate Furniss.
As she unfolds the densely written pages, she is gasping, tears already stinging in her eyes, spilling down her cheeks and splashing onto the words. Impatiently she dashes them aside and begins to read.

———◦◦◦———

She doesn't know how long she sits there. Time becomes fluid, abstract, and she tumbles back through the years to that sultry summer. Looking back, it seems it was a time suspended between two worlds: the Victorian one occupied by Sir Henry Hyde—a world of candlelight and carriages, and this modern age of motorcars and machine guns. A time of brief and shimmering happiness.

He takes her back there, and the emotions she has carefully folded away and packed into the past come tumbling out, like an old suitcase opened and upended, enveloping her in the textures and scents of that time. When she looks up finally, the families are gone, replaced by a few strolling couples and groups of soldiers on leave—some in Canadian uniforms— looking for amusement. The tide has come in and the light is different.

She is different too. It's like a protective cloak has been wrenched off her, leaving her exposed in the teeth of a savage gale. It is impossible to separate how she feels into distinct emotions—it is everything at once:

relief, joy, love . . . elation, and frustration. Yearning. Astonishment. Bitterness and regret.

She gets stiffly to her feet and swipes at her cheeks. She walks quickly, taking no notice of the Canadians who stare at her with interest and call out. She barely registers where she is going, only aware that it isn't back to Belgrave Place, because Mrs Van de Berg's house is too narrow and hushed and decorous to contain the tornado of her thoughts and the wild drum of her heart. As she walks, some of the confusion falls away and she finds that one emotion emerges, phoenix-like, from the chaos.

Anger.

She turns to go onto the pier, pushing against the tide of people flowing out of the concert hall, where a band has just finished playing. She shoulders through them, past the deckchairs and the amusement machines (*Lady Palmist—Automatic Reading of Your Hand. KNOW THYSELF*) until the crowd has thinned and the gaps between the boards beneath her feet show sea instead of shingle.

How can fate be so cruel? How dare it bring her this glimmer of hope and consolation, only to keep it dangling out of her reach?

It is just a week since he finished writing the letter, hardly any time at all; but it has been a week like no other, when the world has split open and unleashed a boiling lava of chaos and destruction. She feels dizzy with panic as she thinks of the convoys and casualty lists, the mud and the blood and the stunned men at whose bedsides she has sat. *Everyone's dead*, one had said, with a kind of horrified awe, describing how he had returned to his regiment's assembly point on that first day to find only twenty men remaining of the four hundred who had left the trenches that morning. Jem had known he might not survive. That was why he'd written.

But still, it is unthinkable. Impossible.

It is . . . *intolerable.*

She walks as far as she can, to the very end of the pier, and grips the railing as the evening breeze (cooler now) tugs at her hat. Behind her, the beach and the rows of smart houses and hotels along the seafront seem far away, and she leans forward, as much as she can, every fibre of her being straining towards France.

She has got used to being unhappy. She has long since given up expecting anything different, but the letter has thawed her frozen heart. The feeling has returned to it, a thousand times more painful than the blood returning to cold fingers held up to a fire.

'Don't you dare be dead, Jem Arden,' she sobs out loud to the reeling gulls. 'Don't you bloody *dare*. You'd better still be out there somewhere. You'd better still be alive. You can't not come back to me now.'

Later, when it is going dark and she has cooked and cleared away Mrs Van de Berg's dinner (*Rissoles again, Simmons? I know there are shortages, but I'm sure there's no need to let standards fall quite so much*), she walks back to Lewes Crescent.

She is far from certain that she will be allowed to see Joseph at this hour. Visiting times are strictly maintained, and the nurses regard the groups of tremulous mothers, sisters, and sweethearts that shuffle into the wards, the gruff fathers who stand around stiffly, getting in the way, as something of a trial, often leaving the men more unsettled than they found them. However, just as she is trying to explain to the purse-lipped night sister sitting at the desk in the entrance hall, Corporal Maloney appears, on his way off duty.

'If you've come to take me dancing, Miss Simmons, I'm afraid I'm going to have to pass,' he says with a half-hearted wink.

'I've come to see Private Jones,' she says. 'He was brought in earlier. I understand it's not really allowed, but I—I know him, you see. From . . . before.'

Corporal Maloney's face loses its teasing expression. 'Young lad who was on Rodney Ward? Sister'll be pleased to have someone to sit with him. He's been giving out something shocking this afternoon—got an awful bee in his bonnet about going to hell because he's killed someone, which isn't really what the other lads want to hear. We had to move him to a room on his own in the end. The chaplain's been in and he's quieter now. Doped up to the eyes, but I reckon he'd benefit from the company of an old friend.' He makes a weary attempt at a grin. 'Not that I'm saying you're old, of course, Miss Simmons.'

At the night sister's nod of assent, she follows him through the inner hall and along to a small anteroom behind the old dining room, where footmen must once have waited with their dishes and tureens for the butler's signal. It is a box, higher than it is wide, its panelled walls painted that pale green that was fashionable when these houses were built. There are shutters at the long window, and the bottom half has been folded closed while the top half is open, showing the darkened sky.

The room contains a single iron bed with a locker beside it, on which a lamp is lit. Beside the bed there's a canvas-seated chair.

'He didn't like being in the dark,' Corporal Maloney whispers, nodding at the figure in the bed. 'Poor kid. If he's eighteen, I'm Lord Kitchener. Anyway, I'll leave you to it.'

She mutters a thank-you and sits down, waiting until the orderly's footsteps have died away before she looks properly at the figure in the bed. Her heart turns over and, for the second time that day, tears rush to her eyes, though she can't say whether it is because Joseph looks so recognisably the same, or so very altered.

Against the white pillow, his skin is as red and fragile as poppy petals. His blond hair is darker, his brow broader, and his jaw harder; but in sleep his face has the same unguarded innocence of the boy she knew at Coldwell, the one she scrubbed clean of workhouse grime on the day he arrived, revealing the bruises on his bony back. She wanted to believe then that his worst days were behind him, that Coldwell would offer a new start and a place of safety for him, as it had for her.

Frederick Henderson had poisoned that hope for them both.

The starched sheets crackle as Joseph twitches beneath them, his head twisting on the pillow. In the lamplight she can see that his eyelids are flickering, his scabbed and crusted lips moving wordlessly. She wonders where he is, what landscapes he is moving through in his dreams. She wonders if Jem is there, and wishes she could follow.

She folds her hands to stop herself from reaching out to wake him. And settles in to wait as long as it takes.

Chapter 35

Nottinghamshire
July 11th 1916

Eliza walks along the lane from the little country station between high hedgerows frothing with cow parsley. Up above, the swallows are swooping and circling in the fathomless blue, but if they're singing their squealing song, she can't hear it: her ears are still ringing with the clang and clamour of the factory. For twelve hours, while the city slept, she has been stuffing explosive into shell cases and hammering it down, and now her arms ache and her back hurts and her dry mouth tastes of iron.

The shift finished at six o'clock, when a pear-drop sun was rising over the chimney pots. It's high in the sky now, hard and hot on the top of her hat. In the hours in between, she has been back to Elsie's house on Albion Street for a breakfast of strong tea, with bread and jam, as she often does (more so recently, with the news dripping in from France all the time; Elsie dreads going home to find a telegram or a letter from the commanding officer of the Pals Battalion her husband, Bert, joined in the first week of the war). Sometimes Eliza stays there for the day, crawling into the creaking bed in Elsie's tiny back bedroom, when sleep is already dragging at her and the journey back to Lane End Cottage seems too arduous. But today some superstitious impulse has brought her home.

Two days ago, a postcard arrived from a convalescent home in Surrey, with her name written in a stranger's stout hand on the front, and Jem's name on the back. Below it was a list of printed statements. *I am quite well,* and *I am being sent down to the base* had both been crossed out with a firm stroke of the pen.

I have been wounded remained.

So did *A letter will follow shortly.*

That's why she's come back. The thought of a stretch of unbroken sleep in Albion Street before going back to the factory this evening was almost overwhelmingly tempting, but she needs to see if the letter has come. Throughout the night shift, the noise and activity had made it possible not to think about Jem being wounded (where? how?) but in the stillness of the countryside, there is nothing to stop the prickle of dread, like iced water dripping down her spine.

As she walks, her feet kick up dust from the road. By the time she arrives at the gate of Lane End Cottage her skirt is claggy with it, and she thinks wistfully of the hard pavement on Albion Street, swept clean daily by its waiting women. The cottage itself looks like something you might see on the lid of a chocolate box, with rosy bricks and diamond-paned windows and pale pink roses clambering around the front door. The rain a couple of weeks ago has made everything grow like mad, and the grass is lush and glossy, matted with daisies and tumbling over the path. The boughs of the plum and damson trees in the little orchard to the side are already laden with fruit, green and hard now, but promising a plentiful autumn.

But still, she feels a weight settle across her shoulders as she fits her key in the lock and shoves open the front door. Not just at the thought that a letter might be waiting but at the damp fug of neglect that folds around her as she steps inside and the guilt that accompanies it. All those ripening plums and damsons don't feel like a blessing so much as a reproach. A very obvious reminder of her domestic shortcomings.

She thinks, quite suddenly, of the stillroom at Coldwell and its shelves of jams and bottled fruits made by Mrs Furniss. How effortless she had made it seem, that order and neatness. That efficiency. The tasks of each season accomplished on time, the rhythm of the vast house kept ticking with the same constancy as its many clocks.

Eliza has spent the last five years trying to be Kate Furniss, and only managing a tin-plate, ha'penny replica of the real thing. A flat, flimsy paper doll, to Mrs Furniss's painted porcelain.

Her heart catches a little as she sees a letter lying on the floor behind the door. She picks it up. The handwriting on the front is elegant and looping—obviously not Jem's. She stares at it as she carries it through to the kitchen and is oddly reluctant to open it. Leaving it on the table, she goes over to unhook a teacup from the dresser and fills it from the tap at the sink (installed by Jem and Joseph the summer before the war). She swallows the cold water and looks around sadly, taking in the dead flies on the windowsill, the layer of dust furring the stone-cold range, and the spectre of her failure rises up once more.

She tried to make the best of it here. They all did. That terrible winter, when the three of them were still reeling from what had happened . . . Jem had gathered them into a sort of patched-up, makeshift, damaged family and looked after them. Taken the first job he found that came with a house and done his best through the bleak time that followed. (The time she didn't allow herself to think about.)

It wasn't his fault he couldn't love her.

At the beginning she'd thought that didn't matter, and that she would be content just being with him. It wasn't what she'd dreamed of, but it was an awful lot more than she'd hoped for back at Coldwell when he'd barely noticed her. In some ways it would have been easier if he'd turned out to be difficult to live with; selfish or disrespectful, demanding or bad-tempered, but he hadn't.

It just wasn't the life either of them wanted.

It wasn't really any life at all.

She gulps the last mouthful of water and leaves the cup on the draining board. If it hadn't been for the war, they might have gone on like that for years, all of them quietly unhappy, Jem pining for the woman he'd lost, Joseph fighting his demons alone and mostly in silence, her mourning the baby she never even wanted and going quietly mad at the relentless grind of domesticity; the endless battles against mud and dust, cold and heat, shortage and surplus, boredom and loneliness. The constant need to produce meals that took hours to prepare and minutes to consume.

The war jolted them out of their torpor. Though she is as aware as anyone at home can be about the horrors of Over There, she can't help feeling that the changes it has brought haven't been *all* bad . . . not for her, at least. She'd rather fill shells in a factory than be a skivvy in service any day. She might not have a man, but she does have freedom, independence, and a decent wage, and there's a lot to be said for that.

She yawns widely. Today she is going to pack up the rest of her clothes and go down to the farmhouse to leave the key with Mrs Burgess, along with Elsie's address, before heading back to Albion Street for a bit of shut-eye before the evening shift. It was Elsie's suggestion that Eliza should stay there more permanently. She likes the company, to make up for Bert's absence, and she could do with some help with the rent. For her part, Eliza would certainly rather be spared the expense of the rail fare back to Little Langley, and the long tramp through the lanes to an empty house, a cold range, and a damp bed at the end of a long shift. So long as Mrs Burgess doesn't mind forwarding on any post, there's nothing to keep her here, except memories and the last vestiges of stubborn hope.

(*Maybe, when he comes back—if he comes back—he'll be ready to accept that he's not going to find her . . . Maybe he'll have missed me, and realised I was what he wanted all along . . .*)

Her eyes swivel to the letter on the table. She suddenly feels so crushed with exhaustion that it is an effort to push herself away from the sink to retrieve it. The postmark is Brighton, and there is something evocative about the graceful script—it makes her think of well-ordered accounts in a ledger and neat rows of jars on a shelf. Yawning, she tears open the envelope and pulls out another, folded inside it.

Her heart falters.

This one is addressed in Jem's writing. Her name. There is a piece of notepaper tucked in beside it. It flutters in her trembling hand as she unfolds it and sees the name at the end.

Kate Furniss.

That's it then, Eliza thinks numbly. She's found. There really is no reason to stay.

Surrey
July 20th 1916

The sun is warm on Jem's face. He can smell lavender and honeysuckle, and hear the sounds of an English summer: the lazy hum of bees, the murmur

348 · Iona Grey

of voices, and the distant trickle of tea being poured. (Or is it lemonade, on a day like this?)

The convalescent home is an old manor house belonging to a lady gardener of some renown, and apparently the herbaceous borders are some of the finest in England. (He has no mental image of what that might look like.) All he knows is there are no howitzers or Lewis guns, no exploding shells or teeth-rattling volleys of bullets, no shouted orders and no swearing. It unsettles him, the quiet. It plucks at his overstretched nerves as he strains to identify each innocuous sound, to make up for the fact that he can't see.

The creak of a wicker chair beside him. The rustle of starched cotton. He knows the nurse is still sitting beside him, but he jumps as she unexpectedly touches his hand.

'Sorry, Lance Corporal. Did I wake you?'

He shakes his head sharply, registering the needling pain at the back of his head that pounces every time he moves. His eyes are hidden by bandages, which is why she has to ask, but it annoys him even so. As does the kindness in her voice. The pity. He's more comfortable being shouted at.

(*On your feet, man! Forward! FORWARD!*)

He hears paper being folded, and pictures her (a fresh-faced outdoorsy type, he imagines) putting Eliza's letter back in its envelope. 'Well, if you're sure you don't want to reply now, I'll leave this in your locker. Probably best to let things settle for a bit. Think it all over and decide what to say.'

She thinks Eliza is his sweetheart, and the news that she is leaving Lane End Cottage to move in with a friend from the factory will be a knife in his heart. She feels sorry for him, but he imagines she feels sorry for Eliza too, and secretly doesn't blame her for freeing herself from his perpetual bad temper and obstinate despair. Given that it looks like he might be here for some time (*Tricky things, head injuries*, Dr McAllen says; *impossible to predict how long recovery will take*—or, Jem presumes, if it will happen at all), he probably should explain, but in that moment, it seems so overwhelmingly complicated that he wouldn't know where to begin. How much to say. And anyway, if she thinks he's been jilted, it at least goes some way to excusing his surliness.

'It's good news about your friend though,' the nurse goes on brightly. 'The one you carried in from no man's land. That was exceptionally brave, especially when you were so badly injured yourself. It's marvellous that he's doing so well. You saved his life.'

He manages to nod dumbly. It *is* good news, of course. Does saving Joseph make up for not being able to save Jack? He's not sure his mother would think so, though it occurs to him that if he had somehow managed to protect Jack from Hyde's sadistic games and Henderson's cold-blooded cruelty, he couldn't have shielded him from British recruiting sergeants or German artillery.

It was all for nothing.

He had thought it was up to him to keep everyone safe and make everything right. The arrogance and the innocence of that. He has sacrificed his own happiness to discover that, in the end, he could no more control the actions of aristocrats or the decisions of politicians than he could change the course of the tides or bring the moon down from the sky. The only thing he had any power over was how he conducted himself.

And it's too late to change that now.

'Can I get you some tea?'

The way she phrases the question makes it sound like she's asking his permission for something she'd like to do. It seems like a small thing to agree, and the itch of anger it provokes is illogical and unfair. He's aware of her getting up, and wonders if she's sharing a conspiratorial roll of her eyes with one of the other patients nearby, one of the nice ones, who flirt and tease and behave like decent human beings.

He doesn't know why he can't be like that. A decent human being. Perhaps it isn't in him, and never was. Dr McAllen says that anger isn't unusual after an injury like his. (*Severe concussion is where the brain gets shaken inside the skull . . . We can't see the damage, but that doesn't mean it isn't significant and will make itself felt in any number of different ways, both physical and psychological . . .*) He appreciates the explanation but suspects it is overgenerous and not very accurate.

It wasn't the trench mortar explosion that has made him like this, it's everything that came before. Dr McAllen might be right—he may recover from the head injury and regain some vision, but he is afraid the damage sustained by losing Jack, losing Kate, and absorbing the fallout from what Joseph did will be permanent.

In the darkness, behind the dressings, he can suddenly see the bleakness

350 · Iona Grey

of the future in front of him, and his head is filled with the panicked pounding of his heart. It seems he is destined to lose everything he cares about. To be separated from those he loves most and to spend his life trying to find them again. Looking for clues and for answers.

He has even lost her photograph. He can't bear to think of something so precious trampled in the mud, but there must be a lot of mothers thinking the same about their boys. The dragonfly brooch, its wings a little bent now, has found its way back to him with the rest of his things. It's in the locker by his bed, though he might as well have told them to get rid of it.

It's not the prospect of living in darkness he can't come to terms with, it's the prospect of living without hope. Because how can he find Kate when he can't see to look for her?

'Here we are . . .'

The nurse is back, her voice artificially hearty. He is aware that his hands are bunched into fists on his lap and, through the ebbing wave of despair, makes a conscious effort to relax them, to at least attempt to appear like a normal human. He hears a cup being set down on the table at his elbow, a few murmured words he doesn't catch, and the creak of wicker as she sits.

His senses prickle. Just as he is wondering if there is someone else there he catches a whisper of scent. *Vanilla . . . nutmeg . . . roses . . .*

His throat closes and a fist of emotion hits him in the chest. He turns his head and a hand touches his cheek.

'It's me,' she says softly. 'I'm here.'

Epilogue

Two years later

It's over.

After the long night of pain, the dark hours of labouring, he is born as the day is beginning. She has asked that the curtains be kept open throughout it all so she can orientate herself like the ancient sailors did, navigating their way by the moon and stars through dangerous waters, steering their course through uncharted seas. When the sky lightens and the storm of pain inside her has finished raging, she finds herself washed up, exhausted and elated, on the shore of a new land.

Mrs Burgess from the farmhouse has been there all night, her face swimming in and out of focus. It is she who eases the baby into the world and tells them that they have a son, and suddenly they are all crying—Kate, Jem (who was supposed to stay downstairs but has been with her from the first raw shout of pain), and their tiny, perfect boy. Even Mrs Burgess, who has delivered five healthy children of her own and more calves and foals and piglets than you can count, has tears rolling down her tired face.

It's over.

Afterwards, there is the cleaning up—the bundling up of bloodied sheets and the changing of her sweat-soaked nightgown for a clean one. Mrs Burgess shoves everything into the basket of her bicycle to take to the farm for laundering, coming back upstairs to make sure Kate is settled before she leaves, bringing her a cup of sweetened tea.

She has lent them a crib: a beautiful old swinging one that has rocked numerous babies in its embrace, including, more than half a century ago, Mr Burgess. In the slow, ripe days of autumn Kate trimmed it with fresh white linen and took the piece of fine Nottingham lace Miss Dunn gave her for her wedding veil to make a canopy. The dragonfly brooch is pinned to it, and nestles in its delicate folds. She will lay the baby in the crib soon, but for now she wants to hold him against her heartbeat. To gaze at his miraculous face as he sleeps away his first morning in the world, his secretive smile suggesting he knows more about its workings than they do.

'He has your mouth . . .' Her voice is a whisper of wonder as she hands the baby, swaddled in a snowy blanket, to Jem. With infinite tenderness he carries his son to the window and holds him at arm's length, twisting his head to get a look at him.

'He has your dark hair.'

His vision is mostly back. There is a gap—a patch of blankness in his right eye—that means they can't make him pick up a gun again, no matter how long the war lasts and how desperate the army gets. But he can harness a horse and steer a plough and take charge of the harvest. He can fix a roof and chop wood for fires and make a home for them. He can look into her eyes on sleepy mornings in their creaking brass bed and he can see the face of his newborn son.

Between them they can do anything.

'He's called Jack, isn't he?' she says. They haven't discussed it, but it seems obvious—natural—though for a moment he says nothing, and she wonders if it's too painful for him and he'd rather choose something else. But he nods, and she realises that he hasn't spoken because he can't. He comes to the bed and places the baby back in her arms, where he already fits, and kisses her softly on the mouth.

'I love you.'

He goes downstairs to get one of the remaining bottles of champagne from the crate that Lady Hyde bought for their wedding (arranged as soon as she had received a reply to her enquiry about Alec Ross, and confirmation that he had died of dysentery in hospital at Wimereux in March 1917); and Kate lies against the bank of pillows and watches the milky mist lift a little, to reveal the apple tree, where a few fruits cling to the topmost branches, and the plums and the damsons, still wearing the last of their faded autumn finery. Through the haze of her own happiness she spares a thought for Eliza's baby, born without a cry in the room across the landing. Eliza has made her promise that she will write the minute there is news. She wants to come and visit as soon as possible, though Kate mustn't go to any trouble. She'll bring buns from the shop on the corner, Eliza says. You can't tell the difference between shop bought and homemade, anyway, and she is flush with her factory wages.

Jem brings the champagne up and they drink it from teacups, and it tastes of sunlight and celebration. She is already drunk with exhaustion and happiness, reeling from the perfection of what they have created together. She lays the baby in his crib and slips into a half slumber.

She comes to with the clamour of voices downstairs—Joseph and Davy—and smiles, glad that they have come. Joseph lives up at the farm in a bothy with the farmhands, and has taken over responsibility for the poultry. He walks down several times a week (a little unevenly now, though his limp is less pronounced than it was) and brings eggs, which she exchanges for the cakes she makes with them, and jars of jam and loaves of bread (because it's still impossible to fill him up). Last year, when Mary Wells's heart finally gave out, it was Joseph who suggested Davy as an apprentice. Perhaps it isn't surprising that Davy, who has an animal's instinct, has a way with them too. No one can soothe a flustered hen like he can (the egg yield has almost doubled) or calm a farrowing sow as easily. It's a gift, Mr Burgess says. He's never seen the like.

Jem comes in, and for a moment she can't read the expression on his face. And then he is beside her, kneeling down and taking her face between his hands as he tells her the news that Joseph and Davy have brought—that in the early hours of the morning, while she was caught in the eye of the storm, men were gathering in France to sign a treaty to bring the war to an end. Their son has been born into a world at peace.

Jem gets up and opens the window. The cold air is as clear and sparkling as the champagne. At the sound of the church bells echoing over the damp winter fields, Jack opens his dark blue eyes and blinks.

It is over.

And it is just beginning.

Acknowledgments

I made my first tentative steps through the servants' entrance of Cold-well Hall in the early weeks of 2020, exploring an idea that had been whispering to me for years, and calling on some of my favourite settings and story elements—a huge old house in a remote location, once grand but now in decline, buried secrets and forbidden love. I couldn't know, as I wrote those first chapters, that the rooms of that imaginary house—its corridors and attics, staircases and basement passages, and the characters who inhabited them—would become my world for the next two years, as real life produced the global pandemic plot twist no one had seen coming, and our horizons had shrunk to the boundaries of our own homes.

I'm writing this in the summer of 2023, more than a year after finishing the book, and that time seems like a sort of fever dream. It's hard to recapture the anxious uncertainty of the spring and summer of 2020, the sense of reality being suspended, and it seems odd to remember the rules and restrictions that so quickly became our normal. But for me, something of the spirit of that time remains trapped in the pages of this book; the closed community of characters in the cut-off house, the sense of claustrophobia and isolation, the restrictions on freedom of a life in service. I think if I had been working on this book at any other time, the finished story would have been quite different.

But although writing *The Housekeeper's Secret* was a more than usually solitary experience, its transformation from laptop to printed page has been very much a team effort, and I am enormously fortunate to be part of the most incredible team at St. Martin's Press. I am deeply grateful to my editor, Vicki Lame, for her patience, positivity, and encouragement as well as her sensitive, insightful editing (which makes me aware that I should strip out at least one of the adjectives in this sentence!). And to assistant editor Vanessa Aguirre, who has been a steady and reassuring presence throughout, providing invaluable advice—both practical and creative—on the journey from page to publication. My heartfelt thanks go to the entire team at St. Martin's Press—Hannah Jones, John Morrone, Martha Schwartz (for an incredibly thorough and incisive copyedit that picked up some fascinating language anachronisms I wasn't aware of), Chris Leonowicz, Jen Edwards, and Danielle Christopher for the beautiful cover. To magnificent marketeers Marissa Sangiacomo, Brant Janeway, and Althea Mignone, and publicist Jessica Zimmerman—huge gratitude to you all.

I am indebted to agents Deborah Schneider, Rebecca Ritchie, and Victoria Hobbs for their support and collective wisdom throughout the process of writing this book. I am always aware of the privilege of having such kind, capable, and knowledgeable people around me, and am profoundly thankful for it.

I'm grateful to my mum, who lit the spark of my interest in historic houses by packing childhood summers with days out to National Trust mansions and English Heritage castles, and fanned the flames of my fascination by encouraging me to read and keeping me well supplied with books. And to fellow historical romantic Jenny Ashcroft, to whom this book is dedicated, simply because I don't think it would have reached completion without her tireless encouragement and the bolstering comfort of her friendship.

And, finally, to my husband and daughters, though I can honestly say this book would have been written an awful lot more quickly if we hadn't all been under the same roof, arguing over spaces on the sofa, baking endless variations of banana bread, seeking out ingenious ways to make two potatoes and a tin of chickpeas into dinner for five, doing Zoom quizzes with distant family and yoga with Adriene (who practically feels like family now and should also get a mention).

I love you all to distraction (literally) and I wouldn't have had it any other way.

About the Author

IONA GREY has a degree in English Language and Literature from Manchester University, an obsession with history, and an enduring fascination with the lives of women in the twentieth century. She has three grown-up daughters and lives in Cheshire with the husband she met on the last night of university, more than thirty years ago. She is a firm believer in love at first sight and happily ever after.